THE ONE WHO RAN

INVESTIGATOR KAT CROMWELL MYSTERY - BOOK THREE

NICHOLAS HARVEY

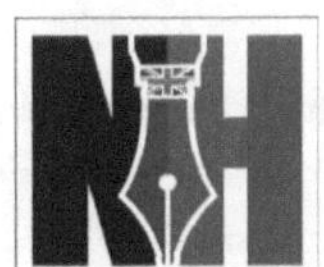

Copyright © 2025 by Harvey Books, LLC

Printed in the United States of America

First Printing, 2025

ISBN: 978-1-959627-38-8

Cover design: Cover2Book

Editor: Chelsey Heller

Author photograph: Lift Your Eyes Photography

PROLOGUE

Thirty-One had been stoned before. Plenty of times. That's how she knew this was different. Time had lost all meaning. Not just tonight. It was dark, so it had to be nighttime, but she couldn't place where or who she'd ever been. Except for Thirty-One. Voices echoed in her head, repeating her name over and over as hands pulled, touched, and cast her aside. She was Thirty-One. The same voices called other numbers, mumbling, discussing, deciding.

Bright lights flashed like hazy strobes, leaving her nauseous. Sounds came and went. She was aware of sitting down, but couldn't remember why or where she'd come from, nor where she'd intended on going. Salty air mixed with the ammonia-like smell of urine. It may have been from her; she wasn't certain.

Groaning with effort, Thirty-One pushed herself unsteadily to her feet. *Why wouldn't her eyes focus?* Blurry buildings and muted colors circled her somehow, yet barely moved, her surroundings in constant agitation. A low rumble came toward her, before receding into the stillness of the night. She looked down at herself, not recognizing the thin summer dress she wore. A cooling breeze made her shiver, yet she felt clammy and overheated. Thirty-One pulled at the dress, hearing the rewarding sound of material giving way, allowing the chill fingers of an ocean wind to brush across her flesh.

An urge inside told her to keep moving, but she wanted to curl up and sleep. To stop the kaleidoscope of sensory inputs from overwhelming her. But going somewhere was more important. Crucial. Yet, she had no idea why.

Another low, droning sound approached, and she instinctively raised her arms to protect herself. Her hands brushed against the fabric hanging at her sides, and she clutched her naked breasts. A louder sound resonated all around before abruptly stopping as the drone faded away.

She stumbled as the ground fell away beneath her, yet the world flew up to meet her. Thirty-One hit the asphalt with a jarring thud, her head snapping forward and striking the solid ground. She groaned as pain wafted through her in slow motion. Rolling to one side, bright lights blinded her as that annoying drone got louder. Until a child screeched. *Was it a child?* The bright lights smothered her, and the droning became constant.

Had she become frozen in time? Unable to open her eyes against the blinding lights, Thirty-One wondered if she was suspended in space. Adrift in a strange universe. Was she dead? But then the voices came once more, and she curled herself into a ball. Incoherent words descended upon her, urgent and challenging.

But the hands that touched her were different. A broad shadow blocked the bright lights, and a softer voice spoke from close by. The fingers on her shoulder were gentle. Thirty-One tried to speak, but no words came out. Something was laid over her, a blanket or a coat, but she tried wiping it away. Her skin was too sticky to be covered. The voices continued. One voice, female, sounded detached, but the other, a man's, kept trying to cover her.

Thirty-One seized his arm and clutched tightly, mustering every ounce of strength and focus she had. Words finally came, but from somewhere beyond the swirling chaos of her conscious mind. She barely knew what she was saying and certainly didn't know why, but she heard herself hoarsely mutter.

"There are more."

1
____

I'd been accused of being many unflattering things. Stubborn, impetuous, rash, to name a few. From where I lay on an old mover's blanket, alone on the roof of my father's boxing gym at two a.m., it was becoming hard to argue with my critics. Feeling dog-tired, my neck ached from staring through the night vision binoculars, and I desperately needed to pee.

Sometimes, circumstances stacked on top of one another like dirty plates in a rest-stop diner until the precarious pile teetered on the brink of crashing to the floor. Looking back over the past few weeks, I could see exactly how I'd ended up on this filthy roof, risking my career like a faltering tower of china. All of which could have been avoided, I was beginning to realize, if I didn't possess many of the unsavory characteristics my detractors attributed to me.

Three hundred and fifty feet from where I lay was a rundown little commercial office building that was smaller than my cottage. It appeared to be a modular or trailer office, but scruffy and old. Located on the corner where Domingo Avenue made a sharp turn and became an alleyway serving a row of equally rundown storage units, a chain-link fence topped with razor wire surrounded the place like a prison compound. A company named Capistrano Holdings owned the property. I'd stumbled upon it after following a thug with an orange and black neck tattoo of a tiger. Emilio Santiago. I knew him from breaking into my cottage a while back and attacking me after scaring the shit out of Roger. A charge Santiago would walk on, as he had an alibi, placing him in a busy bar in Santa Ana.

Roger, the little dude who lives with me, seemed to have recovered from the scare. Santiago worked for the Castillo family, who happened to own a busy bar in Santa Ana, among their assorted assets. Several of which were legal. Most were not. I went to school with Gabriella Castillo, and we were never friends. From evidence I'd come across before my fiancé's unfortunate fatal accident about a year ago, he'd been sleeping with Gabby. So, we would never be friends.

Santiago had visited Gabby's house in Dana Point, which I might have had a surveillance camera pointed at, although I doubted anyone could prove it was mine. Luckily, or probably unluckily, with the benefit of hindsight, I'd been watching the camera feed on my phone when he dropped by. That's how I'd followed the thug and discovered the little building where something illegal was going on.

I knew this because Capistrano Holdings was owned by a man named Trent DeMarco. He was married to Gabriella's cousin. The other giveaway was that the gates remained locked all day, and the only time anyone went there was in the middle of the night. I knew this part because after tracking Santiago, I'd set up a security camera on the roof of Dad's building, aiming it at the corner of Domingo Avenue.

What I didn't know, and hoped to learn by spending half the night on an itchy shipping blanket, was the nature of their illicit activities. Gabriella's grandfather was in jail, but he'd been put away on a series of petty crimes, having avoided the more substantial charges he'd undoubtedly been guilty of. Now his son, Gabby's father Ramon, ran the family's concerns and was adept at keeping himself distanced from the prosecutable offenses. Like using Trent DeMarco's name on company paperwork. Who, in turn, leased the property to some guy who probably didn't even exist. Which all added up to me needing to figure out exactly what was going on and then tying the Castillos to the crime. Without my boss, Captain Bradley, knowing anything about my off-the-books snooping.

The Criminal Investigation Bureau had a task force chasing the family, so I'd be stepping on toes, not to mention the questions over my connection through my dead fiancé, Paul. The bureau wanted to take the Castillos down from the top, which I fully supported, but my personal interest was more focused on figuring out how and why Gabriella had gotten her claws into Paul.

The police radio had been quiet for a while, so it startled me when a voice came through the earpiece. Dispatch was sending deputies to a public intoxication in town. I was listening in to make sure the sheriff's department didn't receive a report of a suspicious person on the roof of Frankie Cromwell's Boxing Gym. I could explain away my presence with an excuse about fixing security cameras, but I couldn't afford to spook Santiago. He'd know his location had been compromised.

Castillo's thug had been inside the little building for over an hour. He'd backed a box van up to the gates, unlocked the chains securing the premises, and reversed the van inside. The courtyard was so small, the nose of the van prevented him from closing the gates, but I still couldn't see what was going on behind the tall, plastic sheet-covered fence. I'd heard the van's roll-up door rattle open, so he was loading or unloading something, but all I could see were the roofs of the buildings and his vehicle.

I used the binoculars to scour the surrounding businesses on both sides of the street. It was pointless. I'd already searched for a way to get closer too many times to count, but I couldn't help myself from looking again. There were only a couple of streetlights on Domingo Avenue and a few entry lights above the doors of nearby businesses, poorly illuminating the street, but a soft light glowed in the courtyard where Santiago's van was parked. I slipped my compact instant camera from my backpack and took a picture. I doubted it would come out clearly, but hoped it would be enough to jog my gray matter if needed.

While the photograph developed, I weighed my options. Going home to bed sounded the most appealing, but that wouldn't land me any answers. My impatience begged me to head down from two stories up and sneak a closer look, but that would be incredibly risky with nowhere to hide outside of a few shadowed doorways. Or I could stay where I was and wait it out. My least favorite option.

My need to use the bathroom was becoming a major contributor to the decision, and staying on the roof meant squatting some-where. Knowing my luck, I'd time it perfectly with a news station helicopter flyover. I was about to retreat to the fire escape ladder when I heard the roll-up door once more. Santiago was on the move. Lifting the binoculars, I zoomed in on the edge of the flat roof of the office, then panned to the van. The top of Santiago's head came into view. He was walking toward the cab from the back of the van.

Keeping low, I stuffed everything I'd brought with me into my backpack, then gathered up the blanket. I scurried across the roof to the ladder and clambered down the side of the building to the backside of the gym. I desperately wanted to go inside and use the bathroom, but that would mean turning off the alarm. A notif-ication would go to my dad's phone, which he wouldn't see until morning, but would raise questions I didn't want to answer.

Running to my car, I tossed the blanket in the back and my backpack on the passenger seat. Making sure the auto headlights were off, I started the engine and waited. The box van appeared at the intersection ahead. Santiago turned right on Doheny Park Road, driving away from me. I waited. He turned right again to join

Pacific Coast Highway, so I followed, switching my lights on now that he couldn't see me.

Making the same right turn, I took the on-ramp to PCH. I could see the van's taillights ahead as the two-lane road crossed San Juan Creek. We were the only two vehicles in sight, so I made sure to stay well behind. If Santiago turned, I'd need to keep going straight, then try to loop back somehow. It would be completely obvious if I followed every turn he made.

I jumped again as a voice spoke in my earpiece. It was a deputy I recognized. Jeff Rodriguez. I'd partnered with him a bunch of times when I'd been a deputy. He was at the scene of the public intoxication.

"This is 15321. We need an ambulance right away. Over."

"Copy, 15321," replied the dispatcher.

After a brief pause, Rodriguez spoke again. "This is 15321. We should probably…"

He broke off, which got my attention. Jeff was a seasoned veteran. He wasn't a man given to hesitation.

Ahead of me, Santiago turned right on Golden Lantern.

"This is Dispatch. Please repeat 15321. Over."

"Sorry, Dispatch. It's just, there's something really strange here. I think we have something more than a public intoxication. Over."

"Bugger," I swore under my breath, stopping as the light for Golden Lantern turned red. I watched the box van continuing up the hill and wondered where he was heading. Could be Gabriella's house.

But now I was distracted by the radio call. For some reason, it bothered me. Maybe it was the concern in Jeff's tone.

I keyed my mic. "15321, this is Sam 54. What's your 20?"

There followed a brief silence in which I was sure Rodriguez was wondering what I was doing on the radio in the early hours of a Tuesday morning.

"Sam 54, Violet and La Cresta. Are you nearby? I could use another set of eyes here. Over."

"Bugger," I muttered to myself once more. "One minute out, 15321. Over," I said over the radio.

The light turned green, and I drove one block farther on PCH before turning right on Violet Lantern. The whole middle section of Dana Point was known as the Lantern District, with streets named accordingly. One long block north, La Cresta ran parallel to Pacific Coast Highway through town. I could see the obnoxious flashing lights of the patrol car long before I reached the intersection.

Apart from a few upstairs lights coming on in nearby homes— the residents no doubt wondering what the light show was about— the area was dead quiet. I parked behind the cruiser and noticed another vehicle pulled over before the intersection. The two deputies stood on the sidewalk in conversation with an older man. A woman, who I presumed was the man's wife, kneeled on the concrete beside a young female wrapped in a silver space blanket.

"Hey, Kat," Rodriguez greeted me as I approached. "What are you doing roaming the streets at this hour?"

"Not what I'd like to be doing at this time of night, believe me," I replied, deflecting the question.

His partner extended a hand. "Graves, ma'am."

We shook. I recognized him from seeing him at the station, but he was new.

"Kat Cromwell."

"Investigator Kat Cromwell," Rodriguez teased with a grin.

"I know who you are," Graves said, grinning, too.

I rolled my eyes. "The crazy English chick with the Polaroid" was how most of the men referred to me at the station. When they talked *about* me rather than *to* me, of course.

"What do we have?" I asked.

Rodriguez nodded to the older man next to him. "Mr. Harris was driving home with his wife when this young woman stumbled into the road half-naked."

"Lucky I didn't hit her," Mr. Harris quickly added. He looked shaken.

The young woman, on the other hand, appeared to be stoned

out of her mind. She was conscious but stared blankly at the road, her arms wrapped tightly around the blanket. Sandy blond hair strayed in all directions, having pulled from her ponytail.

"ID?" I asked.

Rodriguez shook his head. "No shoes, a skimpy dress pulled down to her waist, and she hasn't been able to say a word since we got here."

"Only said one thing to us," Mr. Harris offered. "Poor girl's in a hell of a state."

I looked the young woman over again. She didn't look good, that was for sure. Grubby and disheveled. I doubted she'd showered in days, maybe weeks. I turned my attention back to Rodriguez.

"Blood screen will show quite a cocktail, I'm sure."

He sighed. "I know, but there's something different about this one."

We both turned to the girl once more. As sad and disheartening as it was, even in our little beachside town, drug addiction was a big problem, just like everywhere else. This kid looked like she'd gotten her hands on a bad batch.

"What she say to you?" I asked the witness.

"'There are more,'" he replied.

"That was it?" I asked. "There are more. More what?"

He shrugged. "No idea. But Sharon heard it, too. She mumbled it, but we both heard the same thing."

"Tell Kat what you told me, Mr. Harris," Rodriguez prompted.

The man took a moment and gathered himself. "It wasn't so much what she said, as how she said it," he explained. "The look in her eyes. I mean, I know she's on drugs of some sort, but when my wife and I got to her, she was terrified. Then Sharon managed to soothe her a little, and that's when she grabbed hold of me. For a moment, she was hanging on to me like her life depended on it, and that's when she muttered those words. After that, she went almost catatonic, like you see her now."

I could blame it on the slight chill from the ocean, but I'd be lying. The old man's description gave me goosebumps.

We all turned to look at the young woman once more. If she was aware of our presence or conversation, she showed no sign of it. I took out my instant camera and clicked the button.

"There are more," I repeated quietly to myself as the camera whirred and the picture slowly fed out of the slot.

2

———————

The alarm going off woke me again. For a second time. I'd forgotten to change the setting when I'd crawled into bed at three-something in the morning, so I'd already been woken at five thirty a.m. My usual time to squeeze in a workout before heading to the office. Now it was seven-twenty a.m. If the extra one hundred and ten minutes of sleep had helped, it didn't feel like it.

Dragging myself out of bed, I let my roommate out. Roger, a harlequin cross rescue rabbit, was now four months old. He spent the nights in his hutch, which was actually a fancy converted credenza, but I'd been letting him roam the living area in my cottage during the days. He hadn't chewed a wire and fried himself yet, but I still nervously opened the door each day when I came home until he hopped over to greet me.

Showering, I'd planned on not washing my hair, but after passing the mirror, it was clear that wasn't an option. I kept my hair short so it was more manageable after working out or surfing every day, but the extra time ate into my allotted forty minutes to be at work. I mostly dried myself, threw on clothes, and charged out the door, leaving Roger munching on his breakfast pellets.

Skipping coffee was not an option, so I called PC Beans, my

local spot, and placed my order. They knew me well. I dared not add up my caffeine fix tab every month, but I probably paid the mortgage on the building. Skirting the drive-thru line that wound down PCH, I drove around the narrow alley in the back where my school friend Joanna met me.

"Thanks, Jo. You've no idea how badly I need this," I said, taking the two drinks and bag of treats I shouldn't have ordered. "Looks like you're crazy busy."

She rolled her eyes. "Line's halfway to San Clemente," she exaggerated. "Your mom was by earlier."

"Did she say how the surf was?" I asked.

Jo shook her head. "Didn't say, but she seemed happy."

"She's always happy," I joked.

"True. Gotta get back. Be careful out there, Kat."

"Thanks, Jo," I replied, then drove down the lane to Granada, where I turned left.

Passing by homes on either side, built on leveled lots in steps up the hill, I came to La Cresta. Turning right, I started toward Golden Lantern, the main street leading north out of town, but slowed when I reached Violet Lantern. Reminding myself I didn't have time, I still pulled to the side and looked up the hill. Because of the state she was in, I'd assumed the young woman from last night had come from farther up Violet Lantern. I couldn't imagine her staggering barefoot up the hill from PCH. But it was possible.

On the northwest corner was a small community park. A single lot someone had donated at one time. Maybe she'd been shooting up in there? Hopefully, Rodriguez and Graves had checked for evidence. Regardless, the case would probably be assigned to missing persons. I was with the homicide division, but my partner Hugo and I were based out of the small Dana Point sheriff's office, so we covered other major crime cases sometimes. Fortunately, murders were few and far between in our little beach town.

Driving on, I came to the light at Golden Lantern, waited for the green, then drove the rest of the way up the steep hill to the station. It was 8:06 a.m. when I walked into my office. Hugo was already at his desk. Typical. The one day I'm a few minutes late and he's on time. He was never usually on time.

"That's what happens when you're out trolling the streets in the middle of the night," he greeted me with his hint of a Hispanic accent. "You can't make it to work on time."

Hugo was a lot older than me. A career veteran. So for him, I'd always be the rookie. He was always impeccably dressed in a nice suit with not a single salt-and-pepper hair out of place. He had little time for newbies and subordinates, but he'd softened his demeanor with me now that we had a couple of tough cases behind us.

"That's not the 'good morning, sunshine' I'd expect from a man hoping to get a hot cup of PC Beans coffee and a freshly baked scone," I bantered, taking my seat.

He slid his chair to the side to see me past our monitors. "Great job holding the deputy's hands last night, Kat," he said with more than a hint of sarcasm.

Still, it was the best I'd get from him, so I slid his coffee and scone across the desk.

"*Gracias.*"

"*De nada,*" I replied.

"So what was last night all about, anyway?" he asked before sipping his drink.

I went with the assumption that he was talking about the mystery girl, and word hadn't somehow gotten out about my covert and unsanctioned surveillance.

"Young addict wandering the streets," I replied, then pulled the pictures from my backpack that I'd taken the previous night.

I was careful to toss the right one across the desks.

"She looks young," Hugo commented, studying the grainy photograph while chewing a mouthful of scone. "No ID?"

I shook my head.

"And how was it you happened across this incident?" Hugo asked, staring at me over the disposable coffee cup as he took another sip.

"Alarm issue at my dad's gym," I said, keeping the lie adjacent to the truth. At least I'd established an excuse for being in the area.

Hugo slid back behind his screen, so I'd either appeased him or he was regrouping for another interrogation later. I typed in my password and was about to return my attention to an old cold case we'd been revisiting when a voice came from the doorway.

"Kat, were you on scene when they found a girl wandering around town last night?"

I turned to face Captain Bradley. She was a diminutive fireplug of a woman, with her black hair pulled tightly back in a bun. I nodded.

"Then you two get to the hospital and see what's going on with the vic."

"Is she talking?" I asked, getting to my feet.

"Haven't heard," Bradley replied. "But the tox screen they ran came back with a melting pot of suspicious drugs."

"So, why are we going?" Hugo asked, remaining seated. "Sounds like narcotics ought to handle it."

The captain frowned at my partner. "You're going because I just ordered you to go, Hugo. And my thinking, since you're questioning my motives for a reason beyond my understanding and an inch short of my tolerance, is that Rohypnol was one of the drugs in the mix, so there's a chance she was taken or held without consent."

Hugo didn't say a word, but stood and grabbed his jacket.

"Thank you," Bradley said before walking off.

I'd be bounced down to janitor if I'd questioned her that way. Hugo just shrugged his shoulders.

"Guess we're going to see your girl at the hospital."

"She's not 'my' girl," I muttered, following him out of the office.

Half an hour later, we arrived at Providence Mission Hospital in Laguna Beach. A small facility by modern standards, it had the closest emergency room to most of the South Orange County Beach Cities. We walked through the front doors to be greeted with chaos in progress. Staff were hustling around, mainly focused on one exam room. I approached the reception desk.

"Orange County Sheriff's Department Investigators Cromwell and Fuentes. We're here to see the young woman brought in last night."

The middle-aged woman's anxious expression told me all I needed to know.

"What happened?" I asked before she had a chance to say anything.

"You'll have to wait for the doctor, I'm afraid," she replied. "But he might be awhile."

"Or not," I muttered, turning to Hugo.

"Doesn't look good," he agreed.

Hearing the words "clear" being called out from the exam room confirmed the severity of the situation. I wondered how the woman had lasted the six hours since I'd last seen her, only to crash now.

"We should come back in an hour," Hugo suggested. "Doesn't look like we can talk to anyone for a bit."

"Hmm," I grunted, still transfixed on the hallway. "You know what's weird about this?"

"That Bradley sent us down here," Hugo shot back.

I ignored his jab at our boss. "Our Jane Doe has only spoken three words since the Harrises came upon her last night, yet she had them worried to death about her. Then Rodriguez had a feeling there was more to this than just a strung-out kid—"

"And you're obsessing over her, too?" Hugo offered, finishing my sentence for me.

He didn't use the words I would have chosen, but he wasn't far from wrong. I felt a strong sense of empathy for the kid. Maybe it was because of how vulnerable she seemed, huddled under the emergency blanket on the sidewalk in the middle of the night. I couldn't be sure.

Down the hallway, a doctor and two nurses stepped from the exam room. I couldn't tell if they were resigned or relieved. One of the nurses appeared to be quite upset. Fearing the worst, I strode toward them.

"Kat," Hugo called after me, but I kept going.

"Doctor?" I said as I neared them. "Are you treating the vic brought in last night? I'm with the sheriff's department."

The man turned my way. He looked to be in his thirties. Tall, and not at all unpleasant-looking.

"Dr. Cole," he responded, eyeing me from neck to waist, which I considered rather rude. "Can I see an ID, please?" he asked, and I realized he'd been looking for a badge.

I felt my cheeks blush as I took my department ID card from my pocket and showed him.

"Thank you, Investigator Cromwell," he said, reading my name. "And yes, I'm treating Jane Doe from last night."

I glanced over at the exam room, but the door had been closed. The nurse I'd noticed before was still clearly upset, engrossed in a whispered conversation with her compatriot.

"Is she alive?" I asked.

The doctor blew out his cheeks. "For now, yes. But we had a scare."

I felt a wave of relief. "We were told she had a unique mixture of drugs in her system."

Cole looked at his watch. "Mind if we grab a coffee? I can explain what little I know. It's been a busy morning."

"I never turn down coffee," I replied.

The doctor glanced over my shoulder, and I heard Hugo's footsteps as he joined us.

"This is my partner, Hugo Fuentes," I said, making the introductions. "Dr. Cole."

"Eric is fine," the doctor responded, turning his attention back to me. I blushed a little again.

We followed Cole back to the reception, where he steered us into a small cafeteria. We all ordered coffees and found a table away from the handful of other folks.

"So, what was going on when we arrived?" I asked once we were all seated.

"She flatlined," Eric replied. "Right after receiving meds."

"Is she allergic to what you gave her?" Hugo asked.

The doctor shrugged. "That would be highly unusual. It was a very low dose of lorazepam, and this was the second time she'd received it. She was fine after the first dose."

"So what caused her to crash?" I asked.

"Good question," Eric responded. "We're running another tox screen to see if we missed anything."

I thought back to the scene outside the exam room. "What was the nurse so upset about?"

The doctor glanced down at his coffee cup. "It was a stressful few minutes."

"She the one who gave Jane Doe the meds?" I asked, sensing there was more to the incident.

Eric nodded and sighed. "I was probably a little short with her while it was all happening. A situation like that requires clear thought and immediate action, not blathering responses. Nurse Chen is usually better than that. I'll talk to her later about it."

"She thought she'd done something wrong?" Hugo asked.

"She hesitated," the doctor replied. "We have strict systems and protocols in place for administering any medications. There should have been no doubt."

"But she wasn't sure," I verified.

He nodded again. "So we'll see in the tox screen."

It felt like Jane Doe couldn't catch a break anywhere. But in truth, we knew nothing about her story. I was leaning toward sympathy, but she may have brought all this upon herself. Some would say she was lucky that the Harrises didn't run her over, and maybe the meds were fine, and her heart simply had enough of the abuse she was putting it through. In which case, she was lucky that Dishy Dr. Cole was close at hand.

"What can you tell us about the drugs she was on?" I asked, ready to find answers for the original reason we were there.

"I wasn't on duty when she was admitted, but I talked to the doctor who was, and we looked over the tox screen results together. Either she was grabbing pills from wherever she could find them, or someone has come up with an exotic mix that we have to worry about."

"An exotic mix of what?" Hugo asked.

"We found varying amounts of scopolamine, midazolam, ketamine, and Rohypnol in her system."

"Okay, Eric, you're gonna have to explain the first two. I've heard of them, but I don't know what they are," I said. "The second two, I'm aware of. And why would these be mixed together?"

The doctor took another sip of coffee, appearing to pull his thoughts together. "Scopolamine, which is known as Devil's Breath, is a lesser-known date-rape drug that induces compliance. It's also been used to get information from victims. Midazolam is an anti-anxiety med that is often used to reduce stress before surgery. Ketamine, as you know, is a hallucinogenic with dissociative effects, and Rohypnol, we all know as one of the more popular date-rape drugs."

"Was she sexually assaulted?" Hugo asked.

"She's been recently sexually active," Eric replied. "But there's no indication of abuse. We found lubricant in her pelvic exam, but no traces of semen."

"So someone loaded her up on date-rape drugs and sedatives, then took advantage of her wearing a condom," I suggested.

"Very likely," Eric replied. "But I can't say for sure. There wasn't any vaginal trauma, but that's not uncommon with date-rape drug victims."

"No other drugs in her system?" Hugo asked.

The doctor shook his head. "Surprisingly, no."

"What was the purpose of stacking all those drugs together?" Hugo asked. "Do you think they were blended into one pill or injection?"

"She has numerous injection marks, so we expected to see a narcotic on the tox screen. Some are heavy-handed recent puncture marks with bruising, which suggests someone injected her with the cocktail. But again, it's not conclusive. She may have carelessly administered the shots herself."

"The mixture sounds like a potent date-rape drug," I commented.

Eric winced. "More than that. All these drugs affect memory as well. If she comes around, I can't tell you how much she'll remember about what's happened to her."

"Aren't those drugs usually short-term memory loss?" Hugo asked.

"On their own," the doctor replied. "But who knows with this combination. If she's been given the cocktail over an extended period, there's a chance she'll have that whole portion of memory missing."

"Not to mention she would have been completely out of it," I said. "If the state we found her in is anything to go by."

"No question," Eric agreed, then looked at his watch again. "I have to get back to the ward."

"Mind if I snap a quick picture before you go?" I asked, taking out my instant camera. "Just for our use in the office to keep every-thing square."

"I guess not," he said, and gave me a pleasant smile.

I felt my cheeks blush. Again.

3

"You just wanted a picture of the guy," Hugo ribbed me as we walked to the car.

I laughed. "Tell me you didn't?"

Hugo frowned as he opened the driver's door. "Believe me, he plays on your side of the street, and from the way he was looking at you, I'd say he wouldn't mind ringing your doorbell."

"Hugo!" I exclaimed, annoyed as I blushed once more.

After we'd left the hospital, I shifted the conversation back to the case. "So what now.

"Hand it over to Special Victims Unit," Hugo replied. "Who should have been handling it in the first place."

My first reaction was to argue with him, but I stopped myself for a moment. On the face of it, he was right. This didn't fall under our purview, or our field of expertise. Neither of which made me any less determined to be involved.

"Everything indicates she's a street kid, yeah?" I said, then continued without waiting for his response. "But no narcotics in her system, yet recent injection marks and signs that it's been happening for a while."

"So, she used to be an addict and now someone picked her up

off the street and fed her a cocktail of date-rape drugs," Hugo replied. "Still not our case, Kat."

"Or she was picked up off the street some time ago, and she's been held for a while," I countered. "Which is kidnapping and might fall under us, as it's local."

Hugo looked over and raised an eyebrow.

"We could at least take a first step of looking into it," I continued. "Bradley sent us to the hospital for a reason, right?"

"Checking a box, no doubt," Hugo grumbled.

Rather than carry on arm-wrestling with my partner over whether we should be involved, I took out my phone and made a call.

"Martinez," a gruff voice answered over the car's speakers.

"Sarge, has anyone tried tracking down an ID for our Jane Doe from last night?"

"Of course," he replied.

Our desk sergeant, who never seemed to go home, was hard-nosed, abrasive, and never made things easy on me. I'd be offended if he didn't treat everyone the same way. Plus, he was incredibly efficient and ran the station like a Swiss watch.

"Any luck?"

"No hits from fingerprints. No missing persons matching her description in the system locally. Farther afield has given us a long list. It'll take a while to go through it."

"We're on our way back from the hospital," I responded. "We can help."

I made sure not to look Hugo's way as he muttered under his breath.

"Copy," Martinez said, and hung up.

We drove on in silence for a few minutes while I let Hugo simmer down. Or at least hoped he did. To my surprise, it was he who spoke first. He handed me his phone and unlocked the screen.

"Check my contacts for a Doug Albright."

I did as he said without questioning why. "Call him?" I asked once I'd located the number.

Hugo nodded.

I typed the number into my phone as it was paired to the car. It rang four times.

"Albright," a man answered in a stern voice.

"Doug, it's Hugo Fuentes in homicide. I'm with my partner, Kat Cromwell. It's her phone we called you on."

"Hey, Hugo," Albright said in a lighter tone. "I was about to send it to voicemail as I didn't know the number. Only answered because my eldest has been getting his ass in trouble at school. Figured it was them telling me to come get him again."

Hugo laughed. "Surprised you didn't let it go to voicemail for that reason."

"I thought about it," Albright replied. "How are your two?"

"Growing too fast. Don't see them enough," Hugo replied.

I often forgot about my partner's family. He'd been divorced for many years and only spent time with his kids a few weekends a month.

"I'm just about to walk into a meeting. Is this something quick I can help with?"

"Probably," Hugo replied. "I'll let Kat explain what we've come across, as she can remember all the damn drug names."

"Okay, Kat. What do you have?"

A little warning would have been nice from my partner, but I assumed Doug Albright was in the narcotics division of the Sheriff Department's Special Investigation Bureau.

"We picked up a young woman out of her mind wandering the streets last night. Tox screen came back with a mix of scopolamine, ketamine, midazolam, and Rohypnol. Doc we spoke with this morning thinks it might be a cocktail injected into her system."

The line went quiet for a moment, and the slight echo in Doug's voice changed when he finally spoke. I presumed he'd moved to a smaller room.

"Doc say if he'd seen it before?"

"He hasn't," I replied. "He was guessing. I don't think there's a way to prove all the drugs went into her system at the same time."

"And where did you find the girl?" Doug asked.

His voice had quietened, almost sounding suspicious. Or perhaps cautious.

"In Dana Point," Hugo replied before I could. "What have we stumbled across, Doug?"

The line was silent for several moments.

"We've seen three other cases that sound similar," he finally said, cautiously. "None of our girls were so lucky. We found them all dead. Two on the street. One in a motel room in Costa Mesa."

"When was this?" I asked.

"First girl was a few months back. Costa Mesa was three weeks ago."

I wondered about other similarities. "Had they been sexually assaulted?"

"With the first two, it was hard to tell. They were both hookers. But the motel room girl hadn't been."

"Really?" Hugo responded. "That's odd, isn't it? Someone stuffed her full of date-rape drugs, then didn't do anything."

"We think it was a test gone wrong," Doug replied. "Probably all three were. Look, guys, I gotta run into this meeting, but I need you to keep me informed on this, okay?"

"Sure," Hugo replied. "Our captain has us chasing it down as it happened on our patch, but it really should be a narcotics or SVU case, anyway."

"Listen," Doug said firmly. "Now you're on it, keep the case if you can. I'm going to tell you something, but I don't want this getting around, so careful who you share it with. The least people using this term, the better for now, understand?"

"Not really," Hugo replied. "But sure."

I heard Doug let out a frustrated sigh. "If word gets around, then the next minute, every numbnut drug dealer will be blending, mixing, and trying to sell this shit. And we'll have girls showing up dead all over the place."

Hugo looked over at me and raised an eyebrow. "Alright, I get it now. That makes sense. We'll be discreet."

"Thanks," Doug said, sounding more relaxed. "If your girl's alive, it means they've figured out a blend that works. Is she talking?"

"No," I replied. "She's in a bad way. Almost lost her this morning, but hoping she pulls through."

"I doubt she'll be of any help even if she does make it," Doug said. "That cocktail is designed to knock out any memory of what happened."

"I thought the memory loss was short-term with these drugs," I said. "Leaves them with a hazy recollection, or pieces missing."

I suddenly felt self-conscious talking about memory issues, but Hugo didn't seem to react in any way.

Doug scoffed. "We think this cocktail is not about a one-night party. It's designed to be used for trafficking. Makes them compliant with no memory of where they've been or who they've seen. Perfect for moving a shipment of girls around without them screaming their heads off."

"Needle marks suggest our girl may have been held a while," I offered. "So it aligns."

"She an addict?" Doug asked.

"No traces of other narcotics in her system," I replied.

"Any background on her? She local or foreign?"

"She only spoke three words to the couple who almost ran her over last night," I explained. "But they didn't mention an accent. Mind you, she was so stoned, she was barely coherent."

"What she say?" Doug asked.

"'There are more,'" I told him.

"Shit," Doug muttered.

"Yeah, that plays into your trafficking theory now that we have a new perspective," Hugo said.

"Maybe," Doug said. "I gotta run. Here's the part I'll share, but you need to be careful about, okay?"

"Shoot," Hugo replied. "We'll keep it in a tight circle."

"There's already a street name floating around for this stuff. I'm telling you, the longer we can keep this out of conversation, the fewer bodies we'll have."

"Mum's the word," I assured him.

"You're not from around here, are you, Kat?" Doug queried, his suspicious tone reappearing.

"Raised right here in Dana Point," I replied. "But I was born in England. Never lost the accent."

"You say things kinda funny, too."

"And she's a pain in the ass," Hugo added. "But she can be trusted, Doug."

A backhanded compliment was all I could expect from my partner, but I chose to focus on the positive.

"What are they calling this stuff?" I asked.

"It's called Velvet," Doug replied. "And I have a bad feeling about what's coming with this drug, so keep me posted."

"Thanks, Doug," Hugo said. "We will."

The line went dead, and I looked over at Hugo. "Still want to hand this case off?"

He slowly shook his head. "Not until we know that this shit isn't going down in our beach cities."

My relief at having Hugo on board was short-lived as my thoughts shifted back to Jane Doe in the hospital. If she could pull any thoughts together, I doubt she felt lucky, but it sounded like she might be.

"Velvet," I said under my breath. "And there are more."

Hugo glanced over at me. "You realize that once we get Bradley up to speed, she may well shift gears and want this handed off to narcotics."

"Then best we be careful exactly what we tell her," I replied.

Hugo nodded. "For now."

4

____

After a second stop for the day at PC Beans, this time using their drive-thru, we returned to the office. Sergeant Martinez hadn't lied. He'd used our internal software that accessed the National Crime Information Center (NCIC) database and the National Center for Missing & Exploited Children (NCMEC) database. Once he'd expanded the current missing persons search to nationwide, the number of females reported was 33,289.

"As you kindly volunteered, that's where I stopped," he said without a hint of a smile.

"Thank you, sir," I said, keeping the sarcasm out of my voice. There was no point poking the bear.

Hugo didn't say a word, but held the door for me as we made our way from reception to our office.

"Bloody hell," I exhaled once I'd unlocked my computer and looked at the list we were dealing with. "This is beyond a needle in a haystack, Hugo."

"Fourteen hundred a day," he replied. "That's how many names are added on average each and every day in the U.S."

I let out a low whistle. "Okay, let's start narrowing this down."

"Age," Hugo suggested. "She's sixteen or seventeen, I'd guess."

"Let's use fourteen to twenty to be safe," I replied, using drop-down options in the software. "21,108."

"She's white. That should reduce it some," Hugo said.

I selected Caucasian from another dropdown. "9,831."

"What else do we know?" Hugo said, sliding his chair past our monitors to look my way.

"Sandy blond hair," I said, and checked the menu options. "There's a blond option."

"Natural color?" Hugo asked.

"No roots showing, and we think she's been held a while," I replied. "If they couldn't be bothered to bathe her, I doubt they touched up her roots."

Hugo nodded.

"1,278," I read off from the screen.

"Getting better," Hugo commented. "What else is distinct about her?"

I considered his question for a few moments. I hadn't noticed any obvious scars or tattoos, but I'd only seen her wrapped in a blanket. Digging in my pocket, I pulled out the two instant photos I'd taken and a business card Dr. Cole had handed me before we left.

"He'd love to hear from you," Hugo ribbed from across the desks.

That's because he doesn't know how the last man who dated me ended up, I thought. If the doctor knew a part of Paul washed up on the beach earlier this year, he might not be so keen.

"Sod off," I replied to Hugo with a grin, then texted the doc.

"Investigator Kat Cromwell here. Does Jane Doe have any distinguishing marks/tattoos?"

Setting my phone down, I looked at my grainy, dark picture of the vic on the sidewalk. I didn't have any tattoos, but most people my age had something. Half the girls I'd graduated high school with already had at least a small tattoo they'd talked their parents into allowing.

"I wonder how long she's been missing," I thought aloud.

"Even if she has a tattoo, it could well have been done after she left home."

"Select 'no distinguishing marks' and see what it does to the list," Hugo suggested.

I found the dropdown option and waited for the updated figure. "830."

"There's height and weight options, right?" he asked.

"Yeah."

"The report has her listed as five-foot-four inches and one hundred and twenty pounds," Hugo said. "That sound about right? I suspect these are estimates by the deputies."

"She was curled up under a blanket when I saw her," I replied. "But I can use those numbers, and we'll update once the hospital verifies. If she ever gets out of that bed." I chose from range options the system allowed me to enter. "Okay. Between five-foot-two and five-foot-six, and between one hundred and ten and one hundred and thirty pounds. Narrows it down a bit. 586."

"Still a big number to go through," Hugo replied. "Especially before we know if the parameters we're using are even correct."

He had a point. I was daunted by the task, but still keen to begin searching through details and images. Neither database integrated with facial recognition software, so it was going to be a manual project. It made more sense to wait.

My phone buzzed with a text, and I eagerly grabbed it, hoping it was Dishy Doc. It wasn't.

"When you gym"

If I hadn't seen the name and known it was a message from my dad, I still would have recognized his text. Between struggling to hit the right letters with his banana-sized thumbs, he seemed to work from the theory that he was paying for every digit typed and used as few as possible. The result was usually a garbled, misspelled assembly of words I had to decipher. Punctuation was also far too costly to be involved.

"Tomorrow," I replied, hoping my current state of exhaustion would be negated by a decent night's sleep. I got a brain-exploding

emoji in response. I'd also learned not to ponder on the reasoning behind Dad's use of emojis. In this case, the exploding brain icon was undoubtedly in close proximity to the thumbs-up and got caught in the prod from his oversized digit.

I shifted my tired and wandering focus back to Jane Doe. "I wonder how well the uniforms canvassed the area where she was found."

"Their notes say they checked with all the homes on the block north of Violet Lantern and several south," Hugo replied. "Looks like only half of them were home this morning when they went by."

I stood. "We should bang on some doors. Maybe we can catch a few more."

I heard Hugo sigh. "I'm sure Sarge has them going back later today. Far better chance after five or six this evening."

"We could grab lunch while we're out," I said, knowing what motivated my partner.

He grunted and grabbed his jacket from the coat rack.

My idea had seemed like a good way of doing something other than sitting in the office, but after knocking on a dozen doors and learning nothing more than the deputies had, I was questioning the move. Maybe I would have stumbled across Jane Doe by now if I'd slogged through some of the 586 results. At least it was a beautiful day, and I always preferred being outside rather than cooped up in the office.

We covered a handful of homes on the south side of the intersection, and a few in each direction on La Cresta. Anyone who answered had either slept through the entire event or had been woken by the police lights. No one had witnessed events leading up to Jane Doe's appearance.

North of the intersection on the left was the little park, then a pair of two-story condo buildings and a pair of houses. I noticed that the second residence sitting on the corner of Violet Lantern and Las Robles, a street branching northwest at an angle, had a fancy doorbell camera. There had been no answer earlier in the day when the deputies had checked. I rang the doorbell and waited.

"Lunch after this," Hugo said, joining me from the other side of the street.

"Buena Vista Market," I replied, suggesting one of my favorite taco stops in the shopping center and marketplace between PCH and La Plaza.

Hugo nodded his approval as he took a couple of steps back and glanced up at the second level of the home. It looked like a 1970s build that had been recently renovated and modernized with all-new siding, windows, roof, and trim.

"I hear music from upstairs," he said.

I rang the doorbell again, then banged loudly on the double wood and glass doors.

"They heard you," Hugo confirmed. "The music turned down."

I took out my badge and held it in front of the doorbell camera. A few moments later, a young female voice came over a hidden speaker.

"My parents aren't home. They're at work."

"Okay, but would you mind coming to the door, please," I said, not knowing whether I was supposed to press a button when I spoke. "No one is in any trouble. We're just looking for witnesses of an incident near here."

"Last night?" the girl asked.

"Can you come to the door, miss?" I requested again.

Silence followed, and when I was about to hammer on the door again, I heard footsteps coming down the stairs. The door opened, and a girl I guessed to be around twelve or thirteen stared at me. She had pink hair, a baseball cap on backwards, baggy jean shorts that hit below her knees, and a Santa Cruz Skateboard sweatshirt cut into a crop top.

"OCSD Investigators Kat Cromwell and Hugo Fuentes," I introduced ourselves. "What's your name?"

"Bee," she replied. "This about last night?"

"Did you see anything?" I asked.

"Couldn't miss it. The lights were flashing like a disco for ages."

"What about before the police arrived?"

"What about it?" Bee asked suspiciously.

"Did you see anything odd outside before the police showed up?"

"I wasn't looking outside."

The kid needed to work on her storytelling skills. Her nervous tension gave her away.

"But you weren't asleep, were you?"

She shrugged her shoulders. "So?"

"So how about we take a look at your doorbell video footage from last night, Bee? Maybe it caught something that might be useful to us."

She shook her head. "It doesn't work properly."

Her eyes flicked around everywhere except directly at me.

"So, if I get footage from one of the neighbors' cameras, should I show your parents how you've been sneaking out at night?"

"They don't have cameras pointed right at our house," Bee snapped back far too quickly. The look of dread on her face told me she'd realized her error, too.

"They know you're not in school?" Hugo offered, looking at his watch. "What's your last name? We have a few calls to make."

"I'm out sick, man. Probably contagious. You should step back." She spluttered her best version of a cough.

"Gotta do better than that," Hugo said. "What's your full name?"

The girl gritted her teeth. "I knew I shouldn't have opened the door to the Feds."

I laughed. "We're not the Feds, and I don't give a shit about you sneaking out with your friends. I did plenty of that at your age. We're looking for information about a girl a few years older than you who was found just down the road last night."

I pulled my instant photos from my pocket and showed her the one of Jane Doe in the silver blanket.

"Have you seen her around? Either last night, or before?"

Bee studied the picture. "Shitty photo," she said. "Should've used your phone."

I heard a chuckle coming from Hugo.

"Did you see her?" I persisted.

The girl shook her head.

"Look, Bee. I'm guessing that doorbell camera works just fine. You just don't want us to see you on it, but all we care about is tracking down this girl's movements. It's important, okay?"

She lifted her baseball cap, ruffled her pink-tinted hair, then reset the hat in place, buying herself time to think.

"Don't you need a warrant or something?" she asked half-heartedly.

"Not if you're willingly showing it to us," I replied. "But we can have a warrant back here in an hour. Of course, it'll be for your parents, not you, and they'll see everything."

Bee rolled her eyes. "This sucks," she groaned, but stepped back and nodded for us to come inside. "Close the door. I don't need the old goat over the road asking my mom why the Feds were at the house."

Pulling what looked to be one of the latest iPhones from her back pocket, Bee scrolled and clicked in a blur of thumbs before looking up at me. "What time?"

"Go to two thirty a.m. and work backwards."

More thumb gymnastics, and she held the screen for us all to see. The street was well-lit, quiet, and void of movement except for the subtle strobing of red and blue hues from the unseen police cruiser.

"Rewind until the lights go away," I suggested, and Bee dragged the slider until the view became fixed with only the yellow glow of the streetlights.

She then set the speed to a multiple of eight, still running in reverse. After a minute or so, a figure moved across the screen. Bee hit pause and worked the slider until Jane Doe came into view from the top left of the screen.

"Woah. She's out of it, man," Bee commented, as Jane Doe staggered down the road, occasionally stumbling into the sidewalk curb.

The young woman pulled at her thin cotton summer dress until it fell from her shoulders as if the straps had torn away.

"Damn, she's putting on a show," Bee said, but any humor had vanished from her voice.

Once Jane Doe disappeared off the right side of the screen, Bee hit pause.

"Let's see it again from the beginning," I said.

The girl hit rewind, then the phone pinged, and a text box covered half the screen. Three messages followed one after the other.

"yo B mr franklin trippin fr"

"u ghosted his class AGAIN lol"

"Last time b4 u get wrecked"

"Out sick, you say?" Hugo commented, and Bee quickly swiped the text away.

The footage had continued rewinding, so we were back to looking at an empty street. Until a different figure arrived from the top.

"Shit," Bee mumbled, and went to move the slider. It was unmistakably her in the footage.

"Wait," I urged. "What's the timestamp?"

"2:11," she moaned. "Thought you didn't care?"

We watched Bee walk up her drive with a skateboard under her arm. She breezed past the front door and disappeared. The footage kept rolling. Less than thirty seconds later, Jane Doe appeared, but something was different.

"Didn't she arrive from the upper part of the screen before?" Hugo asked.

"Yup," I agreed, and checked the time. "This is 2:12.09."

Jane Doe paused and looked up at the streetlight shining down. She covered her face with her arm, swung around, and disappeared off-screen again. The footage played on. At 2:12.38, she reappeared from the top left, but more toward the middle of the road. We watched the same scene we'd already watched play out again.

"I think she came down Robles Drive," I said. "She was disoriented under the light and staggered around until she reappeared in the middle of Violet Lantern."

"I missed her by less than a frickin' minute, man," Bee said, letting out a low whistle. "What happened to her down the hill?"

"A car almost hit her, but stopped and called 911," I explained. "She's in hospital, but for what had happened to her before she passed your house. You missing her didn't change anything."

"Okay. Cool. I would have felt like shit if I could have helped her or something."

"We need a copy of this footage," Hugo said.

Bee frowned at him. "I'm so screwed if my parents see this."

"See what?" I replied. "Only thing I see on this video is our Jane Doe."

Bee nodded and let her lips curl into a grin. "Tight. Maybe you can hit me with a note saying I was out performing civic duties?"

I laughed. "Not sure I can commit written perjury for you, Bee."

"Hey," Hugo blurted. "Rewind the footage."

Bee and I had stopped looking at the screen, but apparently Hugo had still been watching.

"What did you see?" I asked as Bee scrolled backwards again.

"There," Hugo said, pointing at the phone. "We must have missed it when we were rewinding so fast."

I watched carefully as the nose of a vehicle crept into view. It stopped just as the windshield became visible. Then slowly backed away.

5

____

With the station only a few minutes away, we picked up lunch from Buena Vista Market and ate at our desks while we strategized. Captain Bradley would be furious if we left her out of the loop too long, but for now, we asked Sergeant Martinez to join us. Maybe if we delayed a little longer, we'd have enough new info to keep the boss appeased and be able to avoid talking about the cocktail of drugs in Jane Doe's system.

"We're not certain of anything," I told Sarge as he questioned our request for a door-to-door search on Robles Road. "We're not even sure she came down Robles, or that she didn't walk all the way down from Selva. It just appears that she arrives from that direction."

"There have to be over forty buildings on that street, some of which are apartments," he responded. "You want every door knocked on?"

"Ideally," I responded.

"Yes," Hugo added with more authority.

"And what should I tell my deputies they're looking for?" Martinez asked pointedly.

"A Ford van," I replied, having searched online for vehicles that resembled the headlight assembly and short hood of the vehicle in the doorbell camera footage. "I think it's blue, but certainly a darker color."

"There," Hugo said. "Have them ask about the van and whether they saw Jane Doe. And have them get names. We can find out the owners of the homes, but many are rentals. We need to check for rap sheets."

"We can do a DMV search for addresses on Robles," I suggested.

Martinez nodded, let out a sigh, and looked at his watch. "Fine. Let me see how many boots I can spare. I'll have them start at four-teen hundred."

"Thanks, Sarge," I said. "We'll meet them there."

"What kind of Ford van?" Hugo asked once Martinez had left.

"The headlight and grille on the top of the hood match a Ford Transit Cargo. They come in panel and minibus styles, but we don't have enough in the shot to tell which this is."

"Got a year?" he asked.

"The picture I found is a 2019, so now I'm trying to see which years they kept the same design."

I heard the crunching of tacos from across the desks as I searched the internet for model years. It reminded me to eat my own lunch as I worked.

"Looks like it has to be 2019 or older," I said, after swallowing a mouthful of fish taco. "The grille detail changed around that time."

"This would be a lot easier if they had a license plate on the front," Hugo commented.

California law dictated having plates on both front and rear, but it had been accepted over decades that most people didn't carry a front plate. Some vehicles didn't even have a provision for one. It was a handy excuse to pull over someone suspicious who hadn't openly done anything wrong, which was probably why it wasn't heavily enforced. Regardless, we wouldn't have been able to read a front plate on the van from the angle we had, anyway.

"Of course there's a million models of these bloody things, too," I groaned. "Panel or passenger with windows. Long or short models. Tall, medium, or regular roof. And three different weight capacities, like pickup trucks."

"A DMV search will bring back more results than our Jane Doe search," Hugo commented, crumpling up his empty wrappers and tossing them in the trash. "But we could see if there are any hits for Robles."

"Good thinking, Sherlock," I quipped. "But no dice. Already checked."

Nothing from my partner. He wasn't big on snappy comebacks. He was more the silent and make-you-wonder kinda guy.

"First year they remade the Transit Cargo was 2015," I added as I verified the model years.

I sat back, picking up my two instant photos and studying them. We still hadn't heard back from Dr. Dishy. I focused on the shot of Jane Doe. What had this girl been through? We were assuming she'd come from the streets, but that was based on how she looked, and the fact that no one had filed a matching missing person report recently. Which gave me an idea.

"We should talk to some of the local homeless people. Maybe they know her."

Hugo rolled his chair to the side of his monitor to look at me. "Send uniforms."

"We've just asked Sarge to gather every available deputy for the house-to-house," I reminded him. "We have time before two o'clock."

I could almost see the gears whirring in Hugo's head as he tried to think of a valid justification not to rub shoulders with people who didn't have the luxury of regular showers.

"I'm going," I said, getting to my feet. "I'll meet you at Robles."

Hugo groaned and stood, too. I was surprised my guilt trip worked, but he reluctantly grabbed his jacket and followed me out.

The unhoused persons crisis in the U.S. had been on a sharp increase for the past few years. While Dana Point had far less of an issue than LA County Beach Cities, there had still been a noticeable rise in less fortunate folks pushing their meager belongings around town in shopping carts. Below the overpasses for Pacific Coast Highway, on either side of the San Juan Creek, was the most popular spot for spending the night. It was early afternoon, so most of the people had dispersed around town to their favorite locations to score money or meals, but I noticed one man still there after we parked in the A's Burgers lot and walked to the bicycle trail.

The name "San Juan Creek" made it sound like a babbling brook amid a wooded pasture. It was not. The creek was a broad concrete spillway designed to funnel heavy rains from the city to the ocean. A four-foot chain-link fence divided the steep concrete slopes from the bike paths on either side. At this time of year, the base of the creek was nothing more than a handful of streams cutting their way through the accumulated muck, the water coming mostly from sprinklers rather than rain.

The man sat next to a supermarket cart full of plastic bags stuffed with everything his life had been reduced to.

"Hi, Dennis, how are you doing these days?"

He squinted up at me, shielding his eyes despite the shade from the overpass. His skin was wrinkled and blemished from the sun, his hair a knotted mess.

"Is that you, surfing cop?"

"Yeah, it's me," I replied, and nodded towards Hugo, who was keeping his distance. "That's my partner, Hugo. He doesn't bite."

Dennis frowned, eyeing the other man. He shook his head and mumbled something incoherent.

"Dennis, could you look at a picture and tell me if you've seen this woman around?" I asked, keen to steer his attention away from Hugo. Maybe it would have been better if I'd come alone. I knew Hugo had empathy for people like Dennis, but his distaste for the foul odors and grime emanated from his presence like the stenches themselves.

I held out my grainy photo of Jane Doe for Dennis to see.

"I got one of them," he said, tapping a grubby finger on the photograph.

For a moment, I wasn't sure what he meant.

"Oh, the blanket," I finally figured out. "Yeah, they hand them out sometimes, right?"

He nodded.

"What about the girl, Dennis? Have you seen her?"

"She had dark hair," he muttered. "Don't remember her having a silver blanket."

I heard Hugo move closer behind me and held out a hand, indicating for him to stay back. Dennis had lost everything when he'd become addicted to pain pills after a cycling accident. The addiction had robbed him of his home and family, but also parts of his mind. There was usually some form of translation required from anything he said.

"You've seen this woman?" I asked. "But with darker hair?"

Dennis shrugged and rifled through a tote bag next to him. After a moment, I realized he wasn't looking for anything to do with my question.

"Hey, Dennis," I said, squatting down. "Can you look at this picture one more time for me?"

"I don't know her," he said without actually looking.

"You said you thought you knew her, Dennis," I said patiently.

He turned to me, then pointed at Sharon Harris kneeling next to Jane Doe. "I don't know her."

"Okay, thank you," I replied. "What about the young woman, Dennis?"

His busy mind seemed to find a moment of clarity, and he looked at the photograph more carefully. "It's not her."

"It's not the girl with darker hair?" I asked him.

He shook his head. "I don't know where she went."

"Dark-Haired Girl went away?" I asked, trying to follow the threads as best I could decipher.

He nodded.

I was about to ask him how long ago, but time wasn't a concept many homeless people maintained a firm grasp on. Their days tended to blend together.

"Did she have a name?" I asked instead.

Dennis's eyes flicked from the picture to me and then to his right. "She was there. That's her spot."

An old shopping cart missing a front wheel sat almost empty, with just a handful of bags and other junk left behind. I guessed it had been picked clean once the woman hadn't returned. I waited to see if Dennis would say anything more. Behind me, I heard Hugo impatiently shuffling his feet.

"I liked Lexy," the homeless man mumbled.

"Lexy?" I responded, telling myself to remain casual so I didn't spook him. "That was the dark-haired girl's name?"

Dennis nodded, then went back to rifling through the bag next to him, finally producing a large folding pocket knife. He opened the blade.

"Hey!" Hugo said, stepping alongside me.

Dennis jumped with a look of panic on his face. I stood and put my arm out, holding Hugo back.

"He's got a knife, Kat!"

"It's okay," I assured Hugo, and pushed him away. "He's just showing it to me."

Dennis cowered, holding the knife away from us as though we were threatening to steal it. He stared past me at my partner.

"It's mine. I traded fair and square."

"You traded with Lexy?" I asked.

Dennis nodded, his eyes still flicking between the knife and Hugo standing a few yards behind me on the path. I took my camera from my back pocket and squatted down once more.

"It's okay, mate. I'd just like a closer look at that knife of yours. It's a beauty."

The man nodded and brought the knife a little closer. It was all metal with a dark scarlet handle and a black blade, like a tactical weapon. I noticed the word "MOVE" etched along the handle.

"Can I take a photograph of your lovely knife, Dennis?"

He held the weapon closer. "Traded fair and square."

"No problem, Dennis, it's okay. I'm not going to touch your knife. I just want to take a picture because it's so nice. Is that okay?"

His eyes warily checked Hugo before he appeared to relax. "Okay," he mumbled, and held the knife out again.

Moving slowly, I brought my instant camera up, made sure it focused on the knife, and snapped a picture. After a few seconds, the motor whirred softly inside, and the photograph began feeding from the slot on the side.

Dennis stared at the device in my hand. "That like a Polaroid?"

"Yes, but it's a more compact version," I replied.

He frowned and looked at me. "Why don't you use your phone like everyone else?"

I heard Hugo laugh behind me.

We still had a few minutes before we needed to meet the deputies at Robles Road, so I persuaded Hugo to drive through PC Beans for the second time for him, third time for me. I wondered if the place would go out of business if I gave up coffee.

On the drive over, I searched the internet on my phone for "MOVE." It returned a bunch of dictionary sites explaining the meaning of the word. I added "knife" to the search, and below a few returns for box knives in house moving ads, I saw a website.

"Manufactured and Operated by Veteran Enterprises," I read aloud to Hugo. "It's a company owned and run by U.S. veterans of the military branches, according to their website. One of the things they sell is those knives."

"This Lexy girl could have picked that up anywhere," Hugo pointed out. "Someone dropped it or gave it to her."

"Maybe," I replied. "But worth a search. Lexy could be former military."

Hugo pulled into the short line for the drive-thru. "If he

compared her to Jane Doe, she's probably too young to be a former much of anything except a high school student."

"Interesting that she's gone missing, though, yeah?"

Hugo nodded. "There's a million explanations for that, but I agree. We should follow up. Her name, Lexy, is probably short for something."

"Alexis, Alexa, Alexandra," I wondered aloud, but my thoughts were interrupted when my phone rang in my hand. I didn't recognize the number. "Investigator Kat Cromwell," I answered over the car's hands-free system.

"Hi, Kat, this is Eric. Dr. Eric Cole. We met this morning."

Hugo grinned at me, and to my annoyance, I felt my cheeks blush once more. My easily triggered embarrassment was embarrassing in itself.

"Thanks for getting back to us. I'm with my partner, Hugo," I said, just in case the doctor intended on mixing business with pleasure on the call.

I then felt stupid for even harboring such a thought. Why would he be interested in me?

"From my examinations, our Jane Doe doesn't have any tattoos or distinguishing marks, I'm afraid. Apart from the injection sites, which look to have been given clumsily."

"Can you tell if she injected herself, doc?" Hugo asked.

"I doubt it," Eric replied. "Unless she gave some of them to herself in the backside, which isn't usual."

"Okay. Thanks, Eric," I said. "Is she stable now?"

"Seems to be," he replied. "But I wanted to update you on the second set of labs we ran."

"Was the dosage wrong?" Hugo asked.

The doctor paused before replying in a quieter tone. "No, the level of lorazepam was consistent with the correct dosage. But the level of midazolam was elevated. A lot."

"Why would that be?" I asked. "Surely it should have been working its way out of her system?"

"Exactly," the doctor replied. "The only way it could be elevated is if more had been administered."

"Did the nurse screw it up?" Hugo asked.

"Not a chance," Eric replied. "I don't know how it got in her system, but it wasn't from the medical staff."

6

"We need to check with the hospital for CCTV," I said after we left the drive-thru with fresh coffees.

Hugo scoffed. "You really think someone snuck in there and dosed her up? Doesn't seem likely to me."

"Ballsy," I admitted. "But if they have cameras pointing down that hallway, we'll see if someone went in the room who shouldn't have been there."

While Hugo drove us up the hill, I called Sarge and asked him to see what footage the hospital had, which he grumpily said he would do. I thought about asking him to put someone in the office on a data search for a missing Lexy, but decided against it. We only had half a dozen administrative staff in our little department, and they were constantly swamped with paperwork. It would have to wait until we returned.

We parked at the bottom of Robles Road, where several squad cars already occupied spots along the curb. Deputy Ripley approached us as we got out of the car. His partner, Hanson, kept his distance. He and Hugo had locked horns in the past, so it was probably a wise move.

"Afternoon, sir. Ma'am," Ripley greeted us. "We have two cars at the top of the hill, so eight deputies in total. We planned to work the street from both ends, if that's good with you?"

"Hi," I responded. "Thanks for doing this. I know it's a pain in the arse. Does everyone know to be on the lookout for a dark-colored Ford Transit Cargo van?"

Ripley nodded. "Yes, ma'am. And anyone who may have seen our vic last night."

"Not just last night," Hugo commented. "If she'd been held around here, it's possible she was spotted a while ago."

"Yes, sir," Ripley replied. "We're on an operational channel. I'll spread the word, and everyone knows to alert you if they come across anything."

I looked at the road before us, branching off from Violet Lantern. Most of the streets in the Lantern District ran north to south in a straight line, but in a few places like this, the contours of the hillside dictated the roads wrap around a steeper slope.

"Should we leave one deputy and a car blocking top and bottom?" I asked, looking at Hugo. "I mean, what's stopping someone from driving away before we get to them?"

Hugo frowned, but I could tell he was thinking it over.

"We'll be down to six deputies, ma'am, so it'll take longer, but we can do it if you'd like," Ripley said.

"Yeah, we should," Hugo agreed.

"We'll be knocking on doors, too," I added. "So we still have eight, and many people won't be home, anyway."

Ripley keyed the radio and relayed the instructions to the other deputies. I watched Hanson roll his eyes, but he went to the trunk of his car and produced a half-dozen traffic cones.

"People won't be happy getting stopped going in and out of their own street," Hugo said to me in a quieter voice.

"That's okay," I replied. "This end will be Hanson taking grief about it, so it's worth it just for that."

Hugo looked at me and grinned. "Why do you think I agreed to the idea?"

Knocking on doors was tedious for everyone. The residents

were usually somewhere between annoyed and freaked out, and we quickly tired of repeating the same spiel over and over. Now that we were here, ringing another doorbell, the exercise was beginning to feel like a waste of time. It had always been a long shot, but with more than half the residents unsurprisingly not home on a weekday afternoon, we were getting nowhere. I made sure to take an instant picture of everyone who answered, just in case I needed to reference them later.

The door before me opened, and a woman in her thirties with her hair pulled back in a tight ponytail looked the two of us over.

"Can I help you?" she asked.

"OCSD Investigators Cromwell and Fuentes," I replied, and we held up our badges. "We're canvassing the neighborhood to see if anyone has seen this young woman."

I held up my phone, showing the picture we'd given to the deputies to use. It was actually two pictures pasted together. One, a now extremely grainy scan of my instant photo, zoomed in closer to cut Mrs. Harris out of the shot. The other was a photo the hospital had emailed us of Jane Doe in her bed. Neither were very clear nor flattering images of the girl.

The woman took a few long moments to study the phone screen. "I can't say I recognize her. Poor soul looks like she's having a bad time of things."

"Do you own the house here?" I asked, tucking my phone away in my back pocket.

"No, just renting," she replied. "Only moved here a short while ago."

"Have you seen a darker-colored cargo van in the neighborhood over the past couple of days?" I asked.

The woman slowly shook her head. "Not that I recall, but I work from home, so it's not like I'm poking my head out the window every five minutes."

"Can we see your ID, ma'am?" I asked. "Simply to make sure we don't bother you again."

She took her own phone out and slid a driver's license from a sleeve on the back of the case. "Sure."

"Sam 54. Sam 23," came a deputy's voice over the radio on my hip. "Can you meet us at 33840? Over."

I heard Hugo unclip his radio, so I glanced at the woman's ID and snapped a photo with my phone.

"On our way. Over," Hugo replied to the call.

"Thanks for your time, ma'am," I told the woman before we hurried back to the sidewalk.

33840 was on the east side of the street, a few homes north of us. As we approached, I noted Ripley and another deputy outside the home with a man standing in the doorway. The guy wore a ratty T-shirt and dirty gray cargo shorts. His face hadn't seen a shaver in probably a week, and his thinning hair looked more like an abandoned bird's nest. The house was an older two-story from the '70s, badly in need of a renovation.

"Mr. Malone here arrived home a few minutes ago, and we suspect he may be under the influence," Ripley explained.

Going by the guy's dilated pupils, he either came from an eye exam or he was certainly stoned. Bad timing on his part.

The deputy stepped to the side in front of the double garage, indicating for us to follow. The rickety-looking door was open, and inside sat a well-used pickup truck. From the ticking sound of a cooling engine, I knew it was the vehicle Malone had just arrived in. That, and it was the only vehicle amongst piles of what appeared to be junk in the garage.

"Tyrone Malone. Got a rap sheet for possession with intent and assault," Deputy Ripley told us. "Hanson ran him through the computer in the squad car."

Hugo shrugged his shoulders. "That's great, but now we're two men down while you arrest this idiot. Doesn't really help our cause, does it?"

As usual, Hugo's delivery was tactless. But he wasn't wrong.

"We figured he might be good for drugging the girl," Ripley said, trying not to sound defensive.

"I doubt this bloke's dealing in the exotic stuff our Jane Doe was dosed with," I explained. "But while we have probable cause, we'd better take a look in his garage."

Hugo muttered Spanish obscenities under his breath as we returned to the front door. I peeked inside and had to agree with his reluctance to step inside Malone's property. It was a shithole.

The other deputy now had the suspect in handcuffs. "I ain't taking a breathalyzer, man. Those things suck. I want a blood test," Malone insisted.

It was the first intelligent thing he'd done, as breathalyzer tests were the least accurate and could swing either way.

"Anyone else in the house?" I asked.

He shook his head.

"Let's step inside for a few minutes and chat, Mr. Malone," I said, and he eyed me over.

"Nice try with your fancy accent, hot stuff, but I ain't inviting none of you inside," he snapped back. "Get yourselves a warrant, and you'd better have a damn good reason, or my lawyer'll have your pretty little ass."

I laughed. "You're a formidable adversary, Mr. Malone. Clearly a man who knows his legal procedures."

"Fuckin-a-right," he replied.

I grinned at him. "Then you probably should have stopped in your driveway instead of parking inside your garage where you left the door open, dipshit. Now we get to look around in there while we search your truck. What will we find, I wonder?"

"Screw you, bitch," Malone growled, straining against the deputy's firm grip.

"Be handy if he had a blue van in the garage instead of this piece of crap," Hugo said, hesitating as we walked back to the garage.

I laughed as I donned nitrile gloves before touching anything. "We couldn't be that lucky."

Opening the driver's door of the truck, a stale smell greeted me. I detected a hint of skunk amid the general stench of body sweat and greasy fast food wrappers. Hugo opened the passenger door and stood back for a moment, cussing some more in Spanish. Checking behind and under the seats, I found nothing illegal, although the accumulation of garbage was certainly breaking laws of sanitation.

"Nothing," Hugo reported from the other side, rifling through the glove box. "Believe it or not, his registration is current."

I would have been surprised, but the deputies had already run a check on Malone and hadn't mentioned an expired license or registration.

"What's the address on the registration?" I asked.

"Here," Hugo replied.

"Makes you wonder how he affords this place," I commented, happy to retreat from the cab of the truck.

A sound of movement made me turn and look at the interior door to the house.

"You hear that?" I whispered to Hugo.

He shook his head from across the roof of the truck.

I pointed to the door. "Someone's in there."

"Maybe the deputies went inside," Hugo offered.

Malone had been adamantly against us entering his home, so I doubted that. I moved quietly outside to where the two deputies stood over Malone, who now sat on his porch step.

"Who else is inside the house, sir?" I demanded.

He shrugged. "No one."

"You have any animals inside?"

He shook his head.

"Someone or something is in there," I said, and watched Malone's reaction.

Both deputies peeked through the open front door, but the suspect didn't even turn around. A sure sign he knew exactly who was in there.

"I heard it, too," Hugo whisper-shouted from outside the garage.

I moved closer to the front door, unclipped the strap on my

holster, and covered the handle with my hand. "This is the police!" I shouted. "Reveal yourself. Move slowly, hands on head!"

For a few long moments, there was silence. Then a figure appeared inside, not moving slowly or with hands on his head. The man charged for the back door at the back of the kitchen, bursting outside.

"Runner!" I yelled. "Out the back!" Sprinting into the house, I called over my shoulder, "Ripley! With me!"

Footfalls on the uneven and peeling linoleum floor told me the deputy was on my heels. I reached the open back door and scanned the yard. It was a mess, like everything else in Tyrone Malone's life. Long grass grew uncut in clumps between bare patches of dirt, and a rotting wooden fence bordered the property. A coast live oak shaded half the yard, and beyond, I noticed a large, empty wiring reel sat under the fence.

"He went over the back," I said, running across the small yard. "Call it in! He's heading for Violet Lantern."

Ripley made the call while I jumped on top of the wooden reel and peered over the fence. The shrubs rustled alongside the neighboring house that backed up to Malone's. Vaulting over, I landed on the slope and took off running again.

"Police!" I announced in case the owner decided the second stranger in their yard needed stopping.

Sirens wailed as the deputies drove around to Violet Lantern while I dodged a slalom of small trees and shrubs alongside the house, quickly reaching a side gate that rattled back on its hinges, having been flung closed. Unlatching the wooden gate, I rushed through to see the first patrol car screeching to a stop on the road. Looking both ways, our suspect was nowhere to be seen. The deputy leaped from the driver's seat and held his hands up.

"You didn't see him?" I shouted.

The deputy shook his head. Behind me, I heard Ripley brushing his way through the shrubs. I turned and opened the gate. On pure instinct born from sparring in my dad's gym, I ducked below the fist coming my way. Pushing with my legs, I threw my counterpunch, landing a solid hit just below the ribs of the man lunging at me. The air left his lungs as his momentum doubled the power in my strike. Coughing and wheezing, he fell to the ground at my feet.

"You okay?" Ripley gasped, running through the foliage alongside the house. "He sprung up from behind a bush when he heard me coming."

I shook my stinging hand and flexed my aching wrist. I was used to being wrapped and gloved when I punched things.

"Yeah, I'm good," I replied. "My own fault for not spotting him. I must have run right by the wanker."

"Guess he panicked when he heard me coming," Ripley said, tugging the man's hands behind his back and securing them with handcuffs. "Thought he'd take you on instead."

"My lucky day," I scoffed.

Ripley laughed. "Not this guy's," he said, hauling the suspect to his feet. "Pretty sure I couldn't have taken him out with one punch."

"Say cheese," I said, snapping a picture of the suspect with my instant camera.

7

Ty Malone and his buddy, Trent Riggs, had completely screwed up our door-to-door sweep of Robles Road. It was after six by the time we'd swept through the house and brought our two suspects to the station. The search had predictably turned up drugs, but all opioids. No sign of the Velvet ingredients we were looking for, or evidence of anyone being detained there.

We left a couple of deputies to conduct a more thorough search, but it felt like a waste of time. Fortunately, we could hand the case off to narcotics, which saved us a boatload of paperwork. Although, I still had to write a report as I'd been involved in a physical altercation with a suspect. I was becoming too familiar with these reports.

"Miss Foreman," Sergeant Martinez ribbed me without a smile as I passed the front desk. "Only a couple of cameras at the hospital. What they had is on the server."

"Thanks, Sarge," I called back as I swiped my card and entered the hallway. "You've earned a discount on one of my grills."

Hugo looked up as I entered the office.

"We have CCTV from the hospital," I told him before taking my seat.

He nodded. "I've started a search for Lexy in the system."

I was hoping to handle that and palm the CCTV task off to my partner, but he'd beaten me to it.

"What were the names you were thinking of?" he asked.

"Alexa. Alexis. I'd try Alexandra and Alexandria with an I," I replied. "Probably a hundred other variations, seeing as people like to give their kids names no one knows how to spell these days."

"Like Cat but with a K," Hugo replied without looking at me.

"Hey, Katherine with a K goes back thousands of years, mate," I said as I logged into my computer. "Ever heard of Catherine the Great?"

"Was that spelled with a K?" Hugo questioned.

"I don't think so, but it could have been in Russia, where she was from."

Hugo may have chuckled, but more likely he just cleared his throat.

"Kate Moss is a Katherine with a K," I added. "And Katharine Hepburn, of course." I took a brief look at the angles and groaned. "This footage is useless," I complained. "There's one camera covering the front entrance and one in reception. Nothing else. If someone did sneak in, I guarantee it was through the back."

"No doubt," Hugo agreed.

I'd been hoping for something more but wasn't surprised a hospital was limited in its camera placements. To be thorough, I fast-forwarded through both sets of footage, covering two hours before Jane Doe crashed. If someone had injected midazolam into our vic's IV, it had been a matter of minutes before she crashed, but I wanted to be sure the perp hadn't entered the hospital earlier. I didn't see anything suspicious, but noted times when people who appeared to be staff entered the building, then emailed the data to the address Sarge had given me for the hospital.

"Any luck?" I asked Hugo before switching my attention to the hunt for Lexy.

"Do you think your buddy Dennis could have invented himself a girlfriend?" he asked.

"It's possible," I admitted. "But he's usually right about what he says, even if it sounds like a riddle sometimes."

Hugo grunted.

"What have you tried so far?"

"I used ages sixteen through twenty-five with military history," he replied. "But we have even fewer details about this girl than we do Jane Doe."

"Except a name," I pointed out.

"We have the nickname she used," Hugo retorted. "For all we know, her birth certificate reads Katherine with a K."

"Ha-bloody-ha."

Opening the missing persons database, I started with females in a wider age group, from fourteen to thirty. I was about to begin trudging through the varieties of full names that could be contracted to Lexy when I came up with an idea. I searched instead for any first name that included "lex." The 507 young women missing around the country seemed like a terrifying number, considering the parameters I'd used. Children weren't on my personal radar, but if I did produce offspring, I decided their names would not include the letters "lex."

"Got a maybe from Michigan," Hugo announced from the other side of our desks. "She'd be eighteen by now. Went missing from home two years ago. Accused her stepfather of abuse, but no charges were ever brought against him. Alexandra Gomez. Possible sighting in Flagstaff, Arizona, six months ago. So she could have been making her way west."

"Okay," I said, wondering how Hugo had narrowed down his search to pick out one name. I would ask him, but I wanted to finish my own search first.

Based on Dennis thinking my picture of Jane Doe might have been his friend Lexy, I selected 100-140 pounds for weight and chose the western states of California, Arizona, and Nevada. Unhoused people sometimes traveled, but usually only within a short period from when they went missing. The longer they were gone, the less likely they were to have money, and not many folks stopped to pick up hitchhikers anymore. Especially the ones who hadn't showered in a while.

My new result gave me sixty-eight names. That was a manageable number to look through.

"How did you find her?" I asked before I began scrolling through my findings.

"The military angle didn't seem to work, so I narrowed down the age and searched using the names you mentioned," he replied. "I had too many hits, so I narrowed by having been missing between six months and a year. Then I used ethnicity and started looking through the list."

"And you pulled one out of that list?" I questioned.

"No. I've found at least two dozen more possibilities, but I wanted to throw out a name, so you knew I was working on it."

I laughed. "Bloody right. I was just thinking you were probably sitting there playing Wordle on your phone."

"Got it in three this morning," Hugo replied.

"What did you say her name was?"

"Alexandra Gomez."

"She's Hispanic. What color hair does she have?"

"Black," Hugo replied in a disheartened tone.

It reminded me to narrow my search further using ethnicity. Although my picture was a lousy shot at night, it was clear Jane Doe had lighter hair. I couldn't be certain Dennis would have been observant enough to notice, but it seemed likely, as her hair was more obvious than any facial features. I narrowed my search to "Caucasian" and looked at a list of twenty-nine names.

"I think I might be getting somewhere," I said, considering my next move.

"What you got?" Hugo asked, rolling his chair over until he could see me.

"I'm down to twenty-nine."

He shuffled his office chair around the desks until he was next to me. I typed "military" into the search bar. Four names remained.

"Alexis Rae Morrison. Nineteen from Oceanside. Runaway.

Father is retired Navy," I read from my screen. "Alexa Jane Whitmore. She's twenty-one and been missing for nearly three years. Former ROTC. Left home in Flagstaff, Arizona, right after graduating high school."

"What did you start this search with?" Hugo asked.

"I used 'lex,' so it covered all the names I could think of."

"Hmm," Hugo grunted. "I wasn't sure if I was happy or disappointed that the deadbeat missed his swing at you, but maybe it was a good thing."

I laughed. "Gee, thanks, partner."

"Well, you went storming off again, doing what the deputies are paid to do."

It was hard to gauge if Hugo was really mad about it or just giving me a hard time. It had been an issue between us in the past. He considered me reckless, which meant I was hard to trust. I didn't feel like I was reckless, but I'd certainly had more than my fair share of incidents and run-ins with suspects in my first year as an investigator. Hugo had accumulated zero since I'd worked with him. Hoping he wasn't lining up to lecture me again, I continued.

"Seventeen-year-old Alexandria Skye Bennett from Henderson, Nevada. Another runaway. Been missing a year and a half. She has an older brother in the Marines."

"She also has a scar under her right eye," Hugo pointed out, tapping a finger on the screen. "Do you think Dennis would have noticed that?"

"We can ask him," I replied. "We can show him a picture of these four, and anyone you found, too, of course."

"I think your search was more productive. Continue," he urged.

I smiled. Apparently, he wasn't upset, which pleased me and made my life easier.

"Last of the four is Alexis Dawn Harper from San Diego. She's twenty and enlisted out of high school. Went AWOL before basic training started."

Hugo pushed his chair back and looked at his watch. "We can

swing by and see your man Dennis in the morning. It's well past time to go home."

"Sure," I replied, but I stayed at my computer and began printing pictures of our four young women.

"Go home, Cromwell," Hugo said, shutting down his computer and gathering up his things. "It'll be here waiting in the morning."

"Yup," I replied, edging my chair back a few inches to give him the impression I was complying.

He shook his head as he walked to the door. "See you tomorrow."

"Have a good evening," I called out, hitting print on the second picture.

Dennis wasn't under the bridge by San Juan Creek, but several other folks were. The sun had set, but the streetlights from Pacific Coast Highway above us lit the pathway on either side of the overpass.

I asked them all if they'd seen either Jane Doe or Lexy, and showed them my selection of pictures. No one had seen Jane Doe. Two people didn't recognize anyone, and a couple who were setting up their tent for the night each picked a different girl from my Lexy choices.

The only useful thing I learned was that Dennis was most likely on his way back from Doheny Beach around this time, so I walked the path toward the coastline. I spotted him where the trail ended by the lifeguard building, rolling his shopping cart from the east park.

"How was your day, Dennis?" I asked.

He shrugged. "Still topside, so I guess it's okay."

"Eaten anything lately?"

Pausing in front of me, he thought for a moment. "I don't think so."

I took a sub sandwich I'd bought on the way over and handed it to him. "I couldn't finish this if you want the other half."

I'd bought the foot-long and had them cut a couple of inches off one end.

"Thank you," he said, taking the sandwich.

"Mind if I sit with you a minute while you eat?" I asked.

Dennis looked around, and then at the path to the bridge. He looked worried.

"I just came from that way. No one is in your spot," I assured him.

He nodded and wheeled his cart to the first of the tables and benches at the edge of the sand. The lights along the front of the state park cast a yellow glow across the seafront, and we were serenaded by the waves lapping against the beach. Dennis took a bite of the sandwich and chewed noisily.

"I have a few pictures to show you, if you don't mind?"

He frowned. "I looked at your pictures."

"I know, and you were really helpful, so I have some more. Is that okay?"

He nodded as he bit off another mouthful.

One by one, I rotated through the pictures I'd printed at the station. Dennis's eyes briefly studied each of them, his focus drifting after a few seconds before returning when I slid the next shot to the top.

"Recognize any of these women?" I asked after he didn't react.

"Lexy," he said. "She gave me a penknife. I liked Lexy."

"Are any of these pictures your friend Lexy?" I asked, slowly rotating through the four photographs again.

The quality varied greatly, from professional school-yearbook-style pics to blurry snapshots. Dennis looked at every page once more, still chewing. When I began another round, he finally reached over and poked his finger at a page.

"That's Lexy?"

He nodded. "Where is she?"

"We're not sure, Dennis. But I'd like to find her."

"She's gone," he muttered, and I turned the page around to read which girl he'd picked.

It was Alexis Rae Morrison from Oceanside, a San Diego County beach town less than thirty miles south of where we sat.

"Do you have any idea where she went?" I asked. "Did she say she was leaving?"

"Left everything," he muttered, licking mayonnaise off his grubby fingers. "Just went away."

"Lexy didn't come back to the pathway under the bridge?" I persisted. "Went out for the day and didn't come back?"

Dennis stopped chewing and looked at me as though I'd asked a dumb question. "No. She just got in that van, and she was gone," he said, waving a hand in the air.

8

By the time I opened my front door, I was too exhausted to think about food. My lack of sleep the night before had caught up with me. I switched off the alarm, closed the front door, then reset the alarm again. I had no plans to venture out. Roger hopped to the edge of the area rug to greet me.

"Bet you're wondering what happened to your dinner snack, huh?" I said, hanging up my blazer and dropping my backpack on the bench by the door.

I walked over, and he lifted his front feet in the air, his little nose furiously twitching.

"It's not me you're pleased to see, is it?" I groaned, getting down on the rug and stretching out on my back. "You only want me for my greens and pellets, don't you?"

Roger nuzzled all around my face, his fur tickling and his frantic sniffs making me laugh. He hopped onto my chest to make sure I wasn't hiding goodies from him, and I petted his head, stroking his long ears. He looked at me with big, glistening eyes on either side of his two-tone brown and beige harlequin face.

"Anyone try breaking in today, mate?" I asked him, my mind drifting back to seeing Emilio Santiago the night before. The man

I'd discovered inside my home a few months back. If Roger hadn't bitten the thug, I wouldn't have been on alert for an intruder, and I dreaded to think how the night would have played out. My dad helped me install the security system shortly afterwards.

"Okay, security rabbit," I said, plucking him off my chest and placing him on the rug. "Let's have some dinner, and then it's time for bed."

Roger munched on greens while I ate a bowl of cereal, and at nine, I woke to find I'd fallen asleep on the couch, spilling the remnants of milk down my pants with the TV still on. Roger had taken himself to bed, so I closed his door, ditched the damp clothes, and stumbled into bed.

When the alarm went off at five-fifteen a.m., I toyed with the idea of grabbing more sleep and skipping the gym. Two things made me get out of bed. The grief my dad would give me, and the crappy feeling I got when I didn't exercise for several days in a row.

Too often, my life felt like a fast-moving train that paused only briefly at stations. I was forever about to miss my ride. I supposed many people felt that way. Never enough time, and a constant fear of being left on the platform. Like Dennis. Or Lexy. Or our Jane Doe. In reality, I was fortunate to have two loving parents who would scoop me up and make sure I always had a roof over my head and food on the table. But not everyone was so lucky.

Roger seemed to have had enough rest as he tore around the living room, throwing in a few leaping kicks rabbit people called binkies. I put down his dish of pellets, gathered up a dry pair of pants along with my other work clothes, dressed, and headed out the door.

"Hello, stranger," my dad greeted me at the gym in his deep London accent. "Got a lot of work on?" he asked in a softer tone, pulling me into a side hug with his bear claw of a hand.

"Yeah. Weird one," I replied. "Not sure if it's even a case yet."

He started to ask me more, but knew he shouldn't and stopped himself. It had taken a lot of coaching on my mum's part, but he'd finally come to terms with the fact that I couldn't talk about my work beyond generalities. Dad was naturally curious, which was a nice way of saying he's nosy, but also concerned about his only kid.

"What you working on this morning?" he asked, looking at his watch.

"Planned on hitting the bag for a bit, then some weights," I made up as I'd arrived with absolutely zero plan whatsoever.

"Got a kid I've been working with for a few weeks now. You can spar if you'd like," he offered.

Which was strange. I'd nagged him forever to let me spar, and he'd finally allowed me to earlier in the year. Reluctantly. Then he'd put me in the ring with his best fighter to scare me off. I was too hard-headed for that to work. His reluctance stemmed from three things. I was his daughter, and he didn't want to watch people punch me. I had a strange, undiagnosed neurological issue that affected my memory, and finally, Mum would kill him if she knew he'd let me spar. That list was probably in reverse order of what worried him the most.

His offer now was out of the blue, as well as out of character. Which made me suspicious.

"Sure," I replied, figuring he'd picked a morning when I looked tired and uninspired so I'd turn him down. I wasn't falling for his tricks. Even if it meant getting smacked in the face.

"Alright," he said casually. "Warm up on a bike for ten minutes, then I'll wrap you, and you can hit the bag for five. Kid'll be here by then."

I walked away with a bad feeling in my stomach and the flutter of nerves. Since Cisco, his top fighter, I'd sparred with a dumb kid Dad had wanted me to knock down a peg or two. I did, which had led to a paying customer leaving the gym. Since then, he'd only let me in the ring a couple of times, and it had been with young newbies to give them a taste of what it felt like to face another human who hit back instead of a dormant bag. Dad was crafty and usually had a plan tucked behind his innocent-looking motives.

After riding hard to wake up my muscles, get the blood flowing in my veins, and air moving through my lungs, I brought my gear out into the main gym. Dad left his assistant trainer working with a group of young boxers getting coaching in before school and joined me.

He whistled a tune as he wrapped my hands and wrists, like he'd done a million times before for the fighters he'd trained over the years. A former British heavyweight champion, Frankie Cromwell had been a household name back in the UK, and a well-known personality in the U.S. After retiring at the top of his game, he'd been hired to commentate for TV in America, which was why he'd moved his family to California. I was six when we'd arrived.

As he continued working on me, I looked up at the tall walls decorated with banners from championships won by fighters coached in the gym. Dad's logo, which my mum had designed for him when he first opened nearly fifteen years ago, held pride of place over the training ring.

My dad was a pretty cool bloke. At least, that was what was going through my mind until I saw my sparring partner walking over.

I'd heard Dad mention a female fighter who'd signed up to train with him, but I hadn't paid much attention other than being pleased for him, as he was excited. He had quite a few women working out at the gym, but only a handful who wanted to fight. Most were there simply to stay in shape, or feel more confident about defending themselves.

Kenzie Frost looked to be an inch or two below my five-foot-six inches, but was packed with lean muscle. Below her shabby-looking cut-off sweatshirt, her abs resembled a granite sculpture. She was already sweating, although I was certain she'd just walked through the door.

"Morning, sir," she greeted my father with a hint of a Hispanic accent.

"Morning," he replied, and turned to me. "This is Kat. She'll be sparring with you this morning."

I reached out my right hand, which Dad had finished wrapping, and we shook.

"Kenzie, right?" I asked.

"Yes, ma'am," she replied.

I laughed. "You can quit with the 'ma'am' part, Kenzie. I'm older than you, but I'm not that *old* yet."

"No, ma'am," she said, then corrected herself. "No, Kat."

"Your uncle here with you?" Dad asked.

"Yes, sir. He's in the car. Said he didn't want to get in the way."

"You go tell him to come inside and help himself to tea or coffee," Dad insisted. "He won't be in the way. I'm almost finished here, then I'll wrap you. You warm up already?"

"Yes, sir. I ran the last mile here so I'd be ready."

"Alright. Fetch your uncle, and we'll get going."

Kenzie left, and my dad finished wrapping my hands before helping me slip on my sparring gloves.

"Her uncle brings her?" I asked.

Dad nodded. "Raised by her aunt and uncle. Her old man's never been around much. Doing time now, I believe. Her mum died when Kenzie was ten. Uncle's a good bloke. Former Marine. Drives her here every morning from Costa Mesa."

"That's a long way to come every day," I commented, thinking about the commute across South Orange County. Even early in the morning, the traffic was awful. It had to be a forty-five-minute drive or more. "Why isn't she training closer to home?"

Dad frowned at me. "Cos she wanted to train with me. Is that so hard to believe?"

I laughed and punched him on his brawny arm. "I just mean that's a big commitment on their part."

"Her old trainer Rudy Mendez brought her to me. Said she had so much potential that he was worried about holding her back. So, she's here on a scholarship."

"What scholarship?" I asked.

"The one I gave her."

"You don't have scholarships, Dad. You mean you're training her for free?"

"That's what a bloody scholarship is, isn't it?"

I laughed again. "I suppose so. No wonder this place never makes any money, Dad. You're a big softy."

He feigned a horrified look. "You wash your mouth out with soap, then hit the bag, young lady. No one calls Frankie Cromwell a softy."

I warmed up on the bag while Dad chatted with her uncle as he prepped Kenzie. When she was ready, we moved to the ring.

"Alright, you two," Dad said as he held the ropes apart for us. "I want to see you both moving all the time. Lively on your feet, right? Kenzie, this is more like the height you'll be fighting, so get used to coming from underneath, and respect the reach."

"Yes, sir."

I now knew why my scheming father had me sparring this morning. I was a useful height. It was nice to know his concern for my broken brain only extended as far as him needing my carcass to train his new fighter. I'd be annoyed if I hadn't nagged him to spar and brought this upon myself.

"Fight on," Dad barked.

We bumped gloves before bobbing on the balls of our feet, circling around the ring, and throwing out little jabs to gauge our distance. I could already tell that Kenzie had great defense. She was compact, kept her elbows in and her gloves high. There was nothing to hit but her arms and gloves, which meant I had to make her punch to have an opening. The tricky part was not getting clobbered while finding that opening.

"Use your reach, Kat," Dad coached from the ropes.

I came over Kenzie's gloves, catching her forehead protected by the padded headgear we both wore. We were sparring for training, so the idea wasn't to hit with full power, but still she seemed to absorb the strike like it was nothing. Cautiously, I stayed just out of reach, and we returned to jabbing gloves and sizing each other up.

After another minute or so, I could sense my dad was about to tell me to use my reach again. Of course, he was right. My height and reach were my advantage. He was staying quiet other than giving us both little pointers on footwork, but I knew what was coming.

Checking Kenzie away from me with a left jab, I followed with another right over her gloves to her forehead. When she made no attempt to back away from my punch, I knew I was screwed. She even stepped into my blow to make sure her counter landed. The air shot from my lungs as her left caught me hard in the chest. I quickly brought my elbows down and protected myself before her right caught my glove. Damn, she was fast. And powerful.

I rapidly moved, keeping her checked at a safe distance while I caught my breath. I needed a better plan, and fast. Kenzie knew she'd rocked me and wanted more. Her feet were constantly moving, and she ducked and weaved around, stepping in closer to jab, trying to get around my elbows to my ribs. On her next right jab, I let go with my left and caught her right cheek. She barely seemed to notice and hammered my ribs a second time, forcing me to drop my elbow to cover up again.

I sensed she'd decided where my weakness lay, and she jabbed with her left, trying to reach my ribs on the other side. Faking a right hook, I dropped my elbow to deflect the blow that I knew was coming. Lifting my left glove to protect my face, I invited her to jab my ribs again on the other side. Kenzie couldn't resist. Her right shot forward and her left dropped, ready to strike again.

I just got my elbow down in time to defend her left, then pushed hard with my legs to carry my right hook. I connected with her cheek, and this time, her head jolted back. We both quickly covered up and guarded against the other's next move.

"Break!" my dad called out. "Good job, both of you."

Kenzie shook her head and spat her mouthguard into her glove. "I left myself open. It was shit."

"You did, but that's why I put Kat in with you. You'll often face taller opponents, and you dropped to work her low. That's okay, but there are more points to be had up high. You're a much better fighter than Kat, but she still caught you a good one."

"Gee, thanks, Dad," I lisped, then spat my mouthguard out, too.

He shrugged. "This kid's been fighting for a couple of years. She should be better."

I knew he was right, and he meant it to encourage his fighter rather than put down his daughter. But it still stung a bit.

"Kenzie, you overcommitted to the ribs," he continued. "Kat saw that and outfoxed you."

Okay, that sort of made up for it.

"You've got some heat in those punches," I confessed. "The one to the chest was solid."

"That was a good one," Kenzie grinned.

I looked over at the clock above the office door. "Bugger. I have to go. I gotta get to work."

"Alright," Dad grunted. "We'll do this again, though. It was good for you, Kenzie."

"Yes, sir," she replied as my dad helped me out of my gloves.

It took me ten minutes to strip, shower, mostly dry, then dress, and when I came out of the locker room, Dad was working with Kenzie in the ring. He still moved agilely for a big man in his fifties, using his padded hands to have her move her punches around.

"Bye, Dad," I called out, and he looked over and waved.

Kenzie jogged to the ropes and stretched out her gloved hand. I bumped it with my fist.

"Thanks," she said. "You really helped me."

I laughed. "You made me feel old and slow, so maybe I should be called 'ma'am' after all."

"No way. You could be good," she replied before jogging back to the center of the ring.

Her compliment made me feel good, but I knew I'd decided to get involved in the sport too late. I walked toward the door and nodded to Kenzie's uncle, who stood outside the offices. I paused.

"I'm Kat," I said, extending a hand.

"Diego," he responded. "I'm Kenzie's uncle."

"That's pretty cool of you to bring her all this way every day."

"I work a night shift, so I pick her up when I leave in the morning," he replied, his accent stronger than his niece's. "Your father is a generous man to make this possible for Kenzie."

I smiled. "Well, she's very talented."

He nodded and beamed. "With your father's help, she'll make the next Olympic team. I'm sure of it."

"I've no doubt she will," I agreed, then remembered something my dad had mentioned. "Are you former military, sir?"

Diego nodded. "*Sí*. Army for twelve years."

"Can I show you something?" I asked. "It's in my car outside."

"Of course," he replied, and followed me into the dawn light.

I unlocked my car, tossed my gym bag inside, then rummaged through my backpack to produce the instant photo I'd taken of Dennis's knife.

"Have you seen one of these before, sir?"

Diego studied the picture. "I didn't know they made this kind of camera anymore. You don't use your phone like everyone else?"

I grinned and shook my head. "No. I'm weird like that."

He nodded and looked at me like I was a little weird. "Sure. I know this knife. MOVE is a veteran-run company. They give part of their profit back into assistance programs for U.S. veterans. They're good people. I have a knife I bought from them."

"So they're quite common?"

He shrugged. "With former military, they are. That one's for a Marine."

I looked at the picture again and recalled the deep scarlet color of the handle. I'd noticed color options on MOVE's website, but hadn't associated them with branches of the military.

"Mine is dark green for Army," Diego added.

I thought back to my missing persons search and Dennis identifying Lexy as Alexis Morrison. Her father was Navy. So why would she have a knife for a Marine?

9

I slid Hugo's coffee across the desk and, after removing my chocolate croissant, handed him his scone in a paper bag. I'd treated myself, using the excuse that my ribs needed fortifying after the punishment they'd taken, courtesy of Kenzie.

Raising my large latte with a sheriff's star drawn on it, I greeted my partner. "Cheers."

"*Salud*," Hugo responded, raising his drink. "You're chipper this morning. I suppose you've been up for hours."

I was about to reply when the captain's voice came from our doorway.

"I heard the door-to-door yesterday turned into a mess."

"If you call arresting a couple of drug dealers a fail, I guess you could say that, ma'am," I replied, far too quickly in a less-than-chipper tone.

Bradley glared at me. "The front desk was inundated with complaints from residents on Robles and Violet Lantern about roadblocks and harassment."

Hugo stood. "It didn't go as we'd hoped in the Jane Doe case, ma'am. But like Kat said, we took a pair of dealers out of circulation."

"Maybe I was wrong about this," Bradley said, and I wondered what was coming next. She'd been the one to assign us Jane Doe. "We don't even know there is a case. We have better things for you two to work on. At least until the woman wakes up and can tell us something."

"But we have a missing persons case potentially connected to this," I blurted quickly. "Alexis Morrison has been missing for weeks, ma'am. She was last seen getting into a van here in Dana Point." I turned and looked at my partner. "Dennis told me last night."

Hugo raised an eyebrow.

"Who reported her missing?" Bradley asked.

"Her father, originally," I replied. "But that was two years ago. A witness spotted her getting into a van that matches the description of the one caught on a security camera near where Jane Doe was found, ma'am."

"That all sounds mighty tenuous, Cromwell," the captain said, and followed her words with a long sigh. "Come back to me by end of day with something more solid, or Jane Doe goes on the back burner until she starts talking."

"Ma'am," I acknowledged.

Hugo and I sat back down after Bradley had left.

"Couldn't wait until this morning, could you?" Hugo said, but I was pretty sure he was grinning behind the coffee cup he now swigged from.

"Bloody good job, too, or her ladyship would have us off the case. You know what else I learned this morning?"

Hugo shook his head, looking amused as he took a bite of his scone.

"Dennis's knife, the one Lexy gave him, is from a Marine."

"How do we know that?" Hugo questioned. "Surely anyone can buy one from that website we looked at."

I thought it over. He was right. "In theory, but you know how the rivalry is between the armed forces. No way a Navy sailor would buy a Marine's knife, right?"

Hugo shrugged. "I wouldn't stake a case on it, but that's probably true."

"Well, here's where I get confused," I admitted. "Alexis Morrison's father is former Navy. They make a dark blue-handled knife for Navy. Dennis's knife is scarlet for a Marine. But Dennis was certain the picture I showed him was Lexy."

"Just because her father retired from the Navy doesn't mean he's the only one who could have given her the knife," Hugo replied. "Wasn't she from Oceanside?"

I nodded.

"Camp Pendleton is a Marine base. Oceanside is swarming with Marines."

"True," I admitted. "And she did run away from home, so I doubt it was because she got along great with her dad."

"Exactly," Hugo replied.

"I guess I'll try to reach the father," I said, bringing up the file on my computer. "See what he has to say about all of this."

"Better come up with something today," Hugo pointed out. "Or we'll be back on robberies and cold cases."

Why Bradley had changed her mind about us handling Jane Doe, I had no way of knowing, but Hugo was right. I tried the phone number listed on the missing person's report. It was no longer active. Moving to DMV records, I searched for the father's name, Raymond Morrison, starting with the address from the report. Nineteen results came back within San Diego County. None at the address I had. We had no picture and no date of birth.

"I've hit a brick wall on Lexy's father," I complained. "What are the chances the detective in Oceanside will remember anything about this case?"

"Worth a try," Hugo replied, and I wondered what he was currently working on. He certainly wasn't offering to help. Maybe he was playing Wordle.

Finding a number for the Oceanside Police Department, I called from the desk phone, putting it on speaker. After I navigated their automated menu of options, someone finally answered.

"Oceanside Police," came a man's voice.

"This is Investigator Cromwell with the Orange County Sheriff's Department. I'm looking for Detective Hernandez, please."

"One moment."

Annoying hold music played while I waited for what felt like several minutes. Finally, the line clicked, and a female voice answered.

"Hernandez."

"Hi, this is Investigator Kat Cromwell with Orange County Sheriff's. Thanks for taking my call."

"Sure. How can I help?" the woman replied, getting straight to business.

"Do you recall a missing person's case from about eighteen months ago involving Alexis Rae Morrison? She was seventeen at the time. It was recorded as a runaway."

"Morrison? Hmm. Yeah, I think I remember something about it. Have you found her?"

"We think she may have been here in Dana Point a few weeks back. There's a chance she's linked to another case we're investigating. I was trying to reach the father, but the cell number on record is disconnected."

After a brief pause on the line, Hernandez said, "Okay, I have the case up on the computer. The kid was seventeen and had dropped out of high school a semester before graduating. Her friends had no idea where she'd gone. A couple indicated the father was a drunk. No mother around. Seemed like the kid was probably better off out of whatever situation was going on, and she was eighteen in six months. We asked around, got nowhere, and didn't have any family screaming to find her, so to be honest, I don't think we chased it too hard. What do you have going on there?"

"That's a great question," I reply with a laugh. "We're not sure. A Jane Doe turned up a couple of nights ago, wandering around town on a cocktail of date-rape drugs and tranquilizers. While trying to figure out who she is and where she came from, we stumbled across a homeless girl going by the name Lexy who went off the radar here a few weeks ago. There's a possible tie-in between the two girls with a van we believe took Lexy and was seen near where Jane Doe was picked up."

"And you think Lexy is Morrison?"

"Got an ID on the picture from your file," I replied. "Homeless guy, but he seemed sure."

"You think Morrison's father can help you?" Hernandez asked.

"Figured I'd ask if he'd heard anything from his daughter since she went missing."

"I'm pretty sure he's the reason she went missing," the detective replied. "Although we had nothing solid to go on at the time, and no vic to press a charge."

I thought for a moment.

"Anything else?" Hernandez asked, obviously keen to get on with whatever she'd been working on.

"Was there a boyfriend involved at all?" I asked. "Or a military connection?"

The line was quiet while I presumed Hernandez scanned her notes in the file again.

"The father was ex-Navy, according to my notes, but otherwise I don't see anything here about a boyfriend. Why do you ask?"

"Lexy had a knife on her, which she'd traded with our witness," I explained. "It likely came from a Marine or a former Marine."

Hernandez laughed. "I'm in Oceanside. All we have here is sea, sand, and U.S. Marines."

It was worth a shot. "Thanks for your help," I said.

"Anytime," the detective replied. "Hey, and let me know if you find the girl. I'd love to close this file."

"Sure," I said, and ended the call.

I took a deep breath. Every law enforcement department in any town bigger than a farming community in the middle of nowhere was understaffed and overworked. A large enough percentage of the population were busy breaking laws from traffic violations to murder to keep us all with more than we could handle. But I hated to hear that anyone had fallen through the cracks like Alexis Morrison seemed to have done.

"She wasn't a big help," Hugo commented.

"No, but I guess I can stop trying to find the father," I replied, peering around our monitors. "What are you up to?"

"Putting together the list of names we spoke to on Robles."

For a moment, I wasn't sure what he meant, but then I realized. Then I felt embarrassed for questioning whether my partner had been working on the case. Thank goodness I'd kept the thought to myself. Of course he had. And more than that, he was following up on something I'd forgotten about. One of the golden rules. Follow every lead to its conclusion. I'd ventured off after a shinier clue that had so far gotten us nowhere.

"Anyone stand out?" I asked.

"Don't know yet," Hugo replied. "I've got a mixture of photos, notes in the file, and scraps of paper to sort through. Once I have those straightened out, I have to look up the owner of every home on Robles to cross-reference."

"And then check to see if they have a record," I said, getting on the same plan.

"Yup. Good times."

"I'll start on the owner list," I volunteered, still feeling bad for having doubted Hugo.

"That would be a big help," he replied, then shuffled his chair to the side so he could see me as well. "Did Dennis give you any more details about the van?"

I shook my head. "None I'd rely on," I replied, thinking over the questions I'd asked him after he'd brought up the van while he'd eaten his sandwich. "He mentioned he waved to Lexy, but he couldn't see her once she was in the van."

"That suggests it might be a panel van rather than the passenger style with windows," Hugo replied. "That would narrow down our search considerably."

"It would," I pondered. "Once we get the Robles list together, we can check DMV records again for the names."

Hugo's brow creased. "I thought you did that before we did the door-to-door?"

"Not exactly," I replied. "I searched to see if a Ford van was registered to an address on Robles. All the landlords will have a different primary address, and the renters might have their vehicles registered to other addresses."

Hugo nodded. "This all adds up to a fun day ahead."

I lifted my coffee cup. It was already empty. "Need a refill?"

"I'm good," Hugo said, rolling his chair back to his computer.

I went to the break room and filled up on mediocre station brew, then returned to my desk. We'd discussed buying a decent coffee machine for our office, but Hugo had pointed out we'd have everyone funneling through to get the good stuff. I felt ready to bear that burden and spring for a single-serve coffee maker. Then hide the pods.

Using county records, I began the tedious process of entering every address on Robles Drive into the search bar to come up with the deeded owners. By lunchtime, I had a complete list. Hugo had completed assembling his names from the door-to-door inquiries, and he'd built a spreadsheet, filling in whatever information we knew. I made a food dash to Lupe's in the Albertsons shopping center at Stonehill and Del Obispo so we could press on while eating lunch.

By three p.m., we had a comprehensive list of ownership and a partial list of tenants on Robles Drive. We couldn't be sure exactly how many renters we were missing, as we could only confirm those who'd answered the door. But we could make a decent guess from the owners who'd listed a different address as their residence on file. We'd then run every name we had through our system to see who showed up as having a police record.

I rolled my chair around Hugo's side to look at his screen with the completed spreadsheet. "That's a lot of names."

"We need to whittle this down," he replied. "Let's disregard all these parking tickets and minor traffic infractions."

Hugo made another column on his spreadsheet and copied over only the major traffic infractions and more serious crimes. That reduced the list considerably.

"What about this woman?" I asked, pointing to a name with a driver's license number and nothing else. "Did you miss her?"

"No. That number isn't in the system."

"Whoever spoke to her must have written it down wrong," I noted. "Who talked to her?"

Hugo shuffled through the papers he'd put aside, then clicked his mouse over to where he'd organized the photos and typed entries.

"Hmm," he said, turning to me. "You did."

I looked at his screen, where he'd brought up a photograph of a driver's license. The name read Tina Holloway. I still drew a blank. Taking out my phone, I looked in my photos, and sure enough, there was the same picture of the driver's license.

"Nothing?" Hugo asked.

I shook my head. "I remember a radio call, and we joined the deputies. Then Malone's mate, Riggs, did a runner and I chased him."

"That's all clear, but you can't remember talking to this woman?"

I looked at my partner. "No. I'm sorry. It's missing."

Gathering up my instant photos from my backpack, I spread them out across the desk. I'd taken eight of people in doorways where we'd spoken to them.

"I don't think you took one of her," Hugo said. "That's right when we got the radio call."

"Bugger," I muttered, feeling a familiar mix of fear and embarrassment. When these moments dropped from my broken brain, it made me question everything. *What else was missing?*

"Regardless," Hugo said, as though he were brushing the incident aside. "It appears Tina Holloway has a fake driver's license, so she should be our first follow-up."

I nodded. "Of course," I agreed.

All I could do was hope our first meeting would come back to me once I saw Tina Holloway again. Or whatever her name really was.

10

I stayed seated next to Hugo while we crafted an application to search the premises on Robles Drive. We had very little to justify a search warrant. In fact, we really had very little to justify anything more than sending a pair of deputies by to seize the woman's fake driver's license. But we had to try. Reading over our request one last time, we agreed it was as good as we could make it, and Hugo hit send.

"Don't hold your breath," he commented, sitting back.

I rolled my chair around to the other side of the desks and logged back into my computer that had gone to sleep.

"Assuming the warrant gets denied," Hugo ventured, "what's next?"

"Bang on the door again, I guess," I replied, accessing the spreadsheet Hugo had put together on the server.

He moved over to look at me. "Okay, so let's work through this. What's the best and the worst thing that could happen if we knock on the door again?"

After the disappointment and shock of realizing my faulty wiring had failed me once again, I wasn't much in the mood for brain teasers. But Hugo had brought up a useful method when trying to decide how to proceed sometimes, so I needed to play along.

"Best case is the woman opens the door and invites us inside."

"Fair enough," Hugo replied. "And the worst?"

I thought for a moment. Of course the absolute worst would be discovering the doorbell was wired to an explosive device, or something as equally outlandish. And unlikely.

"Nobody's home," I said. "We're pretty much stuck with going back another time."

"A car in the driveway or outside the house on the street might help," Hugo pointed out.

"Maybe," I replied. "But if the vehicle is registered to Gladys Doolittle, what does that tell us?"

Hugo nodded. "Good point." He grinned. "Gladys Doolittle?"

I shrugged. "You're getting all kinds of insights into the mad and wonderful world of my mind."

His lips widened again into a brief smile. "Alright, so another alternative would be to contact the landlord and see if he or she would let us in. What's the best and worst of doing that?"

"Worst would be that the landlord is involved in some way with the woman calling herself Holloway."

"True. And what are we thinking is going on in that house beyond a tenant using a fake ID?" Hugo asked.

"Jane Doe came from somewhere in the direction of Robles, and so did the Transit van," I replied. "We'd like to locate where. A woman lying about their identity is hiding something, so like you said, it's the best place to start."

Hugo nodded again. "Sure, and the best scenario of talking to the landlord would be they meet us at the house and let us in."

"Evelyn Chambers."

"That's the landlady?" Hugo asked.

"Yeah. Owned the place since 1981," I replied, and let out a low whistle. "Can you imagine what the appreciation has been on that place? Even taking into account the upgrade expenses over the years."

"Conclusion?" Hugo asked, ignoring my sidebar.

"Sorry. I'd say the potential downsides outweigh the best-case upsides on contacting the landlady, so knocking on the door seems the best option if we don't get the warrant. Or maybe we stake it out for a few hours and see if we get lucky."

Hugo rolled his eyes. "That sounds like the perfect way I like to spend my evenings."

"We need a result by morning," I reminded Hugo.

He nodded, but didn't reply.

"What about the rest of the list from Robles?" I asked, realizing we'd stopped at Holloway.

"Nothing very promising," Hugo replied. "A couple of possessions from way back. One DUI. And those two we brought in, of course."

I looked at my watch. It was almost five. We currently had nothing new or worthwhile to present to Captain Bradley in the morning. I wondered if Jane Doe was doing any better and picked up my phone to text the Dishy Doc.

"Any progress with our patient?"

"Here's what I propose," Hugo said, and I looked across the desks at him. "Let's get out of here on time for once, and get a good night's rest. I'll keep an eye on email and let you know when we hear from the judge. Warrant or no warrant, either way, we show up at the house early tomorrow."

I glanced down at my phone screen, but didn't see the ellipsis blinking. Heck, I didn't even know if he was still at the hospital. It was hard to put the thought of Jane Doe and the other missing girl out of my mind, but there didn't seem much we could do tonight. And at some point, I needed to figure out a life-work balance that wasn't so skewed. But then I'd have to face how truly boring and lonely my personal life had become. Just a girl and her rabbit.

"Sure," I replied reluctantly, already wondering what I'd do with a whole evening to myself.

Driving home, I considered my options. It was an opportunity to spend time with Roger, who deserved more interaction than I'd been able to give him over the past couple of days. But the idea of giving my self-destructive mind a whole evening alone at home to conjure all kinds of reasons to doubt myself didn't appeal. So, I called my mother.

"Hello, darling," she answered. "Did you see the surf forecast for the morning?"

"Hey, Mum. I didn't look yet. Is it good?" I asked, then reminded myself I had an early rendezvous with Hugo. "Bugger. I have to be at work by dawn tomorrow."

"Oh, that's too bad. It's calling for three-foot waves at Doheny and no wind."

I groaned. The one time Hugo wanted to work a case early, and of course the surf was going to be the best day in weeks.

"I'm making fish tacos if you have time to come by," Mom added.

Music to my ears. "Brilliant, I'll see you in half an hour."

We hung up, and I turned left on Selva, then right on Copper Lantern to drop down the hill to my house. Roger hopped out of his credenza and shot across the room to greet me, failing to stop at the edge of the area rug and sliding across the hardwood. Rabbits don't have pads on their feet, just a thick layer of fur, so they struggle for grip on smooth surfaces.

"Hey, mate," I chuckled, watching him slip and slide his way back to the rug.

He'd begun figuring out how to carefully negotiate the hardwood, but on this occasion, his excitement overtook the finesse required. I dropped my backpack on the bench by the door and hung my blazer on a hook.

"How's your day been?" I asked Roger as I kneeled down and petted him.

He ground his teeth in pleasure as I softly ran my hand over his head, ears, and back.

"Okay, we need a few things," I announced, standing up and walking toward my bedroom.

Ten minutes later, I traded my boring, nondescript work-issued car for my 1979 VW bus—the only vehicle I'd ever owned—and drove to my parents' house on the bluffs overlooking the harbor. I had a few memories of the home in England where we'd lived before moving to the U.S., but this single-story, Spanish-tile-roofed house would always be home to me.

Opening the gate on the tall wooden fence at the front of the property, I walked across the courtyard, past my mum's beautiful flowers in planters and large ceramic pots, to the sliding glass doors.

"You brought Roger!" Mum declared excitedly as I set the carrier down on the floor.

"I didn't have the heart to leave him behind for the one evening I actually left work at a decent hour," I replied as Mom hugged me before dropping to the tile to let Roger out and fuss over him.

"Oh, but we're not rabbit-proofed," she said, looking up in concern.

"I'll just keep an eye on him," I assured her.

Roger tentatively hopped out of the carrier, his nose frantically twitching at the unfamiliar smells. He then squatted down and decided to delay his concerns about the strange surroundings until my mother was done petting him.

"You're gonna look like a bloody fish taco if that's all you ever eat," my dad said, walking into the kitchen and dining area from the sunken living room.

I grinned at my mother. "You lied."

She shrugged and smiled. "I may have mentioned something else for dinner before I spoke with you."

My dad wrapped a brawny arm around me and squeezed. "Cost me the one steak she lets me eat a month."

"I'm worth it," I said, and squeezed him in return.

"We'll see," he joked, releasing me and leaning down to tickle Roger's head.

I kept watch over Roger while we chatted as Mom prepared dinner. Dad and I sat on bar stools at the kitchen counter from where we could see the ocean through the window, beyond the backyard.

"How's your case going?" my dad asked when we sat at the table to eat.

I was impressed he'd waited that long to ask. "Frustrating. Won't be our case, or even a case at all by morning, unless we come up with something more than what we have."

"How does that work?" Dad asked. "Either there's a crime or there isn't one, right?"

I paused a moment to consider how to answer his typical black-and-white question. "We have a young woman who appears to be the victim of something, but she's in the hospital and can't say a word," I replied, which reminded me to check my phone for messages. "Then we have another young woman who's potentially missing, but she was already missing, and since she already turned eighteen, no one has really been looking for her."

It was my mum's turn to ask a question, mainly because my dad had a mouthful of taco.

"How is it she's missing twice?"

"She's a runaway," I replied, sneaking a quick look at my phone and seeing I didn't have any texts. "So a case was started two years ago that went nowhere. We believe she was living on the streets here in Dana Point until a few weeks back, when she was witnessed getting in a vehicle and vanishing."

"So how come there's no case out of all of that?" Dad asked, having swallowed his food.

"We don't have a lick of proof of any crime committed. The girl in the hospital was pumped full of drugs, but in theory, she could have done that to herself. Without any evidence, we could be chasing the unfortunate lives of two homeless women who both got themselves in trouble."

My mum shook her head. "So sad. It seems like they'd let you at least look into it a bit more."

"I'm hoping," I agreed, then considered bringing up the other issue that was weighing heavily on my mind. Not the Castillo situation. That was a secret I needed to keep from everyone, but my memory lapse earlier in the day.

My parents were the only people I could openly discuss my memory problem with. They'd lived through it with me since we'd first figured out the issue around the time we'd moved to California. The gift of a Polaroid camera had been a turning point in understanding my forgetfulness was something more than me not paying attention.

They'd taken me to the best specialists available, who'd prodded, tested, and scanned me over many years. The conclusion was an as-yet-unnamed neurological disorder, amongst the hundreds of issues affecting the human brain that science still understood very little about. We'd decided the testing was too disruptive for no net progress, and I was better off managing the situation myself. With an instant camera.

"Had a lapse today," I confessed, deciding their support might help me sleep better. "I lost a key scene in our investigation."

My parents' faces filled with concern.

"Did you have a picture?" Mum asked.

As much as they tried to hide it, they lived in fear that the visual stimulation from the photos would stop working one day. An anxiety I shared.

"No. We were called away, and it didn't seem important at the time. Turns out it might be."

"Hugo know?" Dad asked.

I nodded. My partner was aware of my problem. A secret that, if shared, would have me kicked off the force.

"Anyone else notice?" Dad continued.

I shook my head. "Hopefully it won't matter by the time we reach the office in the morning, but it took me by surprise today. Hasn't happened in a month or so."

My phone buzzed as my parents both gave me their usual

words of encouragement, which were nice, but unheard, as I read the text from Dr. Eric Cole.

"Still heavily sedated. Will reduce meds in day or two. Fingers crossed."

It wasn't the worst news in the world, but I'd been hoping for something more useful. Jane Doe telling us what happened would either assure us we had a case to pursue, or prove Captain Bradley right in her skepticism.

"I have mince pies for dessert," my mother announced from the kitchen.

"She can't," Dad volunteered. "She's in training, trying to keep up with my new girl, Kenzie."

I reached over and punched his arm. "I'll have mine, and I'll take the old man's. Save him from a bloody heart attack."

My dad's playful banter lifted my spirits for a few moments until my phone buzzed again with another text. My stupid brain had me holding my breath, thinking Dishy Doc was following up with something more personal. But of course it couldn't be anything good like that. It was Hugo.

"Warrant denied. See you at 6."

11

Too often, my bright ideas didn't seem as smart when it came down to acting them out. Getting out of my car at four a.m., having parked behind Dad's boxing gym, was starting to feel like one of those times. Dressed all in black: leggings, hoodie, and even tennis shoes, I looked like a stereotypical thief under the glow of the streetlights from Doheny Park Drive. Still, the point was to be hard to identify, and the outfit should do the trick.

Domingo Avenue was dead quiet and far less illuminated the farther I got from the main road. The gates to the corner lot were closed, and there was no sign of activity from what I could see. Which wasn't much with the tall chain-link fence backed with plastic sheeting surrounding the place. I didn't know what I could learn from this risky exercise, but hoped it would be more than the suspicions and bad feelings I knew currently. Something nagged me from the back of my mind that the location would help me tie Paul's involvement together with the Castillos, which currently seemed ridiculous.

I waited in the shadows across the street for several minutes, letting my eyes adjust, and studying the roofs of the two small structures behind the fence. Against the left side was what from satellite maps and my view from the roof of the gym appeared to be a shabby-looking office building. Against the right side was a rusty, old, faded blue shipping container. Between the two was a space only wide enough to pull a box truck inside the yard and walk along either side, as I'd seen the other night.

What I couldn't see were any cameras. There was no chance the Castillos kept illicit goods in a lock-up secured by nothing more than a chain and padlock. Either I wasn't seeing what they'd installed or the property wasn't being used for anything illegal. Which I didn't believe for a second. Why would Santiago only be dropping by at odd times in the night if the buildings were used for storing Christmas decorations and photo albums?

Walking across the street, I looked for the best way to get a look over the fence. They'd certainly made sure the yard was well screened off. The plastic sheeting was a patchwork of various colors and materials, but they hadn't left a square inch open to peek through. A mailbox sat atop a post on the sidewalk about three feet from the fence. Trying to stand on the mailbox and hang on the fence looked like a perfect way to end up in a heap on the concrete. Or cut myself to ribbons on the spiral of razor wire attached to the upper rail of the fence.

I moved around the corner to where the row of little storage garages met the chain-link fence. If I could get on top of the garages, I'd be able to look straight down into the yard.

Jogging along the alleyway, I spotted a camera and kept my head down. It was mounted over one of the six garage doors. At the end of the row, another alleyway led to the left, where vehicles filled a parking area behind the garages. It looked to be a used car dealer or a repair shop. Their fence was a sturdy metal frame, which I knew I could climb.

In short order, I was on the roof above the row of garages. It was pitched at a slight angle to drain rainwater to a gutter along the back edge, but years of slime and dirt made the footing treacherous. The bitumen roof had been repaired so many times that I had to tread carefully in the dark not to trip over ridges and loose corners.

Reaching the end of the garages, I stared down into the Castillos' small compound. Crouching, I risked taking out my flashlight and shining the beam across the yard. While I had the light, I snapped a picture with my instant camera. Setting it down while it developed, I used my phone to take a quick video, panning from one side to the other, taking in both buildings.

The place was a mess. Trash and discarded detritus littered the edges against the base of the fence, and oil and dirt stained the concrete pad between the buildings. The office looked like it hadn't been painted in forty years, with a layer of time-borne grime covering every surface. Except for the door and the two windows I could see, which had been recently replaced with what appeared to be sturdy, modern versions. Odd, considering the glass in the windows was covered from the inside by what I judged to be a dark curtain or blind.

Switching off my flashlight, I allowed my eyes to adjust once more. Curiosity begged me to hop the razor wire to the roof of either building and climb down into the yard. *But then what?* I wouldn't be able to see inside through the windows, and I knew the doors would all be locked. Breaking in would be the only way to learn more. I wasn't sure what I hoped to discover that would clue me in to what role the property played, but at the moment, all I'd accomplished was losing sleep.

What I needed was a drone. I could hover it a few hundred feet over the property at night when Santiago was there and film him. With the nearby freeway noise, even in the middle of the night, he wouldn't hear the buzz of the little motors. I wondered if the camera in one of the consumer drones that I could afford would produce decent footage at night from a safe height above the property.

While I pondered another expensive purchase like the night vision binoculars, the beam of a vehicle's headlights turned off Doheny Park onto Domingo.

I dropped to my stomach in the filth atop the garage roof. My chin touched something sticky, and I dreaded to think what it might be. Behind the two bright white headlights was the silhouette of a large SUV. It slowed and turned left, stopping with its nose at the gates to the little compound. If the fence hadn't been backed with sheeting, the lights would have revealed my outline on the neighboring roof. Which was exactly what would happen when the driver opened the gates. Lying down, I'd be little more than a hump behind the razor wire, but if Santiago, or whoever it was, looked up, they might notice something unfamiliar.

Or were they here because my presence had triggered a hidden camera or alarm?

Hearing the clanking of the chain being removed from the gate, I slithered backwards, feeling my sweatshirt ride up my body. My T-shirt now rubbed against the grubby roof until it rode up, too, leaving my stomach touching the muck and dirt. I stopped once I could only see the very rear of the SUV's roof. And, to my annoyance, my instant camera I'd left near the edge.

The razor wire before me lit up as the gates swung open, and a moment later, the SUV's engine note picked up. The black roof disappeared from view as the driver pulled into the yard. After a moment, the engine cut and I heard a car door open. Then a second door. Beeping sounded from below until the two doors banged closed and quiet returned.

Carefully, I eased myself forward once more until I could peek through the wire at the yard. The SUV filled most of the space, which had returned to shadowed darkness barely lit by distant streetlights. It was good to know there weren't any motion lights in the yard. I noticed movement around the back of the vehicle. Two figures. Men, as best I could tell. The tailgate of the SUV opened, and I heard a hushed voice say something.

One of the men turned on a flashlight, the beam landing on the side of the office, before beginning a sweep of the yard. I dipped my face and shuffled backwards once more.

"You hear that?" I heard one of them say.

I froze, lying still.

"I didn't hear anything," the second man replied in a gruff tone and a heavy accent. I wasn't sure where it was from, but he didn't sound Hispanic.

Raising my head slowly, I peeked from beneath the hood. I could barely see the top of the tailgate in the air, so I figured I was out of their view. But my little instant camera wasn't. Footsteps shuffling in the yard were followed by the flashlight beam searching for the source of the noise. I held my breath as the white light illuminated the rusty razor wire before me, along with my instant camera. But the men must not have seen it as the beam continued around the rooflines until the gruff voice spoke once more.

"You're hearing things." The accent might have been European, but I couldn't be sure.

More shuffling of feet on the dirty concrete, and I finally breathed once more. Slowly, I edged myself forward, listening carefully in case the men detected my presence. I desperately wanted to see whatever it was they were delivering, but first, I needed to get my camera out of sight. Reaching out, I snatched up the device, plucked the developed picture from the slot, and shoved both in my back pocket.

In the yard below, I heard the two men grunting under a strain, then a door swing open. I could just see the tops of their heads outside the office, but I needed to get closer to the edge or raise myself to get a proper look. Pushing up with my hands against the grimy rooftop, I was about to see whatever it was the men struggled to carry when a siren wailed from close by. I dropped flat against the bitumen.

"What the fuck?" the gruff man snapped.

"Hurry!" the other urged.

I turned and looked behind me to my right and saw flashing red and blue lights atop a police car on PCH, where it crossed above Doheny and then San Juan Creek. The deputies were pulling someone over on the road, oblivious to what was going on before me. I raised up again in time to see the second man disappearing inside the office building.

"Bugger," I swore under my breath. Whatever they'd hauled in there had taken the two of them.

Maybe stolen goods of some sort? A big-screen TV? All I could do was guess as they were out of sight, and unless they came back out for a second load, I wouldn't get to know. The second man had closed the door behind him, but I could hear movement from inside the office. They were dragging or moving things around. I took out my phone and set it to video, double-checking that the light feature was off. Then I waited.

Every inch of me felt like I'd been rolled in a filthy gutter. I was more than ready to climb down from this roof and shower at Dad's gym, but what I needed more than anything was some kind of reward from this ill-advised venture. A tie between the Castillos and whatever illicit operation was based out of this crappy place. A video of the two men seemed about the best I could hope for.

Hearing the door open, I risked another peek through the wire. The first man exited the office with the flashlight in his hand, keeping it pointed low. He turned and illuminated the door for the man I could now see was Santiago. Castillo's lackey locked the office. I held my phone outstretched in front of me and hit record. Watching on my screen, I followed the man who'd broken into my house getting into the driver's seat of the SUV. I then switched to his cohort opening the gate, but he was quickly lost in the shadows. I stopped the video and lay flat again when the engine started. The headlights automatically came on.

Once I saw the razor wire wasn't illuminated, I carefully raised up. The SUV backed up, and when its rear tires started down the slope of the sidewalk to the road, the nose of the vehicle pivoted up, along with the headlight beams. I scrambled backwards and buried my cheek in the muck, holding my breath one more time. A subtle clunk sounded as the SUV was put in park, then the driver's door opened.

"Gimme that light," Santiago barked.

From the brightening of the surrounding darkness, I knew he was searching the roofline. *Surely I was low enough to be hidden from his view at this angle?*

"Milo, you're going crazy, man," his cohort laughed. "Probably a cat."

I rolled my eyes. If only they knew.

"Let's go," Santiago grunted.

I stayed pinned to the roof until the sound of the SUV faded into the night. Pushing up to my knees, I was glad it was too dark to see how disgustingly filthy I was from head to toe. Staring down into the yard, I was dangerously tempted by the idea of breaking into the office. *But what would it accomplish?* They'd be warned someone knew of their secret location, and I'd discover whatever their stolen goods might be, yet I could do nothing about it. I wouldn't even be able to come back with a warrant, as I'd have no probable cause to request one.

Which reminded me I was meeting Hugo at six. I stood and began walking back along the roof of the storage garages, tilting my phone to see the time. It was ten past five. I needed to hurry.

Dirty, soggy, and smelling like a dumpster, I questioned once again what the hell I thought I was doing.

12

At 6:07 a.m., I parked behind Hugo's car on Robles. The ration of shit he was about to give me was tempered slightly when I handed him a coffee from PC Beans as I joined him in his car. The paper bag containing a pastry softened him a little more.

"You're late," he still couldn't resist pointing out.

"Figured you'd want breakfast," I used as my excuse, although it was me who desperately craved coffee. He got lucky in the deal. "Any movement?"

He shook his head. "Nothing. We'll wait it out a bit before knocking on the door."

I relaxed into the seat and ate my breakfast pastry. I'd gone from adrenaline rush to frantic urgency over the past few hours, and now my lack of sleep was catching up. After leaving my parents' house, I'd tried going to bed early, but all I'd managed to do was toss and turn and read a book. Somewhere around eleven, I must have dozed off until the alarm had woken me at three-fifteen a.m. Which all added up to this promising to be a really long day.

People left the neighboring houses, heading to work or dropping kids at school, so the vehicles parked by the curb soon thinned. A man walked by with his dog and gave us a suspicious look. A woman shepherded her kids past, probably seeing them to a school bus or a carpool. Still, nothing stirred in the house a hundred feet up the street on the opposite side from where we sat.

At 6:45 a.m., my coffee cup was empty, and I either needed to get out of the car and do something or take a nap.

"Let's knock on the door," I declared. "I don't think anyone's home."

Hugo stared at the house while he took another sip of his coffee. He was oblivious to how close he was to having the paper cup snatched from his hand if he kept nursing the drink. Finally, he put the cup in a holder and opened his door.

"Come on, then," he said.

I got out, and we walked up the sidewalk until we stood across from the home. With too many other things going through my cluttered mind, I'd omitted to think much about the woman calling herself Tina Holloway. But now I felt a twinge of nerves. I was potentially about to meet a suspect I'd conversed with two days before, yet couldn't remember. For me, it could be like meeting her for the first time. Or, the faulty wires might reconnect, and our previous interaction would be back in place as though it had never been missing.

"Okay if you lead this one?" I asked as we strode across the road.

Hugo looked at me. "Still nothing?"

"Not yet," I admitted.

"Okay," he said, and banged on the front door.

Quickly scanning the entryway, I didn't see any cameras. We both listened intently. The street was quiet, but it always surprised me how much ever-present noise there was in the background of the town. Traffic, two dogs barking, a plane going over high in the sky. I tried to shut it all out to focus on any sounds from inside the home. Hugo rang the doorbell and banged on the door again.

"I don't hear anyone inside," I whispered after a long pause.

Hugo took a step back to look up at the upstairs windows. "Got the contact number for the landlord?"

I took out my instant camera and snapped an image of the entryway, determined not to lose this morning's visit, even if it was a waste of time. Handing the camera to Hugo while the photograph whirred from the slot and began developing, I retrieved my phone and logged into the sheriff's department server. After a minute or so of hunting through our case file, I found the number and made the call. It rang five times before a sleepy voice answered.

"Hello?"

"Is this Evelyn Chambers?" I asked.

"Yes."

"Sorry to call you so early, ma'am, but this is Orange County Sheriff's Department Investigator Kat Cromwell. Do you own a property on Robles Drive in Dana Point?"

"Yes, yes I do," the woman replied, beginning to sound more concerned now that I'd startled her awake. "Is there a problem?"

"What can you tell us about your renter, Mrs. Chambers?"

"Oh, she's a nice young woman. Moved in about six or seven weeks ago."

"Can I ask her name, ma'am?"

"Of course, yes, it's Holloway. Tina Holloway. Why are you asking me all this, detective? What's going on?"

I didn't bother correcting her. "Investigator" was an awkward word people weren't used to using.

"We have reason to believe Miss Holloway can help us with a case we're investigating, but she's not currently home. We're standing outside your rental house now, ma'am."

"Oh. Well, I'm afraid I have no way of knowing where Tina is. But she does work from home."

"Do you have a number for her, Mrs. Chambers?"

"Of course. Just a moment, please. I'm afraid I'm still in bed. I'll need my glasses to look."

"Take your time, ma'am," I replied. "And again, my apologies for the early hour."

After some mumbling and beeps from her phone, her voice came back on, albeit sounding somewhat distant. I figured she was reading the number from her contacts. I repeated the number she gave me while Hugo wrote it down.

"Perfect, thank you, Mrs. Chambers."

I looked at Hugo.

"Have her call," he whispered, and I nodded.

"Would you mind doing us a favor and calling your tenant?" I asked. "Ask her if she's home."

"Umm, I suppose. But don't you think it's a bit early to be calling someone? And didn't you just tell me she's not home?"

"I did indeed, ma'am," I said, and couldn't help but grin. From her voice, I could tell she wasn't a young woman, but she was certainly sharp. "Not everyone answers when two coppers are on their doorstep. Just hang up with me, then try her, please. If she says she's home, ask her to answer the front door."

"Okay, but why don't I call her on my landline and keep you on my cell phone?"

I laughed, which earned a frown from Hugo. "That works even better, Mrs. Chambers," I replied, then waited while she called her tenant.

She was back to me after only a few seconds. "That's strange. Maybe I have her number wrong in my contacts, but I've called it plenty of times before."

"Didn't connect?" I asked.

"A recorded message said the user is unavailable. A phone company I've never heard of."

"Just a moment, ma'am," I said, and muted the call, turning to Hugo. "Number's dead. Probably a burner and she's pulled the SIM."

Hugo rolled his eyes, then looked at the front door. "This is probably a complete waste of time down a blind alley," he muttered. "Nothing to do with our case."

I couldn't argue there. We'd ended up chasing the woman calling herself Holloway on nothing more than a long-shot area search and stumbling across her fake ID she'd been stupid enough to show us. Any ties to Jane Doe were based on a general proximity. Beyond tenuous.

"She's probably running some bullshit email or phone scam," Hugo added.

I unmuted the call. "Mrs. Chambers, are you local to Dana Point?"

"I am," she replied. "I have a condo in Lantern Bay Villas."

Maybe we could tie up this loose end and hand it over to another department after all.

"Would you mind coming by Robles, and with your permission, we'd like to have a look around the house?"

"Oh. Well, like I said, I was in bed when you called. But I could be there in thirty or forty minutes."

"That would be brilliant, thank you, ma'am. Any problems, please call back on this number. If not, we'll see you here in half an hour or so."

We ended the call, and I filled Hugo in on the details. He nodded and began walking across the street, heading toward the car.

"Fancy another coffee?" I ventured.

Mrs. Chambers arrived forty-five minutes after we'd hung up. She was at least seventy, but drove herself in a very nice Jaguar SUV and looked like she'd packed a hair and make-up appointment into the limited time she'd had. The woman was perfectly put together. Not that I ever gave myself forty-five minutes to get ready for anything, but even if I did, the result wouldn't be looking ready to have lunch at the bridge club.

"Thanks for doing this, Mrs. Chambers," I said as she gave Hugo a good look-over.

"You've got me worried now," she replied, using her key in the lock. "What is it you think Tina can help you with?"

"We're pretty sure her name's not Tina Holloway, for starters," I shared. "Her ID is fake."

"Oh my goodness," the woman replied, still trying to get her key to work.

"Can I help you with that?" Hugo offered.

Mrs. Chambers gave him a harsh look. "I'm perfectly capable, thank you. Something's not right. See here," she said, holding up the tag attached to the key she'd been trying. "This should be the key to the front and back door."

I looked more closely at the lock assembly. "When did you install this lock?"

"Same lock for years. That's why I don't understand why this darn key isn't working."

I shared a knowing look with Hugo.

"This lock isn't years old, Mrs. Chambers," I said, pointing to the door. "It looks like it's pretty new."

"Oh," she stammered, examining the door. "You're right. She must have changed it and not told me."

"Where's the other entry?" Hugo asked.

She nodded past him. "Up the side."

Mrs. Chambers led us up the steps on the right side of the building, leading to the first floor. Built into the hillside, the home had a double garage and an entryway at street level, then two floors of the actual house. She tried the key in the second door with the same result.

"It appears your renter has locked you out of your own property," Hugo said, earning him another scowl from Mrs. Chambers.

"I'll call my locksmith and have him come by," she said, scrolling through contacts on her phone.

I looked farther up the slope. The place didn't really have a backyard, just a continuation of the hillside and a neighbor butting up to them from the other side of the crest. I noticed a window on the side of the house and stepped carefully up the landscaped rock and flowers until I could see inside. It was the kitchen. The window was over the sink and appeared to be open a crack. I pulled on the edge, and it begrudgingly moved in its old aluminum track.

"Mind if I climb inside, Mrs. Chambers?" I called down.

"Can you get in? Oh, my dear, don't break your neck. I'm sure my locksmith can be here in an hour or two."

"Kat's fine," Hugo answered for me. "She does crazy stuff like this all the time."

"Charming," I muttered under my breath as I removed the screen and hauled myself inside through the window.

The sink and faucet made the maneuver awkward, and the pile of dirty dishes didn't help, either. Starting from a glamorous position with my ass still sticking out the window, I managed to avoid breaking any china by slipping and falling over the other side of the counter and landing with a thud on the linoleum floor.

"Oh my goodness," I heard the old lady gasp from outside, followed by a chuckle from my partner.

Picking myself up, I checked for obvious wounds and breaks. I seemed to be okay other than the bruises that would present themselves later in the day. Stepping from the kitchen into the hall, I opened the front door.

"Are you okay?" Mrs. Chambers asked as she came inside.

"Right as rain," I replied, ignoring the grin on Hugo's face. "Please stay here by the door while we sweep the place. We'll let you know when it's safe."

"Oh. Okay," she responded.

I nodded toward the stairs, so Hugo walked into the living area off the hall. The house didn't smell stale, but not fresh, either. On the landing, there appeared to be a choice of five doors off a central landing. Right away, I noticed something very odd. Two of the doors had extra locks on the outside. Pulling a pair of nitrile gloves from my back pocket, I stretched them over my hands. The first door was ajar.

"Police. If anyone is here, you need to let me know now."

Silence, beyond Hugo moving around downstairs.

I pushed the door open. At first, it appeared to be like any other household interior door, but the weight was wrong. Much heavier. I stepped into what I guessed to be the kid's bedroom with a crude-looking metal-framed bunk bed against one wall. Except there were more bunk beds. One each against three of the four walls.

Leaving the room, I pushed the door across the hall open. It swung slowly, with the same mass as the first one. More like a beefy security door. I noticed the wood frame had also been replaced with a metal version. This bedroom was packed with three more metal bunk beds.

"Hugo!" I called out. "Come up here!"

I heard footsteps on the stairs and waited for him to join me.

"Shit," he muttered, seeing the beds. "Some kind of halfway house, trafficking thing going on here."

I nodded. "I'd say that lines up with young women on Velvet. Would have to keep them quiet in the middle of a busy neighborhood. Our Jane Doe must have found a way out Monday night."

"Can I come upstairs now?" Mrs. Chambers called up.

"No!" Hugo and I answered together. "I'm sorry to tell you your rental house is now considered a crime scene, ma'am," I added.

"Oh my good gracious," the woman muttered from downstairs.

13

———————

Captain Bradley stared at me for what felt like an uncomfortable amount of time before responding to my debrief. Hugo had kindly let me do all the talking so far. As usual.

"So, let me get this straight. After you happened across an incident with this drugged-up Jane Doe wandering our streets the other night, you've discovered another female missing, although no one has reported her so, and now some kind of suspicious bunkhouse in the middle of town. None of which you can connect with any evidence, and none of which would usually fall under a homicide investigator's purview. Am I close?"

"Technically, the missing girl, Lexy, was reported, ma'am," I corrected. "Just eighteen months ago. And we do have a connection between Lexy going missing and Jane Doe being found. The Ford Transit van, ma'am."

Hugo shifted in his chair, and the captain continued staring at me.

"You do understand what actual evidence looks like, don't you, Kat?" she said, then continued before I could answer. Which was probably a good thing. "I know you do because on rare occasions, you have presented me with real evidence we can pass on to the

District Attorney's Office. What you have here is… well, I honestly don't know what you have here, Kat, but I do know there's not a lick of useful evidence so far."

For once in my life, I didn't say what was on my mind. I said nothing at all. Hugo stayed quiet, so I decided to try the same ploy.

Bradley leaned forward with her elbows on her desk. "This is where you two tell me *how* you are going to produce the evidence that will keep this, or these, cases open."

I glanced at Hugo, who was picking at his fingernails.

"Hoping for fingerprints from the bunkhouse, ma'am, and we'll hit the mug shots to see if we can ID the woman calling herself Tina Holloway. We'll update the missing persons on Lexy and put out a picture of Jane Doe. We also have the list of potential matches from missing persons for Jane Doe to go through, and of course, it's possible her prints will be found in the house. That will confirm she was held there."

"Jane Doe's prints aren't in the system?" Bradley asked.

"No, ma'am. Sarge ran them on Tuesday. No luck."

The captain sat back in her seat and sighed, tapping her pen against her other hand. I always had a hard time reading the woman. Her consistently stern expression gave nothing away, and I wondered if she was capable of smiling.

"Connect these three cases with something tangible, or I'm handing them off to the appropriate departments," she ordered, and Hugo's butt was rising out of his seat before the last word left her lips.

"And prove there's even a criminal case with Jane Doe," Bradley added.

Hugo was already halfway to the door, but I'd just gotten to my feet. I should have thrown out a "Yes, ma'am," and been on his heels, but of course that's not what my brain chose.

"She'd been pumped full of Velv—" I began, only just stopping myself before completing the word. "Vexing drugs," I blabbered in desperation.

"Vexing drugs?" Bradley scoffed. "What are you talking about, Cromwell?"

"Sorry, ma'am, poor use of words. I meant a cocktail of drugs no one would give themselves."

The captain shrugged. "So prove who gave them to her."

"Yes, ma'am," I finally managed.

"Don't say a bloody word," I seethed at Hugo once we made it back to our desks.

He threw his hands up. "Every time, Kat. You walk right into it."

"Well, if you'd say something in those stupid debriefs, then maybe I wouldn't be left on the hook."

"You're always keen to do the talking," he said with amusement in his tone.

"Because we'd sit there in complete silence if I didn't!"

He laughed.

"Sod off," I grumbled. "I'm not saying a bloody word next time."

"We'll see," he said with a chuckle.

Blowing out my cheeks, I looked at my watch. It was almost noon. The bunkhouse discovery and subsequent organizing had eaten up the morning. I needed to calm down and focus on the case. Or cases. Although, more than ever, I was convinced they were all connected. The van linked two, and Jane Doe had to have come from the bunkhouse, which tied in the third. But underneath her icy delivery, the captain was right. We were thin on factual evidence. Maybe she'd be keener on the investigation if she knew there was a chance the new drug Velvet was on our streets, but that gem would have to wait.

My cell phone rang, and I checked the caller ID. It was a call I was happy to take.

"Hi, Rosa," I greeted the lead officer with Orange County Sheriff's Crime Lab Unit. "Got something for us?" I put the call on speaker.

"It's good and bad news, I'm afraid," she replied, not pausing long enough for me to choose which one to hear first. "The place has been wiped down."

"Bugger," I muttered. "I'd hoped the woman had been too rushed to do that."

"I'd say she was rushed," Rosa replied. "Or not very thorough. The big items were wiped, the bed frames, bathrooms, kitchen, but we're finding prints on the TV remote, salt and pepper shakers, smaller stuff like that."

"Anything at all from the bunk rooms?" Hugo asked, leaning over from his desk.

"Only partials so far. Like I said, whoever did this wasn't very careful, so we're finding a few on the bed frames, and odd places like the trim around the door and window."

"It's most likely young women who were being held there, and they'd have been heavily drugged," I thought aloud. "So it wouldn't be surprising if they acted strangely. I'd check under the lower bunks, too, Rosa. Maybe they forgot to wipe that down."

"Will do. Just wanted to give you a quick update..." She broke off, and I could hear someone calling to her. She returned to the phone after a few moments. "Okay, looks like we may have our first full print from one of the bedrooms. I'll make sure it's sent your way as soon as possible."

"And the prints you have so far from downstairs, please," I said.

"Sure."

"Thank you," I responded before ending the call. I looked over at Hugo. "Maybe a start."

He nodded. "We need a good thread to pull on. Bradley's not wrong, you know."

"I know," I admitted reluctantly. "But I'll buy you lunch for a week if these three events aren't related."

"Do I have to buy you lunch for a week if they are?" he retorted.

"That's how bets usually work, Hugo."

The corners of his mouth crept into a hint of a grin. "Then I'll pass."

It was good to know we were on the same page.

"I can start going through my list of possible missing persons for Jane Doe," I suggested. "Maybe you search for Tina Holloway in the system?"

"The name didn't come up anywhere as an alias or a record of someone matching her description," he replied. "I already looked. Give me half your Jane Doe list, and I'll knock out a few while we wait on prints."

I nodded. He was probably right. Everything felt like a needle in a haystack, but if we dug into the list of 586 names, we could start making progress. We had the van to track down, too, but that was a bigger task than Jane Doe. At least searching for a person, we might identify her from a picture. All the Transit vans were basically the same. We'd have to get ridiculously lucky to pick out an owner already tied to the case.

"I'll start from the front if you want to start from the rear," I proposed, then we both squared up to our monitors and set to work.

Every file took at least a minute. We had to find the next entry, then open the file itself, which was slow as it was grabbing information across multiple servers, and our station system was embarrassingly slow. Because of the way I'd pared down the search, the majority of details matched, so I went straight to the picture. Or pictures. These also took forever to load, and many of the shots were from the woman as a child or blurry snapshots. One in every four entries, I was keeping as possibilities, simply because I couldn't rule them out.

After an hour, I sat back and realized how hungry I was.

"I need to eat," I announced, then yawned deeply. The lack of sleep was catching up with me, too.

"I could eat," Hugo agreed. "And I'm already sick of looking through these files. Pretty sad to see how little information or pictures there are of some of these kids."

"The best photos are from the foster system as they're usually newer," I said, taking one last look at the case file to see if anything had been updated. "Fingerprints are in the system," I announced. "And Evelyn Chambers emailed me the lease signed by the woman calling herself Holloway."

Hugo stood and looked over our monitors. "My turn to do the food run if you want to press on."

I thought for a moment and noticed my brain was definitely operating at partial throttle. Every change of direction or multitask took extra time to align.

"Sure," I replied. "As long as there's coffee involved. Real coffee, not the naff stuff."

"Do you realize PC beans would go out of business if you stopped going there?" Hugo gibed.

"It's crossed my mind," I admitted.

He gathered his jacket and left, so I returned to my screen and pondered which task to attack next. Fingerprints had to be the best chance of a return, so I opened the file we'd been sent from Rosa's group. They'd given us four sets of complete prints worthy of tracing, and I entered them into the system one by one.

The first hit came back for Evelyn Chambers. Apparently, she used to be a schoolteacher, so her prints were on record from state licensing. The next return showed the prints belonged to one Christina Lowell. Arrested for soliciting fifteen years ago, then charged for possession of a controlled substance for sale three years back. She got away with probation and a $10,000 fine. I opened the picture taken during her arrest and stared at a woman I didn't recognize.

But why would I? I still had zero recollection of our meeting on the doorstep of the bunkhouse. I took a picture of the suspect with my phone and texted it to Hugo.

"Is this Holloway?"

While I waited for a response, I checked the reports on the other two prints. One had no matches, and the other returned a girl from the foster system. Kamaria Ellis. Fifteen when she ran away from a group home in Stockton, California, about a year ago. Her description noted a heart tattoo on the back of her neck. I brought up her picture. A cute black girl who looked like she could be a regular high school teenager, not a runaway who'd recently been held in a house used to… *what?* We were still guessing. If we'd pulled Jane Doe's prints from the house, then it would have sealed the deal in my mind. I still felt like she must have come from the house, but we lacked Bradley's evidence.

My phone buzzed. Hugo replied with a thumbs-up emoji. I typed another message, telling him we also had another missing girl from the prints. Why it couldn't wait until he returned, I wasn't sure. Probably because I liked to know things as they were available. Which reminded me of failing with Holloway. Or Christina Lowell, as we now knew her to be. I had to be more diligent with my pictures.

Which, in turn, jogged my memory about last night. Bringing up the video I'd shot on my phone, I replayed the footage. It was grainy and hard to make out much more than two figures in the dim light of the yard. I recognized Milo Santiago because I'd studied him too many times, but I'd be hard-pushed to make an ID on the other man. The video glimpsed his face as he'd walked toward the rear of the SUV to open the gates.

And what was with the accent? The Castillos hired Hispanics who were related to them or connected through the backstreets of Santa Ana and Costa Mesa. The gruff-voiced guy wasn't Hispanic. It would probably be a pointless task, but while I had the opportunity, I searched our system for known associates of Ramon Castillo, Gabby's father. The tag returned a hefty list. I began working my way through the names, disregarding anyone with a Mexican name. Turned out I was right. Outside of a handful of white and Asian associates, the Castillos stuck to their own. I came up short on finding an Ivan, Pierre, or Gunther.

"Got you something different today," Hugo said, making me jump as he walked into the office.

I quickly minimized the screen I had open and swung around. "You did what?"

"You need variety in your life, Kat. You can't eat the same boring things every day."

Hugo was a big foodie and couldn't understand why I was neither adventurous nor interested in exploring new things to eat. I enjoyed my food as much as the next person, but I was perfectly content sticking to the handful of things I knew I loved. And at this moment, I was too tired and frazzled to deal with Hugo's version of what he thought I should eat.

"Yes, I bloody well can," I retorted. "What did you get me?"

He slid a PC Beans coffee cup across the desk before dropping the bag of food next to it.

"I got you fish tacos, Kat. The world is still on its axis. All will be fine."

I felt more relief than was probably healthy over a lunch order. I spotted the sheriff's badge on the cup, which assured me that my coffee order was my usual latte. I let out a sigh.

"I'm weird. Get over it," I said before sipping my caffeine fix.

"You think?" he replied, shaking his head and chuckling to himself.

14

———————

We put out an all-points bulletin for Christina Lowell, including the best picture we could find and mentioning her known alias of Tina Holloway. I doubted she'd still use the fake name as she knew it had been compromised, but the more details, the better. I updated the missing persons file on Kamaria Ellis and called the foster care worker whose name I found from the file. She hadn't seen or heard from the kid since she'd run away.

I finished lunch and sat back in my chair, clearing my head before tackling more from the Jane Doe search. We were beginning to accumulate several lines of inquiries, but they were all still shots in the dark. I ran through what we knew like a checklist in my mind, then clicked on the case file to make sure I wasn't forgetting anything.

The van. Hugo was right. The vehicle search was another low-odds time suck, but if we believed the van was connected to the bunkhouse, then surely it would show up on CCTV in the area.

"If girls were being ferried to and from the bunkhouse, Hugo, that Transit van would be ideal, right?"

I heard his chair roll to the side. "Sure. But the garage was empty, and none of the neighbors the deputies spoke to have seen a van at the house."

I scooted my chair over to look at Hugo. "Then they must have been doing it in the middle of the night. Those bunks didn't magically appear at the house. They either had to be delivered or brought there in a vehicle large enough to carry them."

"We don't have CCTV in that area, Kat," Hugo replied, but despite his negative comment, I could tell I'd started his gears turning. "Nearest would be Selva and Golden Lantern, or west at Selva and PCH. There are a dozen alternate ways they could drive to avoid those cameras."

I brought up a map on my computer and studied the roads. Hugo was right, of course. We could submit a request to the crime lab techies, but it could take them weeks to get back to us. If we had a license plate, it would be much faster.

An idea came to me, and I picked up my phone, scrolling back through my messages until I found the exchange I was looking for.

"Are you home?" I typed, and hit send.

Ellipsis blinked almost immediately, but after a minute of staring at the screen with no response, I was about to type something else when a reply popped up.

"Why?"

I laughed.

"What you got?" Hugo asked from across the desks.

"That kid, Bee, with the doorbell camera," I replied, looking at the instant picture she'd reluctantly allowed me to take of her. "I was thinking we could check her footage from last night. If the van left south on Robles, it would drive past her house."

"Need your help," I texted.

"Worth a shot," Hugo said, although he didn't sound optimistic. "If that kid will even answer."

"She's answered. But I think we're now negotiating."

Hugo scoffed. "How about we, the police, don't tell her school and her parents that she's skipping class?"

"Trade," came a text from Bee.

"I can get a warrant."

The ellipsis blinked again while I'm sure Bee weighed her options from a position of zero leverage.

"Camera issues 86ed everything."

I laughed again. She'd found her leverage, after all.

I sent, *"I'll owe you one."*

Her reply was immediate. *"Already owe me 1."*

"Are you still negotiating with the skater kid?" Hugo asked, standing up and looking over at me.

"Just arranging when we can see the footage," I lied before texting Bee again.

"$20"

"$50," she texted back

"$40 and we're square."

"I'm home."

Unplugging my laptop from the monitor, I stood and gathered up my things. "Bee will rule this town one day," I said with a laugh. "Not sure if she'll be police chief, mayor, or mafia, but I guarantee she'll be running the show."

"How much did it cost you?" Hugo asked, grabbing his jacket.

"Nothing. She's being a good citizen."

"Bullshit," he said, following me out of our office. "How much?"

"Got a ten on you?" I asked.

"Really? Ten's not bad," Hugo scoffed, digging his wallet out.

I didn't bother telling him I only had thirty on me.

Bee answered the door wearing a Pearl Jam T-shirt and black cargo shorts. I guessed she probably had a figure underneath the baggy clothes that most California fifteen-year-olds would be proud to show off at the beach. Skating all over the hills of Dana Point would keep her trim. I know, as I used to do it.

"You changed your hair," I said, as she waved us inside.

She self-consciously ruffled a hand through the pink mop, which now had purple streaks added. "Yeah. Kinda came out weird."

"I like it," I said, and hoped Bee didn't notice Hugo raising an eyebrow.

The kid closed the door behind us. "So, what is it you need?"

"Doorbell cam footage from Tuesday night."

Bee nodded and began bringing up the app on her phone. "Got a time?"

"No," I replied. "We're looking for a Ford van."

"Is that what we saw before?" Bee asked. "When that chick was wandering down the road? Is she okay?"

I smiled and replied before Hugo had a chance to. I knew he'd be losing his patience by now. "Yes, yes, and recovering. We don't know a time, but we're looking to see if that van passed by anytime Tuesday night."

"Or anytime, period," Hugo pointed out.

"Shit, dude, that's a lot of footage."

"Then send us the file, and we'll look through it," Hugo replied.

Bee scowled at my partner before re-focusing on her phone. She didn't want us seeing her comings and goings.

Even at eight times the regular speed, it was going to take us forever. Any faster, and we'd easily miss a vehicle passing by. Bee set her phone on the kitchen table, propped up by a round stand that popped out from the back. Hugo and I sat down and watched the screen.

"Got any coffee?" I asked.

Bee moved over to the counter and placed a pod in a single-serve coffee maker. She closed the lid and hit the brew button, then moved to the fridge and took out an energy drink.

"If you're cool, I have shit to do. I'll be in my room."

I got up from the chair, leaving Hugo to watch the footage. "Sure. I'll shout if we need you. This may take a while."

"No shit," Bee scoffed, then headed upstairs.

I waited a few minutes until the coffee had brewed, then added milk from the fridge. Hugo had stopped and restarted the player several times, but he hadn't said anything, so I presumed it wasn't the van in question. With the way vehicles blurred by, it was hard to tell a Smart car from a dually, so we had to stop and check anything dark-colored.

I sat back down with my coffee. "I got it for a bit," I told Hugo.

He stretched, blinking to clear his vision after staring at the little screen. "You realize this angle won't give us a license plate, right?" he pointed out.

"Yeah, but maybe we'll get lucky with another detail," I replied absentmindedly as I focused on the dim nighttime footage from the little camera.

We'd been watching for close to an hour when I finally saw what looked like a dark-colored van shoot by on screen. I rewound and played at regular speed. My partner was standing by the breakfast table, looking out the back window.

"Hugo. We have something."

He sat next to me and leaned in closer to see the little phone screen. "Looks like the same type of van," he commented. "No side windows, so that narrows down the model."

I nodded. "Ford made three versions of roof height, too, and this is the standard one."

I played the footage back and forth, hunting for details. The interior was briefly illuminated by a streetlight. The video was far too grainy to identify the driver, but there was only one person up front.

"2:13 in the morning," I read from the timestamp. "And the van's arriving to remove whoever was in the bunkhouse."

"We think," Hugo said. "This only proves the van drove by this spot."

I looked at him and raised an eyebrow.

"I agree," he conceded. "But we need hard evidence, and this is circumstantial."

I returned to the footage and fast-forwarded once more. We both watched for another ten minutes, which meant over an hour of real-time video, before the van appeared again. I could pick out a few more features closer to the camera on the near side of the road. The first was obvious.

"That's a woman in the passenger seat," Hugo said, tapping on the screen.

"Yup. Christina Lowell," I said, then added, "I know, I know, it's a blurry image of what appears to be a female, but you and I both know it's Lowell."

Hugo let out a breath. "The question is, who do they have in the back of that van?"

"And where are they trafficking them to?" I questioned. "I don't mean now, as they're just clearing out the bunkhouse as it's been compromised, but everything points to them trafficking young, at-risk women. So where to? Dana Point is hardly a hub of the sex slave industry."

"Maybe it's not sex trafficking," Hugo offered. "Could be an illegal immigration thing."

"Alexis Morrison and Kamaria Ellis are U.S. citizens," I responded.

Hugo shrugged. "Fair point. Although we can't prove Lexy was in the bunkhouse, or this van."

"Yet," I added, then squinted at the paused screen. I rolled the footage back and forth. "There's a dent in the side door."

"That'll be a help if we ever find it," Hugo said, looking closer for himself. "Damn it, why are we killing ourselves looking at this tiny screen? Have the kid send us the footage so we can see it better on a computer."

I got up and went to the bottom of the stairs. "Bee!"

There was no response. I went up the stairs, and from the landing, picked out the teenager's room immediately. She had a "Keep out!" sign hanging on the door.

I knocked and called her name again. Still no response, so I opened the door and looked inside.

Posters and drawings adorned every square inch of the walls. The ceiling was painted with a celestial sky that could have been straight out of a science fiction movie. An electric guitar covered in stickers leaned against the wall. The bed was unmade, and Bee sat at a desk under the window, sketching in a large art pad. Her head rocked back and forth to the music I could hear thumping through her headphones from across the room.

"Bee!" I yelled, and the girl jumped, spinning around.

"Shit, man. You freaked me out," she grumbled, slipping the headphones off and pausing the music playing from her laptop.

"Sorry. I tried calling from downstairs and knocking on the door." I looked up at the ceiling. "Did you paint that?"

She nodded.

"And all the art?" I asked, pointing at the drawings pinned up all over the place. Most were cartoon street-art-style images of skateboarding, and some were ethereal science fiction designs.

She nodded again.

"You're good," I said.

She shrugged. "AI is screwing the genuine artists now, man. I have a few skate mags buying my shit, but they don't wanna pay anymore. My Etsy store just went live. Print-on-demand shirts so I don't have to stock anything. See how it goes."

"I guess school gets in the way of your business ventures," I joked.

"Totally," she replied, and stood up. "You guys done?"

I handed her the cash. "Can you email me the file from midnight to six in the morning?"

Bee nodded. "Sure. You find your van?"

"We did."

"It have something to do with the stoned girl from the other night?"

Now I nodded.

"And the bust up the street yesterday?"

I nodded again.

Bee let out a sigh and held out the money. "I can't take this."

"We made a deal," I replied. "A deal is a deal."

"Something bad happened to that chick, didn't it?"

"Yeah. We think so."

She shrugged her shoulders again. "I can't profit from that, man. That's not cool."

Thinking for a moment, I considered how surprised I was by the kid's empathy. Maybe it would be a good thing for her to run the town, whichever role she took.

"Show me your Etsy store," I said, pointing to her laptop. "I'll buy something from your store."

Bee grinned. "That would be cool. I can go for that."

"Maybe a gift for Hugo," I suggested as she opened a tab with her storefront.

"That the NPC dude downstairs?"

I laughed, finding the gaming reference to a "non-player character" amusing. "Yup. That's Hugo."

"How about a sick skater girl eating an ice cream?"

"Sounds perfect," I chuckled.

15

Arriving back at the station, I was keen to see if we could narrow down local Ford Transit van owners now that we had a few more details verified. But we didn't make it through the reception.

"Cromwell, Fuentes," boomed a voice, halting us in our tracks.

"Sarge?" I said, turning to see him waving us over to the counter.

"We have a possible sighting of one of your girls."

"Which one?" I asked, walking over.

"The fingerprints from the house on Robles," he replied. "Kamaria Ellis."

"Credible?" I questioned, knowing whenever we put out pictures of suspects or missing persons, we always received a ton of time-wasters calling.

"Absolute crackpot with no chance," Martinez fired back. "I love passing on worthless leads to tie up your days."

I smiled in response to the glare he threw my way.

"What do we have?" Hugo asked, taking the heat off me for once.

"A guy in Laguna Niguel called," Sarge replied. "Says he saw her last week at a club somewhere. He's at work but said you can drop by and see him."

"Where's his work?" Hugo asked.

Sarge handed Hugo a sticky note with an address written on it.

"Okay, thanks. We'll check it out," my partner said, and turned to leave.

"Got someone who can chase down van owners in the area?" I risked asking, waiting to be yelled at again. "We know more about the vehicle specs now."

I received another stern look, but he didn't say no, so I carried on.

"Dark blue Ford Transit Cargo van with standard roof and no windows in the back doors. I've uploaded the video we got today to the server, and the timestamps are noted."

Sergeant Martinez nodded, which I hoped meant he'd have someone take a look, so Hugo and I returned to his car.

The guy worked at the Ralphs supermarket on Golden Lantern at Camino Del Avion, only a mile up the road from the station. It took longer to find Jared Munoz in the store than it did to drive there. The witness led us from the bakery section where he worked to a break room in the back. The man was no taller than my five-foot-six with a slight build and what appeared to be a fancy buzzed sides and long-on-top haircut beneath the glamorous hair net employees were forced to wear. Which was fine with me, as I didn't care for stray hairs in my muffins.

"You believe you saw one of our missing persons, Mr. Munoz?" I asked. "Where and when was this?"

"Yeah, man. I swear it was that chick I saw on the news earlier today. Kamaria something."

"Okay, and what makes you think it was Kamaria Ellis?" I asked.

"Chick had that tattoo on the back of her neck, man," he replied. "Like the report or whatever said."

"Most women have a tattoo these days," Hugo said, doubt oozing from his tone. "Describe the woman you saw."

Munoz looked slightly deflated. I wasn't sure if he thought he'd be getting a reward or made famous on the news for coming forward, but I was beginning to share Hugo's skepticism. Our baker appeared to be all enthusiasm and no details.

"Black girl. Pretty fine, too," Munoz said. "Had her hair up, like, in some kinda cool bundle thing. That's how I could see her tattoo and all. This shiny, lacy sort of tight dress number." He let out a whistle. "I'm telling you, that girl is fine."

"Age?" I asked.

"Twenty-five," he replied.

"That's pretty specific, Mr. Munoz. Did you speak with her?"

He looked confused.

"Not *your* age. The girl's age," Hugo said impatiently.

"Oh," Munoz stammered. "No way is she twenty-one, I can tell you that."

"Where was this?" I asked.

The man grinned and shook his head. "I don't want to say, man. This was like a rave, you know? Temporary location kinda gig."

Hugo sighed in frustration. "Here's the thing, Munoz. You called us down here to see you while we're in the middle of several cases involving young women at serious risk, and then you want to tell us a few snippets of some BS story. This isn't helping us or the girl. It's more like obstruction. Are you working for these guys? Do you know a Christina Lowell?"

Munoz threw his hands up. "Easy there, guy! I ain't workin' for anyone, man. I'm telling you, I saw this chick with the heart tattoo."

"So give us the location," Hugo demanded.

"It'll be cleared out and gone by now, man."

"We don't give a shit about the club, Munoz," I replied, keeping my voice down now that several other employees had walked in and were staring at us. "We need to know where she was seen so we can track her movements."

"Oh, well, yeah. It was in a warehouse near the airport."

"John Wayne Airport?" I verified, and he nodded. "Who was she with?"

"Some other chick, but there was also a dude hanging around, keeping an eye on them."

"Describe the second girl," I said.

"Skinny white chick. Brown hair. She was out of it, man."

"Drunk?" Hugo asked. "Did you see them drinking?"

He shrugged. "I guess. Yeah, I mean, everyone has a drink in their hands, right? But she was stoned on something else, man."

"The black girl wasn't?" Hugo asked.

Munoz shrugged again. "Maybe, but not as out of it as her friend."

"Can you describe the man?" Hugo continued.

"Big dude. Looked like a bouncer."

"Black, white, tall, tattoos?" I prompted.

"White. Taller than me," Munoz replied, and I raised an eyebrow. "I know, I know, everyone's taller than me. This dude was taller than him," he said, nodding toward Hugo. "Older guy, and big, but not like a gym rat dude. Just, you know, big and brawny."

"Anything else you can tell us?" Hugo asked. I could tell he was done talking to Munoz and wanted to leave.

I was still curious. There was no guarantee that the girl he'd seen was Kamaria Ellis, but it could have been. I wanted to know more about the other female with her.

"Don't you want to see the video?" Munoz asked, and Hugo and I looked at each other.

"You have video of that night?" I asked.

"Yeah. That's what I told the dude on the phone."

Would have been nice for Sarge to have given us that little snippet of info.

"Let's see it," I urged, and once more, Hugo and I huddled around a phone screen.

Between the flashy lights, thumping music, and unsteady camera work amongst a sea of dancing bodies, it was hard to make out much at all.

"See her?" Munoz said.

"Can you mute the sound?" Hugo demanded.

"Dude, that's the Blazing Boy remix of—"

"Mute the damn racket," Hugo snapped.

Munoz did, and I immediately felt calmer. It was odd watching people dancing in silence, but much easier to concentrate.

The two women, standing by a wall at the edge of the crowd, occasionally came into view as the camera panned around the makeshift club. With the lights pulsating, their movements were like a stop-motion film, making them seem almost mechanical. The first girl never turned around, but I doubted we'd be able to see her tattoo on dark skin in the crazy light, anyway. The second woman danced with her eyes closed most of the time. She laughed when her friend said something in her ear. Neither appeared to be under duress, but apart from the brief burst of laughter, they didn't seem to be having a great time, either.

The video ended, and I asked Munoz to play it again. I noted the timestamp stated Tuesday, two nights ago. On the second time through, I looked for the bouncer. At first, I couldn't spot him, but once I noticed the outline of a larger figure about ten feet away from the girls, it became clear he was watching them.

"Did you speak with either of the women?" I asked.

Munoz scoffed. "I went over there, but the big dude appeared out of, like, nowhere, man. He just shook his head at me, so I bailed. I didn't want no part of screwing with that dude."

"Did you see anyone else talking with the girls?" Hugo asked.

"I moved on, you know? So I didn't pay much attention after that. I mean, the place was crawling with fine skirt, man." Munoz looked at me sheepishly. "Sorry."

"Continue," I told him, reminding myself to never go to a rave, not that it had ever been on my bucket list. Hell, I didn't go anywhere, so there was no danger of ending up in a dance club unless it hid inside a coffee shop.

"Later, I saw a couple of guys talking to them. Flashy types in fancy suits. But I don't know after that."

"You left?" I asked.

"No, man. They did. Me and my buddy went for drinks, and when I came back, they were gone."

"They left with the two guys?" I asked.

Munoz shrugged. "Couldn't say."

I looked at Hugo, who didn't appear to have any more questions. It was too hard to say from the footage if the woman was Kamaria Ellis, and we only had Munoz's word about the tattoo. Still, her face bore a strong resemblance, so the chances were high.

"Can you send me that video, please?" I asked.

Munoz hesitated. "If it gets around that I gave the cops info about the club, man, I'll be blacklisted."

I quickly replied before Hugo had a chance to. I doubted he'd be able to contain his lack of sympathy.

"This is just for us," I assured Munoz. "And if you don't mind, I'll snap a quick pic of you."

I stepped back and took a picture with my instant camera.

"No, wait," he complained. "What's that for, man?"

"Helps me keep straight who we talked to about what," I explained before giving him my number to text the video to.

I waited until my phone dinged with receipt of the footage before thanking Munoz and following Hugo out of the break room. My partner never said a word until we'd exited the supermarket.

"I don't think that's Kamaria Ellis," he said as we walked to the car. "It doesn't make any sense."

I thought for a few moments before answering. "You mean why she'd be out on the town in the same week we believe she was held in the bunkhouse?"

"Something like that," Hugo replied before we got into the car.

We both quickly powered down the windows. The car had been sitting in the hot afternoon sun and was sweltering inside.

"But we don't know exactly when she was in the bunkhouse," I pointed out. "Her prints could be from up to six weeks ago."

Starting the car and cranking the AC, Hugo waited a few beats before answering. "So, you think that's Kamaria Ellis in the video and she's fine and dandy? Out on the town, as you call it, clubbing with her friend."

"I think that's probably Kamaria Ellis, and those two girls weren't just out for a bit of fun. That bloke's there for a reason."

Hugo nodded. "That's true."

"So why would two girls have their own bouncer with them in a club?" I asked, keen to keep the conversation going. And it wasn't a trick question. I was working through the reasons in my own head.

"They're celebrities," Hugo replied. "Except they're clearly not. Or at least, no one at the club has recognized them."

"Their pimp," I suggested.

"More likely," Hugo agreed. "Or they're working a honey trap."

"The thug doesn't usually let himself be seen in a honey trap," I countered. "Maybe the girls are the advertising hoardings for another club, or drug sales."

Hugo shrugged as he waited for a gap in traffic to leave the shopping center. "Could be any of these things, but what it's not is actionable intel. The warehouse will be cleared out, and whoever rented it will have given fake info and paid cash. From the shitty footage, we can't ID any of them, and the witness never even spoke to the girls." He looked over at me once he'd found a gap and pulled onto Golden Lantern. "What am I missing? I just don't see there's anything for us to follow up on. We're better off refocusing on the van and the big list of possible Jane Does."

I couldn't disagree. The only difference between our conclusions was that I had a gut feeling the girl could well be Kamaria Ellis, and Hugo seemed very doubtful.

"As reluctant as Munoz was about getting himself in trouble with the rave crowd, I don't think he's lying about the tattoo," I said, voicing my thoughts as I tried to understand why my gut had an unsubstantiated opinion.

"If we stopped by any tattoo parlor in town," Hugo replied, "I guarantee they'll tell you they've all tattooed hearts on a dozen girls' necks."

I nodded. Once again, I had no reasonable argument for his point.

"Besides," he continued, "we don't even have a picture of this tattoo. It could be an elaborate design or, more likely, a blurry piece of crap where she let a friend practice on her in exchange for a free tat."

I wished I'd asked Munoz to describe the tattoo he'd seen, and I picked up my phone to text him when the device rang. It was Sergeant Martinez. I answered the call through the car's hands-free system.

"Hi, Sarge, what's up?"

"Christina Lowell's been spotted using an ATM in San Juan Capistrano."

16

"18312, this is Sam 54 and 23 en route. Over," I broadcast over the radio to the deputy who'd reported the sighting.

"Copy, Sam 54. Over," came the brief acknowledgement from the female deputy.

I looked over at Hugo. "They've lost her."

He shook his head. "I'm getting that feeling, too."

"18312, this is Sam 54," I said, keying the mic again. "Do you have eyes on the suspect? Over."

There was a long pause, which told us the answer before the radio squawked again.

"Sam 54. That's a negative. Over."

Hugo swore under his breath. "Is it even worth going over there?"

I shrugged. "May as well. If nothing else, we'll get the ATM camera footage and verify it's Lowell."

Hugo nodded and kept driving. We met the San Juan Capistrano deputies in a strip mall at the corner of Camino Capistrano and Del Obispo in downtown.

"Which ATM was she seen at?" I asked once we'd all gathered next to our cars.

A stocky Hispanic deputy whose badge read "Rivera" pointed to a building on the corner. "Bank right there, ma'am."

"Walk us through what happened?" I asked.

She nodded. "We were on foot patrol and noticed a woman in a black hoodie at the ATM. She was nervous, you know? Looking around and what have you, but careful to keep her face down. We kept our distance, and when she left, Hayes followed while I went in to see if I could look at the ATM camera feed."

"Okay, and where did she go?" I asked, turning to Rivera's partner, a tall, broad-shouldered black guy who wasn't about to go too many places unnoticed.

"She walked down Camino Capistrano, used the crosswalk by the fountain, then came back to Ellie's Table on the other side of the street, ma'am."

"You can drop the 'ma'am' stuff," I told them as I led our group to the sidewalk on Camino Capistrano. "Down there?" I asked, pointing to our left.

"Yes, ma'am," Hayes replied. "Ellie's is a block down on the right-hand side."

I raised an eyebrow at him for the "ma'am" before continuing. "So she looped around and spotted you, right?"

Hayes nodded sheepishly. "I'd say she did, ma'am. Sorry, I mean—"

"Okay, what did she do then?" I asked, cutting off his apology. We didn't have time.

"Went inside the coffee shop."

"And what did you do?"

"I crossed over and waited under the trees by the building next door."

Our heads all turned when a train horn sounded in the distance, signaling one approaching the little station.

When the noise stopped, Rivera took over talking. "I got a look at the video and determined it could well be your suspect, Lowell. That's when I radioed Hayes and he told me she was in Ellic's."

Hugo scoffed. "But when you went inside the coffee shop, she was gone, right?"

The two deputies nodded.

"We asked the staff, but no one seemed to notice her," Rivera added.

"Find the hoodie in there?" I asked.

The deputies looked at each other, then both shook their heads.

"Did you check the bathroom?" Hugo asked.

"Yes, sir," Hayes replied.

"Go back and check again. She would have ditched the hoodie before slipping out a back way," Hugo said.

"She had a backpack, sir," Rivera said. "Maybe she took it off and put it in there?"

Hugo nodded. "It's possible, but check the place again. Check anywhere she could have stuffed the garment."

"Before you do that," I said as the two deputies were ready to race off, "what did she take out at the ATM, and from what account?"

"Took the max of five hundred dollars from three different accounts," Rivera replied. "None were in her name."

"Stolen ATM cards," Hugo grunted.

"Appears that way," Rivera agreed.

"Did you call for more bodies to help?" I asked. "If she has a vehicle, I suspect she's long gone by now, but if she's still on foot, the more eyes looking, the better."

"Something went down at a gas station on the north side of town," Hayes replied. "We were about to return to the car and head there when we spotted your suspect. Dispatch were calling for all hands on deck, so I don't think we'll get anyone else."

I thought for a moment.

"She's miles away by now, Kat," Hugo said.

I wasn't ready to give up that easily. "Alright, you two check the coffee shop. Radio once you're done. And keep your eyes peeled. She's most likely changed her look by now. Wearing a hat, grabbed a jacket from somewhere. You know the drill."

The two deputies left, and I looked to our right down Camino Capistrano. "There are three banks at that intersection, Hugo. One on three of the four corners."

"Perfect if she wasn't sure if the cards would work," Hugo commented.

"Or she had more," I pointed out. "May have decided three per bank was safe to use without raising suspicion."

"Which means she probably parked in one of the shopping center parking lots around here," Hugo suggested.

I looked in the other direction. "That way's the mission and old downtown," I thought aloud. "Be a good place to get lost amongst the tourists."

"She didn't walk here, Kat," Hugo replied. "She must have a vehicle."

I nodded. "Most likely. Why don't you do a lap of the parking lots near the banks? I'll walk to old town and see if we get lucky."

"We should stay together," Hugo said impatiently. "We shouldn't be approaching a suspect alone. You know that."

"Yeah, yeah, Hugo. We won't be for long. When the deputies are done at the coffee shop, we'll get one each."

He looked at me and sighed.

"Like you said," I continued, "she's in the wind by now. We're just playing a long shot. We'll be fine."

I heard him muttering under his breath in Spanish as I strode away, keen to put some distance between us before he protested anymore. As usual, he wasn't wrong and wanted to play it by the book, but we needed to find this woman. She held the key to what was going on at the bunkhouse.

Passing by Ellie's on the other side of the road, I kept going. I noticed a bus stop, but hadn't seen a bus come by since we'd been on Camino Capistrano. It reminded me there were a thousand ways Lowell could get away. Finding somewhere quiet and waiting would be one of the best. But people on the run rarely did that unless they'd prearranged a hideout. The urge to get away from the area where they'd been spotted was too great.

At Veterans Park, the foot traffic increased, and I found myself dodging slow-moving pedestrians enjoying an afternoon in old town. Lowell could have ducked into any of the restaurants or antique and trinket stores. Looking up ahead, I spotted the train station sign and remembered the horn sounding. If a train was in the station, there'd be no better way to get miles away from us than buying a ticket. It felt like a stretch, but I hurried around the corner onto Verdugo.

The sidewalk was too crowded between the people and the fancy raised tiled platforms for the lampposts and big terracotta flower pots, so I took to the road. A car honked but quickly backed down when I flashed my badge. I passed the old movie theater and continued to where the street ended in a little turnaround circle. To the left was the newer, two-story parking structure, and to the right, a one-way street behind a restaurant fronting the tracks. Between them, a wide red brick path led past a vintage-looking clock on a tall green stand to the platform where a Pacific Surfliner train sat at the station.

At the platform, I looked both ways. It appeared most passengers had either disembarked or were already aboard, as only a handful of people wandered about. Turning left, I hurried to the little brick ticket booth and pulled up the picture of Christina Lowell on my phone. I showed the attendant my badge and the photo.

"Seen this woman in the last thirty minutes?"

The older man fiddled with his glasses and took my phone from me, trying a variety of distances from his face to study the picture.

"Maybe," he said after a few beats.

What the hell does maybe *mean?*

"Sir?" I questioned.

"Well, there was a woman about five minutes back. Could be her. Tough to tell from that picture."

"What was she wearing, sir?" I asked impatiently.

He shrugged his shoulders and blew out his cheeks. "I can't say.

Nothing weird, I suppose, as I didn't much notice. Tend to remember the odd ones."

"The *maybe* woman bought a ticket?" I asked.

The man nodded. "Asked for a ticket to the next station."

"Which is?" I asked, unclipping the radio from my belt.

"San Clemente."

"Did you see her get on the train?"

"Can't say I did," he replied. "But doesn't mean she didn't."

"Thanks," I said, and keyed the mic. "This is Sam 54. Possible suspect sighting at train station. I'm going to search the train. Over."

"Sam 54, this is 18312. Complete here. Heading your way. Over."

"Sam 54, this is Sam 23. Driving your way. Over."

"Sam 23. Negative. Could be a bluff. Over."

"Copy," Hugo replied, sounding pissed off.

I looked at the train. We often took the train when we visited the UK, but I hadn't ridden one in the U.S. since I was a kid. I ran towards the south end as it was heading for San Clemente and climbed on board the first carriage behind the engine. A conductor shouted at me from the platform, and I leaned back out and showed him my badge. A look of concern swept across his face, but he nodded, and I continued into the carriage.

For the most part, people ignored me as I moved along the center aisle, scanning the passengers for a face I recognized. I was solely basing my search on the photo from Christina Lowell's mugshot, as I still had zero recollection of meeting her on the doorstep of the bunkhouse. The old man in the ticket booth was right. It wasn't a great picture to go on.

Checking the doors to the first pair of bathrooms I came across, I saw both were unoccupied, and I moved to the next carriage. Outside, a whistle blew loudly, and a voice announced we were about to leave the station.

Perfect. Hugo would love this. He'd have to drive to San Clemente to pick me up.

Lowell, or at least anyone I thought might be Lowell, was not in the second carriage, but one of the bathrooms was occupied.

"Police. Please identify yourself," I said, trying not to shout too loudly as I knocked on the door.

"What the hell?" a man's voice came from inside.

"Sorry to disturb you, sir," I replied. "Carry on with… your business," I muttered, moving to the next carriage.

The voice came over the speakers again, announcing we were now leaving the station. A moment later, the train lurched and began moving. I grabbed a seat back to steady myself and looked out the window. I watched the two San Juan Capistrano deputies arrive on the platform a few seconds before the station slipped out of view.

"Sam 54, this is 18312," came Rivera's voice. "We didn't make the train. Over."

"I saw," I replied in a low voice. I wanted to keep the fuss on the train to a minimum. "Search around the station. Target could still be there." I then steeled myself for the next radio call I had to make. "Sam 23. Meet me at the San Clemente station. Please. Over."

"Copy," came Rivera's voice, followed by a long wait.

"Copy," Hugo finally responded.

Maybe I'd have a ride waiting for me in San Clemente. Maybe not. The third carriage was clear, and so were the bathrooms. In the fourth carriage, I ran into a conductor who asked for my ticket. I tried to be subtle in showing him my badge.

"Oh my," he said, louder than I would have liked. He frantically looked around the carriage. "What do we have going on?"

"Calm down, sir," I urged. "Probably nothing." I unlocked my phone screen and showed him Lowell's picture. "Seen this woman?"

He squinted at the photograph, then swung around and pointed behind him. "Reckon I did, back there. Next carriage."

Looking past the man, I caught sight of a face staring my way through the glass in the doors between the carriages. It was a woman. The train rattled and swayed down the track, and between the movement and the two panes of glass between us, I couldn't tell much except that I was sure she was female. I hustled down the aisle, and the face quickly disappeared.

Breaking into a run, my hips glanced off one seat after another as I fought for balance. Reaching the door, I flung the first one open into the section between carriages. I quickly checked through the window in the next door. Everyone appeared to be in their seats, and I pushed it open.

Where had she gone? Maybe it was a curious teenager who'd returned to her seat, but somehow I didn't think so.

I reminded myself that I had Lowell trapped. There was no reason at all to rush. She had nowhere to go, providing Hugo had called ahead to have San Clemente deputies at the platform. The train took less than ten minutes. Hugo would never make it by road in that time.

The rhythmic rattle from the rails changed slightly, and I leaned against the seats to my right as we started into a long left curve. Through the window, I could see the ocean ahead. We were turning to run parallel with the shoreline at Capo Beach. We'd be in San Clemente in a matter of a few minutes. Maybe I didn't have her as trapped as I'd thought. I couldn't cover every carriage once we arrived, and it wouldn't have been much warning for the local deputies to make it to the station.

Moving down the carriage, I checked each row. The seats were half-occupied with passengers, some staring back at me as I continued my search. Near the end, I looked through the windows into what I believed to be the last carriage. Outside the train to my right, the ocean flashed by, with the late afternoon sun glinting off the waves.

Returning my attention to the doors, I noticed movement through the glass. Someone was walking down the aisle. I reached for the handle just as the bathroom door flung open, bashing me in the shoulder and bowling me over into the last row of seats. A woman yelped as I crumpled into her lap, sending her computer crashing to the floor.

"Sorry," I groaned, struggling to get back to my feet. "Police."

By the time I'd regained my footing, whoever had hit me was gone. The bathroom door remained open, but the stall was empty. I grabbed the door handle to the next carriage and stepped into the section between the two. Through the window, I could see people leaping to their feet. I shoved the second door open, unclipped the strap on my sidearm, and charged in.

"Police! Everybody sit down!"

As usual, only a few of the passengers complied, the others too busy switching their phones to video. At the far end, a woman wearing a dark green windbreaker struggled with the emergency exit window, pulling the levers until it released.

"Lowell!" I shouted, and for a brief moment, she looked my way.

In a flash, our first meeting dumped back into my memory as though a floodgate had opened.

Everybody lurched forward as the train began slowing for the station. I grabbed at the seat next to me, then pulled myself down the aisle.

"Sit the fuck down!" I yelled, resisting the urge to pull my gun with so many civilians in such close proximity. "Lowell, stop right now!"

But Christina Lowell didn't stop. She leaped from the moving train while we were still a quarter of a mile from the station.

17

I considered jumping out the window after Lowell, but good sense prevailed. That, and I looked at the ground speeding by and chickened out. Besides, we were pulling into the station, so with my luck, I'd hit the platform.

San Clemente deputies were just rolling in when I disembarked the train, and an exhaustive search ensued. We found nothing. Not a trace. Somehow, Lowell had survived the jump and escaped the area. I figured at some point, we'd get word of a stolen vehicle nearby.

Deputies Rivera and Hayes in San Juan Capistrano had found a black hoodie shoved behind a toilet in the women's bathroom at Ellie's Table. A customer had also complained to the staff that her windbreaker had gone missing from the coat rack by the door.

I'd been so close to arresting her. As usual, I replayed the events over in my brain, beating myself up about letting the woman get away. The only upside was my missing scene had fallen back into place, which I told a grumpy Hugo when we were finally alone in the car.

"The whole thing just reappeared in your mind?" he asked,

driving back to the station in busy evening traffic so I could retrieve my car.

"You know how sometimes you partially recall something, and bits and pieces start coming to you over time?" I asked.

"Yeah," he nodded. "I remember you used the front desk clerk running up and down the stairs, bringing back bits of memories as an analogy."

"Exactly. That's how regular brains often retrieve old memories they haven't accessed in a while, and sometimes it can work that way with me," I explained. "But often, when a scene drops out altogether, like the doorstep with Lowell, it's completely gone for me. I didn't have a single recollection of the event happening. Then, when I saw her on the train, it re-anchored the memory as a complete block. All of a sudden, I could picture talking to her as though it had never been missing."

"And that's how your instant pictures work?" he asked. "They bring a memory back as a complete scene?"

"Not always. Sometimes it's like the desk clerk running up and down and retrieving pieces. It's never exactly the same twice."

We drove on in silence for a while, moving along slowly with the other commuters on PCH. After a few minutes, Hugo looked over at me.

"That doesn't sound like fun."

"I don't recommend it if you're looking for a neurological affliction to adopt," I replied, and gave him a grin.

He didn't smile in return. "You deal with it pretty well, considering."

"I manage with a little help from my partner."

Hugo grunted and nodded. He may also have smiled just a wee bit.

As I reluctantly slid from bed, I wondered why my shoulder hurt, until I remembered being hit with a bathroom door. A glance in the mirror confirmed the reason, reflecting a dark bruise on my upper arm and shoulder. If I hadn't had my arm extended as I'd reached for the carriage door handle, it would have been my face taking the impact.

To save time at the beach, I donned my wetsuit before leaving the house, then loaded my Robert August Wingnut nine-foot long-board into my old VW bus. The sky was lightening from black into a deep blue as the sun rose in the east. It would be another hour before it crested the hills of Dana Point, which would be my cue to get to work.

Parking in the lot behind Doheny Beach, I joined the other early morning surfers trudging through the sand with boards under their arms as I eyed the conditions. Dawn brought the best waves of the day. The still morning left a glassy sheen on the water. There was no wind chop, and the smooth waves looked like they'd been sculpted into the surface.

"I was hoping you'd make it," my mum said, arriving beside me with her board under her arm.

"I need this," I replied as we walked into the cool ocean lapping against the beach.

We nodded, waved, said hi to the regulars paddling out with us or already in the line-up, and settled in to pick our first wave. The conditions my mother had talked about had stuck around, and clean three-foot waves were consistently sweeping onto shore.

Letting most of the surfers take the first three waves in the set, I chose the next one, paddling hard as the swell approached. The tail of my board rose as the base of the wave reached me, and after a final arm stroke, I pushed myself up and leaped to my feet. Stronger and bigger than the average waves we usually saw at Doheny, the swell launched me forward, where I accelerated down the face. Cutting right and adjusting my balance, I reached out and touched the wall of water beside me. A spray of cool salt water streamed from my fingertips.

For me, surfing was how most women viewed a trip to the spa. It always invigorated, soothed, and refreshed me. There was nothing quite like riding a wave. Feeling at one and so connected to the planet. I imagined a mountain climber must enjoy the same sensation. I'd taken my scuba certification in high school and dived a few times since. It gave me a similar sense of awe to be completely immersed in nature. Surfing was my therapy, and lord knows I needed therapy.

I rode the wave until it closed out near the shore, where I swung the board around to face the open water and dropped to my stomach, paddling back out. My mum rode the next wave, her silvery hair flowing behind her as she elegantly maneuvered the board as though the fiberglass, resin, and foam were merely an extension of her body.

She turned out of the wave once she reached me, and we settled in to paddle side by side, ducking under the incoming swells.

"Three days straight it's been like this," Mum said as we both shook the water from our hair after surfacing.

Having cleared where the waves were breaking, we now rode over the crests. At the peak, I stared out across the Pacific Ocean. A hundred yards from us, a dorsal fin broke the surface, and I smiled.

"Dolphin," I said, pointing to where I'd seen the first one.

Several more fins and the sleek, curved backs of the beautiful creatures rolled out of the water as they took a breath.

"What a start to the day," Mum whispered before we glided down the backside of the swell.

"Just what the doctor ordered," I agreed.

Once we'd reached the line-up *outside*—the term used by surfers referring to the area beyond where the waves formed enough to ride—we straddled our boards and were content to hang out. I rolled my shoulder a few times, feeling the tightness along with the bruising.

"Pull something?" Mum asked.

"I had an argument with a bathroom door," I replied.

"At your house?"

"On a train."

"You were on a train?"

"Not on purpose."

Mum looked at me for a few beats. "How can you be on a train without meaning to be on a train, darling? It's not like stumbling into the wrong loo at a restaurant."

I laughed. "No, I knew I was getting on the train. I just didn't know we were about to leave the station."

I scanned the water for more fin sightings, but my mother wanted to know more. Understandable, considering how the conversation had gone.

"Okay, so how did you provoke a bathroom door into attacking you?"

She made me laugh again. "Someone who didn't want me to find them left in a hurry."

Mum shook her head. "I swear, Katherine, you do worry me, running around after all these nasty people. You know I'm incredibly proud of you, but it's terrifying to imagine."

I shrugged. "It's much safer now as an investigator. The uniforms do all the chasing. We swoop in afterwards and get the confession."

"The bathroom door suggests otherwise," she retorted.

"Now you sound like Hugo."

"Hugo seems like a smart man. Besides, didn't you get thrown down a stairwell a few months back? And it was you who jumped off San Clemente Pier to save that girl, right? And what about that other time someone knocked you unconscious?"

"Okay, okay. Now you really sound like Hugo!"

It was a good thing she didn't know about how I was tied up and about to be shot after being bludgeoned over the head. I paddled forward as a set approached, ready to get back to my Zen instead of defending myself for a laundry list of rash actions at work.

"Oh, and don't forget the vegetable garden incident," Mum called after me.

"How could I?" I shouted back as I caught the wave.

We both rode several more waves as the sky continued to brighten. It was getting time for me to go.

"Any more issues?" my mother asked, and while she could have been referring to any number of what most people would consider issues, I knew from the concern in her tone which one she meant.

"It came back," I replied.

"That's wonderful. What triggered it?"

"Maybe it was the bathroom door," I joked.

"The memory came back to you on the train?"

I nodded. "But after the door incident. I saw the suspect again, and our first meeting came back to me."

"All at once, or in bits and pieces?"

"Just fell back in place as though it had always been there," I explained.

My mother thought this over for a while.

"That's not usual, right?"

I shrugged. "It's happened before, but not for anything this big or important. I wouldn't call it usual."

"Maybe a sign of progress," she said with an optimistic smile.

I scoffed. "Unlikely, Mum."

"Stay positive, Kat," she urged. "And who knows when the doctors will figure out what to do next? At some point, they'll come up with a solution."

"If you're suggesting I let them prod and poke me around again, you can forget that idea," I responded, more harshly than I'd intended. We'd been down that path when I was a kid, and no one could ever figure out exactly what was wrong, the cause, and certainly not a treatment. We'd stopped going, and my dad had a doctor friend sign off that I was fine, otherwise I'd never have been allowed to join the sheriff's department. If I let them test me again, it would mean admitting the problem remained, and I'd be done as an investigator.

"I didn't mean that, darling," Mum assured me. "I think it might be a promising sign. That's all."

I smiled at her. "I know. Sorry. It's just frustrating."

"How's Hugo being about it?" she asked.

"Great, actually," I replied. "Things are going well with him."

I hoped saying the words out loud didn't jinx me.

Another set was rolling our way, and I glanced at the bright sky above the hills. It was time to go.

"Beat you to the beach," Mum challenged me with a wide grin.

"Pick the wave," I said.

"We'll take number three," she replied, referring to the third wave in the set.

"Then you'll be last," I laughed, slipping onto my stomach and paddling like crazy.

"Cheat!" she yelled, and I heard her frantically pawing at the water behind me.

We both barely caught the wave and narrowly avoided crashing into each other as we glided toward the shore, laughing all the way.

I raced home, parked the bus in the garage, and hurriedly hosed down my board. Next was a shower, during which I accidentally left the door open, so Roger had a grand time hopping around a previously unexplored room. Fortunately, there weren't any unprotected wires at his level to chew, but he wasn't happy to be evicted before he'd finished thoroughly sniffing every corner of the bathroom. So, he made me chase him around for another minute I didn't have to spare.

Throwing on work clothes, I made sure all the rooms were closed up, his water bowl was full, and he had plenty of hay, then I bolted out the front door. Joanna saved my bacon at PC Beans by bringing out my coffee so I could skip the line, and I made it to the office two minutes before Hugo arrived.

"Thanks," he said, holding up the coffee I'd brought for him. "Any overnight reports on Lowell?"

I shook my head. "First thing I checked."

"Back to the Jane Doe list?" he asked with little enthusiasm.

"I suppose," I replied, and then remembered the van. "Unless Sarge came up with something."

I reached for my desk phone but paused when my cell rang. Caller ID said Dr. Eric Cole.

"Good morning, Dr. Cole," I answered, putting the call on speaker for Hugo to hear.

"Eric, please," he said. "I wanted to let you know our Jane Doe is stirring. We've reduced her sedation, and she seems to be responding okay. I'm hoping she'll be talking sometime this morning."

"That's great news, Eric. Thank you."

I looked at Hugo, who returned a blank stare, so I took the initiative.

"Could we come by? We'd like to be there the moment she can communicate."

"I can't guarantee when or how well she'll be able to talk to you, but you're welcome to stop by."

"Thanks, Doc. If anything changes, please let me know, but we'll plan on dropping by later this morning."

"See you then," he said, and we hung up.

"You just want to go hang out with the doc," Hugo scoffed the moment the call ended.

"Bollocks. We need to know who Jane Doe really is," I quickly replied.

"If you say so."

"Jeez," I muttered under my breath, pondering the fact that he might be right.

18

After a tedious hour of searching through the filtered missing persons list for Jane Doe, I couldn't stand it any longer.

"Let's go by the hospital," I said, getting to my feet.

Hugo looked over his monitor at me and grinned. "You go. I'm making progress on the van owners Sarge gave us. I think we can whittle this down to a manageable number."

"Okay. That's good," I replied, but didn't move. *Were we better off pursuing the van and waiting for the doc to call?* It felt like I'd lost my objectivity. Or that I was so worried about Hugo thinking I had that now I couldn't make a sensible decision. I hated my stupid brain.

"Go," Hugo said, and laughed. "I'll probably have uniforms chase these leads down, but I'll call if I think we should visit one ourselves."

I nodded. "Okay," I replied, but still felt guilty leaving my partner with the monotonous task of hunting through more data. "I'll call you when she tells me her name," I said, forcing a confident tone as I gathered my things.

"Tell the doc I said hi," was the last thing Hugo said as I went out the door.

Which left me regretting telling my mum that things were good with my partner these days. Sometimes, he was still incredibly frustrating.

It would have been rude to go right past PC Beans on Pacific Coast Highway and not stop in to say hello. As I was already there in the drive-thru, I bought another latte to express my thanks. Hugo was right. I probably single-handedly funded their mortgage payment. There were a lot worse things I could be addicted to, was the excuse I constantly told myself.

Friday midmorning traffic was heavy, but I arrived at ten-forty-five and took the last swig of my coffee before heading inside the emergency section of the hospital. At the front desk, I asked if Jane Doe was still in one of their rooms, and she told me the woman had been moved to the ICU. Getting directions, I followed a warren of corridors until I found the correct ward. On the way, I texted Dr. Cole to let him know I was coming.

"Nice to see you again," he greeted me with a big smile.

"You too," I replied without tripping over my tongue. I could hear Hugo chuckling in the back of my mind and see the smug grin on his face. "How's the patient?" I pressed on, getting to business.

"As you can see, she was moved to the ICU once we stabilized her the other day, but I kept her on my roster," he said, leading me down the hall.

I didn't know what hospital protocols and procedures dictated, but it did sound odd he'd stayed with a patient who'd been moved from his department. The ridiculous idea that he'd done this to see me again flitted around my mind like an annoying gnat I missed every time I tried to swat it away.

"Is she awake yet?" I asked.

"Stirring," he replied as his phone vibrated in his hand. "Excuse me one moment," he added, coming to a stop before taking the call.

The ward smelled like every other hospital I had ever visited. That strange mixture of disinfectant and all the flowery air fresheners scattered about the place. No one was ever truly happy to be in a hospital. Even people receiving good news meant they were there because something shitty had happened in the first place. That was relief, not joy. I supposed maternity wards were generally happy places, but the whole baby and birth thing scared the living daylights out of me, so it was hard for me to imagine the joy.

The doctor continued his in-depth phone conversation with a colleague, discussing treatment for a patient who'd been in a car accident, from what I could gather. I looked down the hall, wondering which room Jane Doe was in. Nurses moved in and out of rooms, some pushing their carts with all the equipment for checking patients' vitals. A maintenance man wearing overalls and a face mask carried a small tool roll in one hand and searched the door numbers for a room.

Figuring I'd spot Jane Doe through the door, I started down the hall, checking in each room as I went. One patient had a curtain drawn around her bed, but I could hear her conversing with a nurse, so I guessed it wasn't the one I was looking for. Unless Jane Doe had made an unexpected leap in her recovery.

I reached a closed door on the right and peeked through the square glass window. It was the room the maintenance guy was in. Hearing footsteps down the hallway, I turned to see the doctor approaching.

"Sorry about that," he said. "That's her room. You can go in."

I was about to tell him he was mistaken until I looked through the window again. The curtain was drawn around the bed, and the maintenance man ducked through the hanging fabric, disappearing from view.

"Bugger!" I groaned, and tried the door handle. It was locked or jammed.

Dipping a shoulder, I bowled into the door, but it held firm. I'd have a choice bruise on my other shoulder now.

"What are you doing?" Cole shouted.

"Stay back!" I ordered. "And call 911!"

Looking through the window, I saw the man in the mask turn and step out from the behind the curtain to see what the commotion was all about. I noticed a syringe in his hand. For a brief moment, I contemplated shooting him through the glass pane, but the chances of hitting Jane Doe or the bullet ricocheting through the drywall were too high. Taking three steps back, I charged the door. This time, the strike plate broke out of the doorjamb and the door opened about eight inches. My shoulder screamed in pain, but I had to get inside.

"What on earth's going on?" a nurse shouted, and I sensed a crowd gathering.

"Stay back," I ordered again before crashing into the splintered door with all my might.

This time, it gave enough that I figured I could slip through. The curtain flailed, and I caught sight of the man running toward the window.

"Stop, police!" I yelled, prying myself through the gap.

The assailant never paused, launching his body through the glass, which loudly shattered into a million pieces. Inside the room, I faced a split-second decision. Jane Doe or her attacker. Whatever he'd injected into her intravascular catheter would head straight into her bloodstream.

Choosing our victim, I rushed to her bedside. The young woman was awake and stared at me with terror in her eyes. She tried to speak, but only emitted a guttural rasp. I grabbed the catheter in her wrist, pinning her arm with my other hand, and pulled. The tape momentarily resisted, then gave, freeing the needle from her vein with a thin spray of blood.

"Kat!" Cole yelled. "What just happened?"

"He injected her with something," I replied, and pointed to the floor, where I spotted the discarded syringe. "I don't know how much got…" I trailed off as I looked up at Jane Doe. Her head had lolled to the side, and her eyes were closed. "Bugger! Do what you can for her, doc. I'm going after the bastard."

Pushing my way past the gathering nurses, I ran to the window and leaped through the opening head-first.

To my relief, the shrubs in the flower bed outside the window were relatively soft, but the shards of glass lying on top crunched as

I broke them into smaller pieces. I completed an uncoordinated front roll onto the grass beyond, then sprang to my feet. The suspect was nowhere in sight. A shout echoed above the muted traffic noise from PCH, and I turned to my right. A nurse rounded the corner, waving her arms in the air.

Sprinting that way, I called out to her. "A maintenance man with a mask?"

"Damn idiot nearly ran right into me," she replied, pointing around the curved building.

I raced past the nurse, following the path next to the wall. If I kept going around the curve, it seemed like I'd end up in the courtyard of another part of the hospital, so I came to a stop. Trees filled the upper part of a landscaped area sloping down to the parking lot below. Pushing through the shrubs and bushes, I was soon slipping and sliding down the dry dirt, dodging neatly manicured plants until I came to the edge of a short retaining wall.

Scanning amongst the cars for any kind of movement, I still couldn't see the suspect. A car backed out of a spot with an older lady behind the wheel. A nurse in scrubs walked back and forth, talking on her cell phone. He had to be here somewhere. Sirens wailed as the local police approached, but I hadn't brought my radio into the hospital with me, so I couldn't direct them. Patching a phone call through their station would take too long.

Tires squealed from over by the parking lot exit to the road, but another vehicle reversed out of a spot to my right, grabbing my attention. The young woman in the driver's seat turned my way, and our eyes met. She looked pale and terrified. Leaping off the wall, I ran across the lot to intercept what I could now see was a four-door Jeep Wrangler. She was slowly backing out of the spot. Tears streaked down the girl's cheeks, and I noticed movement from the rear seats. The Jeep stopped, and the woman spilled out of the driver's door, rolling across the asphalt.

Maintenance Man scrambled into the driver's seat, grabbed drive, and hit the gas pedal. The Jeep shot forward, aimed directly for me. I pulled my sidearm and aimed at the steering wheel, going for center mass. The Jeep swerved to the right, away from me, and I lowered my aim, letting out a breath and squeezing the trigger. The big off-road left front tire burst as the sound of the shot resonated around the hills of South Laguna.

The suspect stayed hard on the gas, despite the tire wallowing around on the rim and the Jeep dipping to the left front. He sped past me, and I took aim at the left rear. My second shot rang out, and the vehicle lurched left with two flats, both rims now grinding on the asphalt.

Ahead, the first police car arrived and, seeing the sparking Jeep, blocked the parking lot exit.

Maintenance Man never lifted off the gas, plowing into the driver's side of the patrol car with a resounding crash. Loud bangs came from the inside of the Jeep as the airbags deployed, and I saw the interior suddenly fill with white fabric. The door flung open, and a leg swung out. Beyond the wreck, a second patrol car screeched to a halt before two officers leaped out.

A second leg appeared from the Jeep.

"Step out slowly with your hands in the air!" I shouted, watching one of the new officers taking position behind the hood of the wrecked patrol car. "Orange County Sheriff's Department Investigator Cromwell," I announced before the officers decided I was an armed perp. "Sir, step out slowly!"

"You're surrounded!" the officer bellowed. "Do as she says. Now!"

In a sudden move, Maintenance Man lurched out of the Jeep. Blood ran down his face, coating the white mask, now flattened and hanging askew under his chin. He suddenly raised an arm, and I saw the gun. I badly needed this guy alive if there was any way we could get him to talk. Dropping my aim, I squeezed again, and the parking lot erupted in a deafening cacophony of gunfire.

The suspect wheeled around with several bursts of blood spraying from his head and torso. Before the echoes were done ringing in my ears, he was on the ground.

Behind me, the young woman screamed. More sirens wailed as I quickly approached the body with my gun still aimed at the suspect. Three Laguna Beach officers neared from the other side, two with their guns on the body, and one keeping me in his sights.

"Sheriff's Department Investigator," I urged him before he got a nervous finger and ruined my day worse than the shit show it had already become.

"I know her," one of the others verified, and I recognized him from a case a few months back.

I reached Maintenance Man first and holstered my weapon. "We're clear," I announced.

"You sure?" an officer asked, his voice sounding jittery.

"Unless he can jump up and repack his bloody skull with his brains you splattered across the car park," I pointed out. "Bugger. I needed this wanker alive, guys."

They holstered their weapons.

"As soon as he raised the weapon, ma'am, we had no choice," the man I remembered as being call sign LB531 said.

I looked down at the corpse again. We'd all hit him. My shot had caught him in the hip. Theirs had all been kill shots.

LB531 looked at me. "I remember after the last time saying that calls aren't ever dull around you."

I shook my head and blew out my cheeks. "Yeah. I have that effect on men. They always seem to run away from me."

I took out my instant camera and snapped a picture of the body next to the Jeep.

"That's the other thing I heard about you," the officer said with a grin. "The old-time camera thing."

19

I'd never shot anything more than a piece of paper before. As the mayhem surrounding the scene died down and I had a few moments to breathe, the weight of what had just transpired hit me. The detail that I'd not fired the fatal shot didn't change the fact that the man being hauled away in the ambulance was dead and I'd been intimately involved in his demise.

He'd chosen to pull a gun on the police, which was tantamount to suicide, and I was sure once we figured out who he was, it would reveal a history on the wrong side of the law. But I still felt like shit. The Laguna Beach police detective assigned to the incident, Selena Rourke, finally released me, and I hurried back inside the hospital to find Dr. Cole.

Checking my phone, I'd missed several calls. Captain Bradley could wait, but I hit redial for Hugo.

"You okay?" he asked in lieu of a greeting.

"Yeah," I replied, unsure how else to answer. "We really needed that douchebag alive."

"He pulled a gun, right?"

"Yeah."

"Then he took away any other options, Kat. You had no choice."

"I took him down with a nonlethal shot, but the other two officers didn't," I pointed out.

Hugo groaned. "You know that's a bad idea, Kat. Wounded and armed can be worse than healthy and armed. The guy would have had nothing to lose."

As usual, he was right. Training had taught us to do whatever was necessary to remove an immediate deadly threat. There would be an investigation into the incident, and it would be examined from every perspective by people who weren't there and didn't have to make the split-second call. But as all three of us present had come up with the same conclusion and course of action, I felt confident there wouldn't be any ramifications. From law enforcement, at least. Time would tell how shooting another human being would affect my already inconsistent sleep patterns.

"Yeah," I said again.

"What about Jane Doe?" Hugo asked.

"Trying to find out now," I replied. "I'll call you back."

"Okay. Let me know. And I have a van we should chase down when you get freed up."

"I'll call you once I've found the doc," I replied, and hung up.

Jane Doe wasn't in the same ICU room as earlier. A maintenance man, who I presumed was the real thing this time, was busy sorting out the broken window. I texted Cole, asking where he was.

He replied almost immediately. *"Meet me at the ICU front desk."*

I strode down the hall and found the reception desk for the ward. The administrator behind the desk looked me over.

"Can I help you?"

I showed her my badge. "I'm meeting Dr. Cole here."

"Kat," came his voice from behind, and I spun around. "Are you okay?" he asked.

The man looked frazzled, which I imagined wasn't usual for an emergency room doctor. They had to deal with chaos on a daily basis.

"I'm fine. Is she alive?"

He nodded. "Touch and go, but we think she's stabilizing. Thanks to you."

"I didn't really know what to do," I admitted. "I took a guess."

"Good guess," he replied, blowing his cheeks out. "I'm pretty sure she'd be gone if you hadn't interrupted him. There's half the dose still in the syringe, and by pulling the catheter, you may have prevented some of whatever it is from reaching her blood system."

"We don't know what he was injecting her with?"

"Not yet," he replied. "I know it's evidence, but we need to find out as quickly as possible, so I sent a small sample to our lab and put the syringe in a bag for you."

"Thanks." The news that Jane Doe was still alive added another wave of emotions to my insides, which already felt like a tub of water sloshing back and forth, in danger of spilling excess all over the ground. A sense of relief was taking over from the stress of the shooting, which, in turn, left me feeling guilty for too readily dismissing the incident.

"But she's unconscious and intubated, so even if she pulls through, I'm afraid you won't be talking to her anytime soon," the doctor explained.

Which left the two people we most needed to speak with unavailable. At least we had a chance with Jane Doe down the road. Not so much with Maintenance Man.

"I need to get back to the station," I said, having a hard time organizing my thoughts as they bounced around. "Please call or text me when you get the lab results, or if there's a change in her status."

"I will," Cole replied, then paused, considering his next words. "I heard the suspect was shot in our parking lot."

I nodded, unsure where he was heading with that thought, or if he had a point.

"I'm sorry it came to that," he added.

"Me too," I replied, letting out a breath I hadn't realized I'd been holding. "He panicked and forced our hand."

"That can't be easy to process," he said, his light brown eyes full of concern. "Even when it's someone who deserves it."

I was impressed he'd instantly pinpointed the internal struggle, but then again, he worked in an emergency room. No doubt he'd seen his fair share of victims on both sides of the law. Doctors dealt with death and loss all the time.

"Yeah. First time I've had to do that," I admitted, and immediately wondered why. I wasn't usually a sucker for a handsome face and a caring smile.

A few beats passed awkwardly before he went to speak again, just as my phone rang. It was Bradley. I couldn't blow her off again.

"Sorry, Eric. It's my boss," I said before answering the call as I walked away.

I fended off Captain Bradley by promising to come straight to her office once I returned to the station. Once in my car, a Laguna Beach police officer waved me through the barricade they'd erected, and I drove away from the parking lot. It was a relief to leave the scene where little numbered yellow markers dotted the area around the stricken Jeep.

The light turned green, and I headed south on PCH, dialing Hugo's phone.

"Hey," he answered.

"She's alive. At least for now. The Laguna police are putting an officer at her door."

"That girl knows something somebody doesn't want anyone else finding out about," Hugo replied. "I don't know what she was part of, but it must be big."

"I should have pushed for security on her after the first attempt," I said, thinking of how I'd have already talked to Jane Doe by now if I had.

Hugo scoffed. "Not a chance LB would have put a man on a door based on what we knew, Kat."

Once more, he was right, but I would feel better about it if I'd at least pushed for someone to watch her. Or maybe not. I'd probably be twice as frustrated.

"What's the van lead?" I asked, ready to move on.

"Are you on your way back here?" he asked.

"I'd prefer not to be," I replied. "Bradley wants to see me, so the longer I can prolong going to the station, the better."

"Fair enough. It's a business in San Clemente. I can text you the address."

"Have you eaten lunch?" I asked.

"No, I figured we could eat on the way."

"I have a better idea. Meet me at Buena Vista Market, and we'll grab lunch and carpool from there."

"You really don't want to see the captain, do you?"

"It's unavoidable eventually, but I'd rather not today," I confessed. I'd relived the moment too many times already.

There weren't too many things in this world that curbed my appetite, and apparently I could add shooting someone to the list. I ravenously tore into my fish tacos, burning my tongue a little in my haste. Hugo grinned and shook his head at me from across the hood of his car, which we were using as a makeshift table.

"Sod off," I muttered, returning the grin as I swallowed a mouthful of food. "So, what's the story on the van?"

"Long shot, but year, make, color, and model match, and the guy has a rap sheet," Hugo explained. "Did time for dealing oxy five years ago. Figured all we need is to get a look at the van and see if it has the dent."

I nodded, sipping the third coffee I'd purchased from PC Beans today. "Okay, let's roll. I'll leave my car here. Where do we find this guy?"

"Shane Corbett, thirty-five. Works at a tire store on El Camino Real," Hugo replied, getting in the driver's side.

I dropped into the passenger seat and set my coffee in the cup holder. "Oh, and if anyone else needs shooting today, you'll have to do it."

He frowned at me.

"They took my gun for ballistics."

"Probably a good thing," Hugo said, and gave me a quick grin before starting the car.

Beach Town Tire sat on the inland side of the main drag through San Clemente, backed up to the I-5 freeway. We parked across the street and studied the stucco building. Five roll-up doors were open to car lifts, where the sounds of pneumatic impact wrenches and a compressor mixed with Latino music. The surrounding businesses had to love these guys.

"We really should call for backup," Hugo said, hesitating with a hand on the door.

"I don't even see a blue van," I pointed out. "Let's look around back. If we spot our dented Transit, then we'll bother the locals."

Hugo got out and paused again. "The offices are on the left side where the ramp is. They'll see us walk back there."

"You think your man Corbett works in the office?" I replied doubtfully.

"Probably not," Hugo admitted.

We crossed the street, staying north of the tire shop, where an old gas station had been converted into a repair garage and a used car sales lot. A low concrete wall ran between the two businesses, butting against the end of the repair shop building. We stayed to the right, walking up the sloped driveway alongside a row of cars waiting to be worked on. I avoided glancing in the windows of the tire shop front office, and soon we were out of view around the back of the long, narrow building.

With the building built into the slope, the rear was a blank wall, half the height of the tall front bays, with what I presumed to be employee vehicles lined up in marked spots. Three-quarters of the way along, a blue van towered over the other cars and SUVs. We strode that way, and Hugo double-checked the license plate he'd found in the DMV search for Ford Transit vans.

"This is the one," he verified while I looked down the right side of the van.

"Bloody great," I moaned.

"What?" Hugo asked, following me down the gap between the van and the neighboring car.

We both stared at a series of scrapes that started a little ahead of the rear tire and continued across the sliding side door to the B-pillar. The metal was dented and gouged as though the van had been dragged along the corner of a post or a wall.

"No rust," I noted aloud. "This is recent."

"How recent will be our first question," Hugo said as he turned and began walking away.

I thumped the side of the van in frustration. "So much for an identifying dent."

20

I strolled around the rest of the van, looking for any other distinguishing marks that might help us confirm or rule out the vehicle. All I found was a baseball cap on the top of the dashboard and a crack in the upper right corner of the windshield, neither of which would be of any use. I took a picture with my instant camera before leaving.

Jogging, I caught up with Hugo. "What's the plan?"

"Walk in the office and ask to speak with Corbett," he replied, seeming uncharacteristically keen to march in without deputies to back us up. Swinging the front door open, Hugo flashed his badge to the two people behind the counter. "We'd like to speak with Shane Corbett, please."

The young woman looked surprised, but the middle-aged white guy instantly appeared annoyed.

"What the fuck has he done now?" he barked.

"He may be able to assist us in a current investigation," I interjected, showing my badge. "We're Fuentes and Cromwell with the Orange County Sheriff's Department."

"I see your damn badges, and I'm asking you what has he done now?"

"Are you the owner or manager, sir?" I asked, sensing Hugo wasn't about to give this guy the time of day.

"Owner."

"Your name, sir?"

"Frank. Not that it's any of your business. Now, how about you tell me why you're here?"

"We already told you why we're here," Hugo snapped. "Now go get Corbett for us."

Frank and Hugo glared at each other in a macho scowling contest stand-off. The young woman, who looked like she was about to have a panic attack, scuttled off through a side door into the work bays.

I stepped closer to the counter. "All we need is to have a conversation with Mr. Corbett, Frank. There's no reason to think he's done anything wrong at this stage."

The store owner's eyes left Hugo and flicked my way.

"Mr. Corbett drives the blue van out back, correct?" I asked.

Frank's brow creased even more, but he nodded.

"Looks like he got into a bit of a scrape recently. Do you know when that happened?"

He shrugged his shoulders. "I haven't seen it. But the guy's always got something going on. I don't need the drama. He's a good worker, but we're not curing cancer here, we're changing tires. I don't have time for employees who bring their problems to work."

"There's been incidents before?" I asked.

Frank scoffed. "He's always on his damn phone, or coming and going. People dropping by to see him."

"What people?" I asked.

"Hell if I know."

He didn't seem eager to expand on his off-handed comment, so I didn't push. The work bay door swung open, and the young woman returned with a man in grubby overalls behind her. He wiped his dirty hands on a rag and looked us over. For a second, I thought he might try to bolt, but he let the door close behind him.

"What the hell now, Shane?" Frank barked.

Corbett raised his hands. "Nothing, man. I ain't done nothing. How am I supposed to know what they want?"

"Let's step outside and talk," Hugo ordered, waving for Corbett to come out from behind the counter.

"This counts as your break," Frank muttered to Corbett.

The suspect trailed Hugo out the door, and I waited a moment in case the guy tried anything before following. Once around the side of the building, Hugo turned and faced Corbett. We both showed him our badges.

"OCSD Investigators Fuentes and Cromwell. What happened to the side of your van?"

The man looked puzzled. At a guess, I'd say that wasn't a question he'd anticipated. Which made me wonder what he had expected.

"Why are you interested in that? It was nothing."

"Then tell us how nothing wrecked the side of your van," Hugo replied.

Corbett shrugged. "I was in a tight alley and had to steer around someone coming the other way. Got on the grassy slope and slid into a damn sign pole. Dragged the side along the metal post. Stupid sliding door won't even open now."

"Where was this?"

"Why, man? Did someone complain?"

"Where?" Hugo repeated.

"Behind some apartments in Laguna Niguel. What the hell is all this about?"

"When did this happen?" Hugo pressed.

"Wednesday evening."

"When on Wednesday evening?" I asked, running the timeline through my head. The doorbell camera footage from Bee was in the early hours of Thursday morning. The van we saw only had a dent in the door.

"I don't know. It had just got dark. Eight o'clock, I'd say."

"Where were you for the rest of the night?" Hugo asked.

Corbett shook his head and let out a long breath. "That was two nights ago, right?" he asked, scratching his forehead. "I finished over at those apartments late, so I guess I went home."

"What were you doing at the apartments?" I asked.

"Replacing a sink for a lady. I do handyman shit in the evenings and weekends."

"Can anyone verify you were home after that?" Hugo asked.

Corbett threw up his hands. "I live alone, man. Believe me, by the time I'm done here, then work another three or four hours in the evening, I grab drive-thru dinner and crash."

I'd arrived hopeful that Hugo had put us onto something useful, but none of this was adding up to Corbett being our guy. Of course he could be lying about everything, but we'd get the sink lady's number and at least verify that part of his story. Hugo gave me a look I interpreted as him being done with this guy, but I figured while we were here, we might as well be thorough.

"Can we see in the back of your van?"

"Don't you need a warrant for that, man?" Corbett fired back, looking at his watch, then glancing at Frank staring at us from the front office.

"We don't if you willingly show us," I replied. "Or we can detain you, get the warrant, then take a real good, long look, but you'll miss an afternoon of work."

He rolled his eyes. "You guys are killing me here. Come on then, but this better be quick, man."

We hurried up the sloped drive and around the back of the building to the Transit van. Corbett unlocked the rear doors and swung them open. Inside, the back of the van was a mess. Some kind of home-built wooden cabinet housed a bunch of tools and miscellaneous home improvement items. A large, square metal frame that looked like it attached to the trailer hitch receptacle lay in the very back with a vise attached. The cabinet blocked us from seeing anything farther into the van.

"The side door won't open?" I asked.

Corbett shook his head.

"Can you open the driver's door for me?" I asked.

He let out an impatient sigh, but walked around and unlocked the door. "Knock yourself out."

Opening the door, I climbed up and kneeled in the seat so I could see in the back. Using the light on my phone, I shined the beam around the midsection between the cabinet and the back of the front seats. The space lined up with the front and back of the side door. It looked like a makeshift camper, with a small bed, a pile of blankets, and another smaller wooden cabinet.

"You sleep in this thing?" I asked.

"Sometimes," he replied. "Not so much now that I have a steady job and a place to live."

I slid from the seat and let him close the door and lock it.

"Lived out of the van for a while?" I asked.

He nodded. "I gotta get back to work, man. I can't afford to lose this gig, or I'll be back to living in there again."

"Write your cell number and the number for the lady whose sink you fixed on the back of this," I said, handing him a business card and a pen.

Hugo and I lagged a few steps behind as Corbett fumbled with his phone to retrieve his client's number on the walk back to the office.

"See anything?" Hugo asked in a whisper.

"He could certainly cram three or four people back there to move them," I replied. "But the van we saw didn't have all this damage down the side."

Corbett paused by the door and handed me the business card.

"Thank you for your time, Mr. Corbett," I said, stepping back and snapping a picture with my instant camera.

He grunted another complaint under his breath before hurrying inside where his boss scowled, watching Corbett head back to the bays.

"Sorry, Kat. This was a waste of time," Hugo said as we walked away.

I looked at the card. "Maybe. But let's call this lady and get her address. We need to verify the timing, but we can also look for the bent pole that assaulted his van."

My phone rang as we reached Hugo's car. "It's Doc Cole," I announced as we got in, and I answered the call on speaker. "Hi, Doc. How's Jane Doe?"

"We've stabilized her," he replied. "I think she's out of immediate danger."

"That's a relief," I said, surprised by how much better the news made me feel. I was becoming deeply invested in the girl, which was not a good thing in our line of work. Invested in the case was expected, but emotionally attached to the victims was a good way to drive yourself crazy.

"We got the lab results back," Cole continued. "She'd been injected with propofol."

"Isn't that an anesthetic?" Hugo asked.

"Oh, hi, Mr. Fuentes," the doctor replied.

"Hugo is fine."

"Okay, then. Hello, Hugo. I didn't realize you were there, too."

Hugo smirked at me. I frowned in return.

"You're correct. Propofol is an IV anesthetic we commonly use for surgery and sedation, but it has a very narrow safety margin. An overdose causes respiratory failure. If Kat hadn't interrupted that man, Jane Doe would be dead."

I felt my cheeks blush at the compliment. "So you said she's stable, but what sort of timeframe before she might be able to speak with us?"

Cole took a moment before replying. "Honestly, it's hard to say. She's still intubated and will be for another twenty-four hours at least. Probably longer. Once she's breathing effectively on her own, we can look at bringing her around again. I know that's probably not what you want to hear, but I'm afraid these things take time."

"Understood, doc," I replied. "I'm just glad she's alive after everything she's been through. Thanks for the update, and please keep us posted if anything changes," I added quickly in case he was about to compliment me again.

"Will do," Cole responded before hanging up.

Hugo turned the car around and headed north on El Camino Real. "He was disappointed you weren't alone," he commented.

I shook my head. "Please," I scoffed. "He's just being helpful. Everyone at the hospital is in shock after this morning."

That quieted Hugo down. I had no enthusiasm for discussing any personal connection with the doctor. I was too busy denying it to myself. But now my partner seemed to slip back into the funk he'd been in at the tire shop. He was usually abrupt and intimidating with people, but it had been something more.

"What's going on with you?" I asked.

He kept his eyes straight ahead on the road. "What do you mean?"

"I mean, you were ready to pull that guy Frank over the counter."

Hugo shrugged. "He was being a dick."

"Half the people we deal with every day are dicks to us," I countered. "Something else is going on."

He muttered something under his breath in Spanish, keeping his eyes on the road.

"I'm not trying to pry, Hugo, but we usually have a good one-two punch going when we question people, and you were going for a knockout right from the bell."

He looked over and furrowed his brow at me. "How many boxing metaphors can you slide into one sentence?"

"It was really just one in multiple parts, but you're deflecting. Why are you biting heads off more than usual?"

Hugo sighed. "Maybe the folks at the hospital aren't the only ones shaken by what went down this morning, Kat."

I was stunned into silence. Hugo usually took everything in his stride, and while we'd found a good working relationship, I still considered myself a burden he barely tolerated. To learn he'd been affected by the shooting more than just figuring I'd done something impetuous again was a shock of my own.

"I'm sorry," I said, more as a reflex than a planned comment. I was used to apologizing a lot.

"For what?" he replied. "You did what you had to do. I hate the perp put you in that position." Hugo added, then took several moments before continuing. "It's a reminder of how dangerous this job can be, that's all. It could have gone down very differently."

"Thank you," I uttered softly, still caught up in my surprise.

"For what?" he echoed.

"For… caring, I guess."

He shook his head as though I'd said the dumbest thing in the world. "Of course I care, you idiot. Now are you calling this woman to get an address, or am I just driving around Laguna Niguel for the rest of the day?"

21

The line rang four times before a woman answered. "Hello?"

"Is this Francine Latham?" I asked.

"Are you one of those scammers? Cos I won't fall for it!"

"Ma'am, this is Orange County Sheriff's Department Investigator Kat Cromwell. Can you please confirm you are Mrs. Francine Latham?"

"Oh," she muttered, sounding surprised. "But how do I know you are who you say you are?" she asked, regaining her defensive stance.

"Because I'll show you my badge and my ID card when we see you."

"You're here at my house?" she asked, switching back to sounding surprised.

"We will be once you give us your address, ma'am."

The line went quiet.

"Mrs. Latham?"

"If you're with the sheriff's office, surely you'd know my address? I think you're one of those scammers my daughter warns me about. You should be ashamed of yourself, young lady."

I forced myself not to laugh. It was good she was being careful.

"I could access DMV records and narrow down the Francine Lathams in Laguna Niguel, but that would take a while, and we're driving your way now, ma'am. Shane Corbett claims to have done some work for you, and we need to verify that as part of an inquiry."

"Shane? What's he done? He's such a delightful fellow."

This was becoming a lot harder than it should be. "Ma'am, if you'd kindly give me your address, we can discuss this with you in person."

"He's done several things for me," she said, continuing to ignore my request. "He's very handy, you know."

"You can show me when we come round, ma'am. Now that address, please."

"I suppose it's okay," she said. "If you know Shane."

How having an association with a convicted felon gave us legitimacy was beyond me, but she finally gave me her address.

"We'll see you in about fifteen minutes," I said, and hung up.

The apartments were older by Laguna Niguel standards, which meant they were probably built in the '90s. Francine's condo was near the back of the complex in a block with three other units. Looking between the buildings, I could see a row of garages behind them and then hillsides. We banged on the door and held up our badges.

"Let me see the fellow's one a bit closer," came her voice from behind the door.

Hugo held his badge near the peephole. After a moment, the door opened, revealing a petite lady in her seventies. The lenses in her glasses resembled the bottoms of soda bottles, making her eyes appear enormous. She wore her gray hair in a tidy bun on top of her head. The bun may have put her over five feet tall, but without it, she was well short of that mark.

"Thanks for seeing us, Mrs. Latham," I greeted her. "I'm Kat, and this is Hugo. I promise we won't keep you long."

"Come inside. Would you like a cup of tea, or maybe a coffee?" she asked, retreating to her living room.

The place was immaculate but stuffy. The furniture old, and shelves crammed with photo frames and keepsakes.

"We're fine, thank you," Hugo answered for us before I had time to accept the offer of coffee.

I closed the door behind us. "We have a couple of questions, and then we'll be out of your hair, Mrs. Latham."

"Francine is fine," she said, looking disappointed. I got the feeling now that she'd allowed us in, she was hoping for an extended visit. "Please sit down."

I really didn't want to commit to a seat as it always lengthened the stay, but it would be rude to deny her every offer. I took one end of the old green sofa, and Hugo reluctantly took the other. Francine settled into a well-worn recliner with lacy covers on the arms.

"Can you tell us when Shane Corbett was last by?" I asked.

Francine furrowed her brow in thought. "Dare say it was Wednesday evening. He replaced my kitchen sink for me. Would you like to see?"

I waved her off as she began to push her little frame out of the chair. "That's alright, Francine. Can you tell us what time he left here?"

She took her time, staring at the wall behind us as the wheels turned and she tried her best to recall. "After seven-thirty, but before eight."

That struck me as an odd reply.

"What show?" Hugo asked, and I wondered what he meant.

"*Entertainment Tonight*," Francine replied. "I missed the bit about the new movie with that hunky fella from Hawaii or some exotic island somewhere."

"Jason Momoa," Hugo said helpfully.

"That's the one," Francine replied with a distant look in her eyes and a wry smile. "He's quite the looker."

While it was entertaining to watch my gay partner and an old lady drool over Hollywood hunks, it was not why we were here.

"Did you hear from Shane again after he left between seven-thirty and eight, Francine?"

She turned and looked at me as though I'd ruined her day. "No, why? Should I have? The sink has worked fine."

"Where did he park his van while he worked on your sink?" I asked.

Francine pointed out front where Hugo's car sat by the curb. "Where you parked."

I looked at my partner. Corbett had described a narrow alley behind the apartments. Hugo raised an eyebrow.

"Shane didn't drive his van around back?" I asked. "There are garages back there, correct?"

"Are you Australian?" she asked. "You say 'garage' funny."

"I was born in England," I replied, trying to hide my impatience.

"You do sound like those shows on PBS," Francine said with a chuckle. "I liked that one with the big country house and all the staff running around."

"*Downton Abbey*," I replied. "Now, did Shane drive his van around back?"

"How would I know? He parked out front, replaced my sink, and by the time he drove away, I was watching *Entertainment Tonight* again."

I stood. "Thank you very much for your time, Francine. You've been a big help."

"Are you sure you wouldn't like a tea or coffee?" she asked, unsteadily rising to her feet. "It's no trouble."

"We have to go," Hugo said, coming to my rescue. "But thank you for being so helpful. You have a lovely home."

"Oh, thank you."

"Mind if I snap a quick photo for our records?" I asked, putting on a pleasant smile.

Francine frowned at me and patted her hair. "Oh, must you?"

"It's just for our notes," Hugo assured her, so she smiled, and I quickly clicked the button.

She mumbled her grievance as she followed us to the front door, then patted Hugo on the arm. "You can come back anytime."

I paused when we reached the car, looking over the roof at Hugo. "Your girlfriend confirms Corbett's story about being here and the time, but why would he drive around the back of the apartments before leaving?"

"I doubt he did," Hugo replied, ignoring my playful jab. "Let's go look."

We followed the curving street to the end, where it wrapped around the next set of buildings on the left. To the right, a driveway went behind the row we'd just visited, and on the backside were adjoining single garages with beige doors. The driveway was wide enough for two vehicles to pass each other, and the outside lane was bordered by a concrete curb, then a short stretch of grass before a hedgerow and a waist-high wooden fence. The only slope was on the far side of the fence.

"Corbett told us a porky pie," I commented, reliving the conversation in my mind to make sure I hadn't misinterpreted something.

"That's one of those cockney slang things, isn't it?" Hugo said as he drove to the far end of the garages and began winding our way out of the complex.

"Porky pies, lies," I confirmed.

"Yeah, I got that. So what's our move now?" Hugo asked.

We rode in silence for a minute while I thought it over. My lack of sleep was joining forces with the craziness of the day to mire my mind in quicksand. All my thoughts churned over slowly and refused to stay in any useful order.

"I don't bloody know," I finally moaned. "I think there's a good chance Corbett is up to something, probably drugs, but I'm not convinced that's our van."

"We have to follow up on it," Hugo countered.

"No question," I agreed. "But it feels like this case has escalated in a big way, yet we're still nowhere with any of it. We can't even ID Jane Doe."

Hugo was about to respond when my phone rang. I answered the call through the car's hands-free system. "Hello, Sarge."

"Fuentes with you?"

"Yup," Hugo answered.

"Good, I only have to say this once. Laguna police have an ID on this morning's perp from the hospital. I've dropped the details in the case folder on the server, but his name is Dmitry Kalinovich from Belarus."

"Where the hell is Belarus?" Hugo asked.

"Eastern Europe," I replied.

He rolled his eyes. "I know that much, Kat."

"North of Ukraine, west of Russia. Does that help?"

He smirked. "Not really. Don't know why I asked, to be honest. They're all somewhere between Russia and Germany, right?"

"Are you two done playing pin the tail on the country?" Martinez snapped.

"Sorry, Sarge. Carry on," I urged. "Belarus."

"He's here on a tourist visa, which was automatically granted, according to the report, as he already had a UK tourist visa."

"So the U.S. didn't run any background checks?" Hugo asked.

"Correct. In theory, Cromwell's people did, but who knows?"

As a dual citizen, my "people" were also the ones who skipped any further checks, just like the two men in the conversation, but I didn't point that out to Martinez.

"How long had he been in the country?" Hugo asked.

"Ten weeks. Drove across the border from Mexico," Sarge replied.

"Any known associations here or in Europe?" I asked.

"He wasn't on anyone's radar here, and I believe Laguna PD has reached out to Interpol, but as the Brits granted the guy a visa, I'm guessing he's not on their books, either."

"Do we know how long ago he was granted the UK visitor visa?" I asked.

I heard the clicking of a keyboard while Martinez searched the documentation for an answer. After a few moments, I heard him grunt something under his breath before speaking to us again. "Files are on the server. You'll have to hunt through them to see."

"Okay. Thanks, Sarge," I said, but before I'd finished speaking, the line was already dead.

I now had a name to go with the face of the man I had helped kill today. The new information hit me harder than I'd expected. He was from a foreign land. I didn't know why that fact bothered me. After all, so was I. My mind conjured up a little old lady wrapped in knitted garments, crying over the news of her son's death at the hands of another nation's police force. I hoped she'd also learn of the circumstances.

"You okay?" Hugo asked, stirring me out of my exhaustion-induced stupor.

"Yeah," I lied. "Just trying to wrap my head around why a guy from Belarus visiting the U.S. would try to silence Jane Doe."

"Because he was paid to would be my first guess," Hugo ventured.

"Sure," I agreed. "But I doubt Christina Lowell and her people would have too much trouble finding a local thug to do their dirty work. Why import muscle?"

"Hmm," Hugo murmured, then lapsed into thought.

Dmitry Kalinovich. I wondered if I'd ever forget that name. In the moment, it was unimaginable, but I also knew too well how human memory could be fickle and unpredictable. I shouldn't ever forget the man's name. The instant picture of his body on the ground would be one I kept out of the file boxes I stored in my spare bedroom.

"Have you ever had to shoot anyone?" I asked Hugo.

My question surprised me more than I thought it surprised him.

He shook his head. "Thankfully, no. I've only had to discharge my weapon twice in the line of duty. Neither time was directly at anyone. Still hoping I never have to again."

"Me too," I breathed.

"If you took it lightly, then this job wouldn't be for you, Kat. It's no trivial thing what happened today. You know there are plenty of resources these days. People you can talk to."

I nodded. "I know. We'll see. Right now, the best therapy will be seeing Jane Doe up and about, and catching Lowell."

"There's a fair chance this Belarus guy was the van driver," Hugo said.

"Maybe. But it could still be Corbett, too."

"We'll go see him again in the morning," Hugo replied. "Or have uniforms bring him in. That may jar his memory loose as to where he really wrecked the side of his van."

I tipped my head back and closed my eyes. "We're guessing on the van, Lowell is in the wind, Jane Doe still can't tell us anything, Dmitry Kalinovich can't talk because he's dead, and we have zero creditable leads, Hugo."

"Get some rest," he replied. "Kalinovich didn't just appear at the hospital. He had to have driven there or been dropped. Either way, there's a vehicle involved, which means if we can identify it, then we can track its movements and ownership. We'll drag Corbett into the station and see what we can squeeze out of him. And on the plus side, considering the recent developments, I don't think Bradley will pull us off the case any time soon. So, we're not dead in the water, Kat."

I rolled my head to the side and looked at my partner. "You're alright sometimes."

He grinned. "Don't let word get out."

22

———————

An evening with Roger and '90s reruns kept my mind distracted enough that when I went to bed at eight-thirty, exhaustion won over and I slept soundly until five. Dmitry Kalinovich guaranteed I wouldn't get any rest after that. The ifs, buts, and maybes found their way into my thoughts, and those brief moments in the parking lot began looping like a movie reel.

Was he really going to fire his weapon? Had he been raising his hands in surrender and just holding the gun?

I hadn't seen the bodycam footage from the officers myself, but hopefully they held the answers. And that answer confirmed what the three of us perceived at the time.

Dressing for the gym, I made coffee and gave Roger his breakfast. Driving to Capo Beach, I went over Hugo's words from the night before, determined to enter the day in a positive frame of mind. For Jane Doe's sake. For my own sanity.

Dad opened the gym at six, but was usually there ten minutes early. He always parked around the back, so I wasn't sure if he was there yet until I saw the lights flick on inside the building. Retrieving my bag from the backseat, I unlocked the front door and walked inside.

"Hey, love," he called across the gym, his deep voice echoing around the tall, concrete space. "You're extra early."

"Roger woke me up barking," I replied.

Dad stopped arranging the weights on the racks and looked at me. "What, now?"

"I went to sleep early," I replied rather than explain my odd humor.

"Oh." He nodded and went back to what he'd been doing.

I smiled as I dropped my bag in my locker, then began warming up on a treadmill. I jogged for a quarter of a mile, then sped up for another three-quarters. Rock music blasted through my earbuds, and between following the lyrics and concentrating on not falling off the treadmill, I drowned out work for a few minutes.

Sweating and panting, I moved onto one of the heavy bags hanging from a framework I'd helped my dad build a few years back. Tugging on my lightweight bag gloves, I punched the leather-covered bag filled with dense foam, causing the chain it hung from to jangle. The gym steadily filled with customers, some there before work, like me, and others starting a morning of training.

I noticed Kenzie come in, sweating like she'd been the other day. She wore the same faded red sweatshirt with the sleeves and lower third cut off. Her black capri leggings were also well-worn, as were the once white and blue tennis shoes on her feet. At a guess, I'd say the gas money to bring her every day was a stretch for her family.

Spotting me, she walked over, but waited nearby.

"Morning," I said, stepping back and taking a breather.

"Hey," she said. "I don't want to interrupt your workout."

"It's fine. I'm just letting off a little steam."

"I was hoping you might train with me for a while this morning?" she asked. "But it's okay if you're doing your thing. I don't want to mess up your plan."

I laughed. "My plan is to come in three or four times a week and do *something*. That's the extent of my regimen."

"You're not going to fight in competition?" she asked.

I shook my head. "No." I was about to say my parents wouldn't let me, but that sounded incredibly lame, albeit true. My neurological issues weren't up for discussion, and it wasn't a great ad for the gym to say my dad refused to let me do what he was training dozens of others for. "I don't have the time to take it seriously," I said instead.

"That's a shame. You'd be good."

"I don't know about that, but thanks. And sure, I'm happy to help you in any way I can."

Kenzie gave me a brief smile. "Great."

She was so polite and respectful, but also shy. It was as though she didn't consider herself worthy of being in Dad's gym, or perhaps it was bigger than that. The beach town, or the other people here at the gym. The clientele was a mixed bag of locals and a few younger fighters from less well-to-do neighborhoods. That wasn't to say that all locals were from wealthy families, because that certainly wasn't the case, but working class in Dana Point wasn't the same as working class in the rougher parts of Costa Mesa or Santa Ana.

We walked over to where my dad stood near the ring.

"Kat said she'll help, sir," Kenzie said.

"Are we sparring?" I asked, the thought launching a few butterflies into flight around my stomach.

"Not in the ring," Dad replied. "But get headgear, sparring gloves, and mouthpieces. Chop-chop. I know Kat can't stay too long."

Five minutes later, we were both geared, wrapped, and laced up. Dad then explained the drill, and we began what he called a fifty percent version of sparring. It was about body positioning, footwork, eyes, and punch placement, not strength or power. Kenzie was working on protecting herself while placing her punches. My job was to try not to get hit, but more importantly, countering whenever Kenzie was on offense.

It was a good drill for us both. Everything happened at full speed, and Kenzie was quick on her feet. She was also lightning-fast with her blows, and for the first few minutes, all I could focus on was not getting smacked. We paused after each exchange, so the tension didn't escalate, maintaining a training drill feel.

My dad was patient, coaching us both, and pretty soon I was able to apply more thought to countering each time Kenzie threw a meaningful punch. Even at what we both interpreted as fifty percent effort, her blows stung, so it wasn't easy to concentrate on my punch when one of hers was about to land.

Obviously, the objective in a fight was to deflect your opponent's attack while mounting your counter, but Dad's exercise was all about training your brain to process both situations. It was nothing more than multitasking. Except we were being physically attacked while trying to accomplish those multiple objectives.

"The brain can only process one thought at a time," Dad said as we took a breather. "Mental multitasking is how efficiently your noggin can switch back and forth between two processes. You can't think about your feet and your fists at exactly the same time," he explained. "The brain doesn't juggle, it jumps. So what we're doing is training it to jump faster."

My dad seemed like an old-school fighter who'd rely on the tried-and-true ways he was taught growing up in London, but in truth, he was quite forward-thinking. He studied and read everything he thought might be pertinent, and introduced new methods from other sports. He spent a lot of money on equipment like a reflex-training light board and vision-training goggles. My dad never ceased to amaze me.

"You rather get hit in the face or the belly?" he asked Kenzie after another run where I'd caught her twice on the forehead.

Kenzie shook her head. "Neither, sir."

Dad laughed. "Well, unless you're growing another arm or making the ones you have longer, you're gonna have to choose one or the other."

"Stomach, sir," Kenzie lisped through her mouthguard.

"Good choice," Dad said, then glanced my way, indicating I should go low with a flick of his eyes.

I guessed what he was up to, so when Kenzie and I touched

gloves again and began jabbing each other, I countered to her body each time. Dad let us go longer than before, building up momentum in the spar, and I mostly deflected Kenzie's blows to my head while I continued punishing her abdomen. As I knew my dad had predicted, Kenzie's elbows soon dropped as she tired of being hit in the gut. I fired one over the top and caught her in the left eye.

"Break," Dad said quickly, stepping in.

Kenzie spun around and growled like a caged animal, swearing under her breath. Dad gave me a wink. He read his fighters like open books, and while it was a lesson Kenzie needed to learn, I felt bad being the tool used to drive the point home. Literally. After a few moments, the young woman turned back to us and took in a deep breath.

"I know, sir," she huffed. "Let's go again."

"That's good for today," Dad said.

His fighter frowned at him from behind her headgear. "I need to get this right, sir."

My dad's voice was calm and encouraging. "You will, I have no doubt. But right now, you're more likely to knock my daughter's block off, so we'll go again later."

The blazing fire in Kenzie's eyes came off the boil and softened. She looked from her trainer to me. I'd been ready to go again, but that was the adrenaline talking. I was no match for Kenzie Frost in kill mode, and I realized my dad had just saved me from a pummeling. Reaching out a glove, Kenzie bumped it with hers, and we nodded to each other.

"Take a break and get some water," Dad said, freeing the Velcro on Kenzie's gloves so he could pull them off for her. He did the same for me, and we both spat out our mouthguards, then took off our headgear.

Sitting on a bench by the wall, I guzzled from my water bottle. Kenzie sat next to me and sipped hers.

"You're a smart fighter," she said. "I'm telling you, you'd win matches."

"I've grown up around boxing, Kenzie. I couldn't help but absorb stuff I didn't even realize I was learning. Besides, I have the inside track on a decent trainer."

She laughed. "Your dad is the best."

"Even when he pisses you off?"

Her smile faded, and she looked worried. "I didn't mean to get mad. You think he's pissed?"

I laughed this time. "He knows. He's a frustrating old bugger. You feel naked around him." I quickly held up my hands. "Not like *naked*, naked! I mean, he sees through you and knows what you did and what you're about to do."

Kenzie nodded. "No shit. And I'm sorry about that."

"About what?"

"About, you know. I did get mad back there. I might have forgotten the fifty percent rule if we'd kept going."

"Lucky for us both ol' Frankie Cromwell knows his stuff, then," I replied with a grin.

We sat and sipped water in silence for a few moments.

"Are you in school?" I asked as I wondered more about Kenzie's life away from the gym.

"Graduated high school a year ago," she replied. "I work afternoons at an auto repair shop. Sometimes evenings, too. I take any hours they give me."

"You're a mechanic?"

She shrugged her shoulders. "Learning. Mostly I clean stuff and help strip the cars apart for repair. The guys put the new shit on, but they're letting me do more and more. You're a cop, right? Or something with the police."

"Orange County Sheriff's Department, but yeah, I'm law enforcement."

"What's the difference?"

"Police are city-run and funded, OCSD is county-wide, and my department is contracted by the city to take care of law enforcement in Dana Point. Different uniform, badge, and pay stub, but basically the same job."

She nodded. "Someone said you're a detective."

"OCSD calls us investigators, but yes, the same role as a detective. I'm primarily homicide, but we handle other cases, too."

"No shit? That's hardcore."

"Doing what I do in Garden Grove or Downtown LA is hardcore. Dana Point is less so," I replied, but the image of Dmitry Kalinovich sprawled on the asphalt flashed through my mind, blood spilling from three bullet holes. "Most of the time," I added.

"You handle missing persons?" Kenzie asked.

"Not usually, but my current case happened to start that way."

"You find her?"

I thought about how best to answer that question, noting Kenzie had assumed the victim was female. "Technically, she found us, but it's a complicated case. Why do you ask?"

"My friend's cousin is missing. Been gone ten days now."

I turned to the young woman. "The family has reported her missing, right?"

Kenzie nodded. "Yeah, but I don't think Costa Mesa PD is doing too much."

"What makes you say that?"

Kenzie shrugged again. "Kaylee is kinda messed up. She's been back and forth, living at home. She shared an apartment in Newport with a bunch of other girls. More like a crash pad in one of those shitty places behind the hospital. Costa Mesa says it's Newport's case, and Newport don't want to deal with it."

I told myself to shut up and tell Kenzie I hoped her friend found her cousin. But as usual, I heard the words spilling out of my stupid mouth when I knew it was probably a hopeless case of a kid making bad choices.

"Give me her full name and whatever addresses you have. I can't promise anything, as I have no jurisdiction in either city, but I'll make a call."

23

Hugo arrived at the office. Seeing a PC Beans coffee beside his keyboard, he placed a twenty-dollar bill on the desk.

"I have to owe you this or more by now."

"You don't need to," I replied, sliding the bill across to his side. "Buy me lunch one day."

"Fair enough," he said, placing the money back in his designer-brand wallet and taking his seat.

"You were supposed to come by and see me," came Captain Bradley's voice from the doorway.

I swiveled my chair around. Hugo and I needed to rotate our desks so we could both see the door. Maybe then she wouldn't make me jump with her impromptu visits.

"I never came to the office after we spoke, ma'am. We interviewed a suspect about the van, then checked out his story with a witness."

Bradley's expression didn't change. She was looking at me like the very sight of me left an unpleasant taste in her mouth.

"We have follow-up procedures after a shooting, Cromwell. You can't just ignore me and carry on as normal."

Actually, I thought the whole concept of the counseling was to help the officer carry on as close to normal as possible, but for once, I kept my mouth shut.

"We now have several leads on the Jane Doe case," Hugo said, running interference for me. "We're working on how Kalinovich arrived at the hospital, and we have Corbett, the van owner we spoke with yesterday, being brought in for further questioning."

Bradley shifted her gaze to my partner. "I was addressing Cromwell and her obligations post a traumatic incident, Fuentes, but seeing as you brought it up, I don't recall giving you two the green light on the Jane Doe case."

"That was attempted murder at the hospital yesterday, ma'am," I replied with probably too much vigor. "There's no doubt this is a major case."

Her laser stare returned to me. "Which is why I'm officially putting you two on the case, but my point, Cromwell, is that we have procedures and you need to adhere to them. When I ask you to come by and see me, that's a polite way of saying come the hell by and see me, understand?"

"Got it, ma'am."

"And you are officially assigned to a case when I say you are," she continued. "Is that clear to you both?"

"Yes, ma'am," I replied.

"Yes, Captain," Hugo huffed.

"Should I come see you now that you're in, ma'am?" I offered.

She tilted her head slightly as though she were trying to determine whether or not I was being cheeky. I hadn't intended to be, but apparently my built-in aversion to being ordered about may have tinted my question.

"No. I have a meeting," she replied. "I'll email you the details of the shrink you're required to see. Don't screw me around on this, Cromwell. Set up the appointment and don't miss it."

"Ma'am," I nodded.

"Right," she said, letting out a breath. Her tone was softer when she continued. "Keep me apprised on the Jane Doe case. I spoke with Lieutenant Marla DeWitt, who was duty commander last night, and she's making her folks aware you two will be in touch."

Bradley left without another word, so I swiveled my chair back around.

"I respect that woman, but she makes it hard to like her," I whispered across the desks.

"It's not her job to be liked," Hugo replied. "But I do think she overcompensates too much."

I looked at my partner. "Because she's a woman?"

He shrugged. "Sure. And she's black. Plenty of people think she's only in the role because of optics."

"Do you?" I asked.

"Not really. She earned her way up the ladder, and she's been savvy. But if it was between her and a hetero white guy, odds are she'd get the nod these days."

"But not if she was gay?" I asked, curious about Hugo's viewpoint.

He shook his head and scoffed. "We're not there yet." He then shuffled his chair to the side to see me more clearly. "Okay. We have Corbett being brought in this morning. Sarge is handling it with the San Clemente guys, so until he's here, why don't we reach out to LBPD and get the ball rolling on tracking down a vehicle used to drop your buddy off?"

"Sounds good. Want to try to get through to the lieutenant Bradley mentioned?" I asked.

Hugo shook his head again. "If she was duty commander last night, then she's not there this morning. I have a contact I can call."

"Perfect," I replied. "I need to reach out to Newport Beach PD about something, so I'll get that out of the way."

"For our case?" Hugo asked.

"No, it's a favor for a kid at Dad's gym. I said I'd follow up, as this missing persons case might be falling between the cracks."

"Call Fitz," Hugo replied, and slid back behind his monitor.

"I was going to ask you if that's okay," I said, fishing for more detail on the state of Hugo's relationship with the NBPD detective.

They'd dated in the past but had a falling out. A recent case of ours had them speaking again. Or maybe more.

"Of course it's okay," Hugo replied, leaving me none the wiser.

Detective Chase Fitzpatrick's cell phone rang a few times before he answered.

"Hey, Kat, what's up?" he greeted me.

"Morning, Fitz. How's life in the big-name beach city?" I joked, Newport Beach being the more familiar of the Orange County coastal cities to most non-locals.

He chuckled. "We pride ourselves on having a better class of lowlifes. How can I help you, Kat?"

Typical Fitz. Minimal small talk and straight to business. "Are you at your computer?" I asked.

"I am."

"Can you see if you've got a case in your system for a Kaylee Monroe?" I said, then spelled out the name for him.

"Okay, I see it here," he said after a few keystrokes. "What do you need to know?"

"Can you see what's going on with the case, Fitz? A friend of mine knows this kid. She seemed to think it might be held up between Costa Mesa and you guys, but maybe you can tell what's really going on."

I heard a few more keystrokes. "Yeah, she might be right. It hasn't been assigned to anyone here yet. The file shows two addresses, one in Costa Mesa and one here. It's unclear which one the girl was living in when she went missing. The file is thin. And when I say thin, I mean nothing's happened from our end."

"No picture, fingerprints, or anything?"

"Nothing. Let me check here with our sergeant and maybe call over to Costa Mesa and see what's going on."

"I'd appreciate it, Fitz, thank you. Costa Mesa PD are probably on top of it, but I don't see any details in the missing persons data-base yet."

"Yeah, I wouldn't be so sure they're doing anything. I'll call you once I find out what's going on."

"Thank you," I responded, and ended the call.

Hugo leaned over, still on his phone, and mouthed, "Look in the server file."

I brought up the directory for our case file and noticed several new entries. One contained two videos. I opened the first one and used the slider to move ahead to the timestamp noted with the file. The footage was from the traffic light on PCH and 7th Avenue, the road leading to the hospital entrance. A blue Ford Transit van approached from the south and turned onto 7th. I paused the video. The image was surprisingly clear, but I shouldn't be surprised as the camera was intended to record license plates. It needed to be high-resolution to capture the letters and numbers on a passing vehicle. Like most vehicles in California, the van didn't have a license plate on the front, but behind the glare on the windshield, I could make out two people.

Hugo finished his phone call and rolled his office chair around to join me. "LBPD had already found this footage," he said. "They're asking us if we recognize the second occupant and the van."

"Hard to see with the sun reflecting off the glass," I muttered, moving the video back and forth, trying to find a clearer frame.

Right after the van turned and was about to leave the camera view, a shadow replaced the glare, and for a moment, we could see the two figures. Kalinovich was driving. In the passenger seat was a woman. I zoomed in closer, then searched on my phone for the picture we had of Christina Lowell.

"I think that's her," I said, holding my phone up next to the computer screen.

"I wouldn't hang a case in court on it, but I'd say you're right," Hugo agreed. "Now open the other file. It should be the van leaving."

Closing the MP4, I double-clicked the second recording and moved the slider until I found the timestamp noted. The nose of the blue van appeared on the left-hand edge of the shot, coming to a stop. The light on the southbound side of PCH was green, which meant the 7th Avenue light had to be red. We could see hands anxiously tapping the top of the steering wheel. The lights changed, and the van lurched forward, turning left to head south on PCH.

"Son of a bitch," Hugo muttered as we watched the blue van sweep by the camera with scrapes and dents down the right side.

I stopped the video and grabbed my instant photos, laid out on the desk. Choosing the one I preferred not to look at, I held the picture of Dmitry Kalinovich's body in the hospital parking lot. I didn't need the photo for this memory to remain anchored, but the instant pictures sometimes helped my mind recall details, even when the memories appeared intact.

"What is it?" Hugo asked.

"She left him," I remarked, still running through each step from that morning.

I'd jumped from the low retaining wall into the parking lot. An old lady had backed out of a parking spot. I remembered that. There was a nurse talking on her cell phone, but she'd been wearing green scrubs. The woman in the van wore a gray or beige top. A neutral color. The sort of thing you wear when you don't want anyone to notice you.

The sirens. I remembered hearing the local officers getting close. And then the young woman in the Jeep, backing out with that terrified expression. But something else nagged in the back of my mind.

"Bloody hell," I whispered as the aural memory returned. "I think I heard Lowell leaving."

"Heard her?" Hugo questioned.

I nodded. "There were tires squealing just before Kalinovich had the girl back up the Jeep. It had to be Lowell making her getaway."

Returning to the video, I hit play, and we watched the van pull away from the intersection. I zoomed in again and wound the frames back until we could read the license plate on the back of the van. Hugo jotted it down. I hit play once more, and moments later, the police cars arrived, slowing to turn across the intersection against the red turn light.

"Yup. Timing fits," I said.

Hugo began rolling his chair away. "I'll run that plate."

"Hold up," I said, and picked up the instant picture I'd taken of the damaged van behind the tire store. "The plates don't match."

"We can't be dealing with two blue vans with the same scratches and dents," Hugo said. "That's impossible. It has to be stolen plates."

"No doubt," I agreed, then thumped the desk. "Do you realize we went by and looked at the bloody van no more than a few hours after Lowell had dropped the damn thing back off?"

"Corbett sure played it cool," Hugo said, shaking his head. "He gets the Academy Award for bluffing us."

"Which begs the question whether he knew what Lowell and Kalinovich had been up to," I replied as I searched for the tire store's phone number.

I put the call on speaker, then listened to it ring several times before a gruff voice I recognized as Frank answered, "Beach Town Tire."

"Frank, this is OCSD Investigators Cromwell and Fuentes. We met yesterday."

"What the hell do you two want? Are you trying to put me out of business? We're slammed, and your deputies dragged Shane out of here half an hour ago."

"Yeah, sorry about that, Frank, but I wouldn't count on him being back today," I replied, faking a hint of sympathy. "Before we came by yesterday, had Shane been there all morning?"

"What do you mean?" Frank asked in response. I figured he was too wound up to listen to my question.

"I'm asking if you can verify Shane's whereabouts yesterday morning, sir."

"He got in at seven and was here all day," Frank replied. "He may have gone out for lunch. I couldn't swear to that, one way or the other."

"But you're certain he was in your shop from seven until at least lunchtime?"

"I mean, he went out back to meet someone during his morning break, but like I told you before, he's always got shit like that going on."

"Meet who?" I asked, catching Hugo's eye.

"How would I know?" Frank retorted. "I just remember a car drove by the office, and a few moments later, there goes Shane to meet them."

"Do you have cameras outside the store?" Hugo asked.

"Not that work," he replied, his tone even more bristly with Hugo asking. "Too expensive. I figure if the sight of the cameras don't scare 'em off, they were coming in, anyway. I have an alarm, not that your people would get here in time to catch anyone."

Hugo sat back, leaving me to continue the questions. The store owner appeared to merely despise me rather than the guttural hatred he harbored for my partner.

"Is there anything else you can tell us about the car or the people Shane met with?" I asked. "What type of car? Color? Any detail might prove useful."

"I barely noticed," he replied. "I let the guys next door park cars along the side or in the back if they get jammed up, so there's often cars coming and going. Only reason I noted this one at all was because Shane went out right after them."

"And you didn't see it leave?" I asked.

"Didn't notice it, no."

"And Shane came back inside and went back to work?"

"Yeah."

I thought for a moment and looked at Hugo. He mouthed the word "van" to me. At first, I didn't understand what he meant, but then I realized, and ran the timing through my mind again.

"Can I get back to work now? We're slammed."

"One more question, Frank," I replied. "Did you notice Shane's blue van leave or return during the morning?"

I heard a voice in the background, and then Frank responding to the customer or employee. I waited.

"What was that now?" he said, coming back to the phone.

"Did you see Shane's van leave or come back anytime yesterday morning?" I repeated.

"Hell, I don't know," he blathered, and then paused. "Wait a sec. Yeah, I do remember seeing it leave. It was right after Shane came back in. A few moments later, his van rolled by."

24

Shane Corbett's demeanor had dramatically transformed in the past twenty-four hours. Yesterday, he'd been concerned but not nervous, and now, sitting across the table from us in the interview room, he was verging on panic. A court-appointed attorney named Miriam Chu sat beside him.

I opened the interview, letting Hugo coldly stare the suspect down. "Yesterday, Shane, you omitted to mention you'd loaned out your van just that morning, despite our questions about the vehicle."

"You didn't ask," he replied, his eyes darting between Hugo and me.

"Okay, let's talk about that, then," I continued. "Where was your Ford Transit Cargo van yesterday morning while you were at work?"

"Parked where you saw it," he replied.

He lifted his chin and spoke firmly, trying his hardest to appear confident, but his nervous eyes and fidgeting hands told a different story. I spun my laptop around, showing him a still shot of his van entering the intersection as it left the hospital.

"Is that your van, Shane?" I asked.

He leaned forward for a moment, giving the screen a quick look before sitting back. "Can't really tell. There are lots of these Transit vans around."

"With matching scrapes and dents down the side?" I scoffed.

"Where is this image from?" Chu asked, no doubt trying to size up how big of a mess her new client was in.

"We'll get to the where in a moment," I replied. "It's the when we'll concern ourselves with first. As you can see by the timestamp, this footage was captured mid-morning yesterday. When your client claims his van was parked behind the tire shop in San Clemente where he works."

"Can't be my van," Corbett blurted, shaking his head.

Chu held up her hand to keep him quiet. "Do the plates match?"

"No, the van has stolen plates on it in the footage, but the damage down the side matches exactly," I pointed out, and slid my instant picture across the table for her to see.

Chu held my shot near the screen. "Who uses a Polaroid these days?" she asked, wrinkling her nose as though the practice was distasteful.

I ignored her. "Did you drive your van here, Shane?"

He nodded.

"We can go outside and look for yourself, but I assure you, this is your client's vehicle in the CCTV footage."

Chu sat back and looked at Corbett.

He shrugged. "I don't know anything about it."

The attorney turned back to me. "I need a few minutes with my client."

Hugo announced he was pausing the interview, then specified the time and clicked off the recording.

"Ten minutes, okay?" I said, getting to my feet.

Chu nodded, so Hugo and I left the room. We headed for the break room and the coffee pot.

"The attorney seems like she's sensible," I said, pouring us both a cup of mediocre station coffee. "Hopefully we can get somewhere when we go back in."

"I've dealt with her before," Hugo commented. "She's tough but reasonable."

"Do you think he's part of the bunkhouse operation?" I asked, pondering the question myself.

Hugo stirred creamer into his cup. "Did time for drugs, so could be. He's connected enough to let them use his van."

"His next move will be that he didn't know the van was gone," I ventured.

"No doubt," Hugo agreed. "Chu will probably need another break to get us past that point."

We both used the restroom and killed a little more time until their ten minutes were up, then we returned to the interview room and restarted the recording.

The attorney kicked things off for round two. "My client is as surprised as anyone to see what appears to be a van similar to his on this tape. If it is, in fact, Mr. Corbett's van and the timestamp on the video is correct, then somebody must have taken it without his knowledge."

Suspects were so predictable sometimes. I gave Chu my best *did you really fall for that* look. "We have a witness who saw the van leave a few moments after your client met with someone behind the tire store where the van was parked. It is Shane's van on the CCTV, and obviously he handed the keys to the person he met with."

Chu looked at her client. He shrugged and picked at his fingernails.

"Enough of this BS," Hugo snapped. "Your van has no signs of forced entry or having been hot-wired and was seen leaving right after you met with the person behind the wheel. Cut the crap, Corbett."

The suspect jumped at my partner's sudden outburst. Now he looked to his attorney for guidance. Chu raised her eyebrows at him. She had to know as well as we did that Corbett was lying. I just hoped she didn't call Hugo out on his intimation that we had more proof than we truly possessed.

Chu leaned over and whispered to her client. He nodded, let out a sigh, then finally looked up.

"I don't really know who they are. A friend hooked us up. They paid me cash to use the van."

"How many of them?" I asked.

"Two."

I waited for him to say more, and after a few moments, the silence got to him, and he continued.

"A dude and this woman."

"Names?"

"The guy never said. She went by Tina."

"Tina? That's it?" I pressed.

He nodded.

"What did they need the van for?" I asked.

Shane shrugged. "Dunno. Didn't ask."

"When did they first rent your van from you?" Hugo asked.

The suspect tensed. "What do you mean?"

"This wasn't the first time," Hugo continued. "Want to see the CCTV of some of the other occasions we know these two used your van?"

"Or maybe you were in the van with them?" I added.

"No!" Shane blurted. "They just paid me cash to use the van."

Hugo scoffed. "So, on multiple occasions, you let two strangers take your van without knowing who they were or what they were using the van for. Is that right?"

The suspect shrugged his shoulders again.

Hugo turned to me. "This guy doesn't want to help himself at all, does he?"

"Seems that way," I replied, then turned my attention back to Shane. "When we spoke yesterday, you told us you had damaged the side of your van the night before at Francine Latham's house, but we checked, and you lied."

Shane furrowed his brow at me but didn't comment. He was scared to say anything now in case he dug himself a deeper hole.

"What is it that this van has supposedly been involved in?" Chu asked.

I smiled. "He knows. Don't you, Shane?"

"I don't know what you're talking about. I just rented my van to some people. No law against that."

"There are insurance considerations, plus I doubt you were planning on claiming the income," I pointed out. "But we don't care about that. What we care about is finding Christina Lowell, Shane, and we think you know where she is."

He tensed again, and his shoulder twitched.

"And who is Christina Lowell?" Chu asked impatiently. "Listen, investigators, if you can't actually tie my client to a crime of some description, then I'm afraid this interview is about to end."

I answered Chu, but kept my eyes on Shane. "Christina Lowell is a wanted suspect in connection with human trafficking and an attempted murder. Tina, as your client knows her, fled the scene yesterday from where her partner, who was the man your client also met with, was shot and killed by law enforcement after he tried murdering a patient in the hospital. And Shane's blue Transit van can be placed at multiple locations involving Lowell and her partner."

The suspect shrank into his chair, and Chu huffed.

"We need another ten-minute break," she said.

Hugo announced the interview was once more paused, and we left the room.

"He's close," I said as we walked down the hallway.

"I think he's about to give us something," Hugo agreed. "But what I don't get is why he's involved at all."

I poured us two more coffees from the carafe in the break room. "You mean, why do they need this guy or his van?"

"Exactly," Hugo replied, stirring creamer into his coffee. "He's a small-time drug dealer who I doubt has the skills to blend Velvet for them, so why involve him at all?"

I sipped my crappy black coffee and thought for a few moments. "Maybe he's just a connection somehow. Corbett put Lowell and Kalinovich in touch with dealers."

Hugo waved a finger in the air. "That could be it. He sourced the ingredients for them. So who's the chemist concocting Velvet? Lowell? Nothing on her record suggests she's got chemistry skills."

I scoffed. "Like half the guys in meth labs ever graduated high school. Maybe she went to the YouTube school of blending illegal narcotics."

Hugo raised an eyebrow. "More likely than Kalinovich. He was hired muscle."

"Corbett might even be a fall guy for them," I suggested. "Someone who doesn't know too much but will tie us up through the van connection."

Hugo nodded. "We need to impound the van. Lowell knows to cover her tracks and wipe everything down, but she had to have been rushed yesterday."

"Plus, Rosa's team can examine the damage," I said, tossing the now-empty coffee cup into the trash can. "I have an idea about that."

After using the restroom one more time, we returned to the interview room, where Corbett didn't look happy, and Chu appeared to have steeled herself for round three. Hugo restarted the recording and announced those still present.

Chu began again. "My client had no knowledge of what his van was used for when the renters had possession of it. As you already know, he was not present at the hospital, even if that is his van in the CCTV footage."

I looked at Shane. "You didn't crash your van at all, did you? Well, apart from the dent that was already in the side door."

His shoulder twitched again.

"Lowell damaged it yesterday morning, didn't she?"

Corbett looked at Chu, who nodded.

"It came back with the damage," he said, finally looking at me.

Finally. It had been a hunch, but I figured the tire screeching I'd heard could have been Lowell leaving, so maybe she'd hit something. Now we could have LBPD check the parking lot and 7th Avenue for recent damage to a pole. Trace evidence from the van and whatever she'd hit would positively place the van at the scene.

"Where's Lowell?" I asked.

Corbett shook his head. "No idea."

Hugo leaned forward. "You better start figuring out a way to help us. You're already looking at an accessory charge, along with whatever the evidence we pull from your van."

The suspect sat upright. "You can't take my van!" He turned to Chu. "Can they take my van?"

She nodded.

"No way, man," Corbett blathered on. "I have to be back at work."

Hugo laughed. "You're not going anywhere."

"You're formally charging my client?" Chu asked.

"Accessory to attempted murder," Hugo replied. "It's Saturday, so arraignment won't be until Monday."

"I'll lose my job," Corbett groaned.

"Good thing you made all that cash from your friend Lowell, then," I pointed out.

He buried his head in his hands.

"Or you can start helping us, and we'll see what we can do for you," Hugo offered.

"Immunity from any of this," Chu said, jumping on an opportunity.

Hugo laughed again. "Get real. As far as we know at this stage, your client could be behind it all. Human trafficking, attempted murder, kidnapping, the lot."

Corbett picked his head out of his hands. "No way, man. I didn't know about any of that!"

"So you're saying it happened, yet you didn't know about it?" I said.

Chu put a hand in front of her client. "You guys mentioned all those events. He's telling you he didn't know about any of it. He's guilty of loaning his van to people who you're looking for, which isn't a crime if he didn't know what it was being used for. Which he didn't. And where does kidnapping and human trafficking play into any of this?"

"We have multiple young women missing, all tied to Shane's van and Miss Lowell," I replied. "Ever been to the house on Robles, Shane?"

Corbett didn't respond, keeping his gaze on the table.

Hugo stood. "Okay," he announced to Chu. "You can argue your point with the judge on Monday."

"I can't go to jail, man," Corbett complained. "I haven't done anything wrong."

Hugo shrugged. "We'll see what we find in the van."

"Anything found in the van cannot be directly tied to my client," Chu countered. "We've already established he's not been in sole possession of the vehicle."

"But what about his home when we get a warrant to search there?" I said, also getting to my feet.

Chu looked at her client. Corbett groaned. "They can do this shit?"

His attorney nodded again.

"Lowell," I said again. "How did you meet her, and where can we find her?"

Corbett's shoulders sagged. "I'm screwed either way, man."

"If you have information to help their investigation, we can use it in your favor," Chu advised.

"You don't understand," Corbett muttered.

"What don't we understand?" I asked as Hugo and I both sat back down.

"These aren't people to screw around with, man. I wish I'd never met them."

"We need assurances," Chu said, tapping a finger on the table. "What does my client get if he helps you?"

"You know it doesn't work that way," Hugo replied. "All

depends on what your client has for information, and what he's guilty of himself."

Chu once more turned to her client. "Your choice."

Corbett let out a long sigh. "I know where Tina Lowell was last night."

"We're listening," I urged.

The suspect hesitated for a few moments, then finally replied, "At my place."

25

Chances were slim that Holloway would still be at Corbett's home, but we had to check. He denied warning her after he was picked up earlier, claiming he didn't even have a phone number for her, but I didn't believe him. He'd clammed up after that, resolved to the fact he'd be spending the weekend as our guest regardless of what else he said.

Our warrant for his home, vehicle, and phone came through as we drove to Capistrano Valley Mobile Estates on Avenida Aeropuerto in San Juan Capistrano. Where there wasn't an airport. Once upon a time, a small airstrip had been somewhere nearby until houses sprung up all around, and the land became far too valuable for a few light aircraft to call it home.

Now, a large tract of mobile homes in various conditions occupied several acres between the railroad tracks and San Juan Creek. Unsurprisingly, the one Shane Corbett rented was a total piece of crap. Even so, I was surprised he could live there alone on a tire shop salary. Any habitable space in Orange County cost an arm and a leg.

"Busting tires alone won't cover this rent," Hugo said as he parked down the street from the unit, proving we'd been thinking the same thing.

"He does the odd jobs on the side, remember?" I replied in a humorous tone.

"Yeah, that's how he pays for this castle," Hugo scoffed. "I vote we sit here and let the deputies knock on the door."

I looked over my shoulder to see an Orange County Sheriff's Department cruiser park behind us.

"It's the same two from the other day," I remarked, recognizing the San Juan Capistrano deputies, Rivera and Hayes.

Hugo's eyes flicked to the mirror. "Call them up and tell them which unit."

I opened my door and got out.

"Kat," Hugo sighed. "Let them knock."

"I will. I'm just going to say hi," I said, leaning back inside. "You sit tight, old man, and leave this to us youngsters."

I closed my door, grinning as my partner shook his head and muttered Spanish obscenities under his breath.

"Hi, ma'am," Hayes greeted me as they both got out of the cruiser. "What do we have?"

"Fourth home on the right," I replied. "The woman we chased on the train holed up there last night. We currently have the renter as a guest at our station. I suspect she's long gone, but we should tread carefully."

"You did all the chasing on the train, ma'am," Rivera joked. "Figure least we owe you is a door knock."

I rolled my shoulder a few times, still feeling a little sore from my run-in with the bathroom door. "We appreciate it, thank you. I'll wander down with you, maybe keep an eye out back. You never know."

The three of us crossed the road and walked along the narrow sidewalk until we stood outside Corbett's trailer home. It was a standard single-wide that had probably sat in the same spot for at least forty years. Recent times had not been kind to the paint nor the patched-up roof. Most other sites I could see had been replaced with newer, fancier models, many of them modular homes rather than trailers. A gate led to a path up one side, and the other was a ramp to the front door midway along the long side of the home. Neither had much breathing room, so they wouldn't be putting a double-wide on this narrow lot.

The two deputies walked up the ramp and banged on the door. I moved to the gate and tried the latch. It opened, creaking loudly, which made me cringe. I heard the deputies knock again, but no sound came from inside the home. I reached a window and raised on my toes to look inside. The living room was filled with an odd mixture of old and newer-looking furniture. Nothing matched. Then I noticed a table lamp on the floor and a recliner chair that appeared to have been turned at an odd angle.

Rushing through the gate, I met the deputies on the stoop.

"No response," Rivera said.

I produced a key from my pocket. Corbett had been sensible enough to give me his door key once I'd explained how we'd be knocking down the door to serve the warrant without it. I released the strap on my service weapon. My backup I'd brought from home that morning.

"Signs of a struggle inside," I said as I turned the lock. "Be ready."

Shoving the door open, I slipped inside first. "Police! We have a warrant. Show yourself!"

I moved left into the living room area, letting Rivera and Hayes go right to the kitchen and rooms beyond.

"Kitchen clear," Rivera announced.

To my left, the living room filled the street-facing end of the home. A few paces forward revealed the damaged lamp and furniture askew, but no one was present.

"Clear," came the call again from the back of the house, where the deputies had checked the bedrooms.

I snapped the strap back over my sidearm and took a few breaths, letting the adrenaline subside.

"You suck at the letting the uniforms doing the knocking part, Cromwell."

I turned and grinned at Hugo. "Welcome to the party, old man."

The deputies chuckled until Hugo threw them a scowl. Then I felt bad. It was one thing to rib each other on our own, but I shouldn't have done that in front of co-workers.

"Sorry," I muttered, turning back to the room. "Either Lowell left in a clumsy hurry, or she had company over."

"The lock was untouched, right?" Hugo asked.

"Yeah," I acknowledged. "If someone else was here, they either had a key or she let them in."

"Should we canvass the neighbors?" Rivera asked.

I liked her. In fact, I liked them both. If they lacked experience, they made up for it in eagerness to help and keenness to learn.

"That would be great," I replied. "I'm guessing Corbett, the guy we have in lock-up, probably left for work around six-thirty or a little after, so we're most interested in activity after that."

"Check for doorbell cams," Hugo added.

The two deputies left, and I moved closer to the lamp on the floor, looking at the side table it had once sat upon.

"Following the fall-line of the lamp, I'd say someone may have knocked into the back of the chair and flailed an arm."

"Could have grabbed something from the side table in a hurry, knocking the chair and the lamp," Hugo suggested. "Doesn't appear to be anything else out of place."

I nodded. He was right. There were too many plausible explanations, but something unusual had happened. "I'll take the bedrooms if you want to start at this end," I offered.

"Sure," Hugo agreed, and we both fought our hands into nitrile gloves to begin searching the house.

It was tedious work, which, for me, meant my mind tended to drift from the task at hand. I wondered how Jane Doe was doing at the hospital. We still couldn't definitively tie her to the bunkhouse, although I was completely convinced it was where she'd wandered down the hill from. *And what about Lexy?* Dennis had seen her being taken away in a blue van. That couldn't be a coincidence.

I paused my rummaging through dresser drawers full of clothes, and Kamaria Ellis came to mind. Her fingerprints had been lifted from the bunkhouse. But wasn't there something else, too? I reached into my pocket and pulled out my instant photos, shuffling through the stack that pretty soon would be too big to keep in my pocket. I came across one of a guy with a slight build. It took a few beats, but the memory flooded back in. Jared Munoz. He'd filmed who we thought might be Kamaria Ellis at an illegal club.

Sitting on the bed, I used my phone to watch the video Munoz had sent me of the two girls, and in the background, their bouncer —or "minder," as my dad would say. I paused the video and tried zooming in on the figure, but the footage was too grainy to make out details. The man certainly had the build of Dmitry Kalinovich. For a split second, he reminded me of someone I'd seen recently, but the recognition came and went in a flash. I shuffled through my pictures from the current case again, but nothing stood out. Everything felt anchored and, having slipped the interview with Munoz back into place in my mind, it all made sense. Or as much sense as the case could make at this point.

"Any luck?" Hugo said, arriving in the doorway.

I shook my head. "Nothing yet, unless poor hygiene is a crime."

"Should be," Hugo muttered. "Have you gone through the linen closet?"

"No," I replied. "Second bedroom is done, and the bathroom. I'm almost finished here."

Hugo started to move away.

"Hey," I said, and he paused. "Doesn't it feel like this thing's much bigger than just Lowell?"

"You mean the bunkhouse and Velvet, and trying to stop Jane Doe from talking?"

"Exactly. The bunkhouse was set up with a dozen beds in those two rooms, both of which locked from the outside. We know

Kamaria Ellis was there, and I'm sure Jane Doe was. I wouldn't mind betting the second set of prints could be Lexy's."

Hugo shrugged. "Or one of ten other girls who potentially were held there. And if they're trafficking girls, then that number goes up exponentially. Who knows how long each batch of new victims spent there? So yes, it feels bigger than just Lowell and her thug. Even including Corbett. An operation of this size takes manpower and more than just a Transit van."

"'There are more,'" I said. "Those were the only words out of Jane Doe."

Hugo nodded. "Trafficking always involves sex workers at some point."

I held up my phone. "And we have the video of Kamaria Ellis being escorted by someone who fits Kalinovich's description."

"Proof," Hugo replied. "We need actual proof."

Putting my photos and phone away, we continued the search. I'd been through all the furniture, the closet, under the bed, and checked for false fixtures. I was running out of places to look. Maybe I'd missed something. Corbett had been too nervous when he'd realized we were going to be searching his van and house.

We'd requested a narcotics detection canine, but dispatch had informed us they'd be a while arriving, so we might as well search ourselves. Moving around the edge of the room, I tapped on the baseboard as I walked. No loose board or hollow sound. I'd had luck with a light fixture in the past, but this one was small and in keeping with the others in the mobile home.

Standing at the end of the queen-sized bed, I slowly turned in a circle, studying the room one more time. I'd been through the bedside table and checked the lamp sitting on top. The ancient bedside clock radio with the old flip numbers had made me chuckle, and looking at it again, I still smiled. Until I noticed the time. It read four-fifteen. I checked my phone. It was currently 12:55 p.m.

Walking over to the bedside table, I lifted the clock radio. The weight felt about right for an old box of electronics. Setting it down,

I traced the power lead, getting down on my hands and knees to see where it plugged in behind the bed. The cord lay on the smelly carpet. It wasn't connected to a socket at all. I stood up and picked up the clock radio again, this time giving it a shake. Something moved inside. Flipping it over, I removed the backup battery cover to reveal an empty space where four AAs should be. I clicked the cover back in place, thinking the clock radio was probably just a relic left by the owner and no one had bothered throwing it out, but then I noticed the four screws. One in each corner, holding the base to the housing of the unit. They were far too shiny.

I'd recently taken to carrying a pocketknife around with me after having to borrow one during a search, so I opened the little Phillips head screwdriver and removed the screws. Holding the base in one hand, I shook the housing as I lifted it free, and watched as three plastic bags of pills dropped to the base.

"Hugo!" I called out, and heard his footsteps entering the room.

"What you got?"

"Pay dirt," I replied, holding up my find for him to see.

"I think you've found how Shane can afford to live alone," Hugo said, looking carefully at the bags without touching them.

I placed the base of the clock radio down next to the housing on the bed, took out my instant camera, and snapped a shot.

As the picture slowly whirred from the camera, my phone rang. I set the camera on the bed and looked at my caller ID.

"Fitz," I answered. "Find out something?"

"Took a little work, but yes," he replied. "Are you with Hugo?"

"Yeah," I replied, wondering why he'd ask. This was a favor for me, not one of our cases.

"Can you put this on speaker?" Fitz asked.

I hesitated, but decided the detective must have a good reason. I clicked the speaker icon on my phone. "Okay, we can both hear you now."

Hugo looked at me with a puzzled expression.

"It's Fitz. He's following up on the favor I mentioned," I explained.

Hugo nodded. "Hey, Fitz."

"Hey, buddy. I'll get to the part that interests you both in a moment, but I reached out to Costa Mesa PD, and they'd gathered a few things together but not put them in the system yet. I think you were right, Kat. This fell between the department cracks over who should handle it. Anyway, they'd pulled fingerprints from the girl's room at her parents' house, so I had them enter them in the system."

"Okay," I said. "That's progress."

Hugo shrugged, still unsure what we were talking about or why he was involved.

"We got a hit," Fitz said.

"I think she's been in some trouble before," I replied. "So I'm not surprised."

"That's not what I'm saying, Kat. Her prints weren't in there. The hit I got back was from your case. Some house you raided on Robles in Dana Point."

"Bloody hell," I muttered, looking at Hugo. "This kid Kaylee Monroe was the fourth set of prints from the bunkhouse."

26

―――――――

Hugo, as usual, knew of an authentic Mexican food truck in San Juan Capistrano. We sat at the benches and tables beside the truck and ate lunch while the K9 unit checked for more drugs, then Rosa's team from the crime lab processed Corbett's mobile home. We'd already identified the drugs from their markings. One bag containing white, oval-shaped pills with Roche 7,5 on them was Dormicum, better known as midazolam. Another with round, white pills and EP904 markings was lorazepam. These two made up half the ingredients for Velvet. The third bag held round blue pills with an "M" within a square on one side and 3.0 above a break line on the other. These were oxycodone. Genuine, as best we could tell.

"We know Corbett has a history of dealing pills," Hugo pointed out between bites of his carne asada taco. "This isn't proof he was supplying Lowell or whoever is making Velvet for them. They're all drugs with high street value, and he had oxy in there, too."

I nodded, trying to listen while I texted my dad. *"Got a number for Kenzie?"*

"I get it," I replied. "But it might explain why Corbett was involved. Maybe he was supplying some of what they needed.

Multiple suppliers make sense in their game. One gets busted, and it doesn't cripple their supply."

"He also said *these* aren't people to screw around with," Hugo replied. "He knew Dmitry Kalinovich was dead, so why use plural if it was just Tina Lowell? Like you were thinking earlier, this must go way bigger than just the three people we know were involved."

"Maybe it's time to speak with your mate Albright in narcotics again," I suggested as I watched the ellipsis blink on my phone screen. My dad had probably attempted to type the phone number three or four times by now, with his beefy thumbs hitting multiple digits with each tap. Finally, a number popped up, and it appeared to have a believable area code and seven more numbers.

"Thx," I typed in return.

Hugo scrolled through his phone, presumably looking for Doug Albright's number, when the device rang.

"It's Laguna Beach PD," he said before accepting the call. "Fuentes."

"This is Selena Rourke, LBPD," I faintly heard a voice say.

"Hi, Selena," Hugo said, and put the call on speaker. "Cromwell is with me. What do you have?"

"We sent uniforms by the hospital as you requested, and they found a sign pole with recent damage. Do you have the van?"

"We do," Hugo replied. "Our crime lab folks have it now."

"Want them to handle the pole as well?" Rourke asked. "If you'll excuse my phrasing."

I laughed, looking up after sending a text to Kenzie Frost. The detective had seemed all business and quite dry when we'd met at the hospital, but we'd been standing next to a dead body, so it was hardly a great time to judge her sense of humor.

"Ideally," Hugo responded. "Let me see if they have the capacity. This case is expanding by the minute, so my concern is evidence walking away or being wiped before they get to it."

"No worries there, Fuentes," Rourke replied. "We have the pole in custody."

I chuckled again. Hugo even cracked a smile.

"Perfect, thank you, detective," he said. "We'll work on having it extradited to our crime lab."

"It's Selena," she responded. "And call me if you need anything else."

They hung up, and I grinned at Hugo.

"What?" he asked.

"Somebody wouldn't mind a slice of ol' Hugo."

He rolled his eyes.

"Should I tell her she's barking up the wrong tree?" I joked.

"Not necessary, Cromwell," he said, raising an eyebrow.

My phone buzzed, and I looked down to see Kenzie's response. But it wasn't from her. It was from Deputy Rivera.

"They have an eyewitness from this morning," I relayed to Hugo. "Let's head back to the mobile homes and talk to her."

Hugo took his last bite of lunch and gathered up our empty wrappers and soda cans. Five minutes later, we were back in Capistrano Valley Mobile Estates, where Corbett's street had been taken over with law enforcement vehicles.

"Only one witness on the entire street?" I asked Rivera as she met us getting out of the car.

"Yes, ma'am. Lot of folks aren't home. Just a few retired folks answering the door. I suspect some of the people currently at work might have seen something, but we'll have to come back this evening."

"If you can do that, we'd appreciate it," I replied. "Who do you have now?"

Rivera led us to a nice double-wide across the street from Corbett's place, and a few homes farther down the street. The front window curtain fluttered as we approached, and the old lady had the door open before we made it to her stoop.

"Mrs. Stevens, these are the two investigators I told you about," Rivera said once we neared. "Can you tell them what you told me?"

"Kat and Hugo, ma'am," I said, keeping it informal.

"I was walking Truffles this morning," the woman said as a dog began yapping inside the house. She didn't seem to hear it and continued. "It was after that man who lives there left in his van."

"Approximately what time, ma'am?" I asked.

"Well, that fella leaves every day around six-forty-five, so I guess that's when it was."

"Okay, thank you," I said. "And you saw him leave as usual on your way out with the dog?"

"Yes," she replied. "And when we came back, there was one of those big black things parked outside."

I looked at Rivera, who subtly shrugged her shoulders.

"Like an SUV, ma'am?" I asked.

"I think that's what you call them," she replied. "This one was all tinted windows like the TV shows."

"That's great, thank you," I said, thinking what a nightmare we'd have trying to identify a black SUV in Orange County. They were practically required driving for soccer moms. "Anything distinguishing about the vehicle?" I asked, raising my voice over Truffles's ear-piercing bark.

"I thought looking like an FBI vehicle from my TV shows *was* distinguishing."

I guessed Mrs. Stevens didn't get out much.

"Catch the license plate, ma'am?" Hugo asked.

"No," she replied. "Why would I?"

Apparently, Hugo's suave charm and handsome looks weren't working on this old lady.

"See anyone get out or return to the SUV?" I asked.

Mrs. Stevens shook her head. "I made my breakfast when I came home, so I was in the kitchen."

"I think we're done here," Hugo said. "Thank you, ma'am."

He turned and walked away. I smiled at the lady and was about to follow my partner when I thought of something more.

"Mrs. Stevens, did you notice anyone coming or going last night?"

"From that fella's place?"

"Yes."

"I'm not one of those busybodies always watching what the neighbors are up to, you know?"

"The thought never crossed my mind," I replied. "But did you happen to notice anything unusual across the road?"

The old woman shuffled a few steps and licked her lips as she pondered her answer. I wasn't sure whether she was deciding how to phrase a reply or simply digging around, attempting to remember something. I could relate to the second point.

"He had a woman over," she finally said. "Smoker. Saw her sitting out front before I went to bed."

I quickly pulled up the picture we had of Christina Lowell on my phone and showed it to Mrs. Stevens. She retrieved a pair of reading glasses from her pocket but still squinted as though the act of looking at a phone screen was painful.

"Could be her."

"You're not sure?"

"It was dark, and she was all the way over there," she replied, gesticulating with a hand. "You'd have a hard time knowing, and you're barely out of diapers."

I laughed. "Mind if I take a picture for our records, Mrs. Stevens?"

"I would've done something with my hair if I'd known there'd be pictures," she muttered, but I'd already snapped the shot before she was done talking.

"Will this be on the news tonight?" she asked.

"Hopefully not," I replied. "Thank you for your time, ma'am."

Rivera and I left the old woman looking disappointed, and we joined Hugo outside Corbett's house. Studying the poorly maintained planter at the front of the single-wide, I stepped closer and pushed a few of the dead weeds aside to see the dirt below. Rivera sensibly used a pen to do the same thing, starting at the other end.

"What are you looking for?" Hugo asked without hiding the disgust in his voice.

"This!" I declared, spotting a pair of cigarette butts.

Hugo looked over my shoulder. "Didn't smell of cigarettes inside."

"No, he made Lowell smoke out here," I replied as one of the crime lab crew made their way from the house toward their van. "Excuse me," I said to the tech. "There are cigarette butts here that we need to bag and check for DNA, please. Most likely belonged to our suspect."

The tech gave me a thumbs-up.

"Nice work," Rivera said, and I did feel a bit like a sleuth coming up with a gem of a clue.

Hugo shook his head. "Please, don't encourage her."

My phone vibrated in my pocket. I fished it out and saw I had a text from Kenzie Frost.

"That's Kaylee."

"Bugger," I muttered, then looked up at Hugo. "The second girl in the club video is Kaylee Monroe, the seventeen-year-old kid who went missing from Costa Mesa area about ten days ago."

Hugo stood with his hands on his hips, squinting at me in the early afternoon sun, thinking. "If we believe that's Kamaria Ellis with her at the club, then that ties them to the bunkhouse, and means they were both moved somewhere else in the Transit van on Wednesday night."

"The night after the rave on Tuesday," I added, following a timeline in my head. "With whoever else was also being held at the house." I felt my jaw clench. "We need to find Lowell. Without her, this is still nothing but a needle in a haystack. We'll be chasing our arses in circles looking for black SUVs and getting no closer to finding these girls."

"Or what they're doing with them," Hugo said, then lowered his voice. "Not to mention Velvet."

I heard a voice over Rivera's radio, but didn't pay attention to what was being said as Rivera responded. Hugo and I stepped away to decide what to do next. My phone vibrated again.

"Have u found her?"

I wasn't sure how to answer Kenzie. I had to be careful. Whatever I told her would be relayed to her friend and then to Kaylee's family. I thought carefully for a moment with my thumbs poised over the keyboard.

No. Pic was Tue night.

It bothered me to be evasive, but I couldn't say anything about our case or the bunkhouse until we knew more. Besides, it wasn't even my case. Although, maybe it was now that we knew she'd been held in Dana Point.

I returned my phone to my pocket, then looked at Hugo. He was staring at me as though he'd been waiting.

"So, how are we going to find Lowell?" I asked, to kick-start our conversation again. "Do you think we'd have any luck with CCTV around San Juan? Maybe we could get lucky with a plate."

We both turned to Rivera, who was finishing up her radio chatter. Her face looked suddenly pale.

"What is it?" I asked.

She hesitated a few times before speaking. "They're not sure yet, but Hayes is on the trail behind the mobile home estate. He's seen something," she said, indicating east where the San Juan Creek bordered the property. "Maybe we should go look."

"What's he seen?" Hugo asked, hands on hips.

I had a bad feeling. "Let's go, Hugo," I urged, and headed for our car with Rivera alongside.

I heard Hugo muttering behind us, but he came along, which was good because he had the keys. He drove us to Avenida Aeropuerto and turned left. The road dead-ended at the sloped retaining wall for the creek, topped with a few strands of wire to deter kids from climbing over. A dirt trail ran parallel to the creek, running behind the estates.

"Hayes is down there," Rivera said as we got out.

As soon as we rounded the corner and started on the trail, I saw a pair of uniformed deputies at the base of the wall.

"What do we have?" I asked as we approached.

"Hayes went over the wall, ma'am," one deputy replied. "He's checking now."

I scrambled up the steeply sloped concrete, slipping and sliding until I reached the short brickwork at the top and the wire. I hung on to one of the metal poles supporting the wire and peered over. Hayes was ankle-deep in mucky runoff water, making his way to a pile of clothes.

"What is it?" Hugo called up.

I looked down but didn't want to say what I thought the deputy had found. Instead, I vaulted over the wire and slithered down the concrete on the other side, landing at the dry and dusty edge of the man-made river. Figuring I was going to get wet and dirty, anyway, I jogged to where the thin streams of water meandered through a mess of sand, trash, and natural detritus, then kept going. I reached Hayes's side about the same time he stopped at the elongated pile of what at first appeared to be discarded clothes. Except for the hand dangling in the dirty water.

"What do we do, ma'am?" Hayes asked me, his voice tense and distressed.

The big man's face contorted now that he knew he'd indeed found a body.

"I'll look," I said. "Call it in. We need the crime lab team here right away."

"Yes, ma'am," he replied, clearly glad to step back.

While Hayes talked into his radio, I took a nitrile glove from my pocket and wriggled my clammy hand inside. The body had been wrapped in what appeared to be an assortment of clothes, held in place with bands of duct tape. I opened up my pocket knife and sliced the tape from around the area of the victim's neck. Moving to the other side, I could see where a T-shirt or blouse swaddled the victim's head, and I carefully unwrapped the material as the filthy water continued to run around the body like a river splitting either side of a long, narrow island.

Steeling myself for what I was about to see didn't stop me from gasping. From the jagged and messy exit wound in the victim's forehead, it appeared the vic had been executed from behind with a large caliber round. But despite the disfigurement, I could still recognize her as Christina Lowell.

27

______

Taking care of everything in San Juan Capistrano ate up most of our afternoon, which was probably okay. It took me that long to stop seething and begin thinking clearly again. Not that I felt much empathy for Lowell. From what we'd seen, she'd likely gotten what she deserved, but once again, our case had hit a brick wall. Just as it had become clear we were dealing with something much larger than we'd initially believed.

"What if it's like a corporation with subsidiaries," I said as Hugo and I waited in the station break room for Miriam Chu to finish consulting with her client so we could begin the new interview. "Corbett told us these were not people to screw with. Maybe they just severed a division."

"You mean like Lowell and Kalinovich ran the honey trap division?" Hugo said, following my point. "I guess that could be the case. Or we've only come across the foot soldiers so far. Whoever is truly in charge drives a black SUV and took care of a loose end."

I shrugged. "It's possible. But Jane Doe wasn't at the club, and Lexy is still missing, so where did they take them?"

"Wherever Black SUV Guy is based, I suspect," Hugo replied. "Look, I'm not saying your theory's wrong. I'm just pointing out that we don't have any evidence indicating a larger operation. More people than we know of, yes, but they could all be part of the honey pot scheme. If that's even what Lowell and Kalinovich were up to. The bunkhouse still suggests trafficking."

"Which could be another branch. And what about Velvet?" I asked. "You think they were formulating it or buying it just to subdue the girls enough to work for them?"

Hugo thought for a moment. "Doesn't explain Corbett's role, does it?"

I shook my head. "That's my thinking. Crime lab didn't find any other drugs at his mobile home, so if he was just supplying half the ingredients, then we're missing another source and a lab."

Hugo's phone buzzed with a text. "They're ready," he relayed. "Let's pile on this guy and let him know how bad it is. See what he gives us."

We walked down the hall and entered the interview room, taking our seats before Hugo started the recording.

"Mr. Corbett," my partner began. "We retrieved Schedule IV and Schedule II narcotics from your home yesterday. This presents you with a very serious problem based on the quantities, along with your prior conviction."

"My client had no knowledge of those drugs in his home," Chu countered. "Christina Lowell could well have left them there."

Hugo nodded. "I thought you might say that. Then explain your client's fingerprints on the clock radio they were stashed in, and on the bags containing the pills. No other fingerprints were present."

"Did you find Tina there?" Corbett asked.

"She was not there," Hugo replied, then quickly moved on. "This is your opportunity to help us out, Mr. Corbett. Give us actionable information, and if it helps our investigation, it will be taken into consideration in our case against you."

Clearly Chu had prepared her client for this eventuality, as she gave him a subtle nod, then Corbett sat back in his chair, letting her talk.

"My client already handed you Lowell. That should be taken into consideration."

"I said actionable information that helps our investigation," Hugo replied. "She wasn't there. What we're interested in now is who Lowell works for?"

I noted his use of present tense. The last thing we needed was Corbett getting wind of Tina's demise. It was possible he'd tell us more to make sure the threat was locked up, but far more likely, he'd clam up out of fear.

Chu looked at her client. "If you have something to give them, I can negotiate on your behalf."

"I'm screwed either way," Corbett muttered.

"We can help steer where you'll do your time, Shane," I said. "That could make a big difference."

He scoffed. "I better not do *any* time if I give you this name, man. I gotta find myself a different place to live. Like, I mean, a different country."

"Second offense for dealing," Hugo pointed out. "We can help, but we can't perform miracles."

"You'd better come up with a fucking miracle if you want me to say anything else, man."

Hugo threw his hands up. "You want to explain to this dipshit how the process works?" he directed at Chu. "He's busted on dealing serious street drugs, not to mention harboring a fugitive, and whatever else the prosecutor dreams up to call loaning a van to commit felonies. That shit doesn't just evaporate when he tosses a name out. If we're able to move our case along based on what you tell us, Shane," Hugo continued, turning his attention to the suspect, "then you'll receive leniency based on how good that info proves to be. If you want no jail time, you'd better give us the shooter on the grassy knoll. So how about you cut the crap and let's start with who Lowell works for?"

Corbett shook his head some more and rubbed his forehead with both hands. Finally, he let out a long breath before he spoke. "*El Pastor*. That's all I know him as."

"Have you met this guy?" Hugo asked.

Corbett scoffed. "Hell no. Tina was freaking out, man. I heard her mention the name when she was talking on the phone last night. I asked her who it was, and she told me to forget I ever heard the name."

"Who was Tina talking to when the name came up?" I asked.

He shrugged. "No idea. She wouldn't say. Told me the less I knew, the better. But I got the impression whoever it was worked for *El Pastor*."

"Do you know if this person gave her any instructions?" Hugo asked.

"Stay put," Corbett replied. "She calmed down some after she talked on the phone and told me she had to stay the night. Someone would come get her in the morning. I told Tina it was all getting too crazy for me, man. She said it would be fine. They'd pick her up tomorrow, and it would all be over."

"So, what was your role?" I asked. "How did you meet Lowell?"

He swallowed and looked at Chu.

"Go ahead," she said. "The more you help, the better chance we have of reducing your sentence."

"I'd been selling product to the Russian dude," Corbett reluctantly admitted. "He introduced me to Tina."

I didn't bother correcting the suspect regarding his nationality error.

"But I had no idea what they were doing, man. You gotta believe that."

"Which drugs did Lowell buy from you?" Hugo asked.

"Midazolam and lorazepam. That's all she cared about."

Hugo leaned over the table. "And you never asked why?"

Corbett laughed, although there was little humor in his tone. "You don't ask, man."

"How did you meet Kalinovich?"

The suspect shrugged. "A guy knew a guy and, you know, I was introduced."

Hugo sat back. "Okay. Where can we find *El Pastor*?"

The suspect shook his head. "Can't help you. I gave you what I know, man. I didn't get a name of who she spoke to, and I only overheard her say *El Pastor*. That's it."

"Did you ever go to the house on Robles in Dana Point?" I asked again.

Corbett looked at his attorney, but she was busy studying something on her cell phone.

"We have CCTV for the traffic in and out of Robles, Shane, so think carefully before you lie to us."

That was pretty much a lie in itself, but I could argue Bee's doorbell cam counted as something.

Corbett was about to reply when Chu held out her hand in front of him. "Whose body did you discover earlier today in San Juan Creek?" she asked pointedly. "Was it Christina Lowell?"

"You know we can't discuss an open case with you," Hugo quickly rebutted.

Chu gritted her teeth. "The creek behind my client's mobile home park."

"What the fuck?" Corbett gasped. "You found Tina dead?"

We were done. It was pointless denying it, but we couldn't admit it was Christina Lowell, so we were forced to blather on about not disclosing victims' names, which Chu saw right through. Corbett freaked completely out. Ending the interview, the suspect was hauled back to his cell, and Chu cornered us in the hallway.

"That's pretty shitty not to reveal Lowell had been murdered."

"We never said it's Lowell, and certainly didn't mention anything about murder," Hugo replied.

"Come on, you two," Chu vented. "I was trying to work with you in there, but I have to represent the best interests of my client."

"And his best interests are to give us something useful," Hugo retorted. "Regardless of Lowell. Telling us some ghost-like gangster calling himself *El Pastor* doesn't do shit for us."

Chu shook her head and walked away. "I'll speak with my

client on Monday morning and see what he says then, Fuentes. But my guess is you've got all he'll say because it's all he knows."

The door at the end of the hall swung closed behind her, and I turned to Hugo. "Except he was about to admit he'd been to the bunkhouse."

Hugo nodded. "I think so, too, but I doubt he saw anything there except Lowell and Kalinovich. They wouldn't have invited him upstairs."

"*El Pastor*," I said. "Sounds like a mastermind villain from a James Bond movie."

Hugo sighed as he took out his phone. "Yeah. I'll probably regret this when he laughs at us, but I'll call Doug Albright and see if the name means anything to him."

We moved to our office and closed the door before Hugo dialed the number. Albright answered after two rings.

"Got something, Hugo?"

"Maybe," my partner answered cautiously. "The name *El Pastor* mean anything to you?"

There was a brief silence on the line, and I could hear Albright was moving somewhere as the background voices faded. "What on earth are you getting yourself into down there?" he finally replied.

"A rising body count, I can tell you that," Hugo said. "Otherwise, we don't know exactly what we're unearthing."

"Okay, so give me the context on *El Pastor*," Albright replied. "How did that name come up?"

Hugo gave Doug the Cliff Notes version of what we knew so far, which sounded even more loosely linked and fragile as I listened to his explanation. When he was done, the line went quiet again.

Hugo muted the call and looked at me. "At least he didn't laugh."

"Are you both there?" Albright asked.

Hugo unmuted. "Yeah, and we're in a private office."

"Okay, give me a second, Hugo. I'm going to try to get someone else on the line. Stand by and I'll call you back, okay?"

"Copy."

We waited, and I wondered where this was going. I had a bad feeling our case was in danger of being yanked out from under us rather than assisted, but I told myself to remain optimistic. Although, maybe someone else who was used to moving in these circles would do the girls better justice than the dead ends we kept hitting. But I wanted to be there when whoever caused Jane Doe to end up staggering down the street, and Lexy to go missing, was brought to justice. I guessed the immediate culprits already had been, but I wanted the ones at the top of the food chain.

Hugo's cell phone rang, and he answered the call on speaker. "Hey, Doug."

"I have Tess Salgado with me, guys. She's an investigator with the vice and human trafficking team. I just relayed what you guys told me. Tess, this is Hugo and… Kat, is that right?"

"Yup," I said from across the desk. "Nice to meet you, Tess."

"So the name you were given has been floating around our patch for a few years now," Tess said without wasting time on small talk and salutations. Her voice was gruff for a woman, and she exuded a no-nonsense efficiency. "No one has verified his real identity, and we've been unable to positively tie him to any busts. We had a lawyer who swore his client could lead us to him, and before we could talk to the guy, he was found in the showers at county with his tongue cut out and his throat opened like a Ziploc."

Hugo winced and let out a low whistle. "What's *El Pastor* supposedly into?"

"You name it," Tess replied. "He runs it like a tiered organization from what we can piece together. Each enterprise operates as its own unit, and if we bust them, whoever was involved either gets out on bail and disappears, or winds up dead inside."

"Your corporation theory is on the money, Kat," Hugo said, surprising me with his credit. "So, where do we go from here?"

"Depends," Tess said. "Got anything leading us to this guy?"

"We shot one of them, who we think was running his human trafficking bunkhouse here in Dana Point, and maybe a honey pot scheme. Looks like he took out the other one before we could get to her," I replied. "We have another perp here in our jail, but he's too removed to know much, as best we can tell."

"You squeezed him pretty good?" Tess asked, and I wondered what she meant by that exactly. From her voice, it sounded like her methods might reach beyond a line we couldn't even think about crossing, but I doubted that could actually be true, or she'd never win a case in court.

"He clammed up once his attorney informed him his contact was dead," Hugo replied. "But I really don't think he met anyone of any significance. In fact, I'd say the only two he knew are now in the morgue."

"It appears Corbett was supplying two of the ingredients for..." I stopped myself before I said the word.

"You're okay, Kat," Doug jumped in. "Our two divisions work together all the time. Tess is well-versed in what's going on."

"Okay, good," I said in relief, thinking I'd almost blown any trust in future dealings with the narcotics division. "Corbett was supplying midazolam and lorazepam in pill form, but we've found no evidence of a lab. Only the bunkhouse where they were keeping the girls."

"Well, I hate to tell you this, but I don't think there's much I can help you with unless you can find a connection to another operation, or to *El Pastor* himself," Tess said. "We have a brothel we've been sitting on for a while, hoping to catch the boss there, but no one has shown up yet. We think it might be one of *El Pastor*'s ops, but hell, we're still not sure this dude's even real. Could be a myth to throw us off a syndicate running everything."

"Do they use black SUVs with tinted windows?" I asked, then wished I hadn't. It was a dumb question.

Tess laughed. "Every jumped-up wannabe on the street rides in a blacked-out Suburban, man. Or the new Range Rovers. The brothel we've been watching has a delivery service. They're dropping and picking up all night long in those things. Got an identical fleet of them all registered to a limousine company in Santa Ana. Silver Crest Limousine Service."

"We have one seen at the perp's house this morning," Hugo said. "Good chance they picked Lowell up, drove around the back of the estate, and executed her. Anything distinctive about the SUVs at the brothel?"

"Biggest difference with these and the usual gang rides we see is these are all Chevy Suburbans with all the bells and whistles, except they ride on standard wheels instead of the pimped-out, stupid-looking shit."

"Okay, thanks," Hugo replied. "It's a long shot, but we have San Juan deputies hunting for any CCTV from this morning. You never know."

"If you can tie one of those SUVs to your murder, I'd like to hear about it," Tess said. "Albright can text you my number. Meanwhile, I'll see if any of my contacts know anything about what happened on your patch. Oh, one more thing. These Suburbans run on standard wheels because they're fitted with run-flat inserts like they use for FBI and VIP protective vehicles. You can't really tell from the wheel and tire, but look for the tire valves. They're machined metal valves. Kinda beefier than normal."

Hugo looked at me, and I nodded. I doubted he'd ever checked his tire pressures in his life, let alone fixed a flat. I knew what to look for if we could get a high enough resolution video.

We ended the call, and I looked at my watch. Five-thirty-eight. Taking out a card with Rivera's number, I called her cell. She answered after a few rings.

"Rivera."

"It's Kat. You got anything for us?"

I heard her sigh. "Sort of. I have about twenty-something black SUVs on CCTV in and around San Juan, close to the right time this morning. Can't guarantee any were near the estates, only that they traveled along Camino Capistrano on the stretch near Avenida Aeropuerto."

I glanced up at Hugo, who rolled his eyes. "You want to go over there and look, don't you?" he asked rhetorically.

I grinned. "Too many files to upload. It would take forever. I'll buy pizza."

He let his head fall back, and he gazed at the ceiling. "This is your idea of an ideal Saturday night, isn't it, Cromwell?"

"Not ideal, but better than my average Saturday night."

"Fine," he groaned.

"When does your shift end, Elena?" I asked over the phone.

"About ten minutes ago," she replied. "But I'm good, man. Off tomorrow, so I don't mind. Meat lover's if I get a vote, ma'am."

I laughed. "You get a vote. See you in ten."

28

Focusing on the black Chevrolet Suburbans in the CCTV, we quickly narrowed down the list from twenty-seven to three. The cameras were both on Camino Capistrano, at Stonehill Drive to the south and the I-5 freeway intersection to the north. In the mile-and-a-half stretch, there weren't any other options to escape the area trapped between the freeway and the San Juan Creek. Car dealerships, the mobile home estate, and a bunch of businesses and warehouses offered a warren of streets, but the two intersections were the only routes away from the confined area.

Hugo and Deputy Elena Rivera shared a large meat lover's pizza after the delivery guy came by, while I ate the small cheese and mushroom I'd ordered as we studied the footage. It didn't take long to narrow the SUVs down even further, as two of them passed through the Stonehill camera, then only took a few minutes to appear at the freeway intersection. The third candidate arrived from the north. For a while, it appeared this may have been someone going to work, but the same SUV finally reappeared when we fast-forwarded the recording far enough. The Suburban spent forty-two minutes in the area before leaving the same way they'd arrived.

"Has to be the one," Rivera said, still chewing on a mouthful of pizza. She paused the CCTV and zoomed in on the image. "Same license plate."

"Check DMV for the owner," I said, sitting back and wondering what our next move would be if the name was what I thought it would be.

"I'd say this would qualify under Tess Salgado's 'wanting to know' parameter," Hugo said, clearly thinking the same thing. "Hardly a smoking gun, but might be enough for a warrant to grab the vehicle."

"I can't imagine they're dumb enough to leave trace evidence in that SUV," I replied. "Not if the place's main purpose is running jobs for *El Pastor*."

"*El Pastor*?" Rivera asked. "The Shepherd?"

"You've heard of him?" I asked in return.

"I thought the guy was a myth," she replied. "Cover name for a crew based in Santa Ana."

"How do you know about him?" Hugo asked. "Or them. We'd never even heard that name until a few hours ago."

Rivera shrugged. "I grew up in Santa Ana, man. My family's all still there. Got a cousin we're trying to keep out of trouble, but he's seeing all those flashy rides and dudes with money they shouldn't have, you know. He mentioned *El Pastor* a few weeks back. Swore this dude wasn't no regular gang boss. He's legit and all that bullshit."

Hugo and I exchanged a glance.

"Is your cousin in with *El Pastor*'s people, or just talking?" Hugo asked.

"I don't know, to be honest. I hope it's all talk," Rivera replied, then pointed to her screen. "Here's your SUV owner." She paused and frowned. "That can't be right. Says here that plate belongs to a Ford minivan that was totaled."

"No way they used a legit plate for a hit," Hugo scoffed.

"Roll that CCTV back a few seconds. I need to see the wheels," I told Rivera. "Bingo," I muttered, once I had a better view. "Stock size wheels, and you can see the valve stem."

"I just see a blurry something, Kat," Hugo remarked. "You think that's a valve stem?"

"Pick another vehicle," I urged Rivera, and she found a car arriving on camera after the SUV. I pointed at the screen. "See how you can't even see any sign of a normal-sized valve stem? The Suburban's is much bigger. It's from Silver Crest Limousine Service."

"You know this firm?" Rivera asked.

"Possible ties to *El Pastor*," I replied.

The deputy turned in her chair and looked at me. "So he is real?"

I shrugged. "To be determined. Regardless, this limo company delivers clients to an underground brothel vice have been watching, and now it looks like they may have ferried whoever killed Lowell."

Hugo dialed the number Doug Albright had texted him for Salgado, putting the call on speaker, as the three of us were the only ones within earshot.

"Yeah," the vice and human trafficking team investigator answered. I guessed she was wary of using her name or official title in her line of policing.

"This is Fuentes and Cromwell. We might have something."

"That was quick," Tess replied. "Shoot."

"We have one of your Silver Crest limos on CCTV here in San Juan Capistrano," Hugo explained. "Arrives in the area a few minutes before a black SUV was parked outside the place where the vic was staying. Left forty minutes later. Has the big valve stem things you mentioned."

"Can you positively match the SUV to the one in front of the vic's place?" she asked.

"No," Hugo had to concede. "Eyewitness from across the road just saw a black SUV with tints. No plate, picture, nothing."

"That's thin," Tess replied thoughtfully. "I wouldn't risk

spooking these guys unless you're sure you'll pull something from the vehicle. That's if you can even get a warrant on what you have."

I looked at Hugo and raised an eyebrow.

He sighed. "If they're pros, it'll be wiped and checked."

"That would be my guess," Tess replied. "And I could do without you getting anyone in a frenzy tonight. We're gearing up to raid the brothel we've been watching."

"Is *El Pastor* going to be there?" I asked.

I heard Tess blow out a breath in frustration. "Doubt it. I'm getting heat from above to take it offline, even if we can't get the major players."

"Okay," Hugo said. "We won't bother you anymore tonight, and good luck."

"Shit, my evening is gonna be sitting around in this van for another four hours before we go. You can text or call if you pull a rabbit out of a hat."

"Copy," Hugo replied. "And we'll hold off trying for a warrant on the SUV."

"*Gracias.*"

"*De nada,*" Hugo responded. "Be safe," he added before hanging up.

"Bugger," I ranted under my breath. "We can't take a step forward without going backwards."

"We could try tracking the Suburban's movements after it left San Juan," Rivera suggested. "See which cameras read its plate."

I nodded. "I think you'll find it returned to base in Santa Ana, where they'll have a very well-equipped detailing department."

Rivera turned and looked at me, her face an odd mixture of thought and concern.

"What is it?" I asked.

The deputy took several moments before she spoke, as though making a decision before saying anything. "My cousin, the one I mentioned…"

"What about him?" I prompted after she paused.

"That's what he does."

My brow furrowed. "I don't follow. What does he do?"

"Details cars," Rivera replied. "He started when he was in school. He'd detail cars in the evenings. In fact, he did more detailing than school, and never graduated. Last I knew, he was working for a dealership detailing trade-ins before they went on the lot. He still does side jobs in the evenings and on weekends."

"You think he might be working for *El Pastor*'s limo service?" I asked.

She shrugged. "It would be the obvious role for him. Believe me, he's no enforcer. I know I ain't a skinny girl, but I'm still a girl, and I bet I outweigh him. He ain't about to intimidate anyone. He brought up *El Pastor*, so maybe he's detailing for him."

"Call him," Hugo urged. "Ask him if he's working for the Silver Crest."

I winced. "That's up to you, Elena. It's tough when it's family. But if he's just detailing cars for them, he won't be in trouble, and we need a break."

Rivera took out her cell phone and shuffled it in her hand for a few moments. Coming to a decision, she unlocked the screen and called a number.

"*Hola, Tía.* It's Elena."

I could hear a female voice on the other end of the call, but couldn't make out what she was saying. From the greeting, I took her to be Elena's aunt.

"I'm good. I just had a quick question for you, *Tía.*" After a brief pause and response from her aunt, Rivera continued. "Where is Matty working now? Did he leave the dealership?"

The deputy's eyes flicked my way as soon as her aunt answered. From the concerned look on Rivera's face, I had a feeling her prediction had been correct. She thanked her aunt and promised to see her soon before ending the call.

"Mateo is working for a limo company from noon into the evening every day. Alma doesn't know which one. She says he's getting paid a lot more and is much happier there than he was at the dealership."

"Let's find out which one, then," Hugo said. "There have to be a hundred car services in Orange County, so let's see if this is even the one we're interested in."

Rivera nodded and looked up another contact. She texted rather than called this number. "We'll see if he responds," she said as she typed. "He's usually good about texts."

She was right. Her phone pinged almost right away. Rivera looked at me again. "How do we play this?"

"What'll happen if you get him on a call and tell him you need to see him tonight?"

She shrugged. "He'll be suspicious. I mean, we're tight, but he knows I'm a cop, and I'm always on his ass to stay out of trouble. I've never asked to meet him like this before."

"What if you tell him you're going to be in Santa Ana this evening and want to say hi?" Hugo suggested. "Maybe he gets a break. Make up something about ideas for his mom's birthday or something."

I frowned at Hugo. I wanted to get these guys as badly as anyone, but he was pushing Rivera too hard. She was in a tough position, one that could cause a serious rift in her family.

Hugo just raised his eyebrows at me.

The deputy took a few deep breaths and typed another text to her cousin.

"How old is Matty?" I asked.

"Nineteen," Rivera replied. "His sister is sixteen. Straight-A student. Matty's a smart kid, too, but could never focus in school. Head full of ideas and better things to do."

Her phone buzzed, and she read the message to herself before relaying it to us. "He's getting off work at nine. He said he'd meet me at my aunt's house."

"Does he still live at home?" I asked.

Rivera nodded, and I looked at the time. It was almost seven-thirty. With traffic, even after rush hour, which was closer to three or four hours of bumper-to-bumper, it would take us forty minutes to drive the twenty-five miles.

"We should be at the house before he arrives," I suggested. "He may spook if he sees three cops roll up, even if one of us is his cousin."

Rivera nodded again. "I need to change. Can I meet you back here at eight?"

"Sure," I replied. "We can drive, unless you want to stay longer with your family."

She thought for a moment. "Tell you what, I'll give you the address and meet you there, if that's okay? I need to smooth this over with my aunt first. Can you guys be there a few minutes before nine? Matty won't be home until ten after or so if he leaves on time."

"No problem," I replied, and Rivera wrote down the address for us.

29

———————

Softly bathed by a yellow streetlight, Alma Rivera's house was a classic single-story stucco in the heart of Santa Ana's residential neighborhood. The place was tidy, although the avocado-green paint looked due for a fresh coat. A perfectly trimmed lawn stretched from the sidewalk to the front porch, albeit tainted by a few brown spots from the California sun. An older Honda Accord sat in the driveway beside the house with a newer, mid-size SUV in front.

Elena Rivera, now dressed in leggings and a Los Angeles Angels jersey, opened the front door before we had a chance to knock.

"Come in," she said, stepping out of the way while checking the street for anyone watching.

We walked inside the home to a faint aroma of food and older but clean and tidy furniture. A woman in her late forties stood by the sofa with a tray of glasses in her hands.

"This is my aunt, Alma," Rivera said, closing the door behind us.

"I'm Kat, and this is Hugo," I said, smiling at the lady, who nodded nervously in return.

Alma set the tray down on the coffee table. "Please, help yourself to water," she said in heavily accented English. "Take a seat. Anywhere is fine."

I glanced at Rivera, who gave me a subtle nod. I took it to mean her aunt might be anxious, but had agreed to what was hopefully about to happen.

"Let's sit in the dining room," Rivera suggested, which I agreed would be better. We didn't need the kid walking through the door to a room full of strangers. "Matty just texted," she continued. "He had to stay a few minutes late."

Alma relocated the tray to the dining table off the kitchen, and we all sat.

"Are you hungry?" she asked.

"We're fine, thank you," I replied, although I bet the woman made the best tacos. "We ate dinner earlier. Thank you for letting us visit with your son."

She nodded. "He's a good boy. I don't want him in trouble."

"That's our goal as well," I replied, and she smiled.

Small talk came slowly at first, but Hugo got involved when the subject of food came up. Pretty soon, we were all chatting and even laughing, so for an instant, I was surprised when the door opened and a young man with a slight build walked in.

"Hey, Matty," Rivera greeted him, getting up from the table.

They met in the middle of the living room and embraced, although the young man's eyes stayed on Hugo and me.

"*¿Qué pedo con esto?*" Matty asked.

"Don't be rude, Matty," his mother scolded. "Elena brought some friends for you to meet."

The young man pushed himself away from his cousin, and for a moment, I thought he might bolt out the door.

But his mother stood and pointed to the chair she'd vacated. "Sit down. I'll fix you something to eat."

"It's okay, Matty," Elena assured him. "You're not in trouble. We just need your help with something."

"I ate at work, *Mamá*," he replied, slowly walking over to the table.

"This is Kat and Hugo," Rivera said, following him over. "We work together."

Matty stared at me. "You're cops?"

"Sheriff's department investigators," I confirmed.

"So what's this about?" he asked, still standing.

His mother, apparently ignoring her son's response regarding food, busied herself in the kitchen but called over to him, "Sit, Matty, sit."

The young man did, but kept the chair well back from the table and angled as though he might need to escape at any moment.

Rivera sat down again. "They're looking into the possibility of a connection between a series of very serious crimes and Silver Crest Limousine Service. Just answer their questions, Matty, and you'll be fine."

Her cousin shook his head. "I don't know nothing about nothing, man. I just clean cars."

"Elena was telling us," I said, trying to figure out the best way to approach a conversation with the young man. "You're a mega car detailer. She says you're the best around."

Matty stares back at me without reacting.

"How long have you worked for Silver Crest?" I asked.

"Couple of months. But they're legit, man. It's just a limo service."

"Do you ever do any of the limo driving?" Hugo asked.

It was a key question, as we were telling the kid he wasn't in trouble, but we really didn't know. He could have been driving the Suburban to San Juan Capistrano that morning.

Matty shook his head. "Clean. That's it. They drive them over to my section, I detail them, they take them away."

"I bet you find all kinds of crazy things left behind in the back of those Suburbans, don't you?" I asked with a smirk on my face. "People go nuts in the back of limos."

He smiled. It was still guarded, but I could tell he had stories to tell.

"Sometimes," he replied.

"What's the weirdest thing you've come across?" I urged, grinning as though I was looking for a juicy story.

Matty leaned forward. "One time," he began in a whisper, checking over his shoulder to make sure his mother didn't hear, "some chick left a *toy* behind, if you know what I mean."

"No way," I laughed. "A *toy*, toy? One that buzzed?"

He nodded and grinned. "Yup."

"That is crazy," I replied, wishing Hugo would get a little more on board with the act. He could play the serious guy, but he sucked at jovial. "Gotta be some awful shit, too, right? People partying too much. I couldn't deal with cleaning up someone's barf."

"It totally sucks," he said, cringing. "I have a full-on painter's mask I wear for that."

"What about blood?" I asked, keeping the grin on my face.

It didn't work. Matty immediately sat back and shrugged. "Not really."

I pulled my instant photos from my pocket and shuffled through them until I found the one of Christina Lowell's corpse wrapped in clothes in the creek. Her hand was clearly visible. I slid the picture across the table.

"This woman was picked up by a Silver Crest Suburban this morning, driven around the corner, executed, and then dumped in San Juan Creek. So, Matty, do they ever have you clean blood from any of the vehicles?"

The young man stared at the picture with his face turning pale. He pushed the picture back my way. "I don't know anything about that."

"Want the plate number of the black Suburban they used?" I asked. "The Suburban you probably detailed today. The plate was a fake from a wrecked car, so someone had to switch it at the shop."

"You gotta tell them if you know something, Matty," Rivera urged. "This is heavy shit, dude."

His eyes flicked to meet hers. "It's just a limo service, man. I don't know about anything except I clean the ones they bring me."

"Matty, have you had to clean blood from any of the vehicles?" Rivera asked.

He nodded and swallowed hard.

"What do they tell you when you get one with blood inside?" I asked.

He shrugged again. "I didn't clean out any blood or nothing today."

That wasn't surprising. From what I'd seen, I figured they'd driven Lowell around the back, then shot her on the trail or in the creek. The crime lab would confirm where she'd been executed by where they'd find blood splatter. Regardless, it wouldn't have been inside the Suburban.

"Okay, but when you have had to clean up blood, what have they told you?" I persisted.

"Last time, they said someone had a nosebleed."

"Did you believe them?" I asked.

He shrugged once again, then started to say something, but stopped himself.

"You gotta tell them, Matty," Rivera said. "It'll be okay."

He sighed. "The blood was in the back, that's all."

"On the back seat?" I asked.

He shook his head. "No, in the very back. You know, where the luggage goes."

"That must have seemed odd," Hugo said. "Why would someone be riding back there, especially if they had a nosebleed?"

"They said he was drunk and banged his head."

"Okay, and they have you scrub all that out, right?" I asked.

"Yeah. Then they check with one of them lights," he replied.

"A UV light?"

"I dunno. But my boss checks them every once in a while."

"Every vehicle you clean blood out of?"

He nodded. "And some others sometimes."

"Who's your boss?" Hugo asked.

"Enrique."

"Does he run the place?" Hugo continued.

"No, man. He's like the foreman. He manages all the mainte-nance and detailing. Gustavo runs the place. He's in charge of everything."

Hugo takes out a notebook. "Got a last name for these guys?"

"Gustavo Vasquez. Don't know Enrique's last name."

"Do any other owners come by?" I asked, wondering if we were getting anything more than a simple confirmation of what Salgado had already told us.

"Who knows? I wouldn't know them, anyway. I mean, the shop is just where they keep the limos and do the service and detailing. The drivers take them to pick up the customers."

We couldn't leave without bringing up the name, so I took the plunge. "You've never met *El Pastor*, then?"

Matty tensed. "Don't know anyone by that name."

Rivera gave her cousin a stern look. "Don't bullshit, Matty."

The young man sighed. "I ain't ever met him. Honestly, I don't think he even really exits, man. Enrique says the same thing."

I was beginning to believe the same thing. Glancing over at Hugo, he shrugged, which I guessed meant he was out of useful questions, too.

"Thanks for talking with us, Matty," I said, turning back to the young man.

"Sure," he replied, visibly relaxing once we appeared to be done. "Sorry I made you wait."

"No worries," I said, and began rising from my seat. "Can't turn down the overtime, right?"

"No shit," he replied. "Some big party tonight. We had to detail a few vehicles that didn't come back in until late."

I dropped back into my chair. "A customer party, or the bosses'?"

He looked confused. "The bosses', I think. Enrique said Gustavo was going to whatever it was."

Hugo and I both leaned forward a little more. "Do you know where this party was happening?"

"Santa Ana somewhere. One of the drivers was telling me. He was pissed. He'd worked all day and now had to work late, too. They weren't even picking up people until ten."

"Did he happen to mention where in Santa Ana?" I asked. "Give you any other details?"

I glanced at my watch. It was nine-forty-three.

"Not really. I think he said something about a motel off Main Street, but I was working, so I wasn't really listening."

I looked at Hugo once more. "We need to call Salgado again."

30

I slipped the picture I'd taken of Mateo before leaving the house into my pocket and climbed into the passenger seat of Hugo's car. He sat behind the wheel with his phone in his hand. He'd already texted Salgado.

"Maybe we should just go by the limo place," I suggested. "See if anyone leaves."

Hugo raised an eyebrow at me. "It's a limo service, Kat. I'd expect them to come and go. We don't even know what this Gustavo Vasquez looks like. Besides, it'll be an empty limo that picks him up from his house if he's going to some shindig. He won't go straight from work at ten at night."

I nodded. "Probably right. I'm just antsy to do something."

"As usual," he replied, then cracked the briefest of smiles.

His phone rang.

"Fuentes."

"You two are racking up overtime," came Tess's voice. "Didn't think you beach crew liked to venture out after dark."

"I don't," Hugo replied honestly. "But my partner is keen to drag me all over the place at crazy times of the day."

Tess allowed herself a quick laugh. "What do you have now?"

"We spoke with a source who works for the limo company," Hugo replied. "You may already know this, but apparently there's a big party going on tonight."

"It's Saturday night in Southern California. There's a party on every block."

"I mean, there's some kind of gathering involving the guy who runs Silver Crest. His name is Gustavo Vasquez. There's a chance it's for other bosses of the branches, too. But that's a presumption based on our source's comments."

The line was quiet for a moment. "Keep talking. What else?" Tess asked.

"We think it's at a motel off Main Street. They were scrambling to have enough Suburbans ready."

"A motel off Main Street?" Salgado echoed. "Guys, I can't decide whether you're a help or a pain in the ass."

Hugo looked at his phone in disbelief, and then over at me.

I laughed. "I vote for us being a help, but I might be biased."

"Yeah, well, the brothel is in an old motel off Main Street," Tess replied. "The one I'm watching from a stinking hot van from across the road. And so far, it's been a quiet evening. We were talking about waving off in favor of a busier night, but I'll have some explaining to do with my boss."

"The party starts at ten," Hugo pointed out.

"Then I guess we'll see in a few minutes. Where are you now?"

"In Santa Ana off Broadway just south of Edinger," Hugo replied.

"What are you driving? Do you two look like a pair of cops?"

"Department-issued Ford, and pretty much, yes," Hugo said, looking down at his wrinkle-free shirt and perfectly fitted slacks.

"Well, shit. Alright, there's a Norm's restaurant at Main and 17th Park in the lot and stay in your car. Someone will meet you there. You might as well hang out half the damn night with me, too. Penance in case you're wrong about this party."

The line went dead, and Hugo looked across at me. He had his "I'm barely tolerating you" expression I'd become used to.

"Norm's has excellent desserts," I said, and grinned.

He turned to the front, then pulled out onto South Ross Street without responding.

The drive wasn't far, only three miles, but it took us ten minutes with all the traffic lights through the heart of Santa Ana. The Saturday evening traffic was busy but not congested, and the parking lot for Norm's was three-quarters full. Hugo backed into a spot and left the engine running. Almost immediately, an old, shabby-looking Chevy Astro minivan with faded brown paint and tinted windows pulled up and stopped in front of us. The driver unwound the window and beckoned to us. He looked more like a perp than a cop.

We got out and cautiously walked over. I freed the strap on my sidearm while the man glanced at Hugo.

"Investigator Julián Acevedo," the man said quietly with a Hispanic accent. "Get in."

It would have been nice to see a badge, as we could be stepping into a perfect trap, but as Tess had set the location, I decided to trust the man. The sliding side door operated far more smoothly than I'd expected from the dented and well-used appearance of the Astro Van, but I supposed having a creaky door on a surveillance vehicle wouldn't be ideal for stealth.

"Hurry," Acevedo urged, and Hugo tugged the door closed behind us.

The moment the latch clicked, the minivan moved off, circling the parking lot to return to Main Street. The interior matched the authentic wear and tear of the exterior. Basically, it was a piece of crap. I don't know why, but I'd expected fancy equipment hidden in the rear behind the tints. Maybe I watched too many old cop shows, but the Astro was technology-free. At least as far as anything developed in the past twenty years.

"Have people started showing up?" I asked.

"No," Acevedo replied without turning around.

"Where are we going?" Hugo asked as the driver turned right on 17th Street instead of staying straight on Main.

Acevedo frowned as he glanced in the rearview at us. "Making sure we weren't spotted and followed, man. You two couldn't be more obvious if you were in full uniform."

These guys existed in a completely different world from us, and I wondered how they stayed sane day in, day out. Maybe they didn't. We rode in silence while Acevedo made a series of turns around the city blocks, even pulling into a fast-food restaurant parking lot one time, looping around the building and exiting in the opposite direction. Finally, he pulled into a lot off Main Street that was half-full of vehicles, then backed into an empty spot where a hedge separated us from the road.

I looked over my shoulder. Under the bright streetlights from the four-lane thoroughfare, I spotted the Sunset Palms Motel. Located on the opposite side of Main at the corner of West 20th, the place looked like it was thirty years on from its last refurb. The beige stucco appeared patched in areas and painted over with various shades somewhat close to the same color. I could see an unevenness to the Spanish tile roof, and the windows were the thin aluminum-framed style from the '60s and '70s.

"That the brothel?" I asked.

"Yeah," was all Acevedo replied as he typed on his phone.

"I guess I was expecting something more upmarket," I said to Hugo.

He shrugged. "This isn't Las Vegas."

"Okay, you two," Acevedo said, turning around. "See that gray van closer to the corner of the lot?"

We both looked and nodded.

"Salgado's in there. Walk like you're supposed to be here and pretend to get in the car parked on this side. She'll open the van door for you to get in. If the door don't open, make yourselves scarce. Got it?"

We both nodded again, but I really didn't understand exactly how we'd beam ourselves out of the lot if the van door didn't open.

We got out and began walking that way. I slipped my arm through Hugo's, and he looked down at me.

"We just left a restaurant and are heading back to our car," I said, and laughed as though we were joking about something.

"Okay, we'll go with that," he replied, laughing a little himself, although it sounded horribly contrived. "But I'm not making out with you."

"In your dreams," I told the gay man with another laugh.

We reached the car, which I presumed was a staged prop, and we both walked to the driver's side as though Hugo was being a gentleman and seeing me to my vehicle. To my relief, the van door slid open, and I pushed a black curtain aside so we could both jump inside. The door quickly closed behind us.

"I'm Salgado," a stocky Hispanic woman wearing a ballistic vest over her black uniform greeted us. She had an acne-scarred complexion, which she didn't attempt to hide under any makeup.

"Kat and Hugo," I replied, looking around the cramped interior.

The van was more like what I'd expected. Three computer monitors above a white laminate desk on one side displayed images of the street and the motel. Salgado was the only person in there and sat in a swiveling office chair mounted to the floor, with a radio at the ready and a keyboard in front of her. Another black curtain separated the back from the front seats. It was hotter than an oven inside the van.

We shuffled to the back and sat elbow-to-elbow on a bench seat. "Business picking up?" I asked.

Salgado shook her head. "Not enough to say we're on. Did your source mention the name of the motel?"

"No," I had to admit. "He just heard the driver talk about a motel on Main Street."

The investigator turned our way with doubt in her eyes. "You know how many motels there are along this stretch?"

I nodded, wiping away the sweat already forming on my brow. "And that place is a brothel? How does it work? Do the limos just drop the clients off at the office?"

Salgado clicked a few keys and brought up an overhead drone video on the screen closest to us. It began playing.

"Both floors in this part of the motel," she said, pointing to the section of the L-shaped building perpendicular to Main Street, "are legit motel rooms they rent at higher than market prices to keep them semi-full most of the time. They jack the prices for the days they want them empty. The office at the end closest to us by the road deals with those rooms. The place runs as a legal entity, although there's no way it makes a profit."

We listened to her talk as the screen switched to footage from a camera mounted on a person walking around. The hands were feminine with painted nails. From the perspective, I guessed the camera was hidden in a cap on her head. She pushed a cleaning cart to a room and went inside. It looked like any other cheap motel room, and I could almost smell the stale odor the rooms all accumulated over time. Salgado forwarded the recording until the cleaner went inside another room, but this time she entered from an interior hallway.

"I'll take one of those rooms," I joked, seeing a far more opulent space with modern furniture and lighting.

"These are the rooms along the other part of the building," she explained, pointing to the rear leg of the L, which met 20th Street. "The front doors for each room are a facade. The clients enter from a hallway along the back."

With a few more clicks, the footage moved on once more until Salgado slowed the replay to normal speed as the cleaner pushed her cart into an expansive lounge, which resembled a nightclub with the lights on.

"That's the upstairs," Salgado continued, her eyes dancing between screens as she monitored the motel in real time. "Drinks, dancing, probably drugs, and the clients choose their girl."

"Surely you could bust them anytime for a liquor license violation and a dozen more building code and illegal sales charges," Hugo said. "You're waiting for a bigger score?"

Salgado nodded. "The property ownership is listed in the name of a local liquor store owner, who is no doubt being paid well for the fake front. He has it licensed for events and liquor. It's rented out to a variety of entities for the bigger bashes, and there's a second office in the far building to handle the upgraded room rentals. If we busted the place on a regular night, we'd never touch the real people behind it. That's why I've been waiting, but now my hand is forced by the brass."

"That's two SUVs in the past few minutes," I said, pointing to the monitor showing the motel. "Where is that camera?"

"Traffic light pole in the intersection," the investigator replied with a smirk.

"And another one," Hugo said as we all watched the screen.

I looked at my watch. "It's ten-thirty. Bloody hell," I muttered. "Of course. The driver talked about picking Gustavo Vasquez up at ten. Makes sense that the party starts after that, right?"

We all watched another limo pull in, stop near the far part of the motel building, then pull away, leaving two men smartly dressed in suits by a door.

"That's the second office," Salgado said, picking up the mic for the radio. "All units, this is Mama Fox. Business is picking up, guys. Over."

"Mama Fox, huh?" I chuckled. "That the kind of official call signs you renegades use over here in Santa Ana?"

Salgado grinned at me. "We pretty much write our own rules around here. It's the wild fucking west most days." She nodded to the bench we were sitting on. "There are vests in there. Wear one if you wanna tag along."

"Get up, Hugo," I ordered after he remained still. He gave me another one of those looks, but obliged.

Salgado keyed the radio again. "Twenty-three-forty team. We'll let them get the party in full swing. Go at twenty-three-forty. Over."

She looked over at me as I made sure the vest I'd selected fit me. "Gotta catch 'em with their dicks out."

31

My blouse clung to my body, dripping in sweat, and I wished I'd waited to put on the vest. I hadn't wanted to hold anything up if Salgado gave the word to raid the motel early. Apparently, having the engine running or any kind of generator making noise might give them away, which made sense, but meant the bank of batteries was used for electronics and not air conditioning. Salgado seemed oblivious to the stale, humid heat, apart from occasionally wiping her brow with her sleeve. This was one of the few times I declined coffee in favor of water.

A steady stream of black Suburbans had delivered men, and one woman, to the motel. Salgado had pointed out the people she could identify, bringing photographs up on the computer monitor closest to Hugo and me. Several were known associates of the group suspected of being run by *El Pastor*. Others were prominent business people, along with a few local politicians. Of course. There was always a politician or two involved when it came to inappropriate sexual endeavors. You'd think they'd learn from their predecessors, but I guessed they couldn't help themselves.

"One-minute warning, team," Salgado called over the radio as the clocks on the monitors all registered eleven-thirty-nine. "You two ready?" she asked, turning to me sitting on the bench, sweating.

"Can't wait to get out of this bloody van," I replied.

Salgado grinned, then looked at Hugo.

"Sure," he said, devoid of all enthusiasm. This was not my partner's idea of how to spend a Saturday night.

Butterflies danced in my stomach as the clock ticked down, and when Salgado made the call over the radio to go, my legs felt like Jell-O. I stumbled out of the van behind her and forced my feet to move as she pushed through the thin hedge to the sidewalk. Behind me, Hugo slid the van door closed, then caught up with us as Salgado paused by the busy road.

Kitty-corner across Main Street, a flat black SWAT truck had already pulled into the motel parking lot, and eight armed officers in dark khaki tactical gear streamed out the back. A second armored truck screeched to a halt on 20th Street, where eight more officers carrying assault weapons swarmed the building. Sirens wailed as four OCSD cruisers parked across Main Street, blocking traffic in both directions. The road cleared in front of us like the parting of the seas, and Salgado took off running.

Another cruiser blocked 20th behind the SWAT truck, and within seconds, the scene was a chaotic turmoil of sirens, lights, and radio calls in the earpiece Salgado had given me.

"*Mierda*," Hugo muttered behind me. "*¡Esto parece una zona de guerra!*"

It did feel like a war zone. My throat was dry, and while my legs had found their strength, my stomach knotted and my heart raced.

We crossed 20th, running down the sidewalk to the side entrance into the motel parking lot. Two SWAT team officers stood guard on either side of the office doorway, and the man closest to us gave Salgado a nod, acknowledging her presence.

She now drew her sidearm, assuming the low-ready position as she moved across the asphalt to the doorway. Stopping short, she raised an arm, signaling for us to do the same. I'd been trying to follow along with the radio messages, but they'd been coming in so fast and furious, I'd lost track. Calls referred to subjects and suspects, which, I knew, defined them by potential threat level.

Gunshots suddenly erupted from inside, and Salgado quickly moved to the wall of the building, clear of the doorway and windows. We both followed, and I drew my sidearm.

"Shots fired!" came over the earpiece. "Hostile with firearm, heading out back. I think there's an exit we didn't account for."

"Shit," Salgado spat, and immediately took off around the building. "Back me up!" she shouted over her shoulder before calling her move over the radio.

Our evening had steadily escalated from chatting with Rivera's cousin, to joining a surveillance, to now plunged into the middle of a full-blown live-fire raid. Training and instinct seemed to kick in as I chased Salgado around the building. My head felt like it was on a swivel, catching every movement around us as people peered at the manic scene from a distance.

A narrow parking lot ran along the back of the building with a corral for dumpsters in the corner and a wooden utility hut attached to the motel about halfway along. The door to the hut hung open. Salgado stayed close to the wall, pausing a moment to turn back and signal to me with her hands. She pointed two fingers at her eyes and then across the parking lot, lingering for a second on the wall around the dumpster. I turned to Hugo, who nodded that he'd read the signal.

Salgado continued along the rear wall until she reached the side of the utility hut. I stopped a few yards short and crouched down, raising my firearm a little to be ready. From the corner of the parking lot, something moved by the dumpsters, sending out a hollow, metallic sound that was quickly lost amongst the wailing sirens and shouts from inside.

"I'm covering it," Hugo alerted from behind me, so I kept my focus on the open door of the utility hut.

Salgado swiftly moved to the front of the wooden lean-to, pausing behind the open door. She turned once more to me, indicating she was about to look inside. That's when splinters shredded from the woodwork and two gunshots rang out in the night. Salgado spun around, dropping to the ground as three men burst from inside the hut, cutting at an angle for the dumpsters sixty feet away.

A shot rang out from behind me as I raised my firearm and tracked the figures, pulling the trigger twice. Across the lot, a figure appeared from beside the dumpster with a handgun raised, firing past the three men in flight, aiming our way. Chunks of pavement kicked into the air nearby, and dull thuds echoed as bullets struck the wall behind me.

For a brief moment, my adrenaline-crazed mind absorbed the scene, mentally recording details as I'd been trained to do. Two men in dark gray suits flanked a third man, who wore all black. He had dark, full hair, neatly combed back. The shooter from the dumpster also wore dark gray. He was short, stocky, with a thick beard.

Pumping my legs as hard as they'd go, I grabbed Salgado unceremoniously by the ankle and tried dragging her into the opening to the hut. More bullets ripped into the wood as the trailing suspect also turned and fired. Tess weighed a lot more than me, and her vest refused to slide easily across the asphalt. Holstering my weapon, I used both hands and tugged with all my strength. For once, I was glad of the stupid exercise my dad made me do, pushing and pulling a weighted sled across the gym floor.

As Salgado's head cleared the doorway, I released my grip and took stock of the situation. She'd taken both rounds in the chest, but the vest appeared to have done its job as she wheezed and coughed but sucked in a few breaths. Two of the three suspects must have reached the dumpster as they'd disappeared, along with the fourth man who'd been hiding there. The third of the runners lay a few yards from the dumpster, groaning as he rolled around on the ground, clutching his midsection.

Where was Hugo?

I glanced behind me through an open door in the back of the utility hut, where a narrow, darkened stairwell led upstairs. Voices echoed around the space from above, matching a call I could hear in my earpiece.

"OCSD Cromwell!" I shouted. "Officer down! Bottom of the stairs!" I leaped to my feet and leaned over Salgado. "Hang tough, Tess. Help is on its way."

Stepping over her, I paused at the exterior doorway long enough to scan the perimeter of the parking lot before moving outside.

"Hugo?" I called out, not seeing him.

"Quit yelling, Kat," he replied, stepping from behind the bullet hole-riddled door. "I need to handcuff that *cabrón*."

I let out the breath I hadn't realized I'd been holding. In my ear, calls from inside suggested the motel, or nightclub, or brothel, or whatever we were calling it, had now been secured. A local deputy reached the suspect on the ground, holding his gun on him, and Hugo stopped after taking a few paces, turning to me.

"Damn it, Kat," He said, shaking his head. "I just got through telling you I'd never had to fire my gun at anyone in the line of duty, and now you drag me into this shit."

"You could have stayed in the bloody van," I fired back, annoyed he was blaming me.

My partner stared at me for a moment, his eyes saying more than words could ever express. Disappointment. He turned and continued walking toward the wounded suspect.

"I'm sorry," I muttered, but I doubt he heard me.

"Are we clear?" a voice barked from behind me, and I spun around to face one of the SWAT team.

"Clear," I replied. "Three armed suspects on foot headed east. One down."

"Copy," the man said, then looked down at Tess, who was catching her breath. "You good, Salgado?"

"I will be," she wheezed.

"Should be used to it by now," he said with a grin, then stepped over her and keyed his radio to report that three men had escaped.

I knelt by Salgado. "Ready to sit up?"

She nodded, so I helped lift her into a seated position, propped against the doorway of the utility hut.

"You took that for me," I said, replaying the situation in my head. "You didn't let me have your back."

She frowned at me. "What are you talking about?"

"I should have crossed over you to the other side of the entrance to clear the hut, but you kept me behind you."

"Oh, that," she replied in raspy breaths. "Didn't figure it was fair on your first one."

"Thanks, I guess," I said. "But I was ready."

Her head bobbed a few times. "Yeah. I think you are."

I looked down at the two bullets wedged into the ballistic material of her vest. They were grouped closely together over her heart.

"Help me out of this thing," she said, clawing at the Velcro.

As I pulled the straps free, two more SWAT guys stepped over her legs on their way out.

"You good, Salgado?" one of them asked.

"Just another Saturday night in Santa Ana, Mikey," she replied.

He laughed as the two of them walked away to assist Hugo. A pair of EMTs had also arrived to tend to the suspect.

"How many times have you been shot?" I asked, amazed at how casually they all seemed to take the situation.

"This makes four," Salgado replied, still struggling to get her breath back as she looked at the vest in her hands. "That was the second-worst hit I've taken."

"Bloody hell. What was the worst?"

"The one that missed the vest," she replied, rolling her left shoulder. "Couple of years back."

I helped the woman to her feet, and she stood unsteadily, leaning on me for a few moments.

"I'm good," she finally said, and keyed her mic. "This is Mama Fox. Am I clear to come inside the building? Over."

"Clear, Mama Fox. Over," came a reply.

I turned and saw Hugo was looking our way. I waved him over as Salgado gingerly started up the stairwell. While I waited for my partner, I stepped away from the hut and snapped a picture with my instant camera.

"Salgado okay?" Hugo asked.

"Yeah, she'll be bruised, but fine," I replied, returning my camera to my back pocket. "Look, Hugo. I am sorry… you know, about all this."

He shrugged. "Who knows, maybe Salgado wouldn't be okay if we weren't here, but there's a reason I don't work in Santa Ana or Garden Grove, Kat. I have two kids I already barely see. I'd like to watch them grow up."

I nodded, but didn't know what to say next. This case had exploded into something so much bigger than a doped-up woman wandering the streets of Dana Point.

"You gotta learn when to lift off the gas, Kat," Hugo continued. "Or get yourself on a SWAT team."

"And leave you with no one to look after your pretty arse?" I joked.

"I'm confident I'd be a lot safer on my own, thank you."

I turned away, walking through the hut toward the stairwell so he didn't see me wince. It stung to think that he truly felt that way. Which made me angry. I stopped and turned back. Hugo looked right at me. The edges of his mouth began a subtle curl into his version of a smile. Barely detectable unless you knew the man. And every day, I felt like I knew him a little more. The idea of working without him flashed through my mind, leaving a gaping hole in its wake.

I grinned in return. "I'm sure the SWAT guys will beg me to come onboard, but I'll have to tell them I'm busy helping an old man get to retirement."

Hugo shook his head. "I just shot my first human being, Cromwell. Don't test me. I might get on a roll."

I was about to start up the steps when a thought occurred to me. "Hugo, did you get a look at the guy in the black suit?"

He shook his head. "Not a good look. He turned back once, but my sights were on the henchman shooting at us. He was the VIP, though. The other three were protecting him."

"*El Pastor*," I murmured. "It was him."

"We don't know that, Kat," Hugo replied. "Could have been a guest who brought protection."

He was right, of course, but there was something familiar about the figure. Maybe it was the hair.

"Cromwell!" came Salgado's voice from upstairs. It sounded like she'd gotten her breath back. "Get up here."

Hurrying up the narrow steps, I squeezed through what appeared to be a sliding door in the back of a closet. Beyond was an office. Salgado stood in the doorway across the room.

"This way," she said, beckoning us to follow.

She led us down a hall through another door into a now brightly lit space I recognized from the video. This was the club, with circular booths along one side and a long bar lined with stools on the other. Down the middle, a row of men stood handcuffed, guarded by several SWAT officers. The girls occupied two of the booths.

Salgado, clutching her chest with one hand, strolled along the line of men who were in various states of dress, some in boxers and undershirts.

"Hello, counselor," she said to one man. "County Supervisor Crandall. This one will be a little harder to explain to the voters, sir."

We reached the first booth, and Salgado turned to Hugo and me. "See if you recognize any of the girls. They're all pretty stoned."

"If you get blood samples, we'll match them to the cocktail our Jane Doe was given," I replied as I studied the faces of the young women. They were all in dressing gowns or flimsy evening dresses and leaning against each other, some holding hands. If they looked up, it was only briefly before their eyes darted away again.

Not seeing anyone familiar in the first booth, I unlocked my phone and found the pictures we had of Dennis's homeless friend Lexy and the two girls from the nightclub video, Kamaria Ellis and

Kaylee Monroe. I showed the three pictures to Hugo to refresh his memory.

"I don't see any of them," he said, so we moved to the second booth.

Forlorn and unfocused stares briefly surveyed us before their gazes returned to their laps. None of the three black girls in the booths resembled Kamaria Ellis. I rested my hand on a slender girl at the front of the second booth who'd kept her head down the whole time. She looked up, squinting against the lights above us.

"Kaylee?" I asked, thumbing to the next picture on my phone. She was the girl we had the most recent picture of, but her makeup and hair were very different. Hugo took my phone to have a closer look.

"Do I know you?" she muttered.

I shook my head. "No, but I've been looking for you. Your family has missed you."

A smile crept slowly across her face. "I'd like to go home now."

I squeezed her shoulder. "We'll work on that for you, love. Where is Kamaria?"

Kaylee's smile disappeared. "They took her away."

"Took her where, Kaylee?"

She shrugged. "We don't know."

Several of the other girls looked up now, and a few muttered to their neighbor.

"But when they take them away," Kaylee added, "they never come back."

My mind raced. We now had a tie between the motel and the bunkhouse. Two branches of *El Pastor*'s empire, but clearly there were more. There had to be a drug lab somewhere, and where did the other girls go? Shipped overseas? Out of state?

"Kat," Hugo said quietly, nudging me. "Girl in the back in the red dress."

I glanced at the picture on my phone, still in his hand, then at the girl he'd pointed out.

"Could be," he said.

"Lexy?" I asked, and the young woman in the red dress blinked a few times as she picked her head up and stared back at us. I pulled my pictures from my pocket and found the one I was looking for.

Holding the snapshot out, the girl's face lit up. "That's my knife," she said, tapping the picture with her finger. "My friend Dennis has my knife now."

32

At eight in the morning, I was still dog-tired when I rolled out of bed. My mind raced, so I had no chance of going back to sleep. It had been after three when I'd made it home. Even Roger showed little interest when I'd checked on him in his hutch before I'd gone to bed. Wrapping up at the motel had taken a while, then Hugo had to drop me at my car before I could come home. The paperwork would be another agonizing time-suck over the next few days. But we'd found two of the girls we knew to be missing, and had rescued many more from their sex slave hell, so it was all worth it.

I wish we could have arrested more of the people behind the brothel, but Salgado had nine of them in custody. Some were lower-level henchmen by her estimation, but more were higher-ranking members of the *El Pastor* group. One appeared to be the manager in charge of the motel, and another was Gustavo Vasquez. None of them were talking, of course, but Salgado was still pleased with the bust.

The most puzzling part was that no law enforcement inside had seen the man dressed in black. The SWAT guy who'd called in the men escaping had only spotted two of the Gray Suits. I had a bad feeling we'd watched *El Pastor* escape. Hugo wasn't convinced. Salgado said maybe.

I dressed, fed Roger his breakfast, threw a few things into my backpack, and headed out the door, swinging through PC Beans for a latte on my way to Dad's gym. Driving the VW bus with the windows down allowed me to enjoy the cool breeze and listen to an upbeat tune on the radio.

I was hoping Kenzie Frost would be at the gym, and I wasn't disappointed. Her uncle sat with Dad outside the office, drinking coffee and chatting.

Dad looked at his watch, then at me. "Did you surf this morning?"

"No. Late night on the job. Good morning, Diego."

"Hello, Kat," he replied. "Kenzie is in the weight room. Are you here for working out?" he asked, looking at the casual attire I'd thrown on. Black leggings and a boxing gym sweatshirt.

"Not this morning, but I'd like to speak with Kenzie."

"She'd like that," Diego replied.

I walked around the corner amid the sound of bags being hit, people grunting in effort, and '70s rock music playing in the background. Kenzie spotted me as she powered up and down an impressive amount of weight, doing squats on a machine. I stayed back until she'd finished the set. She slipped her earbuds away and hit pause on her phone.

"Hello," she greeted me.

"Hi. How are you?"

She nodded. "Good." Her answer was short, but her eyes begged me for any information about her friend's cousin. I guessed the word hadn't made it to her yet.

"We found Kaylee last night," I said.

Kenzie's face began lighting up into a smile, then switched to concern.

"She's alive," I quickly continued. "But she's been in a bad situation. It'll be a day or two before she comes home."

Kenzie then allowed herself the smile. "Thank you. Her family has been through a lot. It'll mean the world to them to have her home."

My phone buzzed in my pocket, and I checked the caller ID. It was Dishy Doc, Eric Cole. I ran through the same emotions Kenzie had just experienced. Initially, I felt a warm feeling of hope, then apprehension.

"Sorry, Kenzie, I have to take this. Work call."

She nodded and repositioned for another set of squats.

"Hi, Doc," I answered, walking away. "Everything okay?"

"Morning, Kat. I hope I didn't catch you at a bad time?"

"No, all good," I replied and stopped myself from saying anything more. I was about to sound panicked, and maybe he wasn't even calling me about his patient. Which was a crazy thought, and I felt embarrassed that my brain had even entertained that idea over a girl's well-being.

"I wanted to let you know that Jane Doe is awake this morning."

"That's great news," I replied as my cheeks blushed in further embarrassment and guilt. "Is she talking?"

"Nothing comprehensible yet, but if you want to swing by, I think she might be able to answer a few questions in a while. We pulled her tube last night, so her throat will be sore, and she's still pretty foggy from the narcotics, but she should be more lucid throughout the morning."

"Okay," I said thoughtfully, wondering whether I should let Hugo know.

"I'm sorry, Kat," Eric added. "It's Sunday. This is probably a day off for you. I wasn't thinking. I forget which day of the week it is sometimes."

"Me too," I replied with a laugh. "How do you like your coffee?"

"Real coffee or the stuff we get here?"

"Real coffee."

"I'm partial to a vanilla latte."

"See you in thirty minutes," I replied, and ended the call.

Waving goodbye to Kenzie, I told my dad and Diego I had to run, then texted Hugo as I walked to the bus. Driving through town, I made my second stop at PC Beans, this time going inside to order as I had to pee after downing the first cup. Joanna laughed as she handed me the two fresh cups over the counter. She'd drawn her usual sheriff's badge on the one with my name, and a pair of handcuffs on the second cup instead of a name.

"That'll take some explaining," I said, wondering how I'd hand the cup to Dishy Doc without turning bright red.

Mid-morning traffic wasn't too bad, so I arrived at the hospital in twenty minutes and parked in the lot where I'd shot Dmitry Kalinovich. I noticed a shiny new stop sign had been placed where I presumed Lowell had bashed down its predecessor. Winding all the windows closed on the bus, I locked the doors with the key, grabbed my bag, and walked around the buildings to the main entrance. Unintentionally, I was retracing my steps from the other day when I'd been chasing Kalinovich. The memories steadily threw the good mood I'd assembled on the drive there out the window as my stupid brain insisted on replaying the unfortunate events.

By the time I reached the main reception, I felt anxious and worried about Kamaria Ellis. Kaylee Monroe hadn't been able to offer much more than she'd initially told me, except confirming that she'd been locked in a room with bunks at one point. But Kamaria was gone, and word amongst the girls, some of whom seemed to have been enslaved for months, was that once a girl left, they never saw them again. I'd also shown them Jane Doe's photograph, but no one had recognized her. The most common thread amongst the girls was how little they remembered about anything. My guess was they'd been fed varying concoctions of Velvet since being abducted, and details of people and places had been lost to the foggy, drug-induced haze.

I texted Eric and noticed I'd missed a reply from Hugo.

"Let me know how it goes."

That was okay. He was more likely to put Jane Doe on edge,

anyway. I returned a thumbs-up emoji and looked for the little blinking ellipsis by my message to Eric. Instead, his voice surprised me.

"One of those for me?" he asked, arriving at reception.

"It is," I replied, handing him the drink I'd set on the counter.

Eric immediately looked at the drawing on the cup, and then at me. "What's my charge, Investigator Cromwell?" he said with a grin. "I'll gladly reimburse you for the coffee."

And of course, my cheeks blushed. Spinning my cup around, I showed him Joanna's handiwork. "A friend of mine draws this badge on my order whenever she's working. You got the companion doodle."

"Talented friend," Eric replied. "I was just about to go check on our young lady, if you're ready?"

I nodded. "Lead the way."

Jane Doe's room was at the end of a ward with open doors to rooms on both sides. Her room was easily identified by the Laguna Beach officer sitting in a chair outside.

"Morning," I greeted him, and the man looked up from his phone and nodded.

"OCSD Investigator Kat Cromwell," I said, and shook his hand. "Any trouble or suspicious people about over the past few days?"

He smirked and shook his head. "Not a thing," he replied, clearly bored and wondering why someone had to be there.

"Good. Thanks for keeping her safe," I said, and followed Eric into the room.

Jane Doe was half propped up on a couple of pillows with her eyes closed. She was still on an IV, and her heartbeats formed a zigzag across a monitor screen beside the bed.

"Hi there," Eric said softly, and the young woman's eyes flickered open.

She immediately tensed and opened her eyes the rest of the way, emitting a grunt. Eric held up both hands and took a step back, which impressed me. Most people's natural reaction to help was moving closer, which, in this case, would panic the girl even more.

"I'm a doctor," he said in a soothing tone. "My name's Eric. You're safe. You're in a hospital in Laguna Beach."

Her eyes shot to me, then back to the doctor. Clearly the male was a bigger threat in her mind, which surprised me, considering Christina Lowell's involvement.

"This is Kat. She's here to help you, too."

The young woman had a death grip on the bedsheet, tugging it up to her chin. She wrenched her stare away from the doctor and scanned the room. The sounds of busy nurses chattering and TVs playing quietly filtered through the doorway.

She turned to me. "How did I get here?" she whispered in a hoarse gasp.

"We found you in Dana Point," I replied. "We believe you'd been held against your will at a house nearby with other young women. You must have escaped."

Jane Doe's face was a mask of confusion. Whatever memories she had were most likely a series of distorted clips, none of which made sense.

"Can I show you a picture?" I asked. "It's of other girls who may have been with you before you got away."

She briefly nodded, keeping the sheet pulled up tight.

I slipped my backpack from my shoulder and rummaged inside for my pictures. I'd snapped one of the women in the second booth the night before. Setting my bag aside, I eased closer to the bed and extended my hand with the instant photograph. She tentatively took it from me. Her eyes scanned the picture, and I watched Jane Doe for signs of recognition. Nothing appeared to register at first, but then she squinted harder, and her face contorted. She threw the picture back at me.

"It's okay," I said, picking the photograph up off the floor and setting it by my bag. "I don't mean to upset you, love. We know you've been through an ordeal."

Jane Doe looked at me once more, and whatever haunting vision or memory the picture had stirred up must have faded as her expression softened.

"She was there, too," she rasped.

"In the bunkhouse?" I asked.

Her brow furrowed. The word "bunkhouse" seemed to trigger something. She nodded.

"Which girl?" I asked.

She pointed to the picture.

"I don't want this to upset you again," I said. "Are you sure? Maybe you can remember her name?"

"Give me the picture," she urged.

I held it for her to see, and she pointed to one of the girls sitting forlornly in the booth, elbow on the table so she could rest her head on her hand.

"That's Kaylee," I said.

Jane Doe's eyes flicked to mine, and she frowned, trying to retrieve the memories. I wondered if being on Velvet felt anything like my neurological issue. I doubted it. Stoned on Velvet seemed more like a living nightmare than the pain-in-the-ass issue I dealt with.

Finally, something stuck in Jane Doe's mind, and she nodded. "Kaylee," she whispered. "And Kammy."

"Kammy?" I questioned. "Is she in the picture?"

She shook her head, and I wished I'd taken a shot of the first booth as well.

"Wait, do you mean Kamaria? Kamaria Ellis?"

She nodded. "Kammy."

I shouldn't have been surprised. We had Kamaria's prints from the bunkhouse, but it was nice to confirm Jane Doe was with the other two, or at least they'd crossed paths.

"There are more," she said, and her face tightened again. She grabbed my arm, squeezing harder than I thought possible in her condition.

Hearing the words she'd uttered to the couple who'd found her on the road made me catch my breath, and I doubted I'd be able to forget the look in her eyes as she stared at me. Pure terror.

"Where are the others?" she rasped.

I placed my other hand on hers, and her grip slowly eased. "We found more," I said, reminding myself not to overcommit and make promises too many law enforcement officers later regretted.

"We should probably give her a break, Kat," Eric said, and I glanced his way. My first instinct was to push back, now that finally she was awake, but he was right. Forcing her to relive her ordeal too soon wouldn't help, and at this point, I wasn't sure how much new information she could provide us.

"Two more questions," I replied. "I'll be quick."

Eric nodded, and I turned to the young woman who'd taken the picture from me again.

"What is the last clear memory you have?" I asked. "Do you remember where you were before all this happened?"

She appeared to think my question over carefully before replying, "I'm not going back."

Bugger. I hadn't thought that through very well. We had no clue what life had been like for this girl before she'd been taken. These people weren't snatching sorority sisters from middle and upper-class families. They were preying on the types no one missed. Again, I needed to be careful. Family services would override anything I promised if she was under eighteen.

"Okay, don't worry about any of that for now," I assured her. "But tell me one more thing."

Jane Doe blinked a few times as she looked at me suspiciously.

"What's your name?"

Her brow tensed. "Thirty-One."

"Thirty-One?" I questioned. "That's not your real name. Is that what the people who took you called you?"

She looked confused. "I think so. I can hear voices calling me Thirty-One."

"Think back farther," I urged. "Do you remember what the teachers called you in school?"

The young woman's expression slowly softened. "Zara. My name is Zara Norwood."

"Nice to meet you, Zara," I replied, unable to keep the smile from my face.

"I'm going to update your chart right away," Eric said, walking to the whiteboard on the wall and erasing the standard moniker we'd all been using.

"Who's Jane Doe?" Zara asked, reading the name before it was completely erased.

I laughed. "She was in here before you showed up."

33

———

I texted Hugo and asked if he wanted to meet for lunch, as I was already in Laguna Beach. He agreed and suggested Coyote Grill in South Laguna just up the road from the hospital. As it was close by, I was there fifteen minutes before he showed up, and it took all my willpower not to order a margarita. I had mowed through half a basket of homemade tortilla chips by the time he strolled in, proving my inner strength had its limits.

Hugo looked dapper as always, in jeans, a brand-name polo shirt, and expensive sunglasses. It took me ten minutes to update him on Zara while he sipped on a Pacifico and I stuck with water.

"That's great," Hugo said when I was done. "Now we'll spend all week wrapping up reports and paperwork."

I stared across the table at my partner. The thought hadn't entered my mind that we were done with the case.

"Kamaria Ellis is still missing," I said. "We have to find her."

Hugo shrugged. "Our case was Jane Doe, Kat—"

"Zara Norwood," I interrupted.

"Right. But the point is, we've taken the bunkhouse out of the system, and the two people running it are dead. Zara can go home, or whatever family services decide to do with her. Salgado's group will keep chasing *El Pastor* and his merry men. We're done."

I wanted to argue the point, but apart from my personal longing to find the other name on our list, he was right. Bradley would tell us to move on. Kamaria's missing person file was already updated with a location in Dana Point, and an approximate date we think she was in the bunkhouse. She'd go back to being one of the eighty thousand or so young females unaccounted for in the U.S.

Our food we'd ordered arrived, but my tacos were piping hot and needed a minute to cool. "Norwood," I said, and Hugo looked puzzled. "Right in the middle of the bloody alphabet," I continued. "We started our search from either end at As and Zeds. No wonder we didn't find her. She would have been one of the last names we checked on our list."

Hugo nodded. "She should be safe now. If the only people she could identify are both dead and she doesn't recall anything about any other locations, then *El Pastor*, or whoever this group is, have no reason to hurt her."

"True," I replied. "As long as *El Pastor* knows that."

"He's got bigger things to worry about after last night," Hugo pointed out.

I reached into my backpack, retrieving my bundle of instant photographs. I should have secured them all together with a rubber band as they'd scattered amongst my other stuff. Plucking the last couple, I ran through them, looking for the one with all the girls in the booth I'd just shown Zara. But a different picture brought me to a stop. The photograph I'd taken from my dad's roof of the little compound on Domingo Avenue. My dead fiancé, Paul, Gabriella Castillo, and Milo Santiago had all slipped my mind over the past few days. I was owed time off in the coming week, so maybe I could refocus my effort on the family.

I shuffled through a few more of the pictures, then stopped again. This time, I gasped. The shot was at night, looking down into a courtyard between a shipping container and a scruffy mobile office. I recognized it as the place on Domingo from the earlier picture, but now the image was bringing another memory flooding back. Damn it. My second trip to the compound had been dumped from my stupid brain.

I fumbled for my phone. I'd shot a video.

"Are you okay?" Hugo asked from across the table, pausing with a tortilla in one hand and a fork full of carnitas in the other.

"Yeah. Well, no," I mumbled without looking up. "I have a bad feeling about something."

"About what?" he asked, but I was too busy finding the video I'd shot that night.

The dim footage played on the screen as two men moved around an SUV parked in the compound. One man I now recalled recognizing as Milo Santiago, but the second figure had been a mystery. Until now.

"Dmitry Kalinovich," I said, looking up at Hugo.

"What about him?"

"I'd seen him before," I admitted as my mind whirred on how I could explain myself without confessing to stalking Gabriella Castillo.

"Where?" Hugo asked before taking a sip of his beer.

I hesitated. *Maybe I could say I'd seen Milo Santiago in town and Kalinovich had been with him, but why would I just have remembered that now?* That sounded like bullshit inside my head. Saying it out loud would be cringeworthy.

"Which picture jogged your memory?" Hugo prompted.

He was a detective, after all, so it was hardly surprising he'd pieced together what had just happened in front of him. Even if it was his day off. Unsure how he'd react, or what he'd do with the information I was about to reveal, I handed Hugo my phone and held my breath.

He wiped his hands on a napkin before taking the device. His brow furrowed as he watched the video. "Where was this taken?"

"Capo Beach near my dad's gym."

Hugo stared at the video a little longer before peering over the phone in his hand. "You were spying on these guys?"

I nodded, still scrambling to think of a way for any of this not to sound like the dumb idea it really was.

"And this video just jogged your memory?" Hugo asked.

I nodded again, then corrected myself. "No, this picture did," I said, holding up the instant photo of the empty compound. "I could remember the first night, but this one had… gone." I slowed and muttered the last word as I realized I'd just confessed to doing this more than once.

Hugo sighed. "Kat. What the hell have you been doing?"

I groaned before digging a deeper hole I prayed Hugo would let me climb out of. "The other guy in the picture is Emilio Santiago. He's the wanker who broke into my house the other month."

"I don't know that I could ID either of these guys from this video, Kat. Maybe the one around the front of the SUV. Is that Santiago?"

I nodded once more.

"Okay, but are you sure that's Kalinovich? It's hard to make out his face at all."

"It's him. He had an accent I couldn't place at the time. It's his build, the way he moved… believe me, Hugo, it's him."

"So, when did you shoot this?"

"Wednesday night. Well, technically, Thursday. This was about four-thirty or five in the morning."

Hugo handed me the phone back, continuing to lean over the table. He lowered his voice. "Why were you spying on this guy, Kat? Just to catch him doing something else illegal because he'll probably get away with breaking into your house?"

That was true. The bastard was going to get away with it, despite his DNA in my house, courtesy of Roger's front teeth. The Castillo family had fabricated an alibi for him. So now I faced a decision over Confession Part Two. A much bigger hole from which there'd be no climbing out, no matter how much Hugo cared to help me, if this key detail made its way to Captain Bradley.

I looked into Hugo's eyes, trying to judge how he was taking all of this. *He'd fired back questions and was obviously concerned, but was he simply gathering evidence, deciding whether to destroy me, or contemplating how we could move forward?* I'd come to know him a lot better over the past few months, but I'd be damned if I could tell.

"Santiago broke into my house to send me a message," I replied. "If Roger hadn't bitten the guy, and I hadn't come home when I did, I'm pretty sure I would have walked through the door to find my little fella… well, you get the idea."

Hugo frowned again. "Why? What's this guy got a beef about? Did you bust him before?"

I shook my head. My stomach tightened and my throat went dry as I struggled over what to say next. *Trust my partner, or lie and hope it didn't come back to bite me later?* If it did come out that I'd lied to Hugo, he'd never trust me again with anything. Which might not matter, as I wouldn't have a job with the sheriff's department anymore, so I doubt our paths would ever cross again.

"Santiago works for the Castillo family," I said before I could reconsider my decision. "I went to high school with the daughter, Gabriella Castillo."

Hugo shrugged. "Okay. So, what did you do to her? Steal her boyfriend? Put a dead rat in her locker?"

"My fiancé, Paul," I began, then faltered. "Former fiancé, I guess. Whatever, semantics don't matter at this point. Anyway, I believe Paul was having an affair with Gabby."

Hugo blew out his cheeks. "Jeez, Kat. Are you sure?"

"Shortly before Paul's accident, I was still a deputy in uniform, and helping the Criminal Investigation Bureau with a stakeout. We were watching Gabby's house in Dana Point, and I spotted Paul there. Well, his car, but he was inside her house."

"Which you didn't report, I assume," Hugo surmised.

I shook my head. "I wanted to confront Paul and find out what the deal was first."

"And did you?"

"I'm not completely sure. I think it came up on the sailboat on the day of the accident."

Hugo groaned and closed his eyes. "No, no, no, Kat. Are you

saying you confronted your fiancé about his affair on the sailing trip that he didn't come back from?"

I nodded. "It's all still hazy, but I think so."

"You know how bad that looks, right?"

"No shit, Hugo!" I replied, louder than I'd intended. I leaned forward and lowered my voice. "Look, I didn't kill Paul, okay? When I got a whack to the head in the Russo case, some of it came back to me. It was an accident in the storm. But of course I know how it looks. That's why I couldn't say anything after the accident about Paul being involved with Gabriella. I had to wait for everything to settle down before I could try to figure out the connection. I'd been watching Gabby's place and spotted Santiago leaving, so I followed him to this little fenced-in compound that happened to be down the street from Dad's gym." Pausing, I took a breath. "The important part is we now have a tie between the Castillos and *El Pastor*'s man."

Hugo sighed and went to speak, then thought a few moments longer. "Okay, so what do you think they're doing in this compound?" he asked. "The place looks small."

"It is small, and it's a rundown piece of crap," I replied as a series of thoughts came tumbling through my mind, and a puzzle piece fell into place. "Bloody hell, Hugo. It has to be the lab. It's where they're making Velvet."

Hugo sat back in his chair and finished the last of his beer. "Do you have a stitch of proof?"

"Of course not, but isn't it an ideal location?"

He shrugged. "It's a location where you think you've seen these two men. Could be storing stolen goods, or could as easily be a container full of his mother's furniture."

"Then we need to find out," I urged, knowing this would be a fresh problem.

"Based on what?" Hugo replied, setting his empty bottle down and leaning forward again, keeping his voice low. "What do you have that a judge will issue a warrant for?"

It was my turn to sigh, this time in frustration. I had zero grounds for a warrant. "That black SUV looks a lot like the ones in *El Pastor*'s limo fleet."

"It looks just like a hundred thousand other black SUVs on the road, too," Hugo countered. "No license plate in the video or limousine number, and it's far too blurry to see valve stems. You'll never get a warrant, even after last night's bust. Besides, are you ready to show a judge your video and repeat the story you just told me?"

"I'll show him the video, but you know it'll be my job if I explain the entire story, Hugo. I'm trusting you with this."

"You're burdening me with this, more like," Hugo replied. "You know damn well I should report everything you just told me. If I don't say anything, then I'm as screwed as you are."

"Not if this conversation never happened," I pointed out. "I have a memory issue, you know. Not that you can tell Bradley that, either."

Hugo almost laughed, but it was more in amazement than humor. "You're a piece of work, Kat Cromwell. You're like a grenade with the pin out, and I'm the idiot standing next to you all the time."

"I'm sorry for bringing you into this, Hugo, truly I am, but if we're going to bust the Castillos for their part in the bunkhouse and probably the brothels and drugs, too, we need to find out what's going on in that compound."

Hugo threw his hands up. "You won't get a warrant, Kat."

"I know."

"Then what else can we do?"

"Watch the place again, but official this time. We got an anonymous tip that they're up to something in the place."

"Right, and based on one anonymous phone call, we spend all night staking out the place," Hugo rebutted cynically. "Bradley will never buy it."

"I wasn't planning on asking her permission."

"And there you go again," Hugo replied as he shook his head. "Playing with the grenade like it won't kill us all."

34

I drove back to Dana Point in a funk. After the joy of seeing Zara awake and recovering, my revelation of reconnecting my lost memory took the wind from my sails. After that, the discussion with Hugo had further dampened my spirits, although it could have gone a lot worse. At least he wasn't turning me in to Captain Bradley. But his parting words were, "Don't do anything rash, Kat. Take a beat. We'll figure out a way to go about this tomorrow at the office."

Waiting was not my forte. On my list of character attributes and flaws, which were heavily weighted to the latter, patience, or lack of, would feature prominently on the wrong side. I couldn't get Kamaria Ellis out of my mind. Not to mention all the unnamed girls we didn't even know about. Zara had been called Thirty-One, which left thirty more if she was the last one taken.

The other thorn in my side was the connection between *El Pastor*'s empire and the Castillo family. None of this helped me discover the truth behind Paul's affair with Gabriella, but I'd settle for sending Gabby's father to jail. Implicating her would be icing on the cake. After all, I had followed Santiago from her house.

Roger came hopping over to greet me as I walked through the side door, having parked the bus in the garage.

"Hey, mate," I said, dropping to my knees to fuss over him as he tentatively negotiated the hardwood floor. His fur-covered feet struggled for traction once he left the area rug that covered most of the living area.

"What do you fancy doing for the rest of our day off?" I asked, scooping him up and cradling him in my arm as I stood, dropped my bag on a dining chair, and walked to the kitchen. "It is Sunday, you know."

Opening the fridge door raised Roger's excitement level, and his little nose furiously twitched. He'd already learned to associate the fridge with treats. Tearing off a leaf of lettuce, I set him down on the edge of the rug where he made short work of his snack. I made a coffee, cursing myself for bypassing PC Beans on the way into town without stopping.

"Beach will be packed by now," I said aloud to involve the rabbit in my thoughts. "And the waves won't be great. We could visit Mum and Dad."

Leaving the single-serve coffee maker to heat, I walked back to the dining table and took my laptop out of my bag, booting it up.

"Or, I could check the camera I left on the gym roof and see if we caught anything interesting going on," I continued, then looked at Roger, who'd finished eating and hopped to the edge of the rug to see what I was doing. "Unless you're on Hugo's side, and tell me not to."

I stared at Roger, who wiggled his nose and stared back.

"Okay, then. No objection, so I'm taking a look."

Rolling my eyes at my own childish behavior, I logged into the security system at the gym and brought up the camera recordings. Clicking on the roof camera, I rewound to ten p.m. last night and paused while I retrieved my coffee that had now brewed. Deciding to settle in more comfortably for what could be a long afternoon of boring video review, I placed my coffee on the end table by the sofa and brought my laptop over. Roger preferred this setup, hopping onto the couch and sitting next to me.

Hitting fast forward a few times, I watched the distant view of the little compound at the end of Domingo Avenue. I started with Thursday night to Friday morning. The night after I'd been on the neighboring roof. Starting at eight o'clock after all the businesses had closed, very little stirred, apart from a guy walking his dog and a car turning around. Even at eight times regular speed, it still took me an hour and a half to reach sunrise.

Contemplating a second coffee, I decided against disturbing Roger. He'd settled down with his long hind legs kicked out and his back against my thigh. His little front feet twitched and his eyelids fluttered a few times, as though he were dreaming. I wondered if rabbits had nightmares of being chased by dogs in the way we assumed dogs dreamed about chasing rabbits.

Starting the process over again, I checked the footage from Friday night into Saturday morning. About halfway through, Roger decided he'd had enough of the lazy Sunday afternoon and hopped down. I pressed on, stopping the replay a few times to check out a stray cat or a car slowly driving down Domingo, then along the alleyway behind. No one showed up at the compound. Reaching sunrise on Saturday morning, I got up to use the bathroom, grab a glass of water, and stretch my legs for a few minutes. Roger insisted I feed him dinner, so I obliged before returning to the sofa.

Saturday night held more of the same uneventful and monotonous lack of activity. I could have been fooled into thinking I was looking at a still image if it weren't for the trees in view swaying at high speed. That was until I reached four in the morning. I slowed the playback down and watched a figure step from a black SUV and unlock the gates to the compound. I rewound to see if the camera caught the license plate, but it was too far away to be clear. From the man's movements, I was pretty sure it was Santiago, but it was impossible to tell from the gym roof in the dim light. If I was closer, or he stood near a brighter light, I'd be able to spot his distinctive orange and black neck tattoo of a tiger.

Once the SUV pulled inside, I couldn't tell much of what was happening. The high chain-link fence backed with plastic sheeting and old tarps left me squinting at the roof of the vehicle. The tailgate swung up, and then I caught movement from the top of two heads walking to the little modular office building. All went quiet for half an hour until finally the SUV pulled out. The first man got out, locked the gates, then returned to the driving seat and sped away. For a brief moment, the SUV passed under a streetlight, and I made out two figures up front. There was no way to tell who either person was, but one thing was for sure: the second man wasn't Dmitry Kalinovich.

Fast-forwarding, I sped through the rest of the footage to make sure no one returned to the compound, but by sunrise, one or two of the neighboring businesses showed some activity, and I figured Santiago wouldn't risk returning.

I considered what I'd learned from the early morning visit. It was interesting it had taken place on the night of the motel raid in Santa Ana, but that didn't necessarily mean anything significant. He'd been there around the same time on Wednesday night and Monday at two a.m. But it could signify they were tightening security, or even moving out. With the heat we'd put on the organization this week, it made sense they'd relocate the other branches. Which would mean shifting not only the drugs, but whatever equipment they used to convert the pills into an injectable formula.

I looked at my watch. It was almost seven. Roger was sitting in front of the sofa, looking up at me.

"What? You had your greens."

He squatted as though he was ready for imminent action, then shot off running around the living room at a ridiculous speed. He made me laugh when he had these little crazy sessions, but he went so fast, I also worried he'd crash into something and hurt himself. Everything was fair game in his quest for speed. Walls, his credenza hutch, and the TV stand were all used as backboards for him to launch in the opposite direction. After making three laps, he leaped onto the sofa and sat down, panting.

"Feel better for that?" I asked, and petted his head, stroking his long ears back. "Reckon you may have to hold down the fort alone again tonight, mate. I know Hugo told me not to do anything, but that was because he didn't see what I just saw on the roof camera."

Roger tipped his head to one side as though he were listening intently.

"What's that, you say? I could call him and tell him? That's not a bad idea, my furry friend, but I hate to disturb the man on his night off. Then I should go check it out myself? Funny you should say that. I was thinking exactly the same thing."

I laughed at my ridiculous theatrics and walked to the dining table, setting my laptop down. It was reckless and potentially a waste of time to go sit on the gym roof again all night, not to mention uncomfortable and tedious. But there was no reason why I couldn't watch the camera live from home.

Thirty minutes later, I had my control center set up on the sofa. On the end table sat a packaged pizza, which was still too hot to eat. On the TV, I'd found a James Bond marathon with *Thunderball* just starting, and on the second end table I'd repositioned to my right rested my laptop with a live stream from the roof camera. Roger had joined me and sat looking at the TV as Tom Jones sang the theme song with the opening credits. Rationing myself to one glass of wine on the slim chance I'd have to leave the house at some point, I settled in for what promised to be a long evening.

<hr>

I jolted awake. Sean Connery careened across the TV screen in a moon buggy, escaping into the desert with sirens wailing in his wake. What movie was this? I knew them all. I'd been watching *On Her Majesty's Secret Service*. The George Lazenby experiment. This was *Diamonds Are Forever*. I fumbled for my phone to check the time. Two-thirty in the morning. And then I remembered the camera feed.

"Bugger!" I blurted, looking at the box truck parked in the little compound.

I quickly rewound the footage to see how long it had been there. I was relieved to discover it had only been ten minutes. Scrambling, I put on my dark hoodie and gathered my gun, badge, handcuffs, and wallet, throwing them in my backpack along with the laptop. I also grabbed a bottled water from the fridge and the night vision binoculars.

"You're in charge," I told Roger, who I guessed had gone to bed in his hutch.

The VW bus made a loud and distinct sound, so I took my department car instead, which was perfectly bland for blending in. As long as no one saw the official license plate. Exactly what I had up my sleeve when I got there, I decided I'd figure out on the way, but I couldn't let them clear the place out and do nothing about it.

I weighed up whether to call Hugo. He'd be asleep and not happy about this, but he'd also be angry if he found out later. I could call the station and have backup standing by, but that was going to be hard to explain. Maybe not tonight, as they'd send a car, but tomorrow, I'd be asked to tell them why. I decided to get down there and see what was going on, then decide from there.

Approaching from the northeast, I parked up Doheny Park Road from the gym and walked the rest of the way. The streets were deserted apart from an occasional car along Doheny. I considered going up on the roof, but I had the camera view from up there and knew it was too far away to see anything useful.

I walked across Domingo, then along the sidewalk on the far side to reach the parking behind a car wash. From there, I turned right up the unnamed alley with the rear of the businesses on both sides. At the end was the used car lot and repair place. I used the same section of fence to climb onto the roof of the storage garages and carefully walked towards the little compound on the corner.

Listening for sounds of activity, I crouched and eased closer until I could peek through the razor wire and see the box truck parked in the yard. Light glowed around the edges of the covered windows in the modular office, but I couldn't hear or see anyone in the yard. I took out my phone and snapped a picture, then texted it to Hugo.

"They're emptying the place," I messaged, although I couldn't be sure that was what they were doing.

The door to the office swung open, and I froze. I was probably silhouetted by the glow from the town, but the person would have to look up to their left and through the wire to have a chance of seeing me. I could have ducked, but I was more concerned movement might alarm them, and besides, I needed to see what was going on.

One man walked to the box truck and pulled the rear roll-up door closed. It was too dark to see what was inside, but under the corner streetlight, I recognized Emilio Santiago. He moved to the cab and climbed inside, drove the truck out of the yard, then got back out and closed the gates. He didn't loop the chain around and lock them, but returned to the cab and pulled away down Domingo.

Where was he going? The lights were still on inside the office, so he planned on returning. Maybe he was moving the drugs locally. I stared at the front door to the office. I hadn't seen him lock it, either. This was my chance to look inside.

My phone buzzed with a reply from Hugo. I'd half-hoped I wouldn't wake him and he'd see the picture in the morning.

"What the hell are you doing?"

It was a fair question. *What was I doing?* Breaking protocols and basic police procedures, that was for sure. But I'd come this far. I was committed now. The tenuous connection between Castillo and the property wouldn't be enough. I needed to catch Santiago on the premises to give us a chance of tying the family to the drugs. Or perhaps even the girls. The idea hit me out of nowhere. Kamaria Ellis and undoubtedly other young women were still missing. Maybe they were being held here, too, now that the bunkhouse was out of the picture. I had to know.

Moving to the edge of the roof over the first storage unit, I lay down on the filthy surface and dangled my legs over the side. Lowering myself by hanging from the roof, I dropped to the concrete below, bending my knees to absorb the impact as I landed with a thud. Staying tight to the outside of the fence, I texted Hugo as I moved to the corner.

"Santiago left. Checking inside. Backup coming. Stand by."

I then pulled up the direct station number and contemplated the call. I couldn't go in there without help close at hand. But what if Santiago saw the patrol car? Bugger. I hit the call button and waited while it rang.

"Orange County Sheriff's Department, Dana Point," came a woman's voice I recognized as Sergeant Miriam Raymond.

"Sarge, it's Cromwell," I whispered into the phone. "Do you have a car you can send by Doheny Park Drive? I have a potential situation."

"Sure, Kat. What's going on?"

"I'm uncertain yet, could be nothing, but I got an alarm fault at my dad's gym. I'm checking it out. Be nice to have someone close by, just in case."

"Why don't you let the deputies check it out for you, Kat? I can send them by."

"No, no, that's okay. Ask them to come in quietly. Use Domingo south of Doheny Park and stage in the back of the oil change place on the corner."

The line went quiet. "What the hell you got going on? Why don't we just have them roll up outside?"

Jeez, this was getting messy.

"Please trust me on this one, Sarge. Have them in stealth mode and give them my cell number. Stay off the radio. Okay?"

"I guess, but you're gonna have to explain this to me later, Kat."

"Will do. Thanks, Sarge."

I hung up and blew out a breath. If this place was full of Emilio Santiago's mother's furniture, I was in big trouble. I pulled my holstered service weapon from my backpack and secured the belt around my waist, tucked my badge in my pocket, then looped my arms through the backpack straps once more.

Checking around the corner, I saw no sign of the box truck returning. Jogging to the gate, I went over the cover story in my mind one more time. *I was at the gym checking an alarm issue when I noticed suspicious behavior. I walked down to check and found the gate open. Which is when I discovered the lab and called it in.*

It sounded thin, but it was all I could come up with, so I slipped through the unlocked gate.

35

———————

A sliver of light edged the two front-facing windows of the scruffy-looking modular office. I cursed myself for not studying the camera footage in more detail before running out of the house. I had to presume Santiago didn't leave everything unlocked unless someone else was present, but I had no idea if that meant one person or ten. More likely one, or perhaps two, as that's all who could fit in the cab of the box truck.

Pressing my cheek to the dirty beige-painted siding of the office, I closed one eye and tried seeing inside through the edge of the closed blinds. I couldn't make out any details through the tiny gap, but the view blinked at me. Someone had crossed the room, and I heard the door handle turn.

In two quick steps, I rounded the corner and hid behind the end of the office, the noise of the creaky door drowning out my steps. From the yard, I heard the scuffing of someone's feet and two clicks. *What was that sound?* A moment later, the smell of cigarette smoke wafted past me. It had been a lighter. The person had stepped outside to smoke.

I slipped the strap off my holster and rested my right hand on my sidearm. Carefully and slowly, I leaned around the corner of the office and took a brief look. It was a man, dressed in a pale blue lab suit of some description. His hair was contained in a similar pale blue elasticized cap. This had to be the chemist, or whatever you called a wanker who cooked drugs for the black market.

My phone vibrated, and I eased back out of sight, checking the message with the screen turned away from the yard. It was my former partner on the beat, Jeff Rodriguez.

"We're across from gym. Please advise."

Knowing it was Jeff less than a quarter of a mile away boosted my confidence. He loved to give me a hard time, but he was a solid deputy and would have my back. Which I would need in a few moments, as my choices were limited.

"Wait for white box truck. Let him park at business on Domingo. Then follow."

Undoubtedly, Santiago would return, but I couldn't verify the lab without going inside, and I couldn't go inside with the smoker in my way. Pocketing the phone, I drew my sidearm and slipped around the corner of the building.

"Sheriff's department," I said firmly, not wanting to shout in case there was someone else inside. "Hands where I can see them."

The man jumped in surprise and spun around. He kept his hands clear of his body, the cigarette still glowing between his fingers in the dim light. A packet of Lucky Strikes fell from his hand to the ground. He was probably in his mid to late thirties, with a slim build and a drawn but swarthy face. His eyes looked like a deer caught in headlights.

"Are you alone?" I demanded.

He nodded, his eyes briefly flicking toward the office. I wasn't sure whether to believe him or not.

"Turn around." He did so, and I fished the handcuffs from my bag. "Hands behind your back." He hesitated. "Hands behind your bloody back, mate," I hissed.

I had no choice but to holster my weapon to put him in handcuffs, and he must have heard the steel meet the leather. Whipping around, Lucky threw a punch, which I narrowly dodged. On reflex,

I countered with an uppercut just below his ribs, catching him with a solid hit, knocking the wind from his lungs. Dropping to his knees, I grabbed a wrist, twisting it behind him as he coughed and wheezed.

"Be quiet, you bloody idiot," I growled, snapping the handcuffs in place. "Now get to your feet."

With help from me, he struggled up, and I drew my gun again, keeping an eye on the office. I still couldn't be sure whether someone else was inside, but they certainly would have heard us if they were. Watching for the door to open or the blinds to move, I looked around for a place to stash Lucky while I went inside. I couldn't leave him unattended or he'd shout a warning or run. Coming to the realization he'd have to come inside with me, I moved toward the door, then stopped, hearing the low rumble of a vehicle approaching. My phone vibrated in my pocket. Instantly, I knew it was Jeff telling me the box truck was back.

Veering right, Lucky gasped as I shoved him behind the far end of the office. We both half-tripped over trash and who knew what else in the darkness.

"Not a bloody word. Got it?" I hissed, holding the suspect with his face against the siding.

The box truck stopped, the engine dropping to idle, and a door opened. A few moments later, the sound of the chain being pulled through the gate echoed around in the still night. I remembered Jeff and his partner. I holstered my gun again, keeping my left arm pinning Lucky to the building. Pulling out my phone, I saw I'd been correct about Jeff's text.

"Box truck coming."

"Wait until he pulls in," I messaged in response.

A thumbs-up emoji appeared next to my text.

Tucking the phone away, I drew my gun once more, praying I wouldn't have to use it again. The gates noisily clanked open, and a few beats later, the cab door closed and the engine note rose as Santiago pulled the box truck into the yard. I moved back another step as the flat front of the truck appeared in view.

"Not a word," I repeated to Lucky, who I kept firmly against the siding.

Santiago killed the engine, and the cab door opened once more. His feet scuffed loudly on the filthy concrete as he stepped out, then closed the door behind him. I prayed Jeff and his partner were giving it enough time to let Castillo's man get inside the office, where we'd have him trapped. I glimpsed Santiago as he walked around the front of the truck, sending me farther back into the shadows.

Absorbed in listening for the sound of the patrol car, I was caught off-guard when Lucky lurched from my grip and stumbled clear of the office.

"*¡Milo, la poli!*"

I lunged forward to grab Lucky. "Sheriff's depa—"

But Lucky jerked as I reached him with blood splattering across my cheek as a gunshot rang out. The chemist's body jolted again as a second shot tore into him, and his corpse limply dropped. Releasing my hold, I sprinted ahead as two more shots pierced the still night. Diving, I made it across the front of the box truck, landing hard on my side. Beneath the truck, I saw Santiago's boots in motion and the door to the office swing open. By the time I'd aimed my gun, he'd disappeared inside.

"Sheriff's deputies!" I heard Jeff yell from the street.

"One down, one inside the office!" I shouted. "Armed!"

"Where are you, Kat? Are you okay?"

I wiped the side of my face with my sleeve, my hand shaking with adrenaline. "Yeah, I'm okay. Inside the yard. Two front-facing windows. None on ends. Cover behind the truck."

"Copy," Jeff replied as I heard his partner calling for backup over the radio.

I stood and peeked through the side window of the box truck. I could see the right half of the little building.

"Hey," Jeff said, slipping between the fence and the rear of the truck, which hung over the sidewalk. "I can't wait to hear how this little party came about."

I rolled my eyes and shook my head. "Congrats, Rodriguez. You've stumbled into a drug lab bust. The chemist is the guy leaking all over the yard," I added, nodding beyond the truck.

Jeff dipped down and looked under the truck. "You do that to him?"

"No. Emilio Santiago did. He's the trigger-happy wanker inside the building."

"He shot his own guy?"

"I think Lucky was collateral damage. He was after me."

"Lucky?"

I shrugged. "Turns out I gave him a lousy nickname."

"I'd say," Jeff said, looking under the truck once more. "But I'm glad this Santiago guy missed you."

"Thanks," I replied, wondering what we should do next.

"So, what's the play, Investigator Cromwell?" Jeff asked, grinning at me.

"Well, Deputy Rodriguez, I'd love for ol' Milo to toss his gun out and give himself up, but I'm going to guess that ain't happening."

"We can call in the SWAT guys, but they'll be a while."

I took a few deep breaths. "We don't have that kinda time. I'd say Milo has two priorities at this point. Destroy all the evidence and extricate himself from that building."

"Any other ways into the office?" Jeff asked.

"Not that I've seen."

"Then—"

"Cromwell!" came a Hispanic-accented voice from inside the office.

"He knows you?" Jeff asked.

"Yeah. He dropped by my house once." I stood tall and looked through the truck windows again. "How you doing in there, Milo?" I called back.

"Like you had the guy over for drinks?" Jeff asked.

"No," I frowned at him. "He broke in and my home security rabbit chased him off."

"Your what?"

"You come in here alone, and we'll make a deal," Santiago called out.

Jeff chuckled without humor. "That ain't happening."

I moved around to the front of the truck so I could see through the windshield and side glass, taking in the entire building.

"Why would I want to do that?" I shouted.

"Cos I got something you want."

"I doubt it."

"Gimme your number."

I looked at Jeff in confusion. "Why would he…" Then I figured it out. "He wants to send a picture."

I called out my cell number, shouting loudly as sirens wailed in the night.

"Get them to turn off that racket, Jeff."

"On it," he replied, and turned away to talk on his radio.

My phone buzzed, and I looked at the text. It was a picture of a young woman. Unconscious. The lighting was poor, but I still recognized her. It was Kamaria Ellis.

"She alive?" I texted back.

"She's alive, man!" Santiago yelled from inside. "Let's trade. You get the girl if I get to roll. If not, she won't be alive long."

The sirens had stopped, but I heard cars arriving, and it sounded like Jeff's partner Graves was organizing the deputies.

"If I come in there, you have two hostages," I called back, buying myself time to think. "Why would I do that?"

"I'll trade you for her!" Santiago shouted in return. "She lives. You and me walk out of here, man. I'll let you go once I'm…"

"Once you're what?" I shouted. "There's nowhere to go, mate. I can't get you a jet fueled and ready to fly anywhere, Milo. It doesn't work like that. Your best bet is to hand yourself in and let the girl go."

"No way!" he shouted. "I gotta disappear, man."

"I can help you disappear, Milo," I called out in reply, well overstepping any authority I had. "Give me *El Pastor*, and we'll make a deal."

Santiago didn't respond. My first thought was that he was considering the idea, but after a minute, I began to wonder. Several more deputies were now lined up behind the box truck. They were all looking at me. It was now three-thirty in the morning.

"Did you call in the SWAT guys?" I asked Jeff.

"Sarge did," he replied. "And a hostage negotiator, but who knows when they'll get here."

"Not in time to be of any use is my guess," I muttered. "I gotta do something. He's desperate."

I turned back to the trailer office when Santiago finally spoke again. "You come inside, and we'll talk."

"No way, Kat," Jeff said, grabbing my arm. "Like you said, you'll be his second hostage."

"I can get him to give up *El Pastor*," I replied, pulling my arm away.

"Who the hell is *El Pastor*?"

"That's what I'm about to find out," I replied, taking a step away.

"Kat, wait," Jeff insisted, and I paused. He waved to a female deputy behind us. "Vest."

She took off her ballistic vest and handed it to me.

"Get another one or stay the hell down, okay?" I told her, and she nodded.

"Kat, we should be waiting. SWAT will have cameras to poke under the door, infrared, and all that crap. You're going in blind."

"We don't have time, Jeff," I replied, putting on the vest. "Look, if you hear shots, or me call for you, then get through that door, okay? Otherwise, don't come in, and don't let the SWAT guys go John Wick on the place. I'm going to talk him out of there."

"You're nuts, Kat."

"Yeah, so everyone keeps saying," I replied as I walked around the front of the box truck. "Coming in, Milo," I called out. "Just me."

36

———————

The blind moved in the left window. "Leave your gun outside," Santiago barked.

"Sure," I replied. "You do the same."

"You're not coming in armed!"

"Then I'm not coming in," I replied through the front door. "It's holstered, so you have the drop on me. You want to talk to me or not?"

I heard him swearing to himself in Spanish.

"You can see I'm alone, Milo. Stay back. I'm coming in, and I'll close the door behind me. Okay?"

I waited nervously, feeling my hands shaking again.

"Okay," he finally agreed.

I took two deep breaths to calm myself, checked the holster strap was unclipped, then turned the handle and pushed the door open.

It was brighter inside the trailer office than in the yard, and I squinted for a moment as my eyes adjusted. Santiago stood to my left next to a table, his gun trained on me. I closed the door behind me and glanced around. Immediately, I realized how wrong I'd been. This wasn't a drug lab. Kamaria Ellis lay on a stainless-steel table beside the gunman, a sheet pulled up to her chin. Two other tables in the room had sheets covering what I presumed to be more girls. Each was hooked up to IVs, and a large refrigerator whirred in the corner to my right.

I felt a lump in my throat and my stomach clench as comprehension overwhelmed me.

"You're harvesting organs," I muttered, my eyes landing on Santiago.

He shifted uncomfortably on his feet, and I noticed his finger was on the trigger rather than resting alongside the guard. I needed to tread very carefully.

I pointed to the two sheet-covered tables. "They're dead, aren't they?"

Santiago nodded. Stomach acid rose in my throat, and I fought back the urge to vomit. I'd been here. Twice before. If I'd shut this place down then, those two girls would still be alive. Anger rose, driven by my frustration at myself and the system that tied my hands behind my back.

"But she's not," Santiago said, nodding to Kamaria.

I had to maintain a level head. Rage wouldn't help the one I could save. "Anesthetic?" I asked.

He nodded again. "Let's talk about how I'm getting out of here so you can save her."

"I can tell you how you'll walk out of this trailer, Milo. It'll be with me taking you into custody—"

"No fucking way," he blurted. "That wasn't the deal."

"The deal was I'd come in here and talk to you and you'd let her go. Here I am, so let's get Kamaria out the door, and then we'll talk."

"No, no, no," Santiago replied, then rocked from one foot to the other. "I gotta disappear, man, or he'll disappear me."

"*El Pastor?*"

His glare shot my way. "You don't know shit, man."

"Then tell me. I want to know. And your best way to disappear is to give us *El Pastor*, Milo. Let me take you in and we'll get you a deal."

He laughed and waved the gun at me. "That's real funny, lady. You think I'd last five minutes inside? They got people everywhere."

"They?" I asked, wondering if the rumors were right and *El Pastor* was actually a syndicate of multiple ring leaders.

He shook his head. "Shut up, man. I gotta think."

"Okay, I get it, Milo. But while you're thinking, the SWAT team is on its way, and one of them negotiators who'll have you thinking there is a fancy jet waiting for you. Right before they storm this place."

He gritted his teeth and looked down at Kamaria, then back at me. "I'll take you both with me."

I held up my hands. "Hey, I'm just telling you how these things go, Milo. Once they show up, it's no longer my show. Let's figure out a deal now."

"You don't give a shit about me," he scoffed.

"You're right, I really don't. But I do care about nailing *El Pastor* and tying him to the Castillo family, and you can help me do that. I might not care, but you're valuable to me. And that value goes down the toilet when the SWAT guys put a dozen holes in you."

Santiago looked around the little trailer that was far cleaner on the inside than its shabby exterior appearance. It might not be a true medical-grade facility, but they clearly kept it sterile enough to cut their victims into pieces and produce viable organs for sale.

"I had nothing to do with this shit," he said, his eyes lingering on the sheets covering the two I couldn't save. "I just do what they tell me, man."

"Like breaking into my house."

He shrugged. "She hates you."

Now we were getting somewhere. "She's never liked me. I wasn't in her clique in school, but I don't know why she hates me."

Santiago scoffed again. "You really don't know shit, do you?"

With my mind still reeling from the shock of what they'd really been up to in the compound only two hundred yards from where I worked out most days, it felt like my brain was wading through mud to process what he was saying. *I get it, Gabby never liked me, but why was she actively after me?*

"It's about Paul, isn't it?"

Santiago grinned. "Finally, Cromwell. Took you long enough."

I threw my hands up again, forgetting to move slowly in front of a guy with a gun. "She was the one having the bloody affair with him, damn it. She ruined my relationship!"

"So you offed him," he replied, and I froze.

"It was an accident," I muttered.

Santiago shrugged. "Maybe, maybe not, but she doesn't think so and couldn't stand you having something she couldn't get."

"But she did have him!" I retorted angrily.

He shook his head again. "She tried," he replied, then gritted his teeth once more. "But none of that matters. What matters is how you're getting me out of here."

"Emilio, this is Tom with the Sheriff's Crisis Team," came a calm but authoritative voice from outside. "I just want to make sure everyone stays safe, starting with you. I'm here to listen. We don't need to rush anything. Let's talk, okay?"

My heart sank. This guy was a professional, and no doubt knew what the hell he was doing, but I had my own agenda and was finally getting Santiago to talk.

"Try anything, and they both die!" Santiago shouted. "I'm talking to Cromwell. Stay the fuck out of it, man."

"No problem, Emilio. I just need—"

"I'm fine!" I yelled. "Give us a minute here. I'm perfectly okay, and Kamaria is unconscious but safe."

"Great. Thank you both for that," Tom replied. "I'll give you a few minutes, then check back in. Do you need anything from me right now?"

"I need you to shut the fuck up!" Santiago raged, his whole body tensing.

"It's okay, Milo. Chill, mate," I urged softly. "I won't let them come in as long as we're talking, alright?"

"You said he'd take over once he got here," Santiago replied, waving the gun at the wall facing the yard. "How do you know what they'll do?"

"Because he has to follow protocols and procedures."

"You don't?"

"I'm in here, aren't I? You really think that's playing it by the book? I'll probably be suspended for this."

His eyes darted around the floor, then to Kamaria lying still on the table, before his head jerked up and he stared at me. "Can you get me witness protection? Like, for real, man. New place, ID, the works?"

"Depends on what you give us and who's involved, Milo. If the crimes cross state lines, then the Feds get involved, and they have way more clout for deals."

Santiago scoffed once more. "State lines? Try international, man. Get me a Fed to talk to, and we'll make a deal. But I gotta disappear completely, Cromwell, you understand? They got people everywhere, and I'm now a liability."

"Can you give us the connection between *El Pastor* and Castillo?" I pressed. "That's the big one, Milo."

He shook his head. "What do you mean connection, Cromwell?"

"Anything actionable to tie the two together," I continued. "Between the bunkhouse, the motel brothel, and this place, you have to have evidence we can use. A direction you can give us, Milo. What about the drug lab? They're making Velvet somewhere, right?"

Santiago's breathing became faster. He was getting even more worked up. "Cut off the head, and there's another one grows in its place, man. You want *El Pastor*? You already got him, and look what happened? He's back. She'll be next. You're wasting your time, man. You can't save me now. This is a fail, and he don't tolerate fails."

My mind raced. I had to calm him down or he was about to do something reckless, but I was desperate to keep him talking. "It's cool, Milo. This is great stuff. The Feds will love it, okay? Let's start with who runs this place, Milo? Who controls which girls are sent here?"

Behind me, I heard a faint scratching sound at the base of the door and forced myself not to look. It would be the SWAT guys sliding a camera inside to get a look at the situation. But it didn't matter, it was too late. Santiago's eyes went wide, and he raised his gun. I reached for my weapon, but I knew I'd never make it in time. He was way ahead of me.

This was it. I'd foolishly thought I could handle the situation and came striding in just like Hugo accused me of always doing. A grenade with the pin pulled. And now the lever had been released. The thought of all the people saying, "I knew this would happen one day" flashed through my mind before I pictured my grieving parents. I'd done this to myself, but far worse, I was breaking their hearts.

My eyes reflexively clenched shut as the gunshot boomed more like an explosion inside the confined space of the trailer. Men shouted from outside, and the door crashed into my back, shoving me across a table, where my hands clutched for anything to help keep me on my feet. All I felt was the firm, lukewarm flesh of the body beneath the sheet.

In a blur of dark green tactical gear, men were inside the trailer, shouting and grabbing at me. The last thing I saw as they pulled me out through the door was Milo Santiago on the floor, and the blood splatter across the ceiling above where he'd been standing.

My key witness had shot himself rather than watch over his shoulder for the rest of his life, wondering when *El Pastor* would find him. I'd completely screwed this up.

37

I looked at my Tag Heuer Carrera watch. A gift from my parents when I'd become a deputy sheriff. I wondered if I should give it back if they kicked me off the force.

It was three minutes after ten in the morning. Hugo sat silently in the chair opposite me on the patio outside PC Beans. In the early hours of yesterday morning, he'd arrived at the compound while I'd still been inside the office and was the first one to make sure I was okay after the SWAT guys extracted me. Since then, once he'd learned I was unharmed, he'd been distant and hadn't said much of anything. We didn't speak from Monday lunchtime until I said hello a few minutes ago, greeted in return with a murmur. It was hard to know what he intended, or had already revealed to Bradley, but I was so tired and deflated, I didn't much care.

I fought back a yawn. Monday had been a series of recaps, reports, and interviews after we'd left the property on Domingo Avenue. Fatigue had driven me to sleep Monday evening, but the night had been restless and filled with weird dreams. Mostly second-guessing from the events of the previous night. I still had to face more inquiries and probing into my conduct, but I was more interested in the outcome of the meeting we were about to have.

"Cromwell, Fuentes," a familiar voice said from behind me.

Tess Salgado took the seat between us and scooped up the coffee I'd bought for her. "You two have been busy little beavers, it seems," she said after taking a sip.

"How's your chest?" I asked, choosing not to comment.

"Purple, but didn't crack a rib, so can't complain after stopping a couple of slugs." She looked at Hugo. "Albright apologizes for not making it, but I'll fill him in."

Hugo nodded, then raised his coffee cup to his mouth. His eyes were hidden behind designer-brand shades.

"Santiago said some things before he…" I said, trailing off.

"Heard he took himself out," Tess finished for me.

"Yeah."

"So, what did he have to say?"

I leaned over the table so I didn't have to shout over the traffic on PCH. "Cut off the head, and another one takes its place."

"What the hell does that mean?" Salgado asked. "Who was he talking about?"

"*El Pastor.*"

"So it ain't one guy," she said, nodding slowly.

"Yes and no," I replied. "I think it's one person at a time, but it's handed down. Santiago said we already had *El Pastor*, yet he's back again."

"Any idea what he meant by that?" Salgado asked.

"The Castillos. The grandfather's inside doing time, and Ramon took over the businesses. We have one, but another takes over." I leaned even closer to Salgado. "He also said she'll be next."

"The daughter?"

I nodded. "Gabriella. Santiago's been seen at her place. He broke into my house because she sent him." I hadn't intended to say the last part, but it came out, so I hurriedly moved on. "*El Pastor* isn't a person or a group of people. It's a role. And right now, Ramon Castillo fills that role." I turned to Hugo. "I'd put money on that being Ramon who they hustled out of the motel. The man in black."

Hugo raised an eyebrow but didn't comment.

"This is good stuff, Kat," Salgado said with a smirk on her face. "But the only man to corroborate any of this left his brains all over that trailer."

"Yeah," I replied despondently. "He was talking, and I thought I had him ready to make a deal, but the SWAT boys shoved a camera under the door and spooked him. I guarantee Ramon or Gabriella never set foot in that shitty building, so there won't be a forensic trace of them. But the property belongs to Capistrano Holdings, which is owned by Trent DeMarco, who is married to Gabriella's cousin. It's a leap, but there's a connection."

Salgado shook her head. "We'll follow the thread, Kat, but unless they really screwed up covering their tracks, it'll be nothing more than circumstantial. Crime lab is still processing the motel, but my guess is it'll be the same there. If it is Ramon Castillo, I'm guessing he's smart enough not to leave his prints all over the place."

"He'll claim he stayed in a room some time prior to the bust," Hugo said, speaking for the first time. "And deny paying for any services."

"Any chance you can get the staff you arrested to roll on him?" I asked.

Salgado scoffed. "We've been trying, believe me, but there's a reason Santiago put a gun under his chin. They testify, they die. Or a family member disappears. They stay quiet, their families magically land a decent job that overpays."

My knee hit the table as I bounced my legs in frustration. "He's going to get away with it. Again."

Salgado shrugged. "For now, probably. But you two helped put a big dent in his operation. We've shut down his halfway house, the brothel, his organ harvesting, and we took down a bunch of his lieutenants."

"For how long?" I responded. "He'll have them all back up again in new locations before we prosecute anyone involved."

"Maybe," Salgado said calmly. "But now we know who *El*

Pastor truly is, so we know where to concentrate our attention. These things are all progress, Kat. It's a long, drawn-out war, not a single battle deciding anything. You two made a major contribution this week."

"She did," Hugo said, before taking another sip of his coffee and avoiding my stunned gaze.

The man perplexed me. He'd been shunning me like I'd dishonored his name and shot his dog, yet now he tossed out a compliment.

"We did," I said. "I just stumbled on the property near my dad's gym."

His eyes met mine. "No. You insisted we work on the Jane Doe case, and you pushed us to interview Rivera's cousin, which led to Tess's group waiting and taking down meaningful people. Then you went after Santiago in the middle of the night." He put his cup down. "You break the rules, you're reckless, and you take risks you're not supposed to, but that's why all this happened, Kat. You're like Tess. She's the same, and that's what it takes against the likes of Castillo. I'm not built that way. I want to reach my retirement and enjoy a long life knowing I did a solid job for all these years. We're cut from a different cloth."

For a moment, I was shocked into silence, and I could see Salgado didn't know quite what to say. She looked at me, and then turned to Hugo.

"Thank you… I think," she said with an uncomfortable laugh.

His words held far more in what he hadn't said. Sure, he'd expressed an acceptance in some way that I'd been effective and achieved results, but it certainly didn't sound like he wanted any part of it.

"Hugo, you're the reason this works," I said, struggling to find the right words. "I can't do this without you."

"Sure you can," he replied. "Until you get benched. Law enforcement's a different world these days. Everything is analyzed, recorded, and torn apart by people without their lives on the line."

"That's why we're a great team," I replied, feeling like I was begging for him not to break up with me. "You're the level-headed, balanced one, and I'm the…"

"Grenade with the pin pulled?" he finished for me.

"I get the sense you two are having a moment here," Salgado said, getting up from her chair. "Thanks for the coffee and to *both* of you for the great work. I have to drop by and see your captain, so I'm sure I'll see you around."

Hugo and I both nodded and muttered our thanks in return as we watched her leave. I took a deep breath before returning my attention to my partner.

"Don't make me do this without you, Hugo."

"We go about this job differently, Kat."

"Which is why we work so well. I push, and you rein me in."

"It's exhausting," Hugo replied, and I wished once more that I could see his eyes. "I never know what to expect next."

I chewed on my lip as I considered his words. My standard reaction was defense, but I fought back the urge to justify my actions. As usual, he was right. Time would tell if Bradley would push to boot or reprimand me, or let me continue without a blemish. I'd achieved a result, but four suspects were dead, and even my embellished procedure for Sunday night was questionable by department standards.

"We both know I'd be lying if I said I'll completely change, Hugo, but people can adjust. I need to be more respectful of putting you in difficult positions. And, if you can accept that there'll be times when you just have to let me go charging in and know it's my choice, then we can still make this work."

He sat back and sighed, staring beyond me as he appeared lost in thought. Against every instinct I possessed, I stayed quiet and let him work through whatever conversation he was having with himself. His mind had probably been made up before he'd arrived, but I'd said my piece, and pushing harder wouldn't help.

After what felt like ten minutes but was probably less than one, he stood and looked at me.

"I went to bat for you with Bradley, and she told me that if I felt that strongly about keeping you around, then I must want to remain your partner," he said, then shrugged. "So, for now, I don't have a choice."

And with that grenade of his own, Hugo cracked the briefest of smiles before walking out of the patio toward his car. Once more, I was stunned by his words, only this time, in a positive way. Relief flooded through me, but I reminded myself that I had to practice what I'd just preached. His mind had indeed been made up before he'd arrived. Now it was up to me to prove he hadn't made a mistake.

I checked my watch. I needed to leave, too. Driving my VW bus to my parents' place, I parked and met them in the driveway, where we all loaded into Dad's British Racing Green Range Rover.

Twenty-five minutes later, Dr. Eric Cole greeted us at the main hospital reception, and I introduced him to my parents. A nurse pushed a wheelchair down the hall toward us, and Zara squinted to see who was with me.

"This is really generous of you to do this," the doctor said to my mum and dad. "I don't think she has much to go home to."

"We're happy to help," my mum replied. "She'll be eighteen in six weeks, and we'll see where best to go from there."

"She can't be more trouble than this one was," my dad added, winking at me.

I hoped Zara didn't prove him wrong. She'd been used to doing things her own way for a while, even if it meant living in abandoned buildings. She stood from the chair, which was unnecessary but standard procedure for the hospital, and looked at me.

"Hi," I said. "I'd like you to meet Frankie and Dot."

Mum extended her hand, and the young woman shook, although her expression projected a mixture of apprehension and embarrassment.

My dad just nodded, respectfully careful regarding any physical contact. "Nice to meet you. Can I carry your bag?"

Zara held up a small hospital-issued toiletries pack. "I travel light."

I kicked myself for not organizing more clothes for her, as we were taking her home in cotton pants and a T-shirt I presumed the staff had found for her. Whatever possessions the girl had owned before being abducted were gone now.

I thanked Eric and promised to keep him abreast of her progress, and we walked to the car. From his smile, I thought the doctor might want to stay in touch for other reasons, but I'd probably convince myself I was imagining things by the time we got home.

I helped Zara into the backseat and closed the door. Dad started the car, but Mum lingered near me and put a hand on my arm.

"How are you holding up, darling?"

"Okay, I think," I replied, willing my voice to sound more convincing.

"When do you have to be back at work?"

"Tomorrow. I have paperwork and a meeting with the captain."

"She must be pleased you put a stop to such a hideous enterprise," Mum said, and I peered through the lightly tinted glass at Zara. As best I could gather, the girls had been shepherded through a system. Used as escorts and prostitutes unless they wouldn't play along, even when drugged. In which case, they were harvested for their organs. If Zara—or Thirty-One, as they'd called her—hadn't escaped, which I doubted we'd ever learn how she'd pulled that off, she'd have faced a miserable and hazy existence before ending up on one of the stainless-steel tables.

"Hopefully," I replied, feeling more optimistic having spoken with Hugo. "Oh, one more thing," I whispered. "I don't think Paul was having an affair after all. Some new information came to light."

My mother smiled. "I was surprised when you told me about that, Kat. It seemed so out of character for the Paul I knew."

I smiled in return. My parents had loved my fiancé, and Mum had been the only person I'd told about his apparent infidelity. It felt good to relieve her of that burden.

Which left me back to the drawing board on why my fiancé had been at Gabriella Castillo's house.

Thank you for reading *The One Who Ran*, I hope you enjoyed it!

Looking for more from Kat Cromwell?
For those of you interested in joining my monthly newsletter, I've
created a fun bonus you'll find by using this QR code…

Don't forget to grab the next book in the series,
Her Perfect Time To Die

ACKNOWLEDGMENTS

My heartfelt thanks go to:

My incredible wife Cheryl, our family, and great friends for their unwavering support, love, and encouragement.

The fine folks at the Orange County Sheriff's Department who met with me, emailed, Zoom called, and provided their wonderful advice and knowledge. Any variances from procedure and law enforcement facts are strictly on the author by error or to enhance the story.

Peter Carey of Capistrano Boxing Gym for taking the time to help me with the boxing scenes. Again, any errors in this regard are solely on the author.

My marvellous editor Chelsey Heller for her diligent and detailed work.

My beta reader group for their wonderful support, feedback, and keen eyes, which make each book better before reaching you, and my ARC group for their amazing support.

Above all, I thank you, the readers: none of this happens without your choice to spend precious time with my stories. I am truly in your debt.

LET'S STAY IN TOUCH!

To buy merchandise, find more info, or to join my newsletter, visit
my website at
www.HarveyBooks.com

If you enjoyed this novel I'd be incredibly grateful if you'd consider
leaving a review on Amazon.com
Find eBook deals and follow me on BookBub.com

Catch my chat show, The Two Authors' Podcast with co-host
Douglas Pratt

Visit Amazon.com for more books in the
Investigator Kat Cromwell Mystery Series,
Nora Sommer Caribbean Suspense Series,
AJ Bailey Adventure Series,
and collaborative works:
The Greene Wolfe Thriller Series
Tropical Authors Adventure Series

ABOUT THE AUTHOR

A USA Today bestselling author, Nicholas Harvey's life has been anything but ordinary. Race car driver, motorsports professional, adventure traveller, divemaster, and since 2020, a full-time novelist. Raised in England and resident in America for many years, Nick and his amazing wife, Cheryl, now base themselves in Grand Cayman from where they travel the globe in search of new plots for his novels. He is the author of the Nora Sommer Caribbean Suspense series, Investigator Kat Cromwell Mysteries, and AJ Bailey Adventure series, along with multiple collaborations.

For more information, visit his website at HarveyBooks.com.